Praise...

DRAGONS WILD

"*Dragons Wild* is a lot more straightforward urban fantasy, complete with the semi-standard trappings of a secret race of supernatural beings dwelling amongst, and influencing, normal people. But Asprin pulls it off with skill and style, delivering a thoroughly satisfying, energetic story that begs for continuation. In fact, it's actually one of the best things I've ever read from him in terms of entertainment and atmospheric value . . . Is it fun? Oh yes." —*The Green Man Review*

"Asprin tackles a new kind of comic fantasy, a little more serious and hard-boiled than previous books. Featuring a likable rake and plenty of action and quirky humor, this series opener belongs in most adult and YA fantasy collections." —*Library Journal*

"Colorful." —*Publishers Weekly*

"This is the start of what looks like will be a great urban fantasy series that is funky, funny, and fun . . . Robert Asprin has begun another fine myth with his first entry in his wild dragon culture." —*Midwest Book Review*

"Delightful." —*Monsters and Critics*

DRAGONS LUCK

"Joyous fantasy with continuous action and a creative cast of characters." —*SFRevu*

"[The] paranormal support cast is three-dimensional . . . The whodunit is a fun sort of a paranormal version of Fritz Lang's *M*." —*Genre Go Round Reviews*

DRAGONS DEAL

by Robert Asprin and Jody Lynn Nye

"Another enjoyable addition to the saga of the McCandles family." —*Night Owl Reviews*

"Enjoyable [and] lighthearted . . . With a wild family-affair final twist setting up the next thriller, *Dragons Deal* is a fun fantasy frolic." —*Midwest Book Review*

DRAGONS WILD

ROBERT ASPRIN

ACE BOOKS, NEW YORK

THE BERKLEY PUBLISHING GROUP
Published by the Penguin Group
Penguin Group (USA) LLC
375 Hudson Street, New York, New York 10014

USA • Canada • UK • Ireland • Australia • New Zealand • India • South Africa • China

penguin.com

A Penguin Random House Company

DRAGONS WILD

An Ace Book / published by arrangement with Bill Fawcett & Associates

For information, address: The Berkley Publishing Group,
a division of Penguin Group (USA) LLC,
375 Hudson Street, New York, New York 10014.

ISBN: 978-0-425-27205-3

PUBLISHING HISTORY
Ace trade paperback edition / April 2008
Ace mass-market edition / February 2014

PRINTED IN THE UNITED STATES OF AMERICA

10 9 8 7 6 5 4 3 2 1

Cover art by Brandon Dorman.
Interior text design by Kristin del Rosario.

This novel marks a radical departure from my usual style and subject matter. As such, I would like to dedicate this work to my test readers, whose input and suggestions played such a large role in forming its style and content.

John Vise
Darlene Bolesny
Todd Brantley
Beth Patterson
Toni Ester

and especially Bill Fawcett

My heartfelt thanks to you all!

One

It was early June, which in Michigan meant one could almost count on summer being here to stay. The state was notorious for its "Indian winters," which lingered forever. When the snows melted, it was all mud. When the mud finally dried, it was summer . . . maybe. One could never be sure when the warmth would come for good, if ever. Something about that thought resonated deeply with a young man whose life should be just beginning, but who had no idea where it would, or should, go.

Griffen McCandles, a recent graduate from the University of Michigan—by the skin of his teeth—was about to attempt something unthinkable, unimaginable, frightening. That is to say, he was out to get a job in the real world.

He was sitting in his uncle's office in what was still referred to as Downtown Detroit. The office was impressive, as it was designed to be. As large as a hotel suite, it was plushly furnished for both business and relaxation. Light poured through one glass wall, which provided a view looking out over the tops of lesser buildings to the river beyond. It was a view that testified to and gloried in success, but Malcolm McCandles, the man who dominated the room and the company, ignored it, choosing instead to study his young visitor.

There might have been some similarity between the two in their tall height, light brown shade of their hair, or the strong lines underlying their faces. That was where the similarity ended. Griffen had boy-next-door features and a disarming smile. Where Malcolm seemed to dominate the scene, his nephew barely made a ripple in it. He sat in the pants and shirt from his one suit, tie but no coat. Choosing to look casual with family but coming off as slightly rumpled.

"So, Griffen," Malcolm said at last, breaking the long silence, "what did you think of college?"

"To be honest with you, Uncle Mal," the young man said, leaning forward to speak earnestly, "I wasn't that impressed with it. I mean, the theories and grand concepts were interesting and informative, but now that I've graduated I'm looking forward to learning the hard lessons you can only get from working in real life with real people and situations."

Malcolm cocked his head.

"Cute," he said. "Did you write that and memorize it in advance, or did you crib it from somewhere?"

"Excuse me?" Griffen said, blinking.

"Let's cut the crap, shall we?" Malcolm said flatly. "I'm fully aware of your college career. I should be, since I paid for it.

"It is only by charm and quick wits you've managed to graduate at all. Not seeming to really care about your chosen major, you rarely attended your classes, but seemed to have a knack for writing essays and papers that were exactly what your teachers were looking for. If you've earned anything it's your nickname, 'Grifter.' A name derived from the time you spent playing poker, at further expense of your studies. You seem to have an utter lack of ambition in any terms but the extreme immediate. Now that you've graduated, you're suddenly faced with the horrifying possibility of having to actually work, and you're hoping to land a cushy job with me to maintain your lifestyle with as little personal exertion as can be managed. Correct me if I'm wrong."

The youth held his gaze for several long moments before shrugging and leaning back in his chair.

"As you said, Uncle Mal," he said, "let's cut the crap. You seem to know me pretty well. I guess the next question is, if you have such a low opinion of me, then what am I doing here?"

Malcolm raised an eyebrow at Griffen's directness. He had expected him to evade for a time yet. He considered for a moment and shook his head, sadly.

"You should learn to listen to what is said without injecting emotion or judgment into it," he said. "I never said I disapproved of your actions, simply listed the facts as I see them.

"As to what you're doing here, that gets into why I originally stepped forward to provide for you and your sister after your parents died. You see, I felt a bit guilty, since I was responsible for those deaths."

He paused, waiting for a reaction, but Griffen simply looked at him, levelly. The young man had suspected as much, since this uncle that he barely knew had paid his way through college. Mostly he was worried about what to do with his life. His one interview at Microsoft for a sales position had been a disaster lasting less time than it took for the interviewer to look at his transcript from the University of Michigan School of Business. He was just changing mental gears to react to the part about Uncle Mal causing his parents' deaths when the well-dressed executive spoke again.

"I didn't actually cause them," Malcolm clarified, "but I did nothing to prevent them either. Since my noninterference resulted in the two of you becoming orphans, I felt it was only right that I oversee your survival to your majorities. Unfortunately, I'm a busy man, so that assistance was mainly in the form of financial support, and without direct supervision, both you and your sister have been free to run wild and do things pretty much the way you wanted. Now that you're finally coming of age, however, there are some things you should know."

He paused to organize his thoughts. Reaching into a humidor on his desk, he produced a cigar and unwrapped it, but didn't light it.

"Tell me, Griffen," he said, "what do you know about dragons?"

The youth blinked in surprise at the sudden change of subject.

"Um . . . I don't know," he said finally. "Mythical beasts . . . big lizards that fly and breathe fire. Why do you ask?"

Malcolm smiled at him.

"Wrong on every count . . . except one," he said, ignoring Griffen's question. "Not surprising, really."

"Okay." Griffen shrugged. "We'll just leave it that they're mythical beasts. What does that have to do with anything?"

Malcolm pursed his lips as if to whistle, then exhaled a small jet of flame to light his cigar. Griffen's eyes widened even more as his mind whirled.

"That wasn't the point you were right on," he said.

Two

Like most people when seeing something utterly beyond the depth of their experience, Griffen was trying to rationalize what he had just seen. He wracked his memory for some other time he had seen his uncle do prestidigitation or even card tricks. Nothing came to him. Could this be some vague hint that he was going to get a chance at heading up a magic store division?

"Nice trick," he said nervously, trying to maintain some foothold. Malcolm merely rolled his eyes, but Griffen did his best to maintain a smile. His uncle's expression then faded, becoming distant, as if he was no longer seeing Griffen, but something far beyond the walls of the office.

Whatever minimal control Griffen had felt coming into this meeting had been completely lost. He felt like he was falling, and couldn't even see the ground beneath his feet.

"Dragons have been around a long time. Longer than humans. Their ability to shape-shift gave them a great advantage in the competition for survival, to a point where they had few real enemies. An old race, ancient really. If one believes the oldest legends, no asteroid was needed to take out the dinosaurs. The early dragons just didn't like competition. But without massive and cunning predators, dragons really had no challenges. In hindsight, they became smug and complacent."

The jobless recent graduate could see Malcolm was choosing his words carefully. Malcolm noticed him schooling his features, trying to look attentive. Despite his comments, true though they were, about his nephew's shortcomings, there was a fine mind there if the boy had incentive to use it. Malcolm was about to give him a big push. It had been a while since he had been called on to explain the real world to anyone.

"They disregarded the humans when they first appeared as being too weak and slow to be of importance. But the humans had intelligence, and they bred like rabbits. The dragons bred slow, and arrogantly didn't see this tribe of apes as truly any more special than any other. They busied themselves with what activities they deemed important, and barely noticed the humans spreading over the globe. By the time the dragons recognized them as a threat, it was too late to stop them."

Why was his uncle making him listen to such a fantasy, and where was it leading? Was this all some kind of odd ruse, a test? Griffen thought himself a fair hand at reading people, but Malcolm McCandles revealed nothing, though Malcolm did show a brief smile as Griffen started to fidget. Catching the smile, Griffen made himself stop.

"Many dragons could adjust and change, many actually living near or with humans. Many cultures have very positive legends about the guidance and protection of dragons.

Though not always using that term, of course; it came later. However, some of the European dragons, stubbornly refusing to see the handwriting on the wall, decided to try to fight the humans. They used their shape-shifting to take on fearsome appearances, which gave rise to the lurid images that people today identify as the true form of dragons. The fact that they are now relegated to the status of myth and legend is mute testimony to the effectiveness of their anti-human campaign."

"So what did they look like outside of the frightening guises?" Griffen asked.

"Different, big, depends on who you . . . Don't interrupt." Malcolm snapped, eyes flashing back into focus. Griffen noticed that his manner was now angry, and slightly embarrassed.

He didn't know what to make of it, though. Griffen flushed slightly, but didn't press the question. After all, what was he asking? How dragons are supposed to look? He couldn't believe he was getting sucked into this bizarre narrative so easily. A worried thought flashed through his mind. Did one inherit madness?

Malcolm nodded and continued. "There was another group, however, who went to their Eastern brethren, seeking the secret of size shifting to augment their own shape-shifting ability. You may not know it, Griffen, but Eastern dragons never had wings. When they needed to fly, they would size shift down to tiny dimensions and ride the wind."

Griffen leaned back more in his chair, looking nonchalant. He was aware of his uncle watching each reaction, and decided some input was expected. He hesitated, again worried about letting himself slip into his uncle's delusions, but decided he had little choice but to go along with the flow of the bizarre conversation.

"I don't pretend to know much about the East, and nothing much at all beyond China and Japan," Griffen said, trying to keep things sounding normal and make one more attempt at getting the conversation back on the track of why he came here in the first place. After all, he had attended international business classes . . . once in a while. "But it's been my impression that they are deadly negotiators. At the very least, it's not a crowd I would want to deal with when they knew in advance they had something I wanted or needed."

Griffen stopped again, unsure whether the comment had broken any ice with his uncle. Again Malcolm McCandles's face showed nothing to give the younger man any relief.

"It was brutal," Malcolm said. "It is unknown today what promises and powers the European dragons had to surrender, but they achieved their objective and gained the ability to size shift. They used that new skill along with their shape-shifting to infiltrate and blend in with the humans, even to interbreed with them in some instances. Their descendants survive to this day, dwelling unsuspected among the humans."

"I see," Griffen said carefully. "And now you're going to tell me that you're one of those dragons?"

"That's right," Malcolm said. "More importantly, so are you . . . and your sister."

"That's interesting," Griffen said. "I have to admit, Uncle Mal, I don't particularly feel like a dragon."

"That's because you're only just coming into your physical maturity," Malcolm said. "Your secondary powers haven't put on their appearance yet, but they should shortly."

"Secondary powers," Griffen said, interested despite himself. "Should I ask what my primary powers might be?"

"You've had them all along," Malcolm said, "but you haven't seen them as being extraordinary. First of all, you rarely if ever get sick. What's more, in the few times you've suffered an injury, you heal remarkably swiftly."

Griffen started to speak, then held his silence. He had always been blessed with good health, but he had always assumed it was just good fortune. It hardly made him some sort of inhuman lizard.

"You also have a certain affinity with animals. You can exert your will over theirs to control their actions."

"Animal control," Griffen said, and a smirk twisted slightly at the corners of his mouth. Polite attentiveness wasn't seeming to help him anyway, and he just couldn't help himself. "You mean like Obi-Wan in *Star Wars*?"

"You could say that," Malcolm said. "In a small way. You can draw animals to you, or send them away. You can even calm them if they're excited. Exactly how much control depends on how much of the talent you were born with, and how much you've developed and exercised it. There are some nondragons who have similar powers. Circus animal trainers and some shamans, for example."

Griffen nodded, trying to keep the skepticism from his expression.

"Uncle Malcolm, granted you said dragons were never big scaly beasts, still, I've never looked anything but human when I checked in a mirror."

"Ah, and you are wondering how a disguise, for all intents and purposes, is passed on from father to son?"

"Pretty much."

"Dragons are not fools Griffen. Quite the opposite. What good would trading for a disguise be, if every baby born put its parents in immediate danger? Let's just say that geneticists barely understand their own DNA, and aren't likely to get a dragon sample."

Again Griffen held his silence, but it was more difficult. There was something that disturbed him in that last comment. A hardness in his uncle's voice that was surprisingly intimidating.

"As I was saying," Malcolm continued, "your senses are notably keener than those of humans, particularly your powers of observation. I suspect that would account for your success at cards. Whether it's gambling or business, dragons have always been able to 'read' their opponents, which gives them a sizable edge in conflicts."

"I'll admit I've always been lucky," Griffen said with a smile. "Then, too, I've always been fond of money. Isn't that another trait of dragons?"

"Actually," Malcolm said, "dragons are fond of power. Money or gold is simply one way of gaining it. Some turn to politics or warfare to achieve the same thing. There are several who have gone the route of becoming entertainers. If you look around our modern society, not to mention history, it isn't that hard to spot the dragons lurking there. Usually around power, always at or near the top."

Malcolm's expression darkened. The look he suddenly shot Griffen was filled with greed such as he had never seen. Griffen could hear his pulse beating away wildly as he watched the executive force himself to stay relaxed. Griffen wasn't sure what set him off more, the expression, or the obvious show of iron-willed control.

"Check me on this, Uncle Mal," Griffen said, keeping up

with Malcolm's thought. "I'll be the first to admit that I'm operating with limited knowledge, but I've always thought that your basic power broker wasn't wild about sharing that power with anyone else."

Malcolm raised his eyebrows in pleased surprise. His expression slipped back into his more neutral mask.

"Exactly right," he said, nodding at the youth. "Dragons are as solitary as they are greedy. Oh, they may put on a show of being friendly, and many are quite charismatic, some to a point of using another form of mind control called glamour, but underneath it all they're pretty self-serving. While temporary alliances are occasionally formed, they usually only last until the objective is achieved. There are some ongoing power blocs, mostly to keep track of and counter the doings of other power blocs, but even those are tenuous and prone to realignment.

"That brings us to your situation."

"Me?" Griffen said, suddenly sitting up straighter.

His expression was attentive, but inside all he could think of were the dangers and pitfalls in the current situation. A part of him was curious, but most of him would have been very glad to be anywhere but this room. Thoughts of a job were long past. He was more interested in making sure he got out of the building with his skin intact.

"That's right. You see, your parents were both near purebloods. That's an expression we use to recognize those with minimal human blood in their line. Alone they were each quite powerful, and united they were strong enough to worry some of the power blocs. When they produced not just one, but two offspring, that worry grew to open fear . . . enough to inspire some factions to engineer their deaths."

Griffen's head cocked, body stiffening. He rarely let himself think of his parents, and didn't care for Malcolm's comments about them so far, nor for the dark implications whirling in his mind. He began to suspect that this was the key to this whole puzzle. Malcolm didn't seem to notice the change in his posture, or just didn't care.

"Now that you're coming of age, however, things are heating up again. You see, with two near purebloods for parents, the other dragons are assuming that you'll have rare strength, particularly once your secondary powers develop. Many fear that, despite your youth, you're potentially more powerful than they are. Can you see what that means?"

"I've got an idea," Griffen said, "but tell me anyway."

"You've become a focal point of the dragon hierarchy. Some will be content to wait and see what powers you develop and what use you decide to make of them. Others will make every effort to recruit you as an ally. I fear, however, that there will be others who will simply try to kill you or have you killed just to be sure those powers aren't used against them."

"I see," Griffen said. "Tell me, you keep saying that all this is coming down the road at me. What about Valerie?"

If other dragons might be out to kill him, where did that leave his situation with the "dragon" in the room? If Malcolm was so deranged by guilt over losing his brother that his mind has slipped into this dementia, what would be the next logical step? If logic could apply. Would he wish to kill a rival dragon, even his own nephew? Would the executive have a gun in his desk? Or would he try to rip Griffen's throat out like an animal?

He swallowed, and tried his best to keep his breathing regular. Malcolm had not once taken his keen eyes off of Griffen, and the younger man realized he didn't want his uncle to know just how fast his heartbeat was going at the thoughts of his possible death.

"I'm sure others have kept an eye on her, but your sister has a ways to grow yet before she's a factor," Malcolm said. "Besides, as wild and undisciplined as she is, I believe there are other plans in store for her. Using her for breeding stock without her being aware of it comes to mind. For the moment, however, it would be best to focus on your problems."

Griffen practically ground his teeth at that. He had kept control all through the talk of threats to him, but the callous tone about his sister . . . Again he kept his reactions to himself, still waiting to see how this would unfold. In any other situation, though, he would have left, or bloodied Malcolm's nose.

"All right." Griffen nodded. "So how many of the individuals or blocs are there, and which ones do I have to look out for?"

"Not so fast." Malcolm said, taking a long draw on his cigar. "Filling you in on the general situation falls under my duties as your guardian. Giving you specific information is a whole different ball game. In case you haven't figured it out, I'm one of the players you have to deal with. Like your father, I'm a near pureblood. Unlike him, however, I've gone to great lengths to keep a low profile in the interdragon power struggles. If I give you too much help, take you under my wing so to speak, all that could change."

In other words, Griffen thought, Malcolm protected his own ass (or was that tail?) when he could have helped save his brother. Griffen wondered why he would do anything else for his nephew . . . unless it gained him something.

Griffen realized suddenly that he had been dead wrong, and felt like an idiot. Too many monster movies, not enough sense. This wasn't a trap, it was an attempt to increase his uncle's power. He could see the recruitment offer coming like a train down a tunnel, but doubted it would be anything like what he had been hoping for when he first entered the office building. Griffen felt like an absolute fool.

"Personally, I'm inclined to be one of those who take a wait-and-see attitude. If you want specific help and training, on the other hand, I'd need your reassurance and pledge that you would align with me and not use what I tell you against me."

He leaned back in his chair and flashed a wide smile.

"So I guess the ball is really in your court, Griffen. Do you want to sign on with me here and now, or do you want to play it as an independent for a while?"

Three

It was notably early in the day to drink, but Griffen figured he deserved one. Not that he needed one, mind you, but it would be welcome nonetheless. Besides, the ground-floor bar in Malcolm's office building was irresistibly convenient.

Sliding onto a stool, he absently gave the bartender his order . . . Irish whiskey on the rocks (beer was so working class) . . . and settled down to think.

He had come to the meeting with such high expectations, and now it seemed he had to recalculate his entire future. Only one thing was sure. The cushy job he had hoped for with his uncle Malcolm was a bust. He had known all along that rich, successful people tended to be a bit odd, but his uncle, in the words of Raymond Chandler, was as crazy as three waltzing mice.

Dragons! Power blocs! Executions and assassinations!

If Griffen had owned any stock in any of his uncle's corporations, he would be thinking seriously of dumping it. Of course, to date he had steered clear of such legalized gambling, preferring the kind when you got to see your opponent face-to-face.

The nerve of Malcolm! Never mind this dragon nonsense. From his own words, he left his own brother to hang for his own profit, and held out his hand to Griffen for the same reason. When he figured Griffen was the most vulnerable, dreading the thought of working and the real world. There was no way Griffen wanted part of a businessman, or business dragon, with those kind of priorities and those sort of tactics.

At least he wasn't totally stranded. He had maybe $20-25,000 he had squirreled away between his poker winnings and what he had skimmed from his monthly allowance. That and his car, which ran most of the time. Originally he had figured on using the stash on his wardrobe and maybe to furnish a nice bachelor pad, but he could live on it for a while until he came up with a viable option.

Unfortunately, most options he could think of at the moment involved working, something he had managed to fastidiously avoid in his life to date.

Maybe Mai would have an idea.

Mai!

He suddenly remembered that he was supposed to meet her back at the hotel room with a report on how his meeting had gone. It wouldn't do to keep her waiting too long. Mai was not a girl to be kept waiting.

They had been playmates and occasional lovers back in school, and when he had mentioned the meeting with his uncle to her, she had offered to tag along . . . a combination of moral support and a chance for her to do a little shopping. He had always known that he was more emotionally involved than she was. It was one of the things she found endearing about him, which would worry him if he let himself dwell too much on it. She never said much about her own background, but the way she went through money it was a cinch her family wasn't exactly hurting. Not a bad person to consult with about his future. She might even provide a contact or two.

His mind invaribly came back to Uncle Malcolm. For the first time he wondered if it had all been some kind of complicated joke. Again, he hadn't had all that much direct contact with the man, but from what he knew Malcolm was not the practical-joking kind. Something was very wrong. Griffen didn't have a glimmer as to what was really going on.

Tossing a couple bills on the bar, Griffen finished the rest of his drink in one long swallow and eased off the stool. The confused young graduate left the building, feeling lost and more than a bit sorry for himself.

He tried to console himself that at least now he had a plan of sorts. Hook up with Mai and pick her mind a bit. Even if nothing came of it, they could enjoy a night on the town and he could attack the problem fresh in the morning.

Emerging into the daylight, he paused for a moment to squint up at the sky. There were a few clouds up there, but the temperature was pleasant enough. He'd go ahead and walk the five blocks back to the hotel. Taxis should be an avoidable luxury for a while until he settled his future finances.

"Mr. McCandles? Griffen McCandles?"

Blinking with surprise and from the sun, Griffen redirected his attention from the sky to the man who had addressed him.

Actually, there were two of them, though only one had spoken. They seemed ordinary enough, to a point where he probably wouldn't have noticed them on the street if they hadn't approached him. Viewing them now, however, there was a sameness in their stance and posture that suggested either military or police, regardless of their tailored suits.

"Yes? Can I help you?" he said, glancing back and forth between the two men.

For a moment, the characters from *Men in Black* flashed through his mind, but he shrugged the image off. If nothing else, their suits were gray, not black, and neither of them was wearing sunglasses. Apparently his discussion with his uncle had affected him more than he had realized.

"There's someone who would like a few words with you, if you can spare a moment."

The man speaking took a step backward and gestured toward a limousine that was standing at the curb. His partner took a step sideways, so that they effectively had Griffen bracketed, blocking his movement in either direction along the sidewalk.

Griffen glanced around quickly. None of the other pedestrians on the street seemed to take notice of what was going on. Perhaps such occurrences were normal in this town.

He decided nothing could be as strange as his uncle, but didn't feel like getting in a stranger's car. Unless this was how the CIA recruited, he really wanted nothing to do with them. He turned as if to push past the men, only to have a heavy hand with an iron grip fall on his shoulder.

"We really must insist, Mr. McCandles," the man said, and squeezed with his hand.

Griffen fought back a yelp, this man was strong! So much for Uncle Malcolm's comments about tough skin, Griffen felt like his shoulder socket was about to be ground to dust. Of course, he realized grudgingly, that had little to do with the skin.

With an offhand shrug, he tried to shake the hand off. Tried, and failed. The other man nodded pointedly to the limo, squeezed once more, then let him go with a little push.

Straightening, Griffen tried to maintain some dignity, and walked over to the limo. As he did, the back door opened as if in greeting. Not breaking stride, he stepped into the air-conditioned interior and sank into the nearest seat.

"Mr. McCandles. So good of you to join me." A warm, resonant voice came to him from the depths of the vehicle. "I don't believe we've had the opportunity to talk before."

Griffen was so surprised, he barely noticed the two suits entering behind him and closing the door before the limo eased into traffic. He wasn't particularly up on news and politics, but one would have to live in a barrel not to recognize the man addressing him.

"Senator Langley," he said, inclining his head in a polite nod. "An honor to meet you, sir."

"Ah, so you know who I am." The man beamed, flashing the smile that the newspapers and TV cameras loved.

"It would be hard not to, considering your distinguished career," Griffen said. "I'm just a little surprised that you know who I am . . . or care, for that matter."

"I've known your family for a long time." The senator waved, negligently. "Congratulations on your graduation, by the way."

"Thank you," Griffen said. "So, what was it you wanted to talk to me about?"

"More curiosity than anything," Langley said. "I heard you were meeting with your uncle today, and I just wanted to hear how the two of you got along."

Griffen wasn't sure which was more unbelievable. The idea that Senator Langley was aware of his movements, or the fact that he had been waiting outside his uncle's office in a limo for an unspecified length of time to find out the results of his meeting.

"We got along well enough, I guess," he said cautiously. "It's the first time we've really sat and talked, you know. Of course, he didn't need an 'escort' to get me to talk to him."

"Yes, yes," the senator said, leaning forward impatiently and ignoring the younger man's dig. "What I want to know is whether or not you've signed on with him."

This was getting just too bizarre. Griffen decided that he wanted to draw this discussion to a conclusion.

"No, I haven't," he said. "Frankly, I found Uncle Malcolm too unorthodox for my comfort."

Langley sat back and stared at him.

"Unorthodox?" he echoed. Then a smile warmed his face. "Oh. I see. You mean about the dragons."

Griffen frowned at him. Was the whole world going crazy?

"Yes. I guess that was it," he managed. "And please don't tell me that you're one, too. I've heard enough about dragons for one day . . . if not for a lifetime."

The senator blinked, obviously startled.

"Me? No. I'm not a dragon. Some of the principals I represent are, however. They're very interested in . . ."

"Senator," one of the bodyguards said.

Somehow he managed to crowd both an admonishment and a warning into the one word. Griffen made a hasty revision of his interpretation of the relationship between the senator and his two escorts.

"Well, the less said about that, the better," the senator said hastily. "For both our goods."

"Excuse me?" Griffen said, now totally confused.

"Nothing, nothing." Langley smiled, regaining his composure. "So, you turned Mal down, eh?"

"Well, actually I told him I'd think about it," Griffen said, "but I'll admit I just can't see us working together."

"Only one to a hill, eh?" the senator said. "I guess that's wise. Courageous to the point of being foolhardy, perhaps, but wise nonetheless. Well, I guess that answers my questions. Don't want to take up any more of your time. I believe this is your hotel."

The limo pulled smoothly over to the curb in front of Griffen's hotel.

Griffen was starting to have a few questions of his own, but it was clear the discussion was at an end.

"Right. Well, it was great meeting you, sir," he said, reaching for the door handle.

"Just one thing, Griffen . . . if I can call you that," Langley said. "A friendly word of advice. Get used to hearing about dragons. They aren't going to go away just because you don't believe in them."

It wasn't until Griffen had almost reached the entrance of the hotel that it occurred to him that the senator had never asked where he was staying. He had already known.

Pausing, he glanced down the street in the direction the limo had gone.

It had stopped a half block away. The door opened and one of the "bodyguards" emerged to stand beside the vehicle. Though he carefully did not look at Griffen, his posture was unmistakable to one who knew how to read people. His pose was calculated, threatening, and quite possibly lethal. He held the pose for a moment, then stuck his head back into the limo, apparently conferring with someone inside. He straightened and stared directly at Griffen for a long moment, then reentered the vehicle, which then moved off.

Despite the day's warmth, Griffen felt a sudden chill, as if he had just had a close call with an unseen, but no longer unknown danger.

Four

Mai looked like a doll and ate like a cannibal.

Even though she was second- or third-generation American, her Asian ancestry apparently yielded strong enough genes that she could have walked into a role in *The Flower Drum Song* or maybe *The World of Suzie Wong*. She had that tiny, athletic physique one normally associates with gymnasts or dancers, and radiated enough energy to power an entire city block. Her dress and manner were pure American, though, and she exuded a rich, sophisticated aura that brought boutique clerks out of their comas and had any four-star restaurant head waiter snap to attention as if she were slumming royalty.

Griffen loved being with her, if for no other reason than her dominating presence meant that he could give his sincere naivety pose a rest. No one even looked at him when he was with her. More than that, he enjoyed her company. Even now, watching her demolish a whole lobster, he took pleasure in her boundless enthusiasm.

"What is it, lover?"

Her sudden question roused him from his reverie.

"Excuse me?" he said, caught off guard.

"You were looking at me with a funny expression," she said. "Have I got something stuck on my nose again?"

"Not this time," he said, smiling at the shared memory. "I was just trying to figure out how you can stuff so much food into such a small body and not gain any weight."

"I'm a high-energy person and I burn off a lot of calories," she replied, negligently waving a forkful of lobster. "You know, kinda like a hummingbird. If I don't eat a couple times my weight every day, I shrivel up and die."

"That must be it." He smirked, watching the lobster disappear into the depths of her tiny mouth.

"You certainly aren't eating much," she said, prizing another morsel of lobster from its shell. "Anything bothering you?"

"Other than being unemployed with no immediate plans for the future, no," he said with a grimace.

"I told you not to worry about that," she scolded, swirling her prize in the cup of melted butter. "I'm sure Daddy can find something for you. He owns a bunch of companies and employs zillions of people. If he doesn't have an opening for someone with your talents, he's bound to know someone who does."

"And what talents are those, pray tell?"

"I don't know. Maybe he can set you up as a male prostitute for bored housewives," she said, giving him a bawdy wink.

That got him to laugh out loud.

"All right. You win," he said, holding his hands up in surrender. "It's impossible to stay depressed around you. So tell me about your father. What's he like, anyway?"

"Oh, he's the typical Hong Kong businessman type," she said, returning her attention to her meal. "Obsessed with finding new ways to make money. Still kinda old-fashioned in a stuffy sort of way, but he still knows how to have a good time. At least you don't have to worry about him hassling you about being a dragon."

Griffen froze, staring at her.

"Why did you say that?" he asked carefully.

"Well, isn't that what you said was your problem with working for your crazy uncle?"

"No. What I said was that he had some weird notion that he was a half-human superbeing. I didn't say anything about dragons."

"Sure you did," she insisted. "What's more, he tried to convince you that you and your sister were dragons, too."

"No," Griffen insisted doggedly. "If anything, I've made a point of not using that word. It's such a crazy notion I don't even like to think about it."

"So what?" Mai shrugged. "Maybe what you were describing sounded like a dragon and I just put a name to it. No big deal."

"But why that particular word?" he pressed. "I mean, when I think of crazy people, I don't automatically think of dragons. At least, I didn't used to."

"Look. We're getting way off the subject," Mai said firmly. "Let's get this job thing settled right now."

She tossed her napkin on the table and rose to her feet, fishing her cell phone from her shoulder bag.

"I'm going to duck outside, call Daddy, and explain the whole situation to him. He'll come up with a job, and we'll have something to celebrate instead of arguing about your loony uncle."

Griffen started to stand politely, but she was already on her way, weaving her way majestically through the other tables. Settling into his seat once more, he stared morosely at his barely touched dinner.

What was wrong with him? He was letting this dragon thing bother him way too much. He had never really been that close to Uncle Malcolm. Why should his obsession with dragons matter one way or the other?

Still, he was sure that he hadn't mentioned dragons to Mai when he told her about the meeting. The casual way she referenced it didn't seem like a spur of the moment label she had just made up. How could she know about the whole dragon thing. Unless . . .

He shook his head as if trying to forget a bad dream.

He was doing it again. He didn't really believe what his uncle had said for one minute. Did he? It was true that the senator's apparent knowledge and belief had given him pause, but he didn't believe it himself.

What was it Uncle Malcolm had said about the Eastern dragons? That they stayed apart from their European counterparts and their descendants, but were suspected to be secretly monitoring Western dragon activity?

Now that was really getting silly. The "Yellow Peril" thing went out with Fu Manchu. Besides, Mai was as American as he himself was.

He found himself staring at the half-finished lobster on her plate. Now that was really unusual. Once she started eating, Mai didn't let anything interrupt her meal short of a nuclear attack . . . and even then she'd ask for a doggie bag. Yet when he started pressing her on the dragon thing . . .

Suddenly restless, Griffen stood up and went looking for his dining companion.

Before he could reach the door of the restaurant, however, he was intercepted by their waiter.

"May I help you, sir?"

Griffen was suddenly aware that it looked as if her were trying to duck out on the bill.

"No, everything is fine," he said with a smile. "I was just checking to see how my date's phone call was going is all."

"Phone call?"

"Yes. She stepped outside to get better reception on her cell phone."

The waiter frowned.

"Umm . . . I think there must be some mistaken communication here, sir," he said hesitantly. "The young lady you were dining with has left. I was a bit surprised myself, since she didn't seem ill or upset, but I saw her hail a cab just outside our door."

Five

Mai wasn't in their hotel room when Griffen returned. Also missing were her bags and clothes.

He knew from previous outings with her that she was far from the world's fastest packer. That meant that she must have been particularly motivated to have gotten back to the hotel, packed, and departed before he had figured out her ploy and returned himself.

This did little to put Griffen's mind, already in a turmoil, at ease. What had started out as a clever ploy to try to land a cushy job had turned out to be the most disruptive day of his life.

First his uncle Malcolm, instead of offering him a job, had given him a load of nonsense about dragons. Then there was the conversation with the senator and his bodyguards that weren't. Now, on top of it all, his old playmate Mai not only turned out to be aware of the whole dragons thing, but had done a disappearing act rather than answer any questions.

Maybe he should have taken Malcolm more seriously . . . or, at least, listened closer.

What all had he said about dragons again?

They were long-lived, and resistant to illness or injury. Did that mean that he could have taken on the two body-guards if they had come after him? Resistant didn't mean invulnerable. Besides, what if they were part dragon them-selves? That grip had *hurt*.

Griffen shook off that train of thought. Was he really ready to accept his uncle's delusion? Had his lack of options made him that desperate? He already had his doubts, and half blamed himself for scaring off Mai. Who wouldn't run off at such crazy talk?

Animal control. Something about animal control. Actu-ally, that could be kind of neat . . . if it were true. Unfortu-nately, there weren't any animals in the hotel room for him to try it out on. What was more, he had no inclination to head out onto the city streets to look for subjects. Then again, could it possibly work on weaker-minded humans . . . like those without any dragon blood in them? Didn't Malcolm specifically mention that dragons were charismatic and able to influence people to a disproportionate degree? Was that just another form of animal control?

Despite his scattered thoughts, Griffen had to smile. "These aren't the droids you're looking for. Move along." No. It was just too silly to be taken seriously. But wasn't he doing precisely that?

Griffen was pacing the limited confines of the room now, moving from the window facing an air shaft to the bath-room door and back. Idly, he found himself wishing that he smoked, if for nothing else than a hand prop. As a poker player, he had never developed the habit. Too many tells were possible just from lighting a cigarette, as he knew from exploiting the same in others. On the other hand, if what Malcolm had said was correct, getting cancer was the least of his worries currently.

He made himself stop pacing, leaning his forehead against the wall. The cool plaster did nothing to ease the ache in his head. It was too much. Dragons, he was actually running through the characteristics of dragons. His thoughts were colliding, his heart pumping, pulse as loud in his ears as the absurdity in his brain. If it had just been his uncle. Even just his uncle and the senator, though the latter was harder to brush off. Then Mai, leaving him like that. Instantly, without hesitation, as if he were . . . nothing.

Or as if he were a threat.

A dragon?

What else? Heightened senses. Now that was something Griffen could relate to. Of course, up until now, he had always assumed that everyone else had the same powers of observation that he had, but never developed them or used them. Maybe he was something special.

Leaning away from the wall, he stood still, trying to calm himself. He let his concentration go out of focus and stretched out his senses to "feel" the hotel around him. The task proving a focus for his calm. It was so easy to do and . . .

There was someone outside the door of his room!

Now that he was "listening," Griffen could hear the minute sounds of breathing and clothes rustling in the hall. What was more, they weren't passing by. They were just standing there.

His first thought was that it was Mai, but he quickly discarded it. Mai would have simply used her key and come in, or, at least, knocked. Besides, it didn't sound like Mai. It sounded like someone who was trying hard not to be heard.

He never even considered the possibility that it might be someone random trying to remember their room number. With all the other weird stuff that had happened today, that would be too much of a coincidence.

No, someone was specifically trying to check up on him. But who? Other than Mai, who knew where he was staying? Malcolm had never even asked. The senator! Or, for that matter, the two so-called bodyguards.

Or worse? Griffen suddenly realized, he only knew of three that seemed to be watching him, but how many knew of him? He wouldn't have known about the senator if he hadn't been summoned into the limo. Was this another party interested in the new dragon? Another recruitment attempt?

Or one of the ones who thought recruitment was too risky?

He had sudden visions of someone waiting outside with a gun. Or maybe just teeth and flaming breath. Terror and absurdity and indignation all flared up in him suddenly. He was torn between a sudden fear of opening the door, and a burning desire to confront whoever was out there and settle things once and for all.

And, like a dam breaking, all emotions eased away into sudden calm.

They had left.

As he had weighed the pluses and minuses of his choices, his senses had still been tracking the figure. Whoever it was seemed to have moved off while he was sorting out what to do. The threat, real or imagined, was gone. His body had relaxed accordingly.

Moving to the door, he first checked the crack of light showing under the entrance, but could see nothing. Cracking the door, he looked out cautiously, then boldly stuck his head into the hall. The corridor was empty. Whoever it had been had vanished completely.

Closing the door, Griffen turned the night lock, then put on the security bar for an added safeguard. His hand shook slightly, and he realized he wasn't all that calm after all. At this point, he wasn't even going to try to pretend that he wasn't spooked.

Turning away, his foot hit something on the floor. It was a small piece of paper, possibly a note or an advertisement had been slipped under his door. He felt another small wave of relief. That would explain why a stranger had approached his room.

He stooped and picked it up. Examining it, it turned out to be a tarot card . . . the Knight of Swords to be specific. It was from a small deck, so the card was barely the size of a business card. There was no writing or other message on it.

Griffen frowned at the card. Instead of finding an explanation to the presence in the hall, he was presented with a new mystery.

The phone rang; the sound like a fire alarm, loud in the stillness of the room.

Griffen collected his nerves from where they were clinging to the ceiling like a velcro cat and reached for the phone. An inch from the receiver, he hesitated. There was no way this was going to be anything good . . . unless it was Mai.

Cursing himself for being a nervous Nellie, he picked up the phone.

"Hello?"

There was a moment's hesitation on the other end.

"Griffen? Are you alone?"

Griffen relaxed as he recognized the voice.

"Hi, Uncle Mal. Yes, I'm alone. What's up?"

"I wanted to warn you," his uncle said. "Things have changed since we talked earlier."

"Changed how?"

"Some of the other dragon factions I mentioned know you're in town."

"No kidding," Griffen said with a sarcastic laugh. "I've already run into some of them."

"What happened?"

Griffen proceeded to narrate his meeting with the senator, including his suspicions about the bodyguards. As he did, he found himself waving his arms wildly and pacing with the phone next to his ear. Here, alone in the hotel room, he allowed himself the physical release, though he was sure his voice would match it with at least a little strain.

There were several moments of silence after he finished.

"Not good," his uncle said at last.

"It gets worse," Griffen said. "I think there was someone outside the door of my room a little while ago. They're gone now, but it creeped me out a little. Whoever it was left a calling card. They slipped a tarot card, the Knight of Swords, under my door."

"The Knight of Swords?" Malcolm's voice was suddenly very sharp. "Are you sure?"

"I'm holding it in my hand right now," Griffen said. "Why? What does it mean?"

"I'm sorry, I can't tell you that," his uncle said. "It would be too much like interfering. I shouldn't even be talking to you, Griffen, but family's family. All I can do is give you a warning. Get out of there now. Don't wait until morning. Get out right now. As fast as you can."

"But where should I go?" Griffen said, taken aback. He glanced at the door, the window, even the door to the bathroom.

"I don't know, and if you think of someplace, don't tell me. What I don't know, they can't get out of me. Good luck."

Griffen started to ask something but realized he was talking to a dial tone.

Replacing the receiver, he started gathering up what few clothes he was traveling with. If nothing else, his uncle Mal had convinced him he had to get out of the hotel and out of town as soon as possible . . . like, right now.

As to where he was going, he had no plans to return to his old campus. The few items he had been planning to pick up later were unimportant. No, he was thinking of something truly precious. His sister. Valerie's school was still in session, and he wanted to talk things over with her. Something about what Malcolm had said about the dragons "having other plans for her" didn't sit quite right in his mind.

Six

Tooling down the expressway with the morning sun rising on his left, Griffen realized he wasn't in the least tired despite his driving through the entire night. Other than a couple stops for fuel and a quick stop at a Waffle House to stretch his legs and grab a bite, he had been behind the wheel for nearly ten hours and felt as fresh as when he had started.

He found himself wondering if this was one of the so-called dragon powers that Uncle Malcolm had talked about, then caught himself and forced the thought from his mind. He had promised himself that he wouldn't fret over the whole dragon thing until after he had a chance to talk to his sister. Besides, it was more likely that he simply enjoyed driving his car.

A state trooper eased up beside him with customary predatory smoothness, paused to look him over, then glided on ahead.

Griffen was neither worried nor surprised. It was the third or fourth time that had happened during this run alone. He knew he was well within the speed limit, being in no particular hurry, and was used to his vehicle drawing attention.

It was an old Sunbeam Tiger with its original British racing green paint, with a black top and trim. A few people recognized the body as being the same kind of car that Maxwell Smart had driven during the opening of the old *Get Smart* television series. Except Max had been driving a Sunbeam Alpine, not a Sunbeam Tiger. Only a few sports car fanatics were aware of the difference.

The Alpine was a sporty little two seater with a four-cylinder engine. The Tiger, on the other hand, used the same body, but had a Ford V-8 engine crammed in under the hood. Basically, it was an engine on wheels with a thin candy shell, and could hit 120 mph with comfort.

Griffen had lusted after the car the first time he set eyes on it, though even now he felt a twinge of guilt recalling how he acquired it.

It wasn't really his fault, he told himself for the hundredth time. The kid who owned it was legally an adult, and no one had put a gun to his head to get him to sit in on a high-stakes poker game. Definitely no one was to blame that the kid hung in until he was deep in the hole. It had been a fair game, and there was no reason for Griffen to feel any guilt over his winnings.

Even as he reviewed the evening, however, Griffen found himself again shaking his head in disgust. His oft-recalled justifications didn't nearly take into account the whole story. Fair game or no, the kid had no business being there. He was perhaps a decent frat or dorm game poker player, but he had been way over his head that night. The only reason he had sat in at all was that he was flattered that Griffen had invited him to play. Even then, he might have bailed out after a while if Griffen hadn't encouraged and flattered him, loaning him the necessary cash to hang in while "waiting for his luck to change." When the debts were totaled up at the end of the evening, however, it was clear that the kid would never be able to come close to buying back his IOUs. That was when Griffen had offered to tear up the chits and give the kid an additional five grand in exchange for his car.

Griffen still felt twinges of remorse over that deal. It certainly wasn't the last time he had used his poker and people skills to further his own ends, but it was the most blatant gambit he had ever pulled simply to get something he wanted. He felt bad about it, but not bad enough to give the car back. The car, which he named the Goblin, was his pride and joy, and he had taken his share of trophies driving it in gymkhanas, those amateur races where you run a driving obstacle course against a stopwatch.

Two pickup trucks were cruising along in the slow lane ahead of him. Without changing speed, he switched to the passing lane to ease past them.

As he passed the lead truck, he glanced over at the driver, thinking to give him a pleasant nod of the head as a road courtesy. Instead of meeting his gaze, the man responded by accelerating, matching Griffen's speed so he couldn't pull ahead.

Annoyed, Griffen glanced in his rearview mirror, thinking to pull back in behind the suddenly awake trucker. The trailing truck, the one he had already passed, had switched lanes and was now sitting on his rear bumper, also matching his speed.

A small trickle of alarm woke in Griffen's mind. Whether they had intended to or not, the two trucks now had him boxed in against the soft shoulder.

Easing up on the gas pedal, he tapped his brakes lightly

so his taillights would flash, trying to signal to the truck behind him that he wanted to slow down and return to his original lane.

Instead of slowing to let him escape, the truck behind him suddenly accelerated, ramming his rear bumper and forcing him to speed up. The truck alongside him matched the move, not only increasing its speed, but edging over until its left wheels were crossing the center stripe.

Griffen was fully alert now and more than a little scared. What were these jokers trying to do? If they weren't in a clear stretch of road . . .

Glancing ahead, he saw there was a gentle curve to the right less than a mile ahead. If he didn't do something, the two trucks could potentially run him off the road and into the ditch that ran along the median.

For a moment, Griffen was tempted to floor the gas and try to outrun them, but he decided against it. He didn't know what these two had under their hoods, and if he failed to outrun them, they'd all hit the curve at an even greater speed.

There was, of course, another option.

Wrenching his steering wheel to the left, he took the Goblin onto the soft shoulder, then stood on the clutch and his brake pedal simultaneously.

The Tiger slid and fishtailed a bit, but came to a halt as the two trucks swept past and into the distance.

Heart racing, Griffen saw them slow to their original speed and reassume position one ahead of the other.

That should have been it. He was out of danger and could either sit for a few moments until they were out of sight or follow at a distance until he found an exit.

Instead, he stared after them through a red haze.

"So they want to play, do they?" he said out loud.

Dropping his shift lever to low, he popped the clutch and stood on the gas, charging back onto the expressway with a spray of dirt and a roaring engine.

It didn't take him long to overtake the pickups. They were driving below speed limit now, back in their old formation one behind the other in the slow lane.

Dropping his speed, Griffen slid in behind them, making it a line of three vehicles. He figured if nothing else, it would make them nervous enough to spark a reaction. It didn't take long.

Studying his opponents at leisure, he noticed something he had missed before. Both truckers had CB radios, and were talking back and forth as they watched him in their rearview mirrors.

Apparently they reached a decision. They reduced their speed, seeing if he would fall into the old trap and try to pass them.

No deal. Griffen lowered his speed to match theirs, sitting about ten feet behind the tailing truck.

The lead truck pulled out into the fast lane, then started to drop back as his buddy held his speed. Unless he dropped his speed even further, Griffen was going to end up in the same box he was in before, with one truck ahead of him and the other alongside, pinning him against the soft shoulder.

This time, he had something else in mind. Instead of dropping back, he moved onto the soft shoulder and eased up on the truck in front of him. This placed him in the blind spot of the second truck, while that truck in turn was blocking the line of sight of the truck dropping back. For a moment, neither driver could see him.

Confused, the driver in the trailing truck craned his neck around trying to get a fix on Griffen's position, while his partner dropped back quickly to try to establish the box.

With a tight smile, Griffen dropped down a gear and floored the accelerator. With a snarl, the Goblin responded, darting along the soft shoulder to pass the truck alongside. Startled, the driver shied away for a heartbeat, then gunned his own engine and moved toward the soft shoulder, trying to crowd Griffen into the ditch.

Too late. The Ford V8 engine was wide open and Griffen slid past, pulling back onto the highway ahead of his attacker.

Glancing in his rearview mirror, Griffen could suddenly see only one truck.

Not having encountered the expected resistance, the truck which had tried to run him off the road had itself gone into the ditch. Its front wheels were mired and twisted at a painful angle, and the hood had popped open.

That only left one.

The truck still on the road slowed momentarily, as if hesitant. Then roared to life again, surging forward. With his lead, Griffen could outrun him, but his blood was still up. Anger and adrenaline making him act foolish. He let the truck gain.

Not even Griffen knew what he was thinking. No longer was he acting off a plan, but merely following the heat of the moment. He let the truck start to pull up along his side, not quite at an angle to run him off the road yet. He only had ill-conceived notions of taunting his adversary before flooring it and leaving him in the dust. He glanced back, catching sight of the driver through the window.

Caught sight of the driver, past the length of a shotgun.

Startled, Griffen almost wrenched himself off the road in

shock. That involuntary jerk was the only thing that saved at the very least some damage to his car, if not preventing total disaster. His engine screamed, drowning out the roar of the blast behind him, and the shot went wide as the Goblin tore down the road, finally outdistancing his attacker. In his rearview mirror, a now thoroughly panicked Griffen watched the truck slow. His last glimpse of it was to see it turn, pushing over the divider, presumably to go rescue the other driver.

Putting his car back in gear, Griffen continued along his way at a much more reasonable speed. His fingers gripped the steering wheel, knuckles white, as his pulse pounded through his ears.

As his heartbeat slowly returned to normal, he found himself wondering at his recent actions. Even though things had eased considerably in Michigan since the late sixties, when the crumbling auto industry inspired frustrated laid-off line workers to retaliate by running imported cars off I-94, it was not unheard of for such incidents to occur even today. Griffen himself had survived three such attempts in the Goblin. In those cases, he had dodged the initial attack, then pulled off at the next exit, shaken and glad to be alive.

He had never felt moved to retaliate . . . to counterattack the way he had just now. It had been a mistake, a nearly fatal one. Even though he had no way to know just how hostile the truck drivers had been, it had been utterly reckless to give up his lead without a clear plan of action. This sudden shift in his reactions both puzzled and bothered him.

What bothered him even more was not the final attempt, but the quick burst of savage glee he had felt when his initial plan had worked and he saw his first attacker in the ditch.

It wasn't until he pulled off the expressway to refuel that he noticed his steering wheel was bent slightly out of round.

Seven

As he approached his sister's apartment, Griffen spied her striding down the sidewalk ahead of him, obviously bound for the same destination. He'd know that rump anywhere.

Not that the rest of her was unremarkable. While he had never actually lusted after her, being her brother did not keep him from noticing that Valerie had a stellar bod.

A bit over six feet in height, his sister's shoulders were a bit too broad and her face a bit too round to be considered a classic pinup beauty. Still, she was short waisted with ample breasts and legs that ran forever so that she had no difficulty drawing male attention whether she wanted to or not. What was more, Valerie moved with the easy, confident grace of a natural athlete, which she was. Whereas Mai always reminded Griffen of a doll, Valerie always made him think of a panther . . . or a wide receiver after a really good sex-change operation. With her blond hair, it was easy to see why he thought of her as Valkyrie rather than Valerie. Especially when she wore her hair in braids.

Passing her, he pulled his car over to the curb and got out, leaning against the vehicle as he waited for her.

She spotted him a dozen yards out and lengthened her stride to an easy lope.

"Hey, Bro!" she called. "What are you doing here?"

Still moving at speed, she swept him up in a bone-crushing hug and held him aloft.

"Val . . . I . . . QUIT!" Griffen managed, prying himself from her grip.

He tried to recompose himself, while not making it too obvious he was trying to get his breath back. His sister's greetings always left him feeling like he knew what Godzilla was like as a puppy.

"Hey, brat," he said finally. "Still working out, I see."

"My God, Grifter. What happened to the Goblin?"

She was staring at the recent damage to his vehicle. He had been avoiding looking at it too closely, himself, and her attention made him uncomfortable.

"A couple guys in pickups decided to contest my right to use their road," he said quickly. "I'll tell you about it some other time. Right now, we've got to talk."

"Yeah? What kind of trouble have you got yourself into now, Big Brother?"

Instead of answering immediately, Griffen peered closely at the hand she was waving.

"Speaking of trouble, Val," he said, "would it be impolite to point out that you're bleeding?"

Valerie glanced at her hand briefly, then licked the wet and drying blood from her knuckles like an animal before answering.

"No big deal," she said. "Just some muscle flexer who wouldn't take 'No' for an answer."

"Some things never change," Griffen said, shaking his head.

"Now don't change the subject," Valerie pressed. "What's up that brings you my way . . . and while the sun's up, even."

Griffen glanced up and down the street before answering.

"First, let's find somewhere we can talk without being interrupted. Someplace other than your apartment, if possible. I have a lot to tell you."

Over an hour, and several coffees, later at one of the campus hangouts, Griffen finally concluded his narration of what he had heard and experienced since visiting their uncle.

Valerie leaned back in her seat and sipped at her lukewarm beverage.

"Huh," she said at last. "That's got to be the weirdest thing I've heard in a long time. So what are we going to do?"

"I dunno," Griffen admitted. "I'm still trying to figure out if I believe it at all."

"Does it matter?" His sister shrugged.

"What do you mean, 'Does it matter'?" he said sharply. "Either the world has just been redefined for us, or a lot of people including our uncle have gone round the bend."

"And I repeat, does it matter?" Valerie shot back. "Whether this dragon thing is for real or not, enough people seem to believe in it that it already *has* redefined our world. I mean, if they're trying to pressure us or kill us, does it matter if they're right or wrong? It makes a difference to us and we've got to decide what we're going to do."

"You know, Val, that's why I wanted to talk this out with you." Griffen smiled. "You always manage to cut through the bullshit and get right to the heart of the matter. You're right, of course."

"So what are we going to do?"

He had missed it the first couple times, but it finally sank in.

"What do you mean 'we'?" he said. "I'm the one they're after. I just wanted to get your opinion and give you a heads-up."

"This affects both of us, doesn't it?" Valerie said stubbornly. "First of all, I'm not going to let you try to deal with this alone. Second, if they'll be after both of us eventually, it's easier to plan a defense if we stick together. Besides, I don't like the sound of that 'We have other plans for her' bit. If they're thinking of trying to use me for breeding stock, they've got another think coming."

"But what about school? You can't just pick up and go."

"Why not?" she said. "The semester's nearly over, and my grades are good enough that I can skip the finals without serious consequences. I couldn't concentrate anyway with this thing hanging over our heads."

"Val, look—"

"No, you look." Valerie cut him off abruptly.

Griffen was used to her changes in mood, but her sharp tone surprised him. She seemed to sense this and her tone softened.

"Forget school, school isn't important. This sounds important, and you need someone you can trust. Oh, sure, Uncle Malcolm was never exactly hands-on with our lives, but a betrayal is a betrayal. Not to mention your little . . . friend Mai."

He couldn't help but wince. When he had been telling her the story, she had been most furious over Mai. At this point, Griffen had doubts he would ever see Mai again, but if he did, he'd have to see about keeping Valerie away from her.

"And the senator, that makes this serious, even if it's ridiculous," Valerie continued, smiling a little. "I'm with you, Big Brother. Period."

Griffen couldn't think of a good argument for her reasoning. Truth to tell, he rather liked the idea of her coming along, even though he hadn't thought of it originally. Still, something nagged at him.

"I know you too well, Sis. Do you know something else that is prompting you?" he said.

"No . . . maybe. Just thinking back. How many times would I catch some guy staring at me or following me, and how often was it just your average stalkeresque loser? Maybe, just maybe someone was keeping an eye on me for more than my looks."

Griffen shivered.

"Recently?"

"No, not recently. Still, you're stuck with me. Accept it."

"Oh, darn, do I have to?"

He grinned and she chucked him affectionately on the shoulder. He managed not to wince from impact.

"So what now?" she said.

"Well, all I can think of is for us to find a safe place to go to ground while we try to figure out a game plan," he said. "Someplace no one would think to look for us."

"Sounds good for a start," Valerie said, rising to her feet. "Just swing by my place so I can pack a few things and we'll be off."

"Actually, Val, I'm kinda beat from driving all night," Griffen admitted, suddenly not relishing the thought of hitting the road again so soon. "Why don't I drop you off and check into a motel so I can sleep a couple of hours before we take on the great unknown."

"If you worked out once in a while, you'd have more stamina," his sister chided him. "Okay then, that will give me a little time to pick and choose what I'm bringing. A girl's gotta look her best, even if she's on the run."

Eight

There was a motel only a few blocks from where his sister lived. The clerk gave the crumpled back of his Sunbeam a hard look, but when Griffen carded over twenty-one and paid cash in advance there was no problem. His room was on the first floor on the back side of the long, low bulding. Throwing his bags on the floor next to a bed covered by a garish purple quilt, the young man turned and left the room. He should be tired, but somehow he wasn't. He went back outside and paused in front of his room to just stare at the stars. They were reassuringly the same.

A chill ran up his spine and the hint of a sound caused the young man to look to his right. A figure a hundred feet away was silhouetted in distant streetlights. There was something about the way the man stood there that set off alarm bells. Griffen backed into a shadow near his doorway and watched. The dark figure paused and then took a few steps. It seemed to the young man that he could sense the

dark man was smiling, but he was equally certain there was
no humor in that smile.

Both stood perhaps a hundred feet apart and half-visible
in the shadows of the badly lit back of the college-town motel. The sounds of traffic and a dog baying a few blocks away
seemed to get louder. Then it happened.

For the first time, Griffen understood what was meant by
a fight or flight reaction. The need to do something screamed
inside him. The man, thing, dragon, or whatever it was, had
seemed to be bigger and taller now. Without knowing it, he
took a step back.

Then it hit him. If he was a dragon, there would never be
a better time to become one. Which only left one urgent
question. How did you change into a dragon?

He tried willing himself to change. Nothing happened.

So Griffen decided he would command himself to
change, complete with a sweeping arm gesture. No dragon.

Risking closing his eyes for a moment, Griffen tried to
picture himself as a dragon. "Be the dragon, be the dragon,"
he intoned mentally, but all he got was the image of Chevy
Chase in *CaddyShack* intoning, "Be the ball."

Frustration led to anger. Okay, if he was going to get
mashed by a massive supernatural monster in the back of a
motel, he might as well go down fighting. He felt rage rise
inside him. It seemed to take hold and his vision blurred.
Everything was out of focus, and the sidewalk seemed to re-
cede. He reached for the wall and steadied himself while
desperately trying to see what his attacker was.

A car came around in the lot. The headlights speared
brightly across the sidewalk and the man disappeared around
the corner of the building. Then the lights swung away as
the car pulled into a space.

Griffen slumped against the wall and discovered he was nauseous. After two tries the key worked in his door. Minutes later the shaking stopped and Griffen risked a look out the door. The parking lot was pleasantly empty.

Tired as he was, Griffen was far too wound up now to sleep. The surge of adrenaline from his mysterious encounter had left him feeling shaken and wired up. After checking one more time to make sure the coast was clear, he made his way into the motel's lobby bar and settled in for a short drink and a long think.

Valerie was right, of course. It didn't matter if Uncle Malcolm was crazy or sane about the whole dragon thing. If there were people out there who believed it and were ready to act on it, then he and Valerie had little choice but to take it seriously as well. The only trouble was, he didn't have the vaguest clue as to what he should do next.

With school behind him, he had gambled heavily on getting a job with his uncle Malcolm only to have that crumble completely. Now he was homeless, adrift with all his worldly possessions in two suitcases, in what was left of his car. What was more, now he had Valerie in tow.

Hooking up with his sister completed the only agenda he had when he blew out of Michigan. Short of throwing a dart at a map, he had no idea of where they should go from here.

"Yo! Bartender! A Jack and Coke for me and another Irish for my man here!"

The familiar voice pulled Griffen out of his reverie and he craned his neck around to view the figure striding toward his table.

"Jerome?" he said. "Man! What are you doing here?"

The lean, dark man held up one finger signaling for Griffen to wait a moment as he detoured by the bar to gather up their drinks. As always, Jerome was stylishly dressed, with a tan sports coat worn over a cream-colored shirt with dark brown slacks that set off his coffee-colored skin to perfection. No matter what situation they were in when they ran across each other, Jerome always made Griffen feel underdressed.

Fast on the heels of his recognition, however, Griffen felt a sudden stab of suspicion. What *was* Jerome doing here?

They were passing friends on campus. Mostly, their relationship had grown from Jerome serving as his on-campus bookie on the rare occasions that he bet on football or other spectator sports. They gained a mutual respect for each other over the poker tables, as Jerome was one of the few that could hold his own against Griffen even when he was trying his hardest. None of this would help to explain what Jerome was doing here, hundreds of miles from their mutual stomping grounds.

"Here you go, Grifter," Jerome said, setting a fresh Irish down next to the half-finished one already on the table and pulling up a chair. "Nice to know someone else who always drinks the same thing. Simplifies things."

"Thanks, Jer," Griffen said, forcing a casualness he didn't feel. "I sure didn't expect to see you here. What brings you to these parts?"

"Lookin' for you, of course." His friend smiled, leaning back. "Fortunately or not, you aren't hard to find. We need to talk, my friend."

Griffen's head was spinning, and he held up a restraining hand.

"Slow up a minute, bro," he said. "I've been driving all night and so I'm a little slow. Why are you looking for me, and what do you mean I'm not hard to find?"

"To tell the truth, Grifter," Jerome said, dropping his

voice, "after the word got out that you had turned Mal down, Mose, that's the head of my crew, gave me a call and told me to look you up. Now, I remember you talking about your sister and her bein' in college here, so I . . ."

"Hold it. H-o-l-d IT!" Griffen said, waving his hand. "Jerome, are you going to tell me that this is about the whole dragon thing? And that you're one, too?"

"'Course it's about dragons," Jerome shot back. "And yes, I'm one, too. I'm way down on the totem pole from where you are, though. Near as I can figure, I'm maybe an eighth blood at best, which is pretty powerful for my crowd but nowhere near what you've got behind you."

"Uh-huh," Griffen said. "And how long have you known about this?"

"About you or about me?"

"Both."

"I've known about it most of my life," Jerome said with a shrug. "I was raised knowin' it and expected to live up to it. Fact is, I'm slated to take over Mose's business when he retires, or at least be the right-hand man to whoever does."

He cocked an eyebrow at his friend.

"I understand that they kept you in the dark until yesterday, so I guess it's kinda hard for you to get your head around it. Even so, you had the instincts and the moves as long as I've known you. Anyone who knew what they were lookin' for could spot it."

"So you've known all along," Griffen said, not even making it a question. Somehow, his first drink was empty, and he reached for the next. "And you never said anything."

"Not my place to," his friend said. "I didn't know what they had planned for you or how they were gonna go about it. Like I said, I'm just a little fish and I don't mess with the big boys. I just did what I was told and kept an eye on you."

"You make it sound like the only reason you were on campus was to keep tabs on me," Griffen said.

"That's about the size of it." Jerome nodded. "To tell you the truth, Grifter, I'm older than I look. I got my degree a long time ago. I got sent there specifically to size you up and report back to my crew . . . and I'll tell you, I wasn't the only one watching."

Griffen's mind flashed back to Mai.

Aloud, he said, "But why, Jerome? I mean, even if everything you say is true, what makes me so important?"

"Like any longtime group, dragons have their legends and prophecies," Jerome said. "Oh, they're not written down or painted on some cave wall or anything, but everybody knows them. One of the long-standing ones is that someday a near pureblood will come along and change things for dragons forever.

"Now 'change' is a pretty nebulous word. It could mean for the better or for the worse. Of course, for those who are comfortable with things the way they are, change is something they look at with distrust if not outright fear. The odds of change improving things for them aren't nearly as high as that it will really mess things up."

In his head, Griffen was hearing his uncle's words: They'll try to recruit you or kill you.

"You may or may not be the one who's gonna do all this," Jerome continued, "but the legend's strong enough that anyone with a stake in things is gonna want to check you out, then try to figure out how to deal with you."

Griffen shook his head. "Let's put all that on hold for the moment," he said. "Now, what did you mean I was easy to find?"

"Like I said, I remembered you had a sister here, so that's where I looked for you." Jerome smiled. "Figured you'd want to talk things over with her once you were enlightened. After that, it was just a matter of cruising until I spotted the Goblin. Man, if you want to move around without bein' noticed, you've *got* to get a different set of wheels. That ride of yours is way too easy to spot."

While he knew Jerome was right, Griffen bristled at the thought of giving up his beloved Goblin.

"So it's distinctive," he said. "What are the odds of someone being in my vicinity to spot it if they don't know where to look? If you hadn't known about Valerie, would you be here looking?"

Jerome threw back his head and laughed.

"Man, you have no idea what you're up against," he said. "I said our crew was small and weak compared to the big boys. Let me give you an idea of what can be done. One of the top dragons on this continent is Stoner. You know what he does for his nine to five? He's one of the high lords of the new Homeland Security. That means that if he wants, he can put your name, description, and the description of your car out on the computers as 'suspected terrorist associate—do not detain but report location and movement' and every cop and federal agent will be keeping their eyes peeled for you."

An image suddenly appeared in Griffen's mind. A picture of a state police car pulling up beside the Goblin and looking it over.

"And you can forget using credit cards," Jerome was continuing. "For that matter, there are rumors that cell phones—"

"Wait a minute, Jer," Griffen interrupted. "Do you know this Stoner guy?"

"Only by reputation." His friend shrugged. "Like I say, we don't travel in the same circles."

"In your opinion," Griffen said, "is he the type to arrange a car accident for someone he's got a problem with?"

"That sounds kinda specific," Jerome said, cocking an eyebrow. "Anything in particular you have in mind?"

Griffen filled him in on the morning's highway skirmish.

"I dunno," Jerome said when he had finished. "That doesn't really sound like Stoner's style. Dragons, particularly big ones like Stoner, tend to avoid open confrontations. Too high profile. I'll tell you what it might be, though."

He leaned forward and lowered his voice.

"Even though law-enforcement types are supposed to co-operate when called on, the truth of the matter is they don't like anyone trespassing on their personal jurisdiction . . . especially not Feds. If Stoner *did* put out a tracker on you as a terrorist associate, I'd say there's an even chance that while the boys in uniform would follow the letter of the law, they wouldn't be above calling some of their buddies, maybe retired buddies, to take an unofficial hand. That would be especially true down here in the South. The good old boy right wingers would love to get a bead on a terrorist . . . especially since 9/11."

"Doesn't sound like someone who would slide a card under the door of my motel room," Griffen said almost to himself.

"A card?" Jerome said. "You mean like a business card?"

"No, I mean like a tarot card," Griffen said, and produced the card from the motel, which he was still carrying in his wallet.

Jerome leaned forward and studied the card, then leaned back with a scowl.

"I don't know for sure," he said carefully. "I just hope that isn't what I think it is."

"What's that?" Griffen said.

Jerome shook his head.

"I think you should wait and talk to Mose about that," he said firmly. "He knows more about that stuff than I do. Last thing I want to do right now is to give you bad information."

"Speaking of information, let me ask you something else." Griffen said uneasily. "When my uncle Malcolm first told me about being a dragon, he said something about how my secondary powers should be appearing soon. I think that's what might have happened this morning."

"Could be," Jerome said. "Sounds like it took some pretty fancy driving to get out from under all that. 'Course, faster reflexes and above-average strength are part of the normal package deal."

"That isn't what I was talking about," Griffen said. "I was thinking more about my temper. I mean, it should have been over, Jerome. I drove my way out and was sitting safe on the soft shoulder. I could have just let them drive away. Instead, it was like something clicked in my head, and I took off after them. I really don't remember clearly what all happened after that, but one of them ended upside down on the median with the other backing up to try to help. That just isn't like me."

"I don't know if dragons have tempers any worse than anyone else," Jerome said, shaking his head. "The problem is, with their powers, they can't afford to give in to it. You'd better start learnin' to get a handle on yours, Grifter. If you start drawing too much attention to yourself, then you're gonna have the whole pack of 'em down on your case. The one thing nobody wants is to have the humans get wise to the fact there are dragons walkin' around among 'em."

"Which brings us to another interesting point," Griffen said, leaning back in his chair. "Or rather, it brings us back to the original point. You keep talking about Mose and your crew. Just what is it that you want, Jerome? You said he sent you to look for me. Is this another of those 'recruit him or kill him' deals?"

"Actually, it's the other way around." Jerome grinned. "It'll be better when you hear about it from Mose in person, but the skinny is that we want to sign on with you."

That caught Griffen totally by surprise.

"Come again?" he said.

Jerome laughed.

"Remember when I told you that the big guys who were fat and sassy with the status quo would assume any change was bad? Well, my crew have been bottom dwellers so long, we figure any change will be an improvement for us. Especially if we line up early on the side of the one doin' the changin'."

"But I don't know anything at this point," Griffen protested. "And there's sure no guarantee that these so-called powers of mine are going to develop at all."

"Mose knows all that," Jerome said. "We've talked it over and we're willing to take the chance. Look, right now there are a lot of things you need: a place to hole up, time to decide what you're gonna do, and information to base your decision on. Eventually, you're also gonna need some financing and manpower to back up whatever it is you decide. We can provide all that. All we ask is that when all is said and done, you remember who it was that stepped forward first to side with you."

"Yeah, but what if I come up empty?" Griffen said. "Then you'll have taken sides against the big dragons and lost."

"We're already pretty much bottom of the heap." Jerome shrugged. "It's kinda like an oh-and-twelve football team gambling on a new coach. We got nowhere to go but up. So, what do you say, Coach? Is it at least worth a listen?"

Griffen hesitated. Even if listening wasn't an actual commitment, it was still a big step. Besides, he was feeling more than a little hurt that Jerome had initiated a friendship under false pretenses. It rubbed the wound of what Mai had done. A very fresh and raw wound.

On the other hand, what were his choices? Was he ready to face more shadowy figures in dark parking lots alone? He had just been considering the fact that he and Valerie had nowhere specific to go and no plan to follow. At least Jerome was offering a base of operation and even some financing. It sounded better than the alternatives . . . especially since he didn't have any.

"Assuming I say yes . . ." Griffen said carefully. "What's our first step?"

"First, I take you home to meet with Mose . . . and we'll take my wheels. No, don't worry about the Goblin," his friend said, forestalling Griffen's objection. "I'll have someone pick it up and put it in storage. Even do a little body work on it to remove the evidence of your little skirmish. She'll be good as new when you want her again."

"Actually," Griffen said, "I was going to say that we had to swing by and pick up Valerie on our way out of town. She's in this, too. Not negotiable."

"You told her about bein' a dragon?" Jerome winced, then shook his head. "Well, I guess what's done is done. You may regret it in the long run, though."

"Why is that?"

"I keep forgetting how new you are to all this," Jerome

said. "Don't tell her this, but it's always been kinda unofficial policy to try to keep the females in the dark for as long as possible about the dragon thing."

"How come?"

"Because female dragons have a bad rep. A *real* bad rep. Now, I won't go so far as to say that all females, dragon or human, are uncontrollable, but female dragons tend to be wild. Dragon powers and short tempers don't make a good mix. Remember how I said that dragons tend to avoid direct confrontation and high profiles? Well, it's because when they *do* square off, folks tend to notice . . . like the Chicago fire and the San Francisco earthquake. Female dragons were at the bottom of both of those little news items."

Griffen tried to imagine his brawling baby sister with dragon powers, and rejected the image with a shudder.

"That's as may be; just now I've got a lot more reason to trust her more than you, old buddy."

"Grifter, I'm hurt," Jerome said, but his eyes twinkled. "You're askin' yourself if you can trust me. You've played me at poker, you know my tells. So ask what's on your mind."

"How much of it was real?"

"Is, not was. Griffen, my man, ignoring that it's in my best interest to watch out for you. I like you, did from our first bar crawl."

Griffen didn't know what to say, but he remembered that night. They had been lucky not to end up in jail on an overnighter. It had been a hell of a night.

"And now here's something to twist your mind around," Jerome continued. "I know how things work, so I could ask, was I liking you, or was I under the influence of a dragon more powerful than I ever would be?"

"Huh. And did you ask yourself?"

"Nope, 'cause it didn't matter. Sometimes questioning doesn't help. Sometimes, Grifter, you just have to go with what works."

Griffen thought for a long minute. Sometimes you have to go with what works. Made sense, and Jerome was right on one thing. He knew Jerome's tells, and he meant every word. Instinct or dragon power, it didn't matter. This was someone he still trusted.

"Okay, I'm in, at least till I've heard the pitch from this Mose."

"Great! We'll get your sister and get started. The less time we are here, the less chance of someone else finding you."

Griffen nodded and finished off the remains of his glass.

"By the way," Jerome said, "have you told your sister about that tarot card?"

"Only in passing," Griffen said. "I really didn't know what to make of it and neither did she."

"Best not mention it to her again until after you've talked to Mose," Jerome said. "And when you show it to him, do it sometime when she's not there. Like I say, female dragons have a rep for overreacting."

"You say we're going to meet Mose," Griffen said, trying to change the subject. "Exactly where is home for you, Jerome? You may have said, but I don't remember."

"Exactly where you need to hide for a while, Grifter." Jerome beamed. "It's got everything you need: nightlife, casinos, loose women, and it's the absolute best place in the country to disappear and has been for over two hundred years. We're talking about New Orleans in general and the French Quarter specifically."

Nine

Griffen excused himself from Jerome, hastily making his way to the bar's small bathroom. The fixtures were the cheapest available, metal instead of porcelain; with a shabby privacy wall between the urinals and the only stall. Shakily, he turned the water on and let it pour, splashing only a bit on his face. He looked up at the mirror, and saw a near stranger looking back.

Despite his stamina on the road and his outward calm, the face in the mirror betrayed just what toll the last day had taken on him. Dark circles had formed under his eyes. Eyes that looked strained and just a bit too wide, like an animal who had only begun to realize the trap it was in. His hair was disheveled, his clothes rumpled, his posture more slumped and tired looking than he ever had imagined.

Dragons. The word kept coming back to him over and over again. His sister was right, it didn't matter what he believed. If others, powerful others, thought dragons were real and he was one, they would respond accordingly. That still left the question, what did he believe?

Staring into the mirror, he didn't see a dragon. He saw a college student, ex-college student, harried and stressed like any other person might be when faced with the prospects of no job or home. That alone gave him some minor reassurance in an odd way. He still looked normal, not like someone who had their whole world turned upside down. The thought gave him some amount of calm, and brought a tight smile to his lips.

What did he believe?

He found himself evaluating the opinions of those he had encountered. Malcolm had always been a distant figure; he didn't know how to read the man. Likewise the senator, who he had only seen through the TV. Mai was really the first real chink in his armor. Someone close to him, someone who had shared his bed. Yet when dragons had come up, she had betrayed her normal characteristics and deserted him.

Now Jerome, another friend. In some ways, a closer friend then Mai. One who seemed to wholeheartedly believe this dragon nonsense. And, perhaps more important to the insecure jobless man, wasn't shunning him or running away, but offering out open hands. His invitation seemed from one angle too good to be true, and from the other angle made perfect sense.

If one believed in dragons.

Griffen had already made his decision to tentatively accept Jerome's invitation. That didn't mean he fully accepted the premise behind it. It was so foreign to anything in his limited experience. He felt adrift, lost, floundering. He searched his own thoughts and feelings for some solution. Any solution. Only one came to mind.

"Okay Griffen," he said to his own reflection. "They claim you're a dragon, a monster, a beast of power. So . . . be a dragon."

He concentrated, willing himself to show some sign, any sign, of dragondom. Inside he kept repeating the phrase "be a dragon, be a dragon," trying to avoid distracting himself by the obvious corollary of "be the ball." He focused his thoughts instead on scales, wings, fiery breath. Trying to force some physical sign that could prove, or disprove, this madness.

So firm was his concentration that his vision blurred, tears forming in the corners of his eyes and further blurring his sight. The image in front of him stared back, features set in concentration, outline going blurry from the tears. He pushed, desperately reaching for something, anything, that he could get a grip on.

A sudden wave of nausea broke over him and his concentration broke. He slumped against the sink, sweat pouring off his forehead from the exertion. There hadn't been so much as a split second where his face in the mirror had seemed to him anything but human. Yet, the effort had left him feeling weak and drained, more so than anything he could remember.

The bathroom door swung open and Jerome looked in. He looked over Griffen, frowning slightly. Something about his eyes made Griffen suspect that he had already known what he would find before opening the door.

"Some things you can't force, my man," said Jerome, confirming Griffen's suspicions.

"How did you know?" Griffen asked.

"You mean 'sides the fact you've been in here a good twenty minutes? I know you, Grifter, and I know what I'd be thinkin, and tryin, if I were in your shoes."

Griffen shook his head to clear it. He hadn't any idea that he had been in there so long. To him it had been five minutes, tops. He thought that he must have been lost in thought.

"I still find this dragons thing . . ."

"Illogical? Impossible? A load of crap?" Jerome said.

"D. All of the above," Griffen answered.

"Still coming with me to New Orleans? If only to find out why so many would be lying about something so nuts?"

"That is just it, Jerome. I can be slow sometimes, but I can read people pretty well. If you are lying, you are better at it than you have ever shown before. I . . . I just don't understand."

"You will, Griffen. So help me, you will."

Griffen nodded and straightened himself up. Carefully, he forced his expression to better hide the tiredness and strain he felt. Jerome smiled and clapped his friend on the shoulder as Griffen walked out of the bathroom and into the bar proper.

Jerome considered the scene for a moment before following and shook his head. His smile was both wry and a touch tired.

"Can't see the forest for the trees," he said to himself and then followed Griffen into the bar.

It would be many hours before anyone sober enough came into that restroom, and noticed the long, finger-shaped dents in the rim of the metal sink.

Ten

Jerome drove a Jeep Cherokee, and the tires sang a high, whiny monotone as they headed west along I-10.

Griffen watched the passing scenery and mentally blotted out the conversation between Valerie and Jerome as he tried to sort out his thoughts. He still hadn't managed to get any sleep, and the last few days were taking on an almost surreal aura in his mind.

Dragons.

He didn't feel like a dragon. In fact, he didn't feel any different than he had two days ago. He hadn't been able to turn into one when he needed to. Still, Valerie was right. It seemed enough other people believed in it and were willing to act on it that he had to take it seriously.

Unfortunately, taking it seriously now had him en route to New Orleans with someone he only knew as a gambling acquaintance.

Before they had gotten into the Jeep, Valerie had pulled him aside. Giving Jerome a none-too-friendly look and asking to talk with Griffen privately. As usual, she cut straight through the bullshit.

"You know you are being an idiot, Big Brother," she said.

"So what else is new?"

She sighed and crossed her arms.

"I know he's your friend, and you trust your friends too much sometimes. That doesn't mean you can trust whoever he works for."

"Maybe we can, maybe we can't, but how can we know till we get there?" Griffen said.

"Okay, but don't you think his showing up is awfully convenient?"

She looked shocked and then angry when Griffen laughed.

"For us maybe. For him, not a chance. He timed this very carefully and spent more time and effort than he wants to admit tracking me down. Not to mention enrolling in a school and putting in a few years. No, frankly I didn't think Jerome had this kind of patience, which makes me want to meet his boss all the more."

He wrapped an arm around her waist and gave her a squeeze.

"Little Sister, you are just mad you can't think of any better ideas."

"Damn straight!"

She grinned, finally relenting, but the first part of the drive had been tense. She had glared at Jerome and it was she who finally asked for more detail about the organization. Griffen didn't stop her, not that he could if he tried. Besides, he wanted to know, too.

"Now, Mose is the man who's been running our crew for a while," Jerome was saying. "Once you get settled in, I'll introduce you to him and he can start teaching you the ropes."

"So, what kind of specialty is your crew involved in?" Valerie said.

"This and that," Jerome said, "mostly on the edge of the law. Our main income comes from gambling."

"Wait a minute," Griffen said. "Are we talking about organized crime here?"

Jerome laughed.

"Like I read somewhere, when you see it up close, it ain't all that organized."

"Does the 'this and that' part include drugs and prostitution?" Griffen said. "'Cause I'll tell you Jerome, I don't think I could be part of that."

"That's up to you," Jerome said. "You might want to take a closer look at it before you make your decision, though."

"Why do you say that?"

"I don't think you'll find it's what you think. The way we do it, it's not like you see in the movies."

"Suppose you tell me about it."

"Well, as to the drugs, we don't do any street sales or anything like that," Jerome said. "If a player in one of our games wants some pot or maybe a little coke, we know some people to call to get him some. That's about the extent of it. If anyone wants the hard stuff like heroin or crack, they got to leave the game and find it on their own, and even then we probably won't let 'em back in. We don't mess with junk like that."

"And prostitution?" Valerie put in.

"Same thing. We don't run strings or do any recruiting," Jerome said. "If a player is looking for company, we know a few girls we can call . . . not full-time professionals, but bartenders or secretaries who turn an occasional trick to supplement their income. Even then we don't take a piece off the top. We make our money from gambling."

"Isn't there a casino in New Orleans already?" Griffen said. "And I know there are some in Biloxi. Why do people sit in on your illegal games when they can gamble legit at a casino?"

"I can answer that in one," Jerome said. "Taxes. You win big at one of the casinos, it gets reported to the IRS. What happens at our games is between us and the players. If you win, it's pure profit without paying a slice to Uncle Whiskers."

"There's another point, too," he continued. "Mose has been running his games for a long time . . . a lot longer than the casinos have been around. Some of the players that sit in when they're in town have been playing in his games since way back . . . some of their daddies, too. It's kind of a tradition with them, and if there's one thing New Orleans is big on, it's tradition."

"So, how are they going to react when you run Grifter here in on them?" Valerie said. "Doesn't that kind of mess up this whole tradition thing?"

"Don't rightly know," Jerome said. "I expect Mose has some plan in mind to ease you in. There might be a few problems, though. We'll just have to see."

"What about you?" Griffen said.

"What about me?"

"I mean, how do you feel about this whole thing with my being brought in. Don't you have any problems with that? I should think this spot that's being set up for me would rightfully be yours."

"Don't worry about that, Grifter." Jerome laughed. "We've been talking about this for a long time. Hell, the reason I was up in Michigan was to keep an eye on you and see how you developed. If I didn't think we'd be better off with you on board, I would have either tried to veto the plan or bailed out myself. No need to worry about me. I'm behind you one hundred percent."

He glanced over his shoulder at Valerie.

"What I'd like to know," he said, "is how all this sits with your sister. She has the same bloodline as you do, and she'll be coming into her secondary powers pretty soon. Is she going to have any problems with your being treated like the big cheese while she stands in the background?"

"Nice of you to think about that, Jerome," Valerie said. "I've never wanted to be the head of anything. I figure to enjoy the city and help out when and if I can. Mostly, I'm here to cover my big brother's back. He isn't always as careful as he should be."

"Well, sure, anyone who's known him for ten minutes knows that," Jerome said.

Valerie smiled despite herself.

"I would like to get one thing straight, Jerome," she said.

"Shoot."

"You are bringing Griffen into this. If you aren't up front with him, if this is a trick, a trap, or some cruel college prank, I'm holding you responsible. And you will answer to me, up close and personal."

There was a moment of silence in the car, broken by Jerome laughing.

"When I said shoot I didn't mean straight from the hip! Hey, Grifter, it's *Big Jake* all over again."

Catching the reference, Valerie grinned.

" 'Your fault, my fault, nobody's fault,' " she said.

They both nodded at each other, and the tension that filled the car seemed to seep away.

"It seems we're in agreement as much as we can be until

we actually see the setup," Griffen said, clearing his throat. "So what's the plan, Jerome? What do we do when we hit town?"

"We've figured to let you take a week or so to get settled in and get to know the town . . . at least the Quarter. Then I'll introduce you to Mose and he can start showing you the operation and answering your questions."

"So where will we be staying?" Griffen said.

"We got a place ready for the two of you," Jerome said. "Actually, you'll each have a place."

"What are we talking about here?" Valerie said. "Rooms at a hotel? That could get real expensive real fast."

"Better than that," Jerome said. "You see, we own a few properties around the Quarter. Mostly, we use them to host poker games and sometimes to give out of towners a place to crash. What we're going to do is have you use one of our slave quarters as a home base until everything gets sorted out."

"Slave quarters?" Griffen said.

Jerome laughed. "You're going to have to get used to how we refer to things in the Quarter. A lot of the buildings you see in the Quarter are built around courtyards. Some of the courtyards were used for gardens, and some were used for carriages or horses. At the back of each courtyard is a smaller building. Way back when, it was used to house the slaves, which is why they're referred to as 'slave quarters.' Nowadays, they're mostly rented out as apartments. Depending on the size, either as a bi-level single apartment, or as two separate apartments, one ground level and one upstairs. We'll be putting you up in one of the two-unit slave quarters. I think you'll like them. They're off the street, and that means they're quiet . . . something that's sometimes hard to find in the Quarter.

"Anyway, I'll drop you off there with the keys and a grand or so walking-around money. We'll get you a couple cell phones so you can stay in touch with each other or call me if there are any problems. Then take your time and start getting a feel for the Quarter. There's enough to do and see that I don't think you'll get bored."

Eleven

The French Quarter was an unending sideshow of tastelessness. It was steamy by day and seamy at night.

Griffen fell in love with it immediately.

The place was incredible enough to pull him somewhat out of his brooding and self-doubts. Failure to change into a dragon, not to mention his troubles coming to grips with the whole situation, faded to the back of his mind as he reveled in his new surroundings. Six blocks wide by roughly thirteen blocks long, it was a world unto itself.

To some, particularly the tourists, it was a Disneyland for adults. Narrow streets lined with old buildings, overhung with flower-bedecked balconies; half-hidden courtyards with picture-book gardens and fountains; antique shops and boutiques mixed with T-shirt shops and adult specialty stores; every corner turned brought new sights and contradictions.

Some tourist towns advertised their scenic nature. When one actually visited them, however, it would be readily apparent that unless one found the exact spot the publicity photo was taken from and hunkered down at precisely the right angle, the scenic wonders would only be visible from between the hotels and office buildings.

Such was not the case in the Quarter. As one walked the streets, the eye and mind were captured again and again by small wonders; the "gaslight" street lamps, the hidden courtyards with flower beds and fountains, the old buildings with their cracked plaster and ferns growing out of the walls, and, of course, the Mississippi River.

While he experienced it, he couldn't prevent a vague feeling of regret. If Griffen had managed to visit New Orleans while he was still in college, he might have been able to enjoy it more. Now, with worries pressed down upon him, he felt more overwhelmed than anything. There was so much in the Quarter to be overwhelmed by.

Then there was the music. It was next to impossible to escape the music in the Quarter even if one wanted to. In addition to the expected blues and Dixieland, there were Cajun and zydeco fiddles and accordions, Chicago blues, piano bars, Irish folk music, rock clubs, and even country/western hangouts. The jukeboxes in the various clubs featured anything from Glenn Miller to Billy Holiday to Janis Joplin to Frank Sinatra to Dr. Hook and the Medicine Show to The Stones, etc., etc. The list was seemingly endless. Even the street musicians were good, supplying hammer dulcimers, Appalachian groups complete with cloggers, jazz flute or violin, and one guy who would play classical music on an array of water filled brandy glasses.

Food was something Griffen had never really concentrated on. Growing up, his diet had consisted mostly of institutional food and restaurant fare, the latter being mostly Chinese or German. It seemed that in New Orleans, food was almost a religion. At the very least, it was a major pastime right along with drinking and partying. There were almost as many restaurants in the Quarter as there were bars . . . which was to say a lot. Along with the upscale Creole and Cajun local food, there were an assortment of other ethnic dining opportunities present, including Chinese, Japanese, Siamese, Tai, Italian, Mexican, and Greek.

Nor were the low-end diners neglected, as there were delis, gyros shops, and the traditional KFC/Pizza Hut fast food assortments. What was more, to Griffen's delight, many places delivered directly to your door and would also provide groceries, cigarettes, a newspaper, and a pint of liquor if you added it to your order. All in all, it was a marvelous place to sleep late, order a brunch delivered while letting the world come slowly into focus, and not have to face the world until you were good and ready. When you threw in the twenty-four hour bars, it was small wonder that the Quarter was such a favorite vacation spot for tourists.

Of course, there were other aspects of the Quarter Griffen had a bit more difficulty adjusting to.

For one thing, there was the custom of "hoo-rawing" people on the street. This consisted of hailing to someone a half block away or on a balcony, then continuing the conversation at the top of your lungs until at least pleasantries were concluded, and often until the latest gossip had been exchanged. As someone who was accustomed to conversing in normal speaking tones, Griffen found this practice vaguely unnerving.

A bit more ominous was the vague feeling of danger that settled over the streets after the sun went down.

Since his normal activities while in school had included countless late-night poker games, Griffen was used to watching his back when he walked alone on the off chance

that one of the other players decided to try to recover his
losses in ways that did not involve skill with cards.

In the Quarter, however, with its round-the-clock bars
and steady flow of drunken tourists, it was apparent to the
most casual eye that there was a thriving cottage industry of
muggers, shakedown artists, and hustlers, ever ready to separate the unwary from the contents of their wallets, purses,
and/or pockets. While the main drag of Bourbon Street was
well lit and closely policed, a mere block off that thorough-
fare and one was on their own. People tended to watch the
other pedestrians as they walked, and were quick to change
sides of the street or to duck into an open bar if they didn't
like what they saw coming toward them.

Griffen was particularly distressed by the terrain in this
claustrophobic community. The campus and small college
town that had been his old stomping grounds were honey-
combed with alleys, doorways, and shortcuts that one could
duck into or through at the least sign of trouble. In the
Quarter, by contrast, all the side streets were narrow and
one-way with parking allowed only on one side. What was
worse, all the buildings were built flush with the street offering no cover at all. Openings into courtyards or passages
between apartment buildings all had locked gates topped
by daunting coils of barbed or razor wire to discourage casual entry. Overall, during his late-night prowls, it gave
Griffen the same feeling of security as a rabbit would feel on
a cut-over field with hawks circling. He made a mental note
that, if the feeling persisted, he would have to talk to
Jerome about the wisdom of carrying a firearm.

He kept thinking, what if something serious came at

him. There was nowhere to hide from someone truly pursuing him. Even the bars that one could duck into had open fronts and many windows. The constant patrol by local police gave some solace, but not enough. If something went wrong, someone really out for a dragon, all a policemen might do was fill out the paperwork afterward.

Still, all this was not enough to detract from Griffen's enjoyment of the Quarter. By the end of a week he had a good feel for the layout of the streets, and he had even found a bar to frequent that was more local service industry than tourist. It was a little Irish pub (that rarely if ever played Irish music) two blocks off Bourbon. It had two coin-operated pool tables that were surprisingly well maintained and had a good selection of Irish whiskey including Griffen's personal favorite, Tullamore Dew. More important, it seemed to be a regular hangout from an interesting assortment of attractive young ladies in their twenties and thirties who did not seem at all adverse to striking up a conversation with a newcomer that went beyond "May I take your order?"

He was sitting at the bar there one night, idly watching a closely contested pool match, when his cell phone went off. He glanced at the caller ID, more for show than anything else as there were only two people who currently had his number, then flipped it open.

"Hey, Jerome. What's up?"

"You got anything planned for tomorrow? During the day?"

"Nothing special. Why?"

"I'll swing by in the morning around noon and pick you up."

"Okay. What's the deal?"

"Figure it's time to take you shopping."

Twelve

"So what's wrong with the way I dress?"

Griffen was mock protesting as Jerome led the way down the stairs from his second-floor apartment in the slave quarters. In the back of his mind, however, he had a horrifying image of Jerome outfitting him in some flashy pimp outfits.

"Blue jeans and T-shirts may be fine for a college boy who's hustling card games," Jerome said. "For what you're going to be doing down here, though, your wardrobe definitely needs an upgrading."

They reached ground level, but instead of heading off across the courtyard, Jerome stopped in front of Valerie's door and rapped lightly on the frame. Almost at once the door opened and Griffen's sister stuck her head out.

"Hi, guys!" she said. "Hang on, I'll be with you in just a couple more minutes."

"How come we're taking Val along?" Griffen asked after she disappeared.

"Couple reasons," Jerome said. "First of all, I thought she

might enjoy doing a little shopping herself. Second, women usually have a better eye for clothes than men, so she can help us out."

Jerome glanced at Griffen and gave him a quick wink.

"Third, having her along will keep you from worrying that I'm going to dress you up like a pimp."

Griffen flushed slightly, then laughed.

"Okay. You caught me on that one," he said. "Seriously, though, what kind of clothes are we looking for?"

"In case you haven't noticed, you can tell a lot about people by how they dress . . . especially in the Quarter," Jerome said, leaning against the wall. "Mostly, we'll be working on what we don't want you to look like. Like I said, the way you've been dressing, you look like some college kid in from LSU to whoop it up on Bourbon Street. That's not good."

"Of course, there are some other looks to steer clear of. Dark slacks and a white tuxedo shirt marks you as service industry . . . either a waiter or a high-end bartender. Loose, baggy pants and comfortable shoes will have people thinking you're a cook. If you wear a suit or a sports coat, you'll either be some kind of a businessman or a conventioneer . . . which is the same thing but on a tighter time table."

Jerome shot another sideways glance at Griffen.

"Of course, the best dressers . . . the ones who pay the closest attention to fabric and cut . . . are the gay guys. Lord knows we have enough of those in the Quarter. By and large pretty good people, but you probably don't want to be mistaken for one."

"So what kind of look are we trying for?" Griffen said, starting to get interested in the proceedings.

Jerome shook his head.

"That's the problem," he said. "I don't rightly know.

There aren't many guidelines for how you should dress. We don't want you to look preppie, but you can't look like you're shopping cut-rate either. I guess that's what this whole expedition is going to be about . . . figuring out what kind of image you should have and how to express it in clothes."

That was the start of one of the strangest afternoons of Griffen's life. While he had occasionally shopped for a shirt or a new jacket, it was nothing like when Jerome and Valerie led him on a frenzied safari through the New Orleans clothes jungle.

There were three big shopping centers within an easy walk of the Quarter: the upscale Orleans Plaza perched across from the casino on the edge of the Quarter, the Riverwalk with its strolling jazz bands and magnificent view of the Mississippi, and the Orleans Center near the Superdome. All three had to be cruised and perused before his guides and coaches were satisfied.

Griffen was quickly numbed by the parade and swirl of names and brands as Jerome and Valerie swept him from one changing room to another. J. Riggings, Banana Republic, Tommy Hilfiger, Rockport, all danced by him in a dizzying array, occasionally punctuated by Jerome saying, "We'll take these two . . . he'll wear this one."

When Griffer tried to comment on the extent of their shopping venture, Jerome just laughed.

"This is nothing, Grifter," he said. "Be thankful you missed being here for carnival, when shopping really gets crazy . . . especially the women and their ball gowns. Just think of this as practice."

As their trek progressed, Griffen's current outfit meta-morphosed noticeably. Toward the end, he could not help but notice that the sales personnel were getting much more attentive and deferential toward him. Of course, that might have been affected by the growing number of shopping bags they were accumulating as they went.

Griffen himself was becoming more and more enamored of his new ensemble. A pair of comfortable walking shoes, a must in the Quarter, had replaced his old, battered running shoes. His blue jeans had given ground to a pair of light-weight wool slacks, and instead of a T-shirt, he was now wearing a raw silk shirt with a slight drape to the sleeves. It was still a casual outfit, but Griffen felt noticeably classier just wearing it. He mentioned this to his guides, and they both smiled at him.

"You're looking really good, Big Brother," Valerie said. "We should do this more often."

"You're getting there, Grifter," Jerome confirmed. "Get used to wearing these clothes, and in a few days we'll go see Mose. In the meantime, wear that outfit into that little Irish bar you've been hanging out at and see if the ladies don't sit up and take notice."

"You know where I've been hanging?" Griffen said, a lit-tle taken aback.

"I like to keep track of things," Jerome said. "You'll see. The Quarter's a whispering gallery. Not hard to keep track of who's who and what's going on."

Thirteen

Whether it was his new clothes, or simply that he had been frequenting the same local bar for over a week, Griffen noticed that it was easier to start conversations than it had been when he first arrived. More and more often, people would recognize him and wave hello when he came in, or wander over with a new tidbit of gossip, or pick up the threads of an earlier conversation they had had with him.

He was pleasantly surprised at how well-read the various people he talked to were. Oh, there was the customary sports talk that went on in any bar, and a certain amount of cross talk that went on about movies and television shows, but there were also conversations about books people were reading or passing back and forth. He had envisioned himself coming to an intellectual wasteland, and was delighted to be proved wrong.

One conversation he had was particularly memorable if for nothing else than what it lead to.

It was with a lanky young man a few years older than

Griffen with shoulder-length dark hair and wire-frame glasses who went by the unlikely nickname of Bone.

It started simply enough, with someone making a comment on the movie that was being shown on one of the bar televisions. Someone came up with the inevitable comparison of the movie to the book it was based on, and the conversation was on. Other books-to-movies were recalled and compared, everyone having their own opinion as to the relative merits of each. By the time it died down, it was clear that Bone and Griffen were the two most knowledgeable on movies, though often their opinions differed widely. Still, they each respected the other's expertise and were delighted to find a fellow aficionado to interact with.

Each bought the other a drink or two, and the conversation drifted into their own backgrounds. Griffen had mentioned that he was new in town, but Bone, waved it off.

"Don't worry about it," he said. "Most people who live and work in the Quarter are from somewhere else. I came down here from San Francisco, myself. Damn few of the current locals were born and raised here."

He paused to take a long swallow of his rum and Coke.

"What you don't realize until you've been down here for a while," Bone continued, "is what a small community the Quarter really is. We have droves of tourists that are in and out of here every week wandering through the bars and shops, but they're just window dressing. In short order, you'll realize that you know damn near everyone who works in the Quarter by sight, if not by name. Every flower peddler, strip bar shill, carriage driver, street entertainer, and Lucky Dog vendor . . . you name it, we all know each other and wave 'hello' when we pass on the street."

"I've noticed a bit of that already," Griffen said.

"You don't know the half of it," Bone said. "Let me tell you, I had only been down here for about three months, and one night at about one in the morning, I was cutting up Orleans about a half block short of Bourbon. These three big, football-jock types stopped me and asked how to find Café Du Monde. That was no big deal, and I told them, 'Straight ahead to the corner, then turn left, then right at the next corner and cross Jackson Square. It's right there. You can't miss it.'"

He paused and grinned at the memory.

"The thing is, in the time it took me to say that, two of the biggest, ugliest shills from in front of the strip joints came up out of the dark behind them, looked at me *over their heads*, and asked, 'These guys botherin' you?' The jocks were freaking a bit, but I just said that I was giving them directions to Café Du Monde. The shills nodded and faded back again and everything was mellow. The point is, though, that all they saw was someone from the Quarter getting braced by three big dudes and they were right there to lend a hand. That's the kind of place the Quarter is. We all know each other. We may not all *like* each other, but we know each other . . . and we form the circle with the horns out."

"Well," Griffen said. "It's always nice to know someone has your back in a fight."

Inside, though, he wondered how far that would extend. A part was wondering about whether the support structure of the area would be enough to protect Valerie if something, or someone, hurt him. Deeper, more buried, Griffen felt the need to unburden his troubles on someone who didn't know enough to judge. Still, if he shared all to someone like Bone, or even part, of what had changed his life lately, it wouldn't be long before everyone knew. Trust and privacy weren't the same, especially in the Quarter.

"Oh, it goes way beyond that," Bone said. "If a suit came in asking about you, it wouldn't matter if you were hanging out here five or six nights a week or even if you were shooting pool on the back table. No one would know anything or admit to ever having heard your name. This has been a pirate community for over two hundred years and the people who are drawn to it aren't real big on authority. Almost everyone has something in their background they would just as soon not have catch up with them, whether it's an ex after back alimony, a parole officer, or the IRS."

Griffen thought about it, and began to realize why Jerome had said the Quarter would be a good place for him to hide out.

"Another thing, people down here look out for each other. There's always someone to help you carry your stuff if you have to move, or if you don't have a place to move to, there's always someone who will let you crash on their sofa until you raise the money for a new place."

Griffen shook his head.

"Sounds almost too good to be true."

Bone stared at him, then set down his drink.

"For a minute there," he said softly, "it almost sounded like you just called me a liar."

"Whoa there, Bone," Griffen said, holding up a restraining hand. "If that's how it sounded, I apologize. All I meant to say was that what you're describing is a lot different from where I just came from."

"And where is that, if you don't mind my asking?" Bone said, slightly mollified.

"Up north," Griffen said. "Michigan to be exact. Little college town named Ann Arbor. Home of the University of Michigan Wolverines . . . the team that can't win a Rose Bowl."

"Michigan? No kidding?" Bone said, all traces of his earlier annoyance vanishing. "Com'on. There's someone I want you to meet."

Grabbing up his drink, Bone led the way to the other end of the bar where an older man with his long hair in a ponytail sat chatting with a young redheaded woman.

"Excuse me, Maestro," Bone said. "I just found another Michigander. Thought you'd like to meet him."

The man turned and ran a curious glance over Griffen. At first Griffen figured him for his midforties, then noted the wrinkles around his eyes and added another decade to his estimate.

"Griffen, this is Maestro," Bone said. "He's from your neck of the woods, except he moved down here about fifteen years ago. Maestro, this is Griffen . . . late of Ann Arbor."

For a moment, Maestro's features froze and his eyes swept Griffen from head to foot. Then he smiled and extended his hand.

"How's the team this year?" he said as they shook hands.

"Too early to tell," Griffen said. "Ask me again in August."

As he spoke, he wondered about the subtle reaction his name had gotten from Maestro. The answer was quick in coming.

"The name's 'Griffen,' right?" Maestro said, still smiling. "Do you by any chance know a guy named 'Mose'?"

Griffen hesitated. Jerome had warned him not to let anyone know where he was living, but nothing had been said about keeping his purpose in town a secret. Still, he wasn't wild about his name being recognized already. If Maestro were a threat . . . or an assassin, but no. Bone had known him, that made him a local, with all the many levels that "local" implied in these parts.

"Actually, we haven't met yet," he said cautiously. "But he's one of the main reasons I'm down here. If everything works out right, I'll be working with him."

"I thought the name sounded familiar." Maestro nodded. "Bone, can I talk with you for a second?"

"Sure," Bone said. "Back in a second, Grif."

The two men moved to the wall, where Maestro spoke to Bone in quiet undertones. Griffen was sure he was the subject of conversation, but had no idea as to what was being said. He hadn't often been cut out of a conversation like that. Like he was an outsider who had no business being there. Though at least part of that was true. He was just starting to build up a bit of indignation, and paranoia, when a voice distracted his thoughts.

"So, new in town?"

It was the little redhead that Maestro had been speaking with. She was about Griffen's age with medium-length auburn hair that she had back in a hair clip.

"I thought I had seen you in here a couple times this last week. I'm Lisa . . . well, Fox Lisa. There are so many of us named Lisa in the Quarter we need nicknames so people know which Lisa they're talking about . . . like guys named Joe or Robert."

He had noticed her before, but only in the passing awareness any man has for an attractive woman in the room. This was the first time he had seen her up close, much less spoken with her, and the effect was startling.

She had a slender build and a heart-shaped face with clear

blue eyes that sparkled when she smiled, as if she were harboring an unspoken joke. She also had a nose piercing and several visible tattoos.

Griffen knew he was in trouble. She was just the kind of woman he was drawn to. She also looked like five kinds of bad news, including the fact that, if she wanted to, she could probably wrap him around her little finger. He decided to set things straight before his fantasies went any further.

"Griffen," he said, shaking her hand. "Have you known Maestro long?"

Meaning: Are you with Maestro?

"Oh, I run into him here and there. We're just bar buddies."

Meaning: No, we're not attached.

He waited a moment for her to elaborate or clarify. Instead, she took a sip of her drink and smiled at him.

Big, BIG trouble.

Griffen chided himself, remembering that he was already plunging into a brand-new situation, one potentially fraught with unknown dangers. This really wasn't the time for him to get involved with a new flame, however tempting.

"I heard you talking with Bone," Lisa said, stepping into the silence. "It sounds like you're as big a movie buff as he is."

"It's an old passion of mine," he said with a shrug. "Things are always clearer and more easily resolved in movies. I guess the romantic in me is drawn to that."

"Well, I happen to have one of the biggest collections of videos and DVDs in the Quarter." Lisa smiled. "And my apartment's only a block and a half from here. Maybe we could watch a movie together."

Griffen felt his resolve weaken.

"That would be pleasant," he said. "When did you have in mind?"

"Actually," she said, wetting her lips with the tip of her tongue, "I was thinking about right now."

For a moment Griffen was taken aback, then he remembered that this was the Quarter, where people would go to a party or head for a different bar at two o'clock in the morning. Then he realized that Lisa was inviting him back to her apartment.

Looking into her bright eyes, his resolve crumbled and he smiled.

"As I said, that sounds pleasant."

They never did get around to watching a movie.

Fourteen

The place Jerome took Griffen and Valerie to was one of those small houses on a side street in the Quarter. It was set back slightly from the street and had its own fence and gate with room to park two cars in front of it.

Even in his brief time getting to know the neighborhood, Griffen knew that he was looking at expensive property, even though it did not look particularly pretentious. Parking was at a premium on these streets, with people paying ninety to a hundred and fifty dollars a month for an enclosed, secure parking place. A home like this one, with its own secured parking, meant money.

Jerome punched a code into the keypad mounted on the pedestrian gate, and led Griffen and Valerie up onto the porch. He knocked once, lightly, then opened the door on his own. Apparently they were expected.

While speculating about this meeting, Griffen had found himself wondering the most about exactly what Mose would look like. His visions of the man ranged from a ponderous fat man to one that was skeletally thin. If this was a movie, that would be how the role was cast. Powerful crime leaders should look dominating . . . or, at least, impressive.

The man sitting in the easy chair of the small living room they stepped into was nondescript. In fact, he looked so ordinary that Griffen would not have looked at him twice if they passed on the street. Medium height and build with short-cropped white hair, he could have been a doorman or cook, or maybe a shop owner. Even his dress, consisting of a plain sports shirt and a pair or khakis with his feet shoved into a pair of slippers, was unremarkable.

Perhaps the only noteworthy feature about him was his face. His milk-chocolate-colored skin was lined with deep smile wrinkles, and his dark eyes twinkled with vague amusement, as if he were waiting for you to catch onto a joke.

Griffen found himself liking the man before a single word had been spoken.

"Mose," Jerome said. "This is Griffen and Valerie Mc-Candles. Grif, Val, this is Mose."

"Griffen. Miz Valerie," Mose said, half rising from his seat. "Been looking forward to meeting you both. Just make yourselves comfortable. Can I get you anything? A drink? Some coffee?"

"Coffee would be fine," Griffen said, taking the lead as they seated themselves on the sofa. "Val?"

She nodded.

Mose nodded to Jerome, who disappeared into the depths of the house.

"Well, before we start talking about our setup here in the Big Easy," Mose said, "I expect you have some questions about being dragons. As I understand it, this is all pretty new to you."

"Very new," Griffen said. "Questions? Oh, only a couple dozen off the top of my head."

Mose smiled.

"Fire away. I probably can't answer them all, but maybe we can make a start of it."

Jerome reappeared with a tray laden with coffee, cups, and the condiments including a small plate of croissants. The conversation paused while they all helped themselves.

"Well, for openers," Griffen said, settling back, "everyone keeps talking about our 'secondary powers' starting to show as we come of age. What can you tell us about these 'secondary powers'?"

"Not much," Mose said. "Don't think I'm trying to hold back information, though. It's just that the powers have been diluted over the centuries, and now it's hard to separate what's fact from what's brag or legend."

"You mention centuries," Valerie put in. "If you don't mind my asking, just how old are you, Mose?"

The old man laughed.

"There them that say everyone calls me 'Mose' because I'm as old as Moses. Truth to tell, I'm not that old . . . and they've been calling me 'Mose' even when I was young. Say I'm over a hundred and fifty years old and you'll be in the right neighborhood. But don't start asking me about the old days or I'll never shut up. Nothing as boring as an old man talking about how things used to be. You've got to realize, though, that a lot of what you learned as history to me are memories . . . and I got lots of memories. Mostly these days I try to keep focused on the here and now. That's enough to keep me busy."

He cocked his head at Griffen.

"But you were asking about the 'secondary powers.'

Again, it's hard to tell for sure, because even those that have some tend to try to keep them secret. Draws less attention that way."

"My uncle Malcolm lit a cigar just by blowing on it," Griffen said.

"Yeah, I've heard that some can do that," Mose said. "Of course, Mal is a half blood. Folks like Jerome and me who are lesser bloods don't have as many powers."

He picked up a cigarette lighter from the coffee table, lit it, then held his hand in the flame as he continued.

"I've always been good with fire. I could hold my hand here all day and it wouldn't burn me. I'd feel some heat, but it wouldn't hurt."

He extinguished the flame.

"Dragon skin is one of the secondary powers that pops up in varying degrees. I don't burn and I don't bruise. Now, if you was to stick me hard with a knife, I'd bleed like a human . . . but even then, it wouldn't penetrate too far. It would be like trying to stick a human through a thick leather coat. You could get through, but not as easily as if you were just dealing with bare skin.

"Some say that the closer to pure-blood you are, the tougher your skin will be. I'm not sure you could get through Mal's skin with a knife at all. A true pureblood is supposed to be able to shrug off bullets. Of course, even though the skin doesn't break, I'm not sure what it would do to the bones underneath if you got hit with a big enough caliber."

While he was considering trying the flame trick, Griffen mentally decided holding off testing whether or not he was bulletproof for as long as possible.

"There are all sorts of things some say dragons can have

as secondary powers." Mose continued. "Dragon skin and breathing flame are both pretty well-known and documented. Size changing and shape-shifting are talked about, but you don't actually see it very often."

"How do those work, exactly?" Valerie said. "I mean, is it like the Human Torch from the *Fantastic Four*? Do you say 'flame on' or 'shape-shift' to trigger it?"

"As I understand it, it's kind of like your voluntary muscles," Mose said. "I mean, the dragon skin, if you get it, will always be with you. As to the others, once you discover you have it, you have to train it and learn control."

"How do you do that?" Griffen said.

"Like I say, it's like a muscle you just learned you have. Imagine if you were just learning to use your arm. With a little practice, you can learn to make it reach out without thinking of exactly how you're doing it. You also learn how far it reaches, how fast, and how strong it is."

"And with exercise," Griffen said, "you can make it stronger."

"To a degree," Mose said. "But it's more complex than that. Sticking with the arm example, if someone hits you unexpectedly, your arm will flinch away without your thinking. Boxers and karate artists learn to control that reflex. If you develop some of the stronger secondary powers, you have to learn to control them as well. An unthinking flinch with a secondary power can not only be noticeable to the humans around you, the actual immediate effects could be disastrous."

"I can see where that could be a problem," Griffen said, winking at his sister.

Mose leaned back in his seat and looked at them both.

"It's no laughing matter," he said. "Now, I want both you

young dragons to listen to me real close. I'm answering your questions about primary and secondary powers as best I can because you've asked and I don't want you to think I'm holding back on you. The truth of the matter is that, for the most part, the various powers don't mean squat. It's how you handle yourself that counts. People should do what you want them to because they're convinced you're right, not because they're afraid of what you'll do to them if they don't go along. Sure, dragons have powers to some extent or other, but mostly it's frame of mind."

Griffen frowned.

"Please excuse me, sir. I didn't mean to act like I'm taking all this lightly. It's just that it's all so new to me that I automatically drop back to old defense patterns . . . like laughing . . . to keep from showing how confused I am. Some of this stuff you're telling me I just don't understand."

"Like what, for example."

"Well, like what you were just saying. I understand that one doesn't use these powers without a good reason, and even then only use them very carefully. It's just . . . well, I keep being told I'm getting this generous offer because of my power potential, but then you say it's a frame of mind, not the powers. If it isn't the powers, or potential powers, and just a state of mind, then what do you need me for? What is it exactly that you expect me to do?"

Mose heaved a sigh and ran his hand through his hair.

"That's a fair question," he said. "It's the answer that's not so easy. Let me try to cover this in pieces. First of all, as you say, you're new to all this. Part of why I wanted you down here is because I've got some things I can teach you."

He held up a restraining hand.

"Let me get through this. I know what you're thinking.

How is that different from what Mal offered when he asked you to sign up with him. Well, the big difference is that you don't have to be subservient to me to learn. This is going to be your operation. We're joining you, not the other way around.

"As to what you'll be doing, first of all we have to teach you the operation. I understand from Jerome you're no stranger to betting or bookies, but I don't think your real familiar with the ins and outs of how it all works. It's going to take you a while to learn what we do and to meet the people who do the day-to-day work."

"Once you get the feel of things, though, you probably won't be that involved in the actual work. You'll be management, and most of what you do will be setting policy and making decisions."

"If I can interrupt for a moment," Griffen said, "could you elaborate a bit on what it is I'll be deciding?"

"I'll give you an example," Mose said. "Something that's just come up that I'm trying to decide how to handle. There are some poker games around town that aren't really a part of our group, but that pay us a percentage to operate. Now one of them that's run by a young kid named Gris-gris has decided to stop paying us that percentage. It's up to me to decide how to react. If it were you in my seat right now, Young Dragon, what would you do?"

"Me?" Griffen blinked, taken aback. "I . . . I don't know. I guess you'd have to arrange for some kind of punishment to make an example of him."

Mose threw back his head and laughed.

"I can see what Jerome means that you truly love your movies. Well, in part you're right. But if you're thinking of roughing him up or shooting up his game, you couldn't be more wrong. We just don't do that kind of thing. The kind of punishment we deal in would be to cut him off from the network."

"The network?" Griffen said.

"That's right." Mose nodded. "You see, we have a whole network of people all through town who operate cabs or work at the hotels. When tourists or conventioneers are looking for a game, these folks check them out to be sure they aren't the law, then send them along to one of our games with an initialed business card to show they're clean. That's where we get a lot of our business and most of our new regulars. If Gris-gris wants to operate independently, his game gets dropped from the spotters' list and he has to make do with locals. That's the kind of punishment we usually deal in."

"That's all?" Griffen said. "I guess it makes sense. I was just expecting something a little more dramatic."

"Uh-huh," Mose said. "Well, it can be a bit more tricky once you really get into it. Like in this case, Gris-gris has been shooting his mouth off about how he's going independent and there isn't anything we can do about it. Now, whether he stays with us or not I figure is his business, but talking that kind of trash is disrespectful. That's a whole different issue to be settled."

"So what are you going to do?" Griffen said.

Mose looked at him and smiled.

"Tell you what," he said. "Why don't you think about it for a day or two, then we'll sit down and talk it out together."

"Um . . . excuse me?" Valerie said. "But before Big Brother here got you sidetracked on the Gris-gris business, you were about to explain how the powers factor in at all."

"That's right." Mose nodded. "Now, realize that not everyone in our organization is a dragon. In fact, most of them know even less about dragons than you do. Those people you should be able to lead and control with nothing but your attitude and presence. There are some folks you'll run into who will stand out as having dragon blood in them, but are totally unaware of it. They're a little more tricky to deal with, because they'll be drawn to you without knowing why . . . some will want to ally with you, some will feel the need for a confrontation. Again, you should be able to handle them without using any kind of powers."

"The problem is the dragons who know what they are and what you are. Most will be willing to leave you alone if you don't pose a threat to them. There are others, though, who will want to test you or simply eliminate you. That's when it will be a good thing if your secondary power potential proves to be true."

"Would this guy Stoner be one of those?" Griffen said.

"Definitely," Mose said. "Jerome told me about your little set-to on the expressway. He would have the contacts to try something like that, but it just doesn't seem like his style. Don't focus all your attention on him. There are others out there that can be just as nasty."

"Speaking of that," Griffen said, "do you happen to know a guy who goes by the name of Maestro?"

Mose and Jerome exchanged glances.

"We've crossed paths a couple of times," Mose said carefully. "Why do you ask?"

"I ran into him at the Irish pub the other night, and he recognized my name," Griffen said. "He even specifically asked if I knew you."

Again Mose and Jerome looked at each other.

"Don't worry about him," Mose said at last. "He's got his own thing going that doesn't affect us one way or the other. Not a bad man to have for a friend, though."

"Is he a dragon?"

"I figure him for one of those I was telling you about," Mose said. "The ones with dragon blood who don't know it."

"Does he have any secondary powers?" Griffen pressed. "Does he use them?"

Mose shook his head.

"No," he said. "He uses a knife."

Fifteen

Mose studied the tarot card Griffen had passed him, then glanced at Jerome.

"Is that what I think it is?" Jerome said.

"Depends on what you think it is," Mose said with a sigh, "but probably yes. My only question is why you didn't tell me about this before?"

"If you mean before today, I wanted Griffen to show it to you himself." Jerome shrugged. "Besides, I figured we had a bit of time, what with him just having hit town and all. I wasn't even sure it was the real thing. If you mean why not earlier, I wanted to wait until Valerie wasn't around."

Valerie had finally gotten bored with the details of even a preliminary briefing on Mose's gambling operation and had excused herself to run some errands.

"Uh-huh." Mose nodded. "I can see why you'd want to keep her out of this until we sort out what's goin' on."

"Excuse me," Griffen said, "but would someone please tell me what it is we're talking about?"

"Could be nothin' but someone pulling your chain," Mose said. "On the other hand, it could be real trouble. Truth is, I've never actually seen one of these before. Only heard about them."

"Since you're the one I heard about it from, Mose, I thought you should be the one to fill him in," Jerome said.

Mose nodded, tapping the card with his finger.

"Sorry to keep walking around this, Griffen," he said, "but I'm having a bit of trouble getting my mind around this. It may be that you've got George on your trail."

"Who's George?" Griffen asked quickly.

"No one knows who he is," Mose said. "But there are rumors about what he is."

He pursed his lips, then continued.

"There's supposed to be some kind of freelance enforcer or hit man that dragons hire when they want something to happen to another dragon. Like I told you, we aren't big on direct confrontation. Now this enforcer isn't a dragon himself, but he's made a study of how to hurt or kill dragons so now it's his specialty. I've only heard him referred to as 'George' or 'Saint George.' You know, the Dragonslayer. He's supposed to charge an arm and a leg for his services, so things usually have to be pretty desperate or someone has to have a big hate on to call him in. That's why all we have to go on is rumors. We've never been big enough or important enough to draw that kind of big league attention."

"That's just great," Griffen said with a scowl. "I've only known about being a dragon for a couple of weeks . . . less than that, actually . . . and I've already got a professional hit man on my trail."

"Don't panic yet, Grifter," Jerome said.

"Why not?" Griffen snarled. "Right now, panicking seems like a pretty good idea to me."

"Because panicking never helps," Mose said. "It only makes things worse and can maybe even get you killed. You should know that if you're as good a gambler as Jerome says."

Griffen thought for a moment, then took a slow, deep breath and blew it all out.

"You're right." He nodded. "So, what do we know about this George? What rumors are there?"

"Well, realize that we may not be dealing with him at all," Mose said. "It may just be someone imitating his style to make you run. Like I say, George is a legend. Almost a boogeyman for dragons. This may be just someone trying to cash in on that legend."

"Okay," Griffen said. "But the question still stands. What do we know about him?"

"Well, first off, he's a bit of an artist," Mose said.

"I always thought he sounded like a bit of a nutcase," Jerome muttered.

Mose shot him a look.

"I thought you wanted me to tell this," he said tersely.

Jerome spread his hands in surrender and leaned back.

"As I was saying," Mose continued, "the man's a sort of an artist. He has his own way of doin' things, and won't change for anyone. Right off the bat, he always lets his victim know he's hunting them. That's what that tarot card is all about. He's not going to just walk up on you or hit you from behind."

"Sounds more like a sportsman than an artist," Griffen said. "He's handicapping himself like a fisherman using a light test line."

Mose hesitated, then nodded.

"You may be right," he said. "Never thought of it that way. Anyways, the other thing he always does is that he'll take a couple of dry-run passes at you before he makes his real move . . . just to show you how vulnerable you are."

"Maybe this guy is a Native American," Griffen said. "That last bit sounds sort of like counting coup."

"Except in counting coup, your enemy has a chance to kill you while you're doing it," Jerome said drily.

"More like a cat playing with a mouse," Mose said. "He wants you on edge and jumping at shadows before he does anything. The way I hear it, though, when he makes his move, you'll know it. It'll be out in the open, face-to-face. What's more, he'll only make one real try. If you survive that, he'll walk away."

"I don't quite get that." Griffen frowned.

"The story is he gets paid to give it one big try. He's paid for the effort, not results," Mose explained. "He's not going to keep coming at you. That is, of course, unless they want to pay him to try again."

"He must be pretty good to get hired on those terms," Griffen said.

"They say he's the best." Mose nodded.

"So what exactly can he do to me?" Griffen said. "From what you were saying earlier, I should be pretty hard to harm, much less kill."

"That would be true for any human that didn't know what they were going up against," Mose said. "That's not the case with George."

Griffen sighed.

"Okay, give me the bad news," he said. "What am I vulnerable to?"

"Well, I've already told you your skin is pretty tough," Mose said. "We haven't really tested you out to see how far your blood has pushed it, but any fire or penetration shouldn't be able to get through."

"I can't help but notice the word 'shouldn't,'" Griffen said drily.

"There are always exceptions," Mose said. "While most edges won't be able to cut you, I've heard of some people getting through with weapons with serrated edges."

"Serrated edges," Griffen echoed. "Anything else?"

"Just remember what I told you earlier," Mose said. "Tough skin, like chain mail, only gives you one kind of protection. Even if your skin isn't penetrated, you can still be hurt. You can suffer broken bones and bruises if you get hit hard enough . . . like, say, by a car."

"Then, too," Jerome put in, "there are things like poisons that could kill you without going through the skin."

Griffen stood up and walked to the window where he stood for a moment, looking out.

"What you're saying overall," he said at last, "is that I'm really not all that invulnerable."

"Let's just say it would be best if you didn't count on it too much," Jerome said. "'Course, it's always best to stay alert and watch out for whatever might be coming at you."

"Let's back up a bit here," Mose said, holding up a hand. "While it may be best to consider and plan for the worst, there are some other possibilities here. The most obvious one I pointed out earlier, that it was just someone running a bluff on you up in Detroit to get you running."

"There's one problem with that, Mose," Griffen said, returning to his seat. "That only works if I recognized the threat, which I didn't."

"But you ran," Jerome pointed out.

"Only because my uncle Malcolm told me to," Griffen said.

"In a phone call that came in conveniently just after the card got slid under your door," Jerome said.

"As to your not recognizing the threat," Mose said, "it could also be a way to make any dragon you tried to hook up with think twice before taking you in. I already told you that dragons can be a sneaky bunch."

Griffen started to speak again, but Mose held up his hand.

"Le'me try a different slant on this," he said. "Let's assume for a moment that this is for real, and that the George is really after you. That doesn't necessarily mean that he's out to kill you."

"But you said he was a hit man," Griffen protested.

"I also said he was an enforcer," Mose said. "See how this sounds. Malcolm told you that you were a bit of a wild card as far as the established dragons were concerned. What if one or more of them decided to hire the George to test you. To put some pressure on you to see what kind of power you have and whether or not you're a threat to them."

"So if I understand you right," Griffen said, "if he tries to kill me and I'm weak, he'll kill me. If he's testing me and I'm strong enough to stave him off, it will alert the other dragons that I'm strong enough to be a threat to them."

"Well, I wouldn't have put it quite that way, but yes," Mose said.

"Somehow I don't find that reassuring," Griffen said with a grimace.

"Cheer up, Grifter," Jerome said. "Mose has already pointed out there's a good chance this is just some elaborate kind of bluff. Even if the George is after you, remember where you are. Right now, he has no way of knowing you're in New Orleans. Even if he finds you here, what with everybody in the Quarter knowin' each other, he'll stick out like a sore thumb."

Everybody in the Quarter knows each other, Griffen thought to himself. Except for the couple of million tourists who roam the Quarter every year. Any of whom could be a killer in disguise. Great. Just great.

Sixteen

Griffen and Jerome were sitting at one of the small tables in the Irish pub waiting to meet with Gris-gris. It was early afternoon, so the place was nearly empty except for them, the bartender, a few people at the bar, and two guys shooting pool on the back table.

Meeting at a public place had been Gris-gris's idea, though he had approved their choice of the Irish pub. Despite Mose's statement that these matters were not handled by rough stuff, apparently Gris-gris was sufficiently worried that he wanted other people around.

The meeting itself was Griffen's idea, just as he had proposed to handle the matter himself. Mose had agreed on the condition that Jerome went along. Everything had progressed smoothly, and now there was nothing to do but wait.

The waiting made Griffen edgy.

With nothing else to do, his mind was free to mull over anything he might have overlooked and everything that could go wrong. Try as he might, though, he couldn't think of anything more to do now to improve the situation.

He had even thought to give the bartender forewarning. All it took was a quiet explanation that he was going to be meeting with someone and that it might get a little noisy. The bartender agreed to stay out of it, on the proviso that if it got rough they would take it outside and that Griffen would make good any damages.

The customers were all regulars and wouldn't need any instructions to keep their distance. It was the Quarter.

Still nervous, Griffen played with his cup of coffee. He had considered having a shot of Irish whiskey, but decided he needed a clear head more than steady nerves.

"So, Jerome," he said at last, just to break the silence, "what do you think of my plan?"

"Doesn't matter," Jerome said, watching the door.

"Excuse me?"

"I said it doesn't matter what I think," Jerome said. "You and Mose came up with this idea, and now it's in motion. I'm just here to back you. If it works, it works. If not, we take it from there."

"I'd still like to know what your opinion is," Griffen said.

Jerome looked at him levelly, then returned his attention to the door.

"Well, I'll admit I'm curious as to why you wanted to handle this yourself," he said. "Would have thought you had more than enough on your plate right now. For that matter, would have thought you'd want to wait a bit and get a feel for things before you plunged in."

"It seemed like the only logical way to play it," Griffen said. "Gris-gris trying to pull out just when I'm coming in is too much of a coincidence. I think his problem is with me . . . and if it is, I've got to square things away with him myself. Hiding behind Mose won't cut it."

"Well, however it goes, it's going down," Jerome said. "Here they come."

Griffen forced himself to take a slow sip of his coffee as the door opened.

The first one to come in was a huge chocolate-colored black man. Easily six foot six or seven, he had a thick massive body that made Griffen think of Fat Albert in the old cartoon show. He recognized him as the one they call Jumbo who works as a shill and bouncer at one of the strip joints on Bourbon Street. Rumor was that he also picked up a bit of extra money as a strong-arm man and debt collector. Despite his size, he was supposed to be very fast.

Pausing just inside the door, Jumbo swept the place with a slow, steady stare. When his eyes met Griffen's, they paused and he gave a small nod of recognition. Meaning: We know each other, but I'm working. It's just a job, nothing personal. Griffen nodded back.

Apparently satisfied, Jumbo opened the door behind him. A small, wiry, ebony black man came in. He was maybe in his late twenties or early thirties, and seemed to vibrate with energy. As he moved, he seemed to throb to the beat of unheard music. Gris-gris.

Jumbo stayed by the door as Gris-gris moved to their table.

"Hey, Jerome," he said by way of greeting. "This the new guy?"

Jerome nodded.

"Gris-gris. Griffen."

"Have a seat, Gris-gris," Griffen said, gesturing to an

empty chair at the table. "I thought we should meet and have a little talk."

"We got nothing to talk about, white boy," Gris-gris said. "What I got to say, I can say standing up."

He pulled himself erect and folded his arms across his chest.

"Since I've been running my game, I've been paying a piece to Mose. I didn't have to, but he's been operating down here forever and I figured it was only respectful to acknowledge that. Then I hear he's bring in some white-bread college boy from up north to take over his operation."

He unfolded his arms and put his fists on his hips.

"Now, Mose is Mose, but I don't figure I owe you anything. I'm going to keep my money and keep running my game and I don't see there's any way you're going to change that. You sure ain't going to do it with talk. That's all I got to say to you."

The bar was now dead quiet as everyone concentrated on not looking like they were listening in on the exchange.

Griffen took another sip of his coffee and set the cup down.

"You're wrong, Gris-gris," he said. "I didn't ask you to come here to threaten you in any way. In fact, I just wanted to let you know that I'm your new best friend."

Gris-gris frowned.

"And just how do you figure that?" he challenged.

"Simple." Griffen shrugged. "I'm the only thing between you and her."

As he spoke, Valerie came off her stool at the bar and grabbed Gris-gris with both hands, slamming him against the wall.

"You listen to me, little man," she hissed, her face close

to his. "I don't give a rat's ass if you run your game or not or if you pay in a percentage. But if you dis my big brother again . . . if I hear about you talking trash the way you've been doing . . . I will personally kick your boney ass up one side of Bourbon Street and down the other. Now, do we understand each other?"

She gave him a small shake.

"I said, do you understand?"

"Um . . . Val?" Griffen said. "He can't answer if he can't breathe."

"He can nod," she said, not looking around.

Gris-gris managed to vibrate his head up and down.

"Fine," Valerie said, setting him down. "I knew you'd listen to reason. Hey, Jumbo. How's it going?"

With that she slid back onto her bar stool and returned to her drink.

Gris-gris straightened his clothes, then looked at Valerie's back.

She ignored him.

Then he looked at Griffen.

Griffen shrugged and gave a little grimace.

Finally, Gris-gris turned on his heel and left the bar, with Jumbo, deadpan, trailing along after him. As the door closed behind them, the bar talk resumed, a little louder than before.

Griffen exhaled a deep breath he hadn't realized he'd been holding.

"I think that went well," he said, leaning back in his seat. "I'm about ready for a real drink. How about you?"

"In a minute," Jerome said. "Did you notice anything unusual happen during that exchange?"

"You saw it, too, huh?" Griffen said. "I was thinking that maybe it was an optical illusion."

"Um . . . what did you see?"

"When Val picked Gris-gris up and pinned him against the wall," Griffen said. "It looked to me like she grew about six or eight inches while she was reading him the riot act. She's back to normal now, so I thought it was just my eyes playing tricks on me."

"If so, then my eyes are playing the same tricks," Jerome said. "But I was talking about the other thing."

"What other thing?"

"While she was working on Gris-gris and everyone was watching the action, you blew a smoke ring."

"I what?"

"You blew a smoke ring. A nice round one until the draft blew it apart."

Griffen looked at him.

"You're kidding me. Right?"

"Well, while you're laughing at that, sneak a peek at your right hand."

Griffen glanced down at his hand that was holding the coffee cup.

At first he thought he was having trouble focusing his eyes, as the image was fading . . . but his hand, for a few lingering moments, was covered with leathery scales.

Seventeen

Even though it was only supposed to be temporary shelter, Griffen found himself growing increasingly fond of the complex he and Valerie were housed in. He had been puzzled at first by the apparent lack of neighbors, but when he asked, the answer was quite simple.

Mose owned the whole complex. He used the apartments to host the occasional poker game if they didn't want the lack of privacy that was the downside of using a hotel room. They also served as "perks" for various out of town high rollers, one of the few concessions made to the new competition of the casino. New Orleans wasn't used to Vegas-style casinos, but with a relatively new Harrah's literally across Canal Street, the locals had to adapt.

The location of the complex was convenient, tucked away on a small street running parallel to Decatur one block into the Quarter proper. It was only a block and a half away from Jackson Square with its wide range of amusements and distractions, and the street itself was lined with small shops featuring used books, small restaurants, craft and vintage clothing shops, and even one small local bar, Harry's Corner, that was open twenty-four hours a day.

The complex itself was impressive. It had been designed and built in the 1800s by the same person who had designed and built Pat O'Brien's, a popular bar and restaurant on St. Peter in the heart of the Quarter. Griffen learned this by listening to the carriage drivers who paused at the entrance-way to rest their mules while regaling their passengers with the history of this particular landmark.

Griffen found himself feeling not only comfortable, but safe. It was as if, nestled as his temporary home was in the surroundings, it was protected by the Quarter itself. He felt himself relaxing, comforted by old brick and the constant swirl of activity beyond the complex walls.

After the inevitable wrought-iron gate on the street, there was a low carriage passage leading to the open-air courtyard. The courtyard itself featured heavily planted gardens, with the apartments in the three buildings surrounding it reaching up two stories. The second floor was circled by a wooden walkway edged by a railing, affording residents a fine view of the courtyard as they emerged from their dwelling.

It was on that walkway that Griffen found himself one morning in the early daylight hours. He was in one of those rare moods that occasionally strike young men. That is, he had abandoned the music and lingering crowds of the clubs to return home, but upon reaching that destination, discovered he was not yet ready to go to sleep. Having noted the clear sky and fresh air still not heated by the new day's sun, instead of watching a DVD or curling up to read, he decided to pull a chair out onto the walkway and enjoy the morning while he read.

Unfortunately, the book he was reading proved insufficient to hold his attention. He had picked it up at the used bookstore down the street, but as he started to read it, he realized it was merely a reprint of a novel he had read before, rereleased under a new title with a new cover.

As his attention wandered, his eye was drawn to a movement in the courtyard below. It was a cat . . . no, two cats, strolling regally along one of the walkways between the gardens.

Griffen had noted them, or other similar cats, in the courtyard before, but had never paid them much attention. They usually kept their distance, or, if one attempted to call them over, they would either run or simply fade back into the shadows.

This time, as he watched them, Griffen remembered what his uncle Mal had said about animal control. On a whim, he set aside his book and descended to the ground level to see if there was any substance to the claim.

As he approached the animals, however, he realized that he didn't have the foggiest idea what was involved in animal control. Pausing about twenty feet away, he stared at them.

They ignored him.

After a few moment's consideration, he tried to focus a suggestion at them.

"Come here."

It was a simple enough order.

One sat down and began to wash its crotch.

"Come here."

Nothing.

Maybe he should try something else.

"Go away."

The washer broke off its hygienic activity, and they both began to saunter toward the carriageway.

Griffen felt his hopes lift. Maybe there was something there after all.

"What are you doing up so early, Big Brother?"

He turned to find Valerie emerging from her apartment. She was decked out in sweat suit and cross trainers, obviously ready to go jogging.

Griffen was suddenly embarrassed at having gotten caught in his animal control attempt. Viewed through a sober and well-rested eye, his actions probably would seem silly. As a matter of fact, it seemed a little silly now even viewed through his own eyes. He was just glad she hadn't seen enough to be able to figure out what he had been attempting.

"Hi, Val," he said. "Actually, I'm just coming in."

"Well, since you're up, want to come running with me?"

Griffen had to admit that the suggestion seemed even sillier to him than animal control.

"You know I'm not much for exercise," he said evasively.

"You sure?" his sister said. "I'll spring for breakfast at the Café Du Monde afterward.

"Actually, it's about time for me to crash and burn," Griffen said. "It's been a good day, but it's time it was over."

"Actually, it's a different day," Valerie said pointedly.

"You know what they say down here," Griffen countered. "Whatever the clock says, the day isn't over till you go to sleep and wake up again."

His sister started her stretching exercises to warm up her legs.

"Isn't that usually for people who work night shifts, like grave shift bartenders and cab drivers?" she said.

"That and people who can pick their own hours of when to sleep and when to be awake," Griffen said.

"If you say so," Valerie said, starting for the front gate. "Anyway, good luck on your animal control. Let me know how it works out."

Watching her go, Griffen had a moment of wry despair of ever being able to put one over on his sister.

"Hey, Big Brother," Valerie called, returning to the courtyard. "Looks like someone left a message for you. This was taped to the front gate."

She handed him a regular white envelope with his name written on it. He took it and stared at it for a long moment.

"Aren't you going to open it?" Valerie urged.

"Not right now," Griffen said, trying to sound casual.

"Don't worry. If it's from a new woman, I won't tell Fox Lisa."

"Uh-huh," Griffen said, tucking the envelope in his back pocket.

"So be that way," Valerie said, sticking her tongue out at him. "I can tell when I'm not wanted."

With that, she turned on her heel and headed for the front gate again.

Griffen waited until he was sure she was gone, then pulled out the envelope again. From the feel of it, he was afraid he knew what was inside. He opened he missive and confirmed his fears.

Inside was a tarot card. The Knight of Swords. A duplicate of the one he had been carrying in his wallet since Detroit. The sense of safety Griffen had allowed himself to be lulled into by his new surroundings crumbled.

George was not only in New Orleans, he knew where Griffen lived.

Eighteen

Despite all the warnings and promises he had received about the rumor mill in the Quarter, Griffen was startled with how far and fast the word of his encounter with Gris-gris had spread. Even though the confrontation had occurred in the midafternoon, by the time midnight rolled around, he had been stopped or approached no less than a dozen times by people who had heard about it.

"Griffen! What's this I hear about you tossing four guys out of the Irish pub this afternoon?"

"Hey, my man! Been hearing talk about how you got in the face of a bunch of bruisers today."

"Here. This one's on me. Heard about how you stepped in and settled a brawl at the pub."

The accounts varied, and none of them were correct. The story being spread was that Griffen had either been in a fight or settled a fight with three to six guys bigger than he was. When he tried to clarify that (a) there had only been two people on the other side, (b) one of the opposition had done nothing but watch, (c) he himself had not been directly involved, and (d) no punches had been thrown and the altercation was nothing more serious than raised voices, he was greeted with exaggerated winks and declarations of, "Yeah. That's always the best way to handle it."

The pattern continued the next day as Jerome was walking him around the Quarter, introducing him to the various spotters and runners who were involved with the gambling network. It seemed that three out of four or four out of five of the people he met had already heard of him. What's more, they all made a point of expressing their approval and support as well as telling him how much they were looking forward to working with him.

After a while, this inflated notoriety began to annoy him, and eventually generated a seed of worry in his mind. Eventually, he expressed his concern to Jerome.

"Don't worry about it," Jerome said with a wave of his hand. "It never hurts to have a reputation for being a bit of a badass, even if the facts get garbled a bit. It's not like you're bragging it up yourself."

"But it was Valerie that actually braced him."

"So? You think Gris-gris is gonna say anything about that?"

"Why wouldn't he?"

Jerome laughed.

"For the same reason Jumbo didn't step in when it all went down. It would look bad all around if it came out that he got backed off by a girl, and even worse if Jumbo had to help him."

"But isn't he going to come back at me over this?"

"Not much chance of that," Jerome said. "That would make it seem bigger and more important than it already is.

Besides, unless I read him wrong, he's more than a little bit afraid of your sister."

"Really?"

"Uh-huh. To tell the truth, I'm a little spooked by her myself. That's one impressive mama you've got there . . . and remember what I told you about female dragons. You really don't want to get them stirred up."

They walked on in silence for a few moments, then Jerome cocked his head.

"Tell me one thing, Grifter," he said. "If you didn't know how Gris-gris and Jumbo would react, why did you set it so it would be Valerie who'd do the talkin'?"

"I don't know," Griffen admitted. "From what Mose was saying, it sounded like Gris-gris had a problem with me. I figured it would be better to play it from the angle of his disrespect than making an issue of the money . . . and that bracing him for respect would sound better coming from someone else, like Valerie. I really hadn't thought about the whole male/female aspect of it. Call it instinct and good luck."

"Well, any gambler needs good luck," Jerome said, resuming his walk. "Just keep listening to your instincts. So far they're the best thing you have going for you."

Jerome's words stayed with Griffen, and he gave them considerable food for thought. He had always been good at reading people and situations . . . something he was now being told was part of his dragon heritage. Now that he was consciously thinking about it, however, his senses and observations seemed heightened to a new level.

Now, whenever he walked down the street or sat down in

a bar or restaurant, he was aware of who was looking at him and who wasn't. More particularly, of those who looked at him, he was building a sense of who was friendly, who was curious, who was neutral, and who seemed to be harboring some kind of hostility.

For the most part, the tourists and conventioneers barely glanced at him, if that. Of the locals, whether if was due to his new found notoriety or simply the fact that more and more people were recognizing him as a Quarter regular, he found an increasing percentage noting his presence and tracking his movements with the casual attention a veld full of antelope will give to a strolling lion.

It was both unsettling and exhilarating at the same time. Back up north when he walked across the campus, he had been all but invisible, his passing noticed by only a scattered handful of acquaintances. Here in the Quarter, while the transients were oblivious to his presence, he was being watched by the locals as a power to be reckoned with.

One night, he was walking Fox Lisa back to her apartment. She had called him from her bartending job and suggested that he pick her up when she got off work so they could spend some time together, and he had complied.

It was a weekday night, so the side streets were virtually deserted except for a few single pedestrians either making their way home or to a late-night club for a nightcap. The weather was pleasant, if warm, and he enjoyed her company as she clung to his arm and chatted about the problems that had arisen on her shift, obviously decompressing now that she was off duty.

All at once, the night felt wrong.

There was nothing tangible or specific that had changed, but he suddenly realized he was feeling edgy and a bit tense, as if there was static electricity dancing just above his skin.

A month ago he would have shrugged it off as a mood swing. Now, however, he surreptitiously swept the street ahead with his eyes.

Nothing in particular caught his attention, but the feeling persisted.

Leaning down slightly to kiss the top of her head, he glanced behind them.

One guy walking alone on the far side of the street about a half block back. No feeling of threat there.

He looked ahead again.

There was a man standing in the shadows twenty feet ahead, partially hidden by the cement steps running up to an apartment door. It looked like he was tying his shoelace, but it seemed to be taking him a long time to do it.

The setup didn't seem to match the way Mose described the George operating, but he figured it was better to be safe than sorry.

He kissed the top of Lisa's head again and murmured in her ear.

"Don't like the looks of the guy ahead, there. Be ready to get behind me."

With that he straightened again and continued walking, casually putting his hand on the knife in his pants pocket.

Angling their path so it slanted closer to the curb, he stopped about eight feet short of the man in question and made as if to kiss Lisa on the lips.

The man came out of the shadows and started toward them, one hand hidden in his pocket.

Griffen moved a step forward, steering Lisa behind him with his left hand.

"Can we do something for you?" he called while the man was still six feet away.

The man continued toward them.

"I was wondering if you could . . ."

"Hold it right there!"

Griffen realized with a start that Fox Lisa was beside him, a small, black, automatic pistol in her hand leveled at the man in front of them.

The man froze in his tracks.

"Let's see your other hand . . . and it better come out empty."

The man slowly removed his hand from his pocket and held it empty at shoulder height.

"I don't want no trouble," he said. Soothingly.

"You got him?"

The call came from the far side of the street. Griffen glanced back and recognized the man who had been walking behind them as one of the two men who had been shooting pool in the Irish pub when he and Jerome had met with Gris-gris.

"I got him," Lisa called back. "Make sure he's alone."

The shadower waved and moved on ahead.

The man under the gun hadn't moved, but he kept glancing nervously down the street behind him and muttering softly to himself.

Fox Lisa took two steps forward, her weapon still leveled, and jerked her head toward Griffen.

"I want you to take a long look at this man," she instructed. "Do you know who he is?"

The man stared at Griffen and shook his head.

"This is Griffen McCandles," she said, drawing the name out for emphasis. "You may have heard of him. He'll be taking over Mose's business."

The man stared harder at Griffen and said something that sounded apologetic.

"Remember him and tell your friends they can save themselves a load of trouble if they walk wide around him. Understand me?"

"Yes'm."

"All right. Get moving and don't let us see you again tonight."

The man turned and sprinted away down the street.

"That was a good call," Lisa said as she returned her automatic to the pocket in the back of the fanny pack she was wearing. "Most people wouldn't have spotted . . . What?"

Griffen continued staring at her.

She cocked her head and frowned.

"Is something wrong, lover?"

"You're carrying a gun," he said.

"Yeah. So? Sometimes it comes in handy . . . like tonight."

"It's just . . . I've never known anyone who carried a gun before."

"That's right. I keep forgetting you're from up north." She flashed him a quick grin. "Well, you're in the South now, and a lot of people carry. It's even worse over in Texas."

"Isn't that illegal or something?" Griffen managed at last.

Again the grin.

"So's gambling, but we do it anyway. No. Seriously. It's not that hard to get a concealed weapons permit here in New Orleans. Especially if you live in the Quarter and have to go out at night. Of course, being a girl helps. Anyway, all you have to do is take a class and get certified so they know you won't shoot anyone including yourself accidentally. Other than that, the only big rule is that you can't carry in a bar."

"But you . . ."

"Think a minute, lover. How often have you seen me peel off my fanny pack as I walked into a bar and asked them to hold it behind the counter for me?"

Griffen realized it was almost a habitual routine for her.

"I thought you were just doing that because it was like a purse to you and you didn't want to have to keep watching it all the time."

"That, too," Lisa said. "Still, it keeps me within the rules. Any other questions?"

Griffen nodded.

"Yeah," he said. "Who was the other guy?"

"Who? The one I ran off?"

"No. I meant the guy on the other side of the street," Griffen said. "The one that was hanging back until the action started. He called to be certain you had things in hand."

"Oh. That guy."

"Uh-huh. You seemed to know each other."

"Yes, we do."

"Let me try to make this easier for you," Griffen said. "Unless I'm mistaken, he was shooting pool on the back table at the Irish pub the afternoon Jerome and I met with Gris-gris. Am I right?"

"Well, yes."

"Let me take this one step further. Am I being body-guarded? Did Jerome or Mose hire you and the others to cover me?"

"Not really hire, even though I have done that kind of work for pickup money sometimes. It was more like Jerome asked for a favor. He asked me and a few others to try and keep an eye on you while you were getting used to the city."

She cocked her head and narrowed one eye. Griffen seemed hesitant.

"Don't even go there, lover. Not if we're going to stay friends."

"What?"

"I'm betting your next question was going to be whether or not Jerome asked me to go to bed with you. That's dangerously close to calling me a working girl. I'll go ahead and tell you so you won't have to ask. The subject never came up. All he asked was that I keep an eye on you, and I can do that without sleeping with you. Clear?"

Griffen winced inwardly at her assumption, but didn't think the truth of what he had thought would be very comforting—a gun against someone who professionally killed dragons didn't seem a fair match. He really didn't want to risk his lover, bodyguard or not, against a true killer.

"Crystal clear," he said.

"Fine. Anything else?"

Griffen thought for a moment.

"Okay," he said. "What do you know about dragons?"

"Dragons?" Lisa said frowning. "What does that have to do with anything?"

He smiled and gathered her arm in his again.

"Just curious," he said.

Nineteen

Yo Mama's Bar and Grill was a shotgun-style bar just off Bourbon Street across from Preservation Hall and Pat O'Brien's. Other than a small upstairs dance floor, there was nothing to distinguish it from any of the dozens of bars in the area except its selection of tequilas and that it served the best hamburgers in the Quarter.

Griffen had discovered it his first week in town and had taken to stopping in two or three times a week. While the local cuisine was interesting and he had made a point of trying the gumbos and jambalayas, he still favored a basic burger or Chinese meal when his stomach demanded something familiar. When he found out that the regular graveyard shift bartender, Padre, shared his love of old movies and trivia, it cemented Yo Mama's as one of his hangouts of preference.

One of the few difficulties was determining exactly when was a good time to drop in. Too early in the evening, and the place was packed with tourists. Too late, and it was full of service industry people stopping in for a drink and a burger before going home or moving on to another club.

Usually, Griffen tried to stop in somewhere between eleven at night and one in the morning. While never empty, the crowd had usually thinned enough at that point that he could chat with Padre without interrupting the flow of service.

This particular evening, he was seated at one of the booths enjoying a Peanut Butter Burger with a baked potato while idly watching a movie on AMC on one of the televisions that bracketed the bar. Specifically, it was *The Great Escape*, which he had seen often enough that he could almost recite the dialogue without the closed caption subtitles at the bottom of the screen.

A heavyset biker type came in and began to walk down the bar with a heavy, almost lurching step.

This in itself was not unusual, as this stretch of St. Peter was a favorite gathering point for the bikers, and they would wander in and out of three or four bars with their beers while joking with each other or comparing the relative merits of their bikes. For the most part, they kept to themselves and didn't hassle anyone, so they were generally treated like any other customer.

Something about this newcomer, however, caught Griffen's eye. Mildly curious, he watched the man, trying to figure out what made him different.

On the surface, he seemed not unlike the standard issue biker. Medium-length dark hair that looked like it could use washing, a thick mustache perched in the middle of a heavy-jowled face with a couple days' beard growth adorning it, black T-shirt with the arms cut off, blue jeans with a chain running from the belt to somewhere in his back pocket, and scuffed black boots. Still, there was something . . .

Griffen suddenly realized that the man was not interacting with anyone. Usually, when one of the bikers came in, he would nod to the bartender and greet any other bikers in the place, even if just with a wave.

This man was just walking along, glancing neither right nor left, with his eyes fixed on something on the back wall. Without looking back, Griffen knew there was nothing on the wall the man was staring at. It was simply that unfocused gaze of someone who was totally out of it . . . or who was watching everything without looking directly at any specific point.

Griffen glanced over at Padre. The bartender was standing blank faced, showing no reaction to the man, not even a glance.

Then he noticed that the group of three bikers at the front of the bar were putting money on the counter and gathering up their beers with a quiet, forced casualness.

At this point, the pieces began to add up, and Griffen was not even a little surprised when the man slid into the booth with him, still not looking at anything.

"Is there something I can help you with, officer?" Griffen said, pushing his plate to one side.

The eyes finally focused and the man gave him a long stare. Griffen stared back. At last, the man gave a small nod as if something had been confirmed to him.

"Detective Harrison," he said. "Vice."

Griffen had not had that much experience dealing with the police. If anything, he avoided them like the plague. While he generally respected them for doing a job he wouldn't touch with a ten-foot pole, it always made him a bit uneasy to be around anyone who held automatic authority over him.

Perhaps if he hadn't just been watching a movie involving Allied POWs outwitting their German captors, he would have reacted differently. As it was, he felt an overwhelming impulse to give this man a hard time.

"I repeat: Is there something I can help you with?"

"You're Griffen McCandles," the detective said, ignoring the question. "Word is that you're taking over for Mose."

"Mose who?" Griffen said, deadpan.

Harrison stared at him for a moment, then heaved a big sigh.

"Look, kid," he said. "I ain't wired or trying to trick you. Don't worry, and don't try to be cute. Just to keep things straight, let me fill in a few pieces for you."

He leaned back in his seat.

"Mose's games . . . the operation you're slated to take over . . . it's protected. Not a grift or payoff, at least not much. I figure some palms are greased somewhere, but mostly he's protected 'cause a lot of the powers that be who run this city also sit in on his games. The word is that we're supposed to leave them be, just in case some politicos get caught in a raid. We couldn't spring them without letting everyone else go and that shit would be too embarrassing to tolerate. For them, and for me . . . us. What I'm tryin' to say is, I'm not tryin' to trip you up or trick you into self-incrimination."

"Okay," Griffen said. "But I still don't know what you're talking to me for."

Harrison's eyes closed slowly, and when they opened again they were flat and expressionless.

"I just thought it would be nice if we met face-to-face," he said. "Clear the air, so to speak. Also, if you struck me as solid, I thought I'd ask a favor of you."

Griffen shrugged.

"I suppose . . . if it's within reason."

The detective leaned forward and gave a humorless grin.

"You're new in town, Griffen. Still getting used to the way we do things down here. All I'd ask is that you don't make it too hard for us to turn a blind eye to your doings."

"Like how, specifically?"

"Oh, nothing much. Don't be too loud and open with illegal games that should be secret. Keep a lid on things much as anyone can around here. And if you should happen to end up with a body at one of your games, could you drag it outside or maybe even break up the game before you call the cops? That way we don't have to ignore what's going on around it. It's a little thing, but we'd appreciate it."

"Sounds reasonable," Griffen said.

"Good. Glad we understand each other."

The detective started to slide out of the booth.

"Is there any chance you could do me a favor in return?"

The policeman froze, then slowly turned his head to stare.

"*You* want *me* to do you a favor?" he said slowly.

"Nothing big." Griffen shrugged. "Obviously you can say 'no' if you don't want to do it."

The detective sank back into his seat and twitched his fingers in a "give it to me" gesture.

"Like you said, Detective, I'm just a kid. I'm still learning how things work." Griffen hesitated a second. "One of the things I've heard, though, is that the police don't like the Feds messing in local affairs. Is that right?"

"Keep talking," Harrison said.

"Well, I've picked up a rumor that I've been targeted by someone in Homeland Security. A guy by the name of Stoner. Word is that he's looking for me and might use his federal clout to have law enforcement across the country help him find out where I am and what I'm doing."

The detective leaned back and cocked his head.

"Exactly what have you done to earn that kind of heat?"

"I really don't know, sir," Griffen said as sincerely as he could manage. "I just graduated from college about a month ago. Other than running a few card games while I was in school to pick up some pocket money, and this thing I am doing now with Mose, I can't think of a single thing that would warrant that kind of attention. That's part of what makes me nervous."

Not as nervous as the George made him, but at least it was clear that Stoner and George were unconnected. Their styles seemed far too different.

"Again," Griffen continued, "I've never experienced it, but I've heard that once the Feds get a bee in their bonnet about someone, it's hard to get them to let go. One version I've heard is that Stoner might try to say I should be watched for suspected terrorist involvement."

"Terrorist?" Harrison snorted. "Yeah. Suddenly since 9/11 every penny-ante pissant they want to mess with gets the terrorist label slapped on. But a terrorist poker game. I'll admit, that's a new one."

He stared at Griffen for a long minute, then got to his feet.

"All right, McCandles," he said. "I'll keep an ear open. Just don't get in the habit of asking for favors. Got it?"

"Got it," Griffen said. "Thanks, Detective."

"Don't mention it," Harrison grunted. "Please!"

"You *did what?"*

"I asked him for a favor," Griffen said into his cell phone.

"Detective Harrison? Harry the cop?" Jerome's voice came back to him over the phone. "I should have warned you about him, Grifter. If there are three cops in the entire city of New Orleans who hate our operation and having to lay off it, they'd all be him. Finding a way to bust us up would make his entire incarnation."

"I don't know," Griffen said casually, smiling as he did it. "He seemed reasonable enough to me."

"Detective Harrison? Are we talking about the same guy? Big white biker-type dude? Looks like a circus bear gone bad?"

"That's him."

"Maybe you'd better tell me about this conversation from the top."

Griffen complied, starting with Harrison sitting down at his booth and ending with his request about Stoner.

When he was finished, there was a long moment's silence.

"That might do it," Jerome said at last. "If there's anything Harrison hates more than our protected gambling operation, it's having Feds come traipsing around what he considers to be his private turf. Particularly if they don't bother to check in first."

"Yeah, and somehow I didn't think our first meeting was the right time to ask his thoughts on the possibility of a professional killer named George being on my trail."

"Yeah, why don't you wait till the second date for that sort of thing, Grifter. Or, ya know, maybe never would be a better idea."

"Probably right. So, you think he'll do it?" Griffen said.

"Fifty-fifty chance," Jerome said. "If nothing else, it might give him something to focus on except us for a while. All in all, I don't see a downside to this."

"Just thought you should know," Griffen said.

"Yeah. Grifter? Remember when we were talking about luck and instinct?"

"Yeah?"

"I'd say you're giving them both a real workout."

Twenty

Griffen was shooting pool at the Irish pub as he waited for Fox Lisa to get off work. He had never been much of a pool shooter in college, but had started taking the game up since arriving in New Orleans. Much of the social life in the Quarter revolved around the clubs, and one of the main pastimes and subjects of conversation was pool.

In the time he had been shooting, he had noticed a marked improvement in his game, which in turn encouraged him to practice more. He had even been asked to join one of the pool-league teams, but had refused because his schedule was so uncertain. The house shooters remained friendly, however, and were more than happy to show him some drills or to advise him on the ins and outs of position play and spin.

He was just lining up what he hoped would be an easy combination shot, when a minor stir rippled through the bar, and he glanced up to check the reason.

Gris-gris had just walked in alone, and was scanning the

place. When he saw Griffen, he held his hands up in a "no hassle" gesture and walked over to him.

Since everyone knew there was bad blood between the two of them, half the bar was watching closely. Some craned their necks to see better, while a few others left their seats to drift a little closer to the action.

Gris-gris stopped a few paces from where Griffen stood.

"Mr. McCandles," he said.

"Gris-gris." Griffen nodded back. "And it's 'Griffen' or 'Grif' to my friends."

Gris-gris's face split with a wide grin.

"Listen. If you got a minute, I need to talk to you. Can I buy you a drink?"

"No problem," Griffen said. "Hey, Steamboat! Can you take over this rack for me?"

Passing the stick over to his replacement, they stepped to the bar, gathered their drinks, and retired to one of the circular tables along the wall . . . the same one, in fact, that Griffen had been sitting at for his last meeting with Gris-gris.

More and more, Griffen found himself sitting with his back to the wall, facing the doors, wherever he was. No sense letting anyone, local or more dangerous threat, have an easier drop on him. He tried not to overthink his new paranoia, especially when it seemed to be justified.

"So, what's up?" Griffen said, settling into his chair.

Gris-gris looked nervous, fidgeting with his drink as he talked.

"There's a couple of things I need to talk to you about," he said. "Let me get the first one out of the way so you don't think the second one has anything to do with it."

"All right," Griffen said. "Shoot."

He immediately wished he had used a different word, but Gris-gris didn't notice and plowed on.

"Well, first of all I wanted to tell you that I've thought about it and decided to keep my game with your organization. I'll be using your network and paying you a percentage like before . . . including the payments I missed during our little difference of opinion."

Griffen kept the surprise off his face and simply nodded.

"That's great, Gris-gris," he said. "I'm looking forward to working with you."

He made a little toasting motion with his glass that Gris-gris returned.

Instead of continuing, however, Gris-gris kept fidgeting uncomfortably, glancing around the room.

"What's the other thing?" Griffen said, prompting him.

Gris-gris seemed to gather himself.

"Well, you see . . ."

He broke off and took another sip of his drink.

"What it is . . ." he began again, then stopped.

Griffen frowned at him.

"You're starting to worry me, Gris-gris," he said. "Talk to me. Are you in trouble with the law? Do you need money?"

Gris-gris shook his head.

"Nothin' like that," he said. "Look. What I'm trying to say is that I want to date your sister . . . if it's all right with you, I mean."

Griffen sat back in his chair and blinked. For a moment, he could think of absolutely nothing to say.

"Hey, if there's a problem . . . that's cool." Gris-gris said hastily, misunderstanding the silence.

"No. It's just . . . you just caught me by surprise is all,"

Griffen managed at last. "You know, this is the first time anyone ever asked my permission to date Valerie. We've always pretty much gone our separate ways."

"Then it's okay?"

"I don't have a problem with it," Griffen said. "I figure it's her decision to make."

Besides, Griffen thought, the rumor mill has been so good that he has worried less and less about her. Here, the town protected his "little" sister.

"I understand that," Gris-gris said. "I just didn't want you to think I was sneaking around behind your back to hit on your sister. Some guys get real upset if they think you're trying to pull a fast one."

"Well, I appreciate you letting me know," Griffen said, finally starting to recover from his surprise. "It's always good to keep communication lines open."

"Speaking of that," Gris-gris said, "I don't have any way to get in touch with her . . . or you for that matter. That's why I came looking for you here."

"We can fix that easy enough," Griffen said. I'll pass you both our cell phone numbers before you leave. In the meantime, let me get the next round here."

As he went to the bar to get the drinks, it occurred to Griffen that he should probably check with Valerie before giving out her cell phone number. The more he thought about it, though, the more he was convinced to let things go as they stood.

Why should he be the only one to have to deal with surprises?

Twenty-one

Fourth of July weekend meant different things to different people in New Orleans.

For some it was the Essence Fest, another of the numerous music festivals that dotted the city calendar.

For others, it meant a long weekend break from work. Weather permitting, an excursion to the beach, the Audubon Zoo, or even just a picnic or backyard barbecue provided a sufficient change of pace.

With the hotels and restaurants full, the service industry dropped it into low gear and worked their tails off. No rest for the wicked.

For Mose's crew, and therefore for Griffen, it meant a high-stakes poker game.

It seemed that this was a yearly event that a group of regular players attended, both local and out of towners. To be accurate, it was one of several yearly games that Mose hosted, usually coinciding with holidays or major local celebrations. This was just the first big game that Griffen had

been invited to play in since he arrived in New Orleans
three weeks earlier.

While he was at college, there were several regular games
that Griffen would sit in on. These would usually be at someone's apartment or fraternity house, and would be held on specific nights of the week. Some of them would begin midday
on Friday and continue through the weekend, with players
sitting in, then leaving to go on a date or sleep, then sitting in
again. Those games were usually at nickel/dime/quarter or, in
some cases, quarter/half/dollar stakes. The host would usually
pull a low chip or two out of every pot to cover the cost of the
cards (they always used new decks) and refreshments. Griffen's
real preference was half/dollar/five stakes as it upped the
power of the bluff, but students were traditionally poor and
games like that were rare unless you were willing to collect
large quantities of IOUs.

The Fourth of July game Mose hosted was nothing like
that.

Instead of sitting around someone's dining room table in
an apartment, they had a suite at the luxurious Royal Sonesta Hotel in the heart of the French Quarter. There was an
open wet bar with top-shelf liquors, and instead of potato
chips and pizza they had trays of sandwiches and potato
skins from room service. They also had a real casino poker
table with two nonplayers (Jerome being one) alternating as
dealers.

The stakes were $25/$50/$100 with $500 chips available if the betting got fierce. It was the highest stakes game
Griffen had ever sat in on, and he was worried that it would
affect his game. While in theory, one should play a blue
chip the same whether it was worth a dollar or a hundred
dollars, it was hard to keep the actual dollar value out of

one's mind. As an example, Griffen had always avoided the penny/nickel/dime games back at school. For one thing, the amount to be won in a single evening wasn't worth the time and effort. More important, the low stakes affected everyone's play. Even if someone raised your bluff the limit on the last card, for a dime it was easy to call the raise just to see if your busted flush and one medium pair would stand up.

There was another worry just as bothersome.

Mose had told him that the word was out through many of the regular players that Griffen was being groomed to take over the operation. When they phoned or e-mailed in to reserve a seat in the weekend's game, they had also commented that they wanted to meet and play against the new wunderkind. This made Griffen very self-conscious and aware of his age. Even though both Mose and Jerome counseled him not to worry about it, he was afraid that the players would consider him too young to run the operation and take their play elsewhere. That would bode ill for his eventual involvement.

There were five players in addition to Mose and himself: a middle-aged businessman and his teenage son from Oklahoma, a solidly built Philippine woman from Los Angeles who was a surgeon, a well-dressed black man who was some kind of politician locally, and a Chinese restaurant owner who Griffen recognized as a semiregular at the Irish pub. He had wondered about the teenager being allowed to sit in, but was told that it was sort of a coming-of-age ritual. The businessman's father had brought him to sit in on one of Mose's games when he was in his teens, and the man wanted to continue the tradition.

As the evening progressed, Griffen began to gradually relax and lose himself in the play of the game. For once, he felt that he didn't have to worry about threats on his life. All of the players were well-known and vouched for by Mose, and no one else came in or out of the room. They were all good players, though the teenager was clearly the weakest, but Griffen found he could read them as easily as he had his old opponents at school.

Mose had the fewest "tells" with the Philippine lady a close second, but everyone seemed to have those little habits and gestures that would signal when they had a good hand or if they were bluffing. In addition, there were changes in breathing patterns and eye blinks that were more telling than the players' betting patterns or table talk. The teenager might as well have been playing his cards faceup.

When a break was called after four hours of play, Griffen estimated that he was several thousand dollars ahead.

"So, Mose. What's this I hear that you're going to be stepping down in favor of this young Turk here?" the businessman said, freshening his drink.

"Nothing goes on forever, Mr. Goodman," Mose said. "I figure it's time I started taking it easy."

"Oh, bullshit," the businessman said. "Com'on Mose. You were old when I was Junior here's age . . . and I keep telling you, it's Hank, not Mr. Goodman. I mean, you call Lollie here Tía, don't you?"

" 'Tía' is a Spanish word," the Philippine woman said. "It means 'aunt' and is a title or honorific, like when he calls you 'mister.' Mose is just being polite."

"Whatever." Hank waved. "And we're getting off the subject here. I want to hear why Mose is thinking of retiring, and I don't think it's just because he's getting old."

"Seems to me that's Mose's business, not ours," the politician put in.

"That's right," the restaurant owner said. "We play here because Mose runs an honest game and we trust his judgment about who he lets play. I don't think we should start questioning his judgment if he wants to step down, much less who he chooses for his successor."

"Gentlemen, please," Mose said. "Mr. Goodman has a right to ask any question he wants, just like I've got a right not to give any answers I don't want. In this case, I don't mind answering him."

He took a small sip of his drink before continuing.

"I've been running these games for a long time now. And I mean a LONG time. That's gotten me kind of set in my ways. You know, thinking, 'It's always been good doing it this way before, so why change?' The trouble is, the world moves on. Maybe the old way isn't as good as it could be. Maybe it needs new blood like Jerome or Griffen here with new ideas to bring some changes in. Just as an example, you know I don't like Texas Hold 'Em, but it's all the rage now. They got tournaments and television shows on it now, not to mention books and magazines. Maybe it's time to give it a try."

"So why bring this kid in?" Goodman said, jerking a thumb at Griffen. "I mean, he's a hell of a poker player, but Jerome's been around these games for a long time. Why bring in some outsider?"

"As a matter of fact, Mr. Goodman," Jerome said from the sofa where he was watching television with the sound turned off, "I was the one who recommended Griffen. I've been playing cards with him for years and have gotten to know him pretty well. I think he can help our network in ways I can't."

"Like how?" Goodman pressed. "By bringing in Texas

Hold 'Em? I don't happen to like that game myself. If I wanted to play Texas Hold 'Em, I'd go to the casino."

"For the record, sir, I don't care for it either," Griffen said. "If we were going to try it, my first thought would be not to bring it into these games, but to set up some separate games on a trial basis."

"So what other kind of changes are you thinking of?" the businessman said, speaking directly to Griffen for the first time.

"Frankly, sir, I don't know," Griffen said easily. "As you pointed out, I'm still very new to this setup. I've got a lot to learn and consider before I'd even start to think about changing anything."

"One thing you might be interested in," Jerome said. "Griffen's only been with us for a few weeks. Mostly, I've been introducing him around and showing him how we do things. In that time, we've had no fewer than eight independent games contact us and ask to join our network. That's more than we had join in the last year. What's more, the ones I've talked to make it clear that they're doing it because they want to work with Griffen. I think that says something."

"There. You see, Goodman?" the politician said. "Mose knows what he's doing. Hell, if they were selling stock, I'd buy some."

Mose caught Griffen's eye and winked.

Twenty-two

Griffen had wholeheartedly adopted the nocturnal schedule of a Quarter rat, but Valerie lacked her brother's tastes and habits. More and more she found herself embracing the Quarter by day.

At first, it had been morning jogs on the Moonwalk to keep her active and in shape. She was used to an active lifestyle, and it felt good to get her heart rate up and pounding with some simple aerobic exercise. Of course, night or day, there were always temptations to be found.

Naturally, after such healthy and worthwhile endeavors, she deserved a healthy bit of indulgence. As often as not, she ended up breakfasting at the Café Du Monde. The inexpensive and delicious beignets, buried under their mountains of powdered sugar, sent a rush through her at least as enjoyable as the endorphins her run produced.

She sat as she always did, right beside the rails marking the boundaries of the open-air café. Though it meant occasionally being hassled by tourists and panhandlers, it provided her a splendid view of Jackson Square. Already, as a lazy Sunday morning flowed over the Quarter, the Square was full of life. As she sipped her hot chocolate, another indulgence more satisfying then the strong coffee preferred by most of the café's regulars, she leaned back in her chair and watched as the street entertainers plied their arts for the scattered groups of ever-present tourists.

Artists hung their canvases on the iron railing of the Square, or set up mobile easels to do quick sketch portraits and caricatures. Valerie knew that on the opposite side of the Square, psychics would have set up small tables to read palms and cards and bones. Performance artists, from men painted as silver robots to jugglers to living statues who never moved, stood in front of hats or boxes or buckets that held the smatterings of bills and coins from appreciative passersby. The snappy patter of a street musician blended into the soft strains of an accordion accompanied by a young girl's voice singing in French, and somewhere in the mix a lonely guitar repeated the same blues riff over and over.

Though she hadn't quite fallen in love with New Orleans as her brother had, she had succumbed to many of the local habits. People watching, for example. She found it fascinating the types of people attracted to the area, day or night, and spent just as much attention on the endlessly changing stream of tourists as she did the more stable performers. Whether it be families weighed down by too many children far too young to enjoy the Quarter at night, or well-dressed professionals on a break from their various conferences, or even the expensively but slovenly decked out retirees just off the cruise ships, each brought their own style, and their own amusement. And that was without the eclectic mix of locals who sauntered across the Square or down Decatur Street.

They nodded to and tipped the performers just as often as the tourists, and knew just how lucky they were to get such a display of humanity anytime they should choose to indulge.

After she had finished with her breakfast, she decided to take a leisurely stroll down Decatur Street. Unlike the tight, channel-like feel of Bourbon, Decatur was split into two lanes to accommodate greater vehicle traffic. Both sides were lined with shops and restaurants, with bars being less common and the Bourbon Street–style strip club nonexistent. Valerie found hours could pass just window shopping the countless shops, which ranged from the tacky T-shirt shops to upscale clothing and jewelry merchants. She usually found many things she wanted, though limited herself to a rare purchase. Shopping was a spectator sport for her.

On the way back, she decide to browse through the many galleries on Royal Street. Again, shops ranged wildly, and not just between paintings and sculptures. There was a cluttered hole-in-the-wall poster gallery a few doors down from a high-class place that seemed to have nothing but Dr. Seuss art. Valerie didn't even pause while walking past the famous "blue dog" gallery. There were some things about New Orleans that she just never would understand.

Of course, above every shop and tucked away in every crevice were houses and apartments for the many living in the Quarter. Valerie stopped, amused, watching a man struggle to pull a couch through a doorway that seemed much too small. What's worse, the couch was white, and the man working alone kept scraping it against the slightly grimy door frame or the ground. Valerie shook her head and smiled, then silently crept up and took the other end of the couch. When he hauled, she lifted, and the couch passed through like magic.

"Hey, thanks! Whoa."

The man had looked up, and caught sight of his assistant. His jaw hung open just slightly, and Valerie fought the urge to reach up and push it closed. Instead she replied, with just a bit of teasing in her voice.

"Now isn't the time to 'whoa,' you've still got to get it to your apartment door."

"And upstairs. Three floors," he said with a sigh.

Like most apartments, there was actually a bit of a walk from the street door to the separate entrances. And the buildings were renowned for spiral staircases of dubious stability. Valerie smiled and cocked her head.

"Well, going to ask for help?"

"Hell, no. I'm going to ask you up to my place for a drink," he said.

"At two in the afternoon?"

"Hey, it's the Quarter. But, oh, woe is me, there seems to be a nasty old couch in your way."

"Ha! Now you are back to the woe again. Well, I suppose I'm far too stubborn to let a couch stand between me and a free drink."

"Great."

The man jumped onto the couch, lying back and grinning up at her.

"Third floor, second door on the left please," he said, and pretended to close his eyes and go to sleep.

Despite the narrow alleyway, Valerie managed to turn the couch enough to dump him on the ground.

"The operative word was 'help,' " she said.

"It was worth a try." The man laughed. "By the way, the name's Kid Blue. I play guitar on Bourbon Street."

"You're a street entertainer?" Valerie said, shaking the offered hand.

"Pul-eeese," Kid Blue said, drawing himself up haughtily. "I play in one of the clubs. I'm with a band. And you?"

"Oh. My name's Valerie. Valerie McCandles," she responded.

"I meant what do you do?" the man said. "What pays your bills?"

"Nothing," Valerie said softly.

Until just now when she vocalized it, she hadn't realized how discontented she was with that situation.

Twenty-three

Griffen had a new resolve as he sauntered down the Moon-walk. He had been sitting around bars and card games too long. It was time for him to get back in shape. Well, get into shape, as he had never been that athletically inclined.

Valerie had always been the fitness freak of the family and, since moving to New Orleans, had taken to getting up mornings to jog along the Moonwalk before the midday heat set in. The other day, however, she had mentioned that she had discovered that someone was teaching a fencing class upstairs at Yo Mama's Bar and Grill on various weekdays. Since the upstairs was only open to the public Thursday through Saturday nights, the owner was letting them use the space for free.

That alone had caught Griffen's attention, as he had done a bit of fencing with a local club while he was at school. He had a wry picture in his mind of him and the George, or at least him versus a knight in full armor, going sword to sword. Of course, nothing like that would happen in real life, even as odd as his "real" life was.

What really piqued his interest, though, was when she mentioned the teacher's name was Maestro. Griffen was pretty sure it was the same guy that Bone had introduced him to the night he first met Fox Lisa. After all, how many people in the Quarter could there be that went by the name of Maestro.

Joining his class would accomplish two things. First, it would give Griffen some much needed exercise, and second, it would give him a chance to learn a little more about Maestro.

Of course, he would have to get in shape first. (Guys getting in shape before joining an exercise class was not unlike the thing women do when they clean up before the maid comes.) Maybe a bit of power walking and light jogging to increase his stamina and lung capacity.

That was enough to set him up for today's errand . . . a shopping trip through the Riverwalk, the small shopping center along the river just outside the Quarter. After all, if he was going to start exercising, he would need some athletic shoes . . . and maybe a warm-up outfit or two.

It was late morning, earlier than he usually was out and about, but late enough for there to be a fair amount of activity along the Moonwalk. The street musicians were out in force, working the inevitable crowds of tourists who were getting an early start on their day's itinerary. The breeze off the river was doing a nice job of holding the ovenlike heat of midday at bay, and a light, high cloud cover kept the sun from being blinding. All in all, a beautiful day, and Griffen enjoyed the relaxed ambiance as he made his leisurely way along.

His reverie was interrupted when his cell phone rang. The caller ID showed an unknown caller, but that wasn't unusual.

Since passing his phone number to Gris-gris, he had gotten several calls from strangers, often setting meetings to ask about joining some satellite card game to his network.

Flipping the phone open, he held it to his ear while casually looking around.

"Griffen," he said into the receiver.

"Mr. McCandles," a male voice said. "I think it's time we talked. I'd like to clear the air between us."

"And you are . . . ?"

"This is Jason Stoner. I believe you've heard of me."

It took a moment for the name to register. Stoner. The man with Homeland Security that was supposed to be hunting for Griffen.

"So talk," Griffen said. "You have my undivided attention."

"I was thinking more of a face-to-face sit-down," Stoner said.

Griffen thought for a moment. He really didn't want to be alone with this man. Still, his curiosity was piqued.

"That might take a while to arrange," he said. "If you don't mind, I'd prefer to meet somewhere in public."

"My thoughts precisely," Stoner said. "How about that bench just ahead of you . . . say, in two minutes?"

Startled, Griffen looked around, trying to see in all directions at once. There didn't seem to be anyone in the crowd paying particular attention to him, but it was obvious he was being watched.

"How will I know you?" he said, stalling for time.

There was no answer. Glancing at his phone, Griffen realized Stoner had broken the connection.

Replacing the cell phone on his hip, he stared at the indicated bench, looked around again, then slowly walked over to it and opted to stand rather than sit.

Pedestrians continued to stream by in groups of two to six, with an occasional jogger mixed in for variety. Nothing there that seemed particularly threatening or ominous.

There were people leaning on the railing watching the river traffic, a couple of tired looking women herding a group of shrieking children from a day-care center, and a trio of sailors in uniform taking pictures of each other, but no one seemed to be paying any attention to Griffen.

Then a man sat down on the bench. There was nothing noteworthy about him. He was dressed tourist casual, opting for the polo shirt and light slacks rather than a T-shirt and shorts, and even had a small shopping bag that he carried in one hand. Griffen wouldn't have looked at him twice if he wasn't expecting to meet someone. Still, there was something about him . . .

Suddenly, Griffen realized what was wrong. The man was sitting absolutely motionless.

If one watched closely, most people were constantly in motion . . . even when supposedly at rest. They would fidget and look around, or shift their position slightly, or fiddle with their clothes, but they were always moving. To a card player, these were "tells" about a person's thoughts or mood, to be noted and studied.

This man just sat, muscles relaxed, eyes unfocused.

Steeling himself mentally, Griffen also took a seat on the bench.

"I assure you, Mr. McCandles, your misgivings are unwarranted," the man said. "I mean you no harm. That's why I wanted to have this conversation."

"Mr. Stoner?" Griffen said.

The man turned his head and looked at Griffen directly.

"That is correct," he said. "It has come to my attention that you are laboring under certain misconceptions regarding our relationship."

"I wasn't aware that we had a relationship," Griffen said. The stilted, formal speech patterns Stoner used were contagious. "I have, however, heard that you might be looking for me. Something about dragons."

Stoner smiled slightly, then his mouth returned to its normal, neutral position.

"Something about dragons," he said. "I suppose that's one way of putting it. What have you heard, exactly?"

Griffen took a deep breath.

"Well, sir, I've heard that you are one of, if not the, most powerful dragons operating on this continent. I've also been told that, now that I'm coming into my secondary powers, I could be seen as an ally or a threat. Specifically, they say that you'll either try to recruit me or kill me. Since I'm brand-new at this dragon thing, hearing something like that tends to make me nervous."

"Understandable," Stoner said, giving the smallest of nods. "Well, Griffen—May I call you Griffen?—I'm here to give you my personal assurance that I currently have no plans to pursue either of those options."

Griffen considered that for a few moments.

"Forgive me, sir, but could you elaborate on that? I can't help but notice the careful use of the word 'currently' in what you're saying."

"Very well," Stoner said. "My main focus is on international events . . . things that could create a threat to this country. If my information is correct, your current activity centers around running a small, local gaming operation. That is of no interest to me at all. Also, as you mention, you are still extremely new to . . . as you put it . . . the dragon game, I can see no point in recruiting you until you have developed considerably beyond where you are now . . . say, in twenty or thirty years. That is the situation as I see it currently. Should either of those conditions change, if you increase the scope of your operation or if your development takes a sudden surge forward, I would have to reconsider my position. If not, I see no reason for us to have any dealings with each other. Is that clear?"

"Crystal," Griffen said.

"Well then," Stoner said, starting to rise, "if there's nothing else to discuss . . ."

"Um . . . since you're here, sir," Griffen said hastily, "might I ask you a few questions? I mean, I'm new to all this and it would be a big help."

Stoner glanced at his watch, then sat down again.

"Very well," he said. "What do you want to know?"

"Well, first of all," Griffen said, "if you weren't looking for me, how did you find me? I find it hard to believe you just happened to be here."

"There was an inquiry submitted to our offices by the local police," Stoner said. "They wanted to know if Homeland Security in general or I specifically had any interest in you and if so, why. That gave me a pretty good idea of where you were. Once I had that, it was easy, with my resources, to find out what you were doing and what your habits were."

Griffen was too good a poker player to let anything show on his face, but inwardly he cursed himself. His clever plan to use Harrison to run an official check for him had backfired. If

Stoner had really been hunting for him, that could have been disastrous. As it was . . .

"So, you've been having me watched?" he said carefully.

Stoner smiled slightly.

"Don't misunderstand me, Griffen," he said. "Just because I mean you no harm does not mean I'm totally disinterested. A dragon is still a dragon."

"Does that mean you're going to continue having me watched?"

"I'll be keeping casual surveillance on you," Stoner said. "Again, more curiosity than anything else. In my position, it's relatively easy to add a few more names to the list of those we're keeping tabs on."

"What about before," Griffen said.

"Excuse me?"

"Was my name on the list before I reached New Orleans?"

Stoner sighed.

"If you're referring to that incident on the expressway, that was regrettable. The attack, such as it was, was spontaneous. Certainly not ordered by me or anyone reporting to me. Your movements were to be noted and reported. Nothing more. Be assured that the officer who leaked the information to some of his friends has been dealt with severely."

Something in the tone of Stoner's voice reminded Griffen that this was not a man to be taken lightly . . . as if he needed reminding.

It also made him reconsider exactly what Stoner's concept of "not having dealings with each other" might consist of.

"One more question, Mr. Stoner," he said. "Are you aware of a person known as George?"

"The George?" Stoner said, cocking his head to one side. "That old myth? I've heard of him, but never felt the need to run down the truth of the matter or look into hiring him. I have my own organization with a carefully audited budget. It more than suffices for my needs. Why do you ask?"

"Just something I heard," Griffen said negligently. "No one down here seems to know much about him. I thought maybe with your resources you might have more information."

"Nothing I'd consider reliable," Stoner said, getting to his feet. "If you're sincerely trying to keep a low profile, Griffen, I'd recommend you leave that subject alone. Asking too many questions could draw unwanted attention."

Griffen was having a Peanut Butter Burger at Yo Mama's when Harrison slid into his booth.

"Hey, Griffen," he said. "You owe me a cup of coffee."

His poker reflexes came to his rescue, and instead of showing his true feelings, Griffen managed to keep a straight face.

"Really?" he said, raising his eyebrows slightly. "How so?"

"I got good news for you," the detective said. "One of the computer whizzes down at the department ran a check for me on that rumor you asked me about. Near as he can tell, Homeland Security doesn't have a flippin' clue who you are. No interest in you at all. That piece of information will cost you a cup of coffee, since that's what I gave him for the favor."

Griffen smiled.

"As John Arbuckle would say . . ." he said.

"Excuse me?" Harrison frowned.

"It's from an old television coffee ad," Griffen explained. "The whole quote is 'As John Arbuckle would say, you gets what you pay for.'"

The detective frowned some more, then shook his head.

"I don't get it."

"They were pushing an expensive blend of coffee," Griffen said. "Their point was that you can get cheaper coffee, but it will be just that . . . cheaper coffee."

"Which means . . ."

"I'll buy you your cup of coffee," Griffen said, "but we're both being overcharged for that information."

"You're saying there's something wrong with what I was told?" Harrison said.

"Let's just say I have additional information and let it go at that," Griffen said with a shrug.

"Let's not," the detective growled. "What have you got and where did you get it?"

"You first," Griffen said. "How do you suppose your computer whiz went about checking the rumor out?"

"Do I look like a computer geek?" Harrison said. "If I knew how to do that stuff, I wouldn't have had to ask someone else to check it out for me. I guess he checked some database or other online. How should I know?"

"Uh-huh," Griffen said. "Well, I think my source is a little more accurate than that."

"And just what would that source be, Mr. Been-in-Town-Less-Than-Two-Months?"

"I spoke directly with Stoner," Griffen said levelly. "You know, the guy with Homeland Security?"

Harrison sat back in his seat and cocked his head.

"I don't get it," he said at last. "If you knew this guy

Stoner well enough to pick up the phone and call him, what did you need me for?"

"I didn't say that I knew him," Griffen said. "And I didn't call him on the phone."

The detective frowned and blinked.

"Then how . . ."

"I talked to him face-to-face, after he stopped me on the Moonwalk and introduced himself."

"The Moonwalk?" Harrison said. "He was here? In New Orleans?"

"That's right," Griffen said. "Oh, and you'll like this part. When I asked him how he found me, he said that someone from the NOPD had sent an inquiry about me to his offices. Said it made it easy for him to know where to look."

Harrison's face fell as the full impact of the information registered.

"Shit, I'm sorry, Griffen. Never occurred to me my computer man would be so blatant. I should have warned him to be more careful."

Griffen shrugged with a carelessness he didn't feel.

"What's done is done," he said. "What's interesting is that Stoner said the same thing your man did . . . that he wasn't interested in me and there was nothing to worry about."

The detective's eyes narrowed.

"He came all the way to New Orleans to tell you that personally?"

"Not only that," Griffen said, "he had my cell phone number and knew enough to catch me on the Moonwalk at eleven o'clock in the morning. Do I need to tell you that's not my normal prowl pattern?"

"The bastard was having you watched before he approached you," Harrison said flatly. "He had a surveillance operation in my city and didn't even have the courtesy to let us in on it . . . even after we asked."

"Not 'had,' Harrison. 'Has.' He told me flat out that they were going to be keeping tabs on me 'just out of curiosity.' Isn't that cute?"

"'Cute' doesn't start to cover it," the detective said, sliding out of the booth. "Keep your coffee, Griffen. If anything, I figure I owe you a couple for fingering you. In the meantime, we'll just see what we can do about this 'casual' surveillance team the Feds are running on my turf."

Twenty-four

It was a beautiful evening as they emerged from Irene's. Griffen had resisted coming out, as he was still uneasy about the idea of Stoner's men shadowing him, but the others had insisted and, in afterthought, he had to admit that it had been one of the most pleasant evenings in his memories.

Irene's was a small neighborhood restaurant frequented mostly by locals and a few tourists willing to wander off the beaten track, and it had a family-run feel to it. The decor was nothing to brag about, but the food had been excellent and reasonably priced.

There were only four of them, Griffen, Jerome, Valerie, and Fox Lisa, but the conversation had been easy and as enjoyable as the food. Griffen had been surprised at the range of subjects they had touched on, from books to Broadway theater, to food, to music, to the inevitable gossip of who was doing what to who in the Quarter. By now he was used to Jerome and Fox Lisa holding their own on an amazing number of topics, but Valerie had surprised him by her knowledge and depth of perception. He realized now how seldom he had actually sat down and talked with his own sister.

They lingered over coffee and dessert of bananas Foster, a flaming ice cream concoction that he had never heard of before but had just become one of his favorites. He was informed that it had been invented right here in the Quarter at Brennan's. Their waiter, overhearing their discussion, commented, "That's right. They invented it at Brennan's, and we perfected it here." That earned him a round of applause from the diners and an extra large tip.

A rare cold front had come through while they were dining, and, while it was still warm by Griffen's standards, they walked out of the restaurant into a light fog that thickened slowly as they made their way down Chartres Street to Jackson Square. Despite the hour and the chilly damp, the Jackson Square street entertainers were still working. A hammer dulcimer player was working a small audience, flanked by several tables with tarot readers.

"That reminds me, Big Brother," Valerie said, glancing at the readers, "did you ever find out anything about that tarot card that got slipped under your door back in Detroit?"

Involuntarily, Griffen and Jerome glanced at each other.

"Nothing definite," Griffen said with forced casualness. "I'm still looking into it."

Valerie had caught the glance between Griffen and Jerome, and cocked a suspicious eyebrow at her brother. Warnings about female dragons aside, Griffen still agreed with Jerome's and Mose's earlier advice. Sometimes ignorance was bliss. It certainly would keep Valerie from rushing toward danger.

"I still can't believe how good the food was at Irene's,"

Griffen said, trying desperately to change the subject. "A little place like that."

"You've got to get out more, Grifter," Jerome told him, picking up on the cue. "I shouldn't have told you about phoning out for food. You've been living on ho-hum junk food just like you used to up in Ann Arbor. New Orleans is a prime dining town. It's almost impossible to get a bad meal unless you're stupid enough to eat a Lucky Dog. Places that don't have good food and big helpings don't last long down here."

A figure emerged from the fog, shuffling toward them. The reminder of the George still fresh in his mind, Griffen eyed it suspiciously for a moment, then recognized it. It was one of the street people who seemed to exist by begging money from tourists. The hair was so short and the face so wrinkled that, with its body wrapped in a shapeless jacket, for a while he had been unable to tell if it was a man or a woman. He had always brushed off advances in the past and got ready to do it again.

"Is that you, Mr. Jerome?" the figure said. "Praise Jesus. I was hopin' to see you tonight."

"How you doing, Babe," Jerome said, coming to a stop. "You liking this cold weather we've got now?"

"Oh, I love it," the beggar said. "Mr. Jerome, can you help me out a little? I just need another seventy-five cents to get into the shelter tonight."

Her voice took on a slight whine, and she glanced around as she spoke. The police did not take kindly to beggars who bothered tourists in the Quarter.

"Sure, Babe," Jerome said, passing her a bill. Griffen caught sight of the corner of the bill, and it was a five. "But you watch out for yourself now. Hear? There are folks out that will take that away from you if you give 'em half a chance."

"Praise Jesus. Thank you, Mr. Jerome," the lady said, backing away with a smile. "You have a nice night now. You and all your friends there."

The fog swallowed her up as though she had never been there.

"Why do you do that, Jerome?" Griffen said.

"Do what?"

"Give money to the street people," Griffen clarified. "I've seen you do it a dozen times."

Jerome was silent for a few moments.

"Have you ever been hungry a single day of your life, Grifter?" he said finally, in a soft voice.

Griffen hadn't, but fought off the moment of guilt.

"That isn't the point," he said firmly, almost as much to himself as to Jerome. "I mean, I've always known you as a savvy guy. Somebody would have to be pretty sharp to put one over on you, and I'd be willing to bet they never caught you with the same scam twice."

Jerome flashed a smile.

"I like to think that's true."

"So how come you're willing to give away good money just because someone walks up to you on the street and just asks for it?" Griffen pressed. "I mean, I don't want to sound like a hard case, but somebody down here told me that begging down here is a real racket. That some of these supposed beggars pull down a good buck from sympathetic tourists. I hear some of them have their own cars that they drive down to the Quarter and park on side streets before putting on their homeless act. Aren't there all sorts of government programs to help the homeless that our taxes are paying for?

Why should we reach into our pockets again to pay for their booze or drug habits?"

"Nice to know you don't want to sound like a hard case, Big Brother," Valerie said sarcastically.

"Hey. That's why I'm asking," Griffen protested. "I know Jerome, and I know he usually has a reason for whatever he does. When I see him do something that doesn't seem to make sense, I ask him. That's one of the ways I learn things. Okay?"

They all walked along in silence for a while, and Griffen wondered not only if Jerome was going to ignore the question, but if he had inadvertently put a damper on the mood of the whole evening.

"I'll tell you, Grifter," Jerome said at last. "One of the legends . . . stories they tell in voodoo is how sometimes one of the gods . . . Changul, I think . . . takes on the form of a beggar and walks among normal people to test their charity. It's a way of seeing whether people really feel compassion, or if they just pay lip service to it because the doctrine demands it."

Griffen didn't know what he had expected as an answer, but this one caught him by surprise.

"Come to think of it," he said, "I think there's something similar in Norse mythology. I think it's Odin who is supposed to disguise himself as a . . ."

He came to an abrupt halt.

"Wait a minute, Jerome. Are you saying that you believe in voodoo? That you're a practitioner?"

"Why?" Jerome said, raising an eyebrow. "Would that be a problem?"

"Well . . . no . . . I don't know," Griffen managed. "I guess I never gave it much thought. We've never talked much about religion. I guess I just never thought of you as a religious person."

"I'd have to say you're pretty much right on that one," Jerome said. "Just keep in mind the difference between religion and spirituality."

Griffen shook his head.

"I'm afraid you're going to have to clarify that one a bit, Jerome," he said. "I'm not sure I'm clear on the difference."

"That's two of us," Valerie chimed in. "What are we talking about here?"

Jerome turned his head.

"You want to take a shot at this, Foxy Lady?" he said. "I've never been too good at explaining things."

"There are a lot of very spiritual people around who are turned off by organized religions," Lisa said. "They may be in tune with the world and believe deep down in a higher power or plan, but they are repelled by the ritualization that's superimposed by so-called religions, particularly when the priesthood uses it to dabble in politics or for monetary gain."

"I think it was John D. MacDonald in one of his Travis McGee novels," Jerome said. "In it, the main character describes his view of organized religion as being marched in formation to look at a sunset."

"That's right," Fox Lisa said. "For some, religion is going to church once a week and paying five dollars while paying lip service to things they don't really believe in. For others . . . and I think both Jerome and I fall into this category . . . there are certain teachings that, while they may fall under the heading of religion, provide a code or a way of life. It's not a matter of 'practicing' a religion, it's living it day in and day out."

"If you open yourself up to it," Jerome said, "you'll feel

it. You know how, as each new religion gained domination, they would build their new temples on top of the places used by the old religions? That's because there are certain focal points of energy in the world, and those who are sensitive can sense them. New Orleans in general, and the French Quarter specifically, is one of those kind of places. It practically vibrates with energy, and different people react to it differently. That's why it's always been a gathering point for creative people who express themselves with art or music . . . or theater. It's also why we have so many people who are strongly religious or spiritual . . . or both."

"Is that why everything down here is divided into parishes instead of districts?" Valerie said. "I wondered about that."

"That's part of it," Jerome said, "but that's only been because Christianity or Catholicism has been the dominant religion here for a long time. Another thing you can look at is Mardi Gras. Around the country, people think of Mardi Gras as the world's biggest open party that runs for weeks with everyone getting drunk and flashing for beads. They miss completely that it's a carnival and celebration for the start of Lent. I will guarantee you that on Ash Wednesday, most of the locals you've seen partying and working triples manning the bars and restaurants will be crowded into that cathedral right there and several dozen other churches around town for Mass."

Griffen shook his head again.

"I don't know, Jerome," he said. "Like I said, we've never really talked about any of this before. You've given me a lot to think about. I always figured that if I ignored religion, it would ignore me. Isn't there something in voodoo that says if you don't believe in it, it can't affect you?"

Jerome laughed.

"Actually, what they say is that if you don't believe in it, you can't summon the powers even with rituals or charms. Then again there are others who will tell you that just because you don't believe in the gods doesn't mean the gods don't believe in you. I told you this is a focal point. Well, things that can't be explained by science have a way of reaching out and tapping you on the shoulder down here. Wait until the first time you run into a ghost."

Griffen and Valerie looked at each other, then looked at Jerome.

"Com'on, Jerome," Griffen said. "Ghosts? Like white sheets and chains?"

"More like disembodied spirits," Jerome said. "We've got a lot of them down here. Especially in the Quarter. Haven't you seen those Haunted History Tours that are out on the street every night?"

"Of course," Griffen said. "They're hard to miss. But I always thought it was pure tourist hokum. Do you really believe in ghosts?"

"Look at it this way, Grifter," Jerome said. "Every religion throughout time in all parts of the world have different burial customs. One thing they all have in common, though, is the basic purpose of the ritual. That is to lay the spirit to rest. As in if you *don't* lay the spirit to rest, it will potentially hang around and cause you grief. That's a lot of people believing essentially the same thing that can't be explained by science. To me, that goes way beyond superstition. Think about it."

Griffen did. For a long time after the evening was over.

Twenty-five

Griffen spotted Jerome's Jeep Cherokee parked on the street as he walked down Rampart. Without breaking stride, he strode up to the vehicle as his friend rolled the window down.

"Is he still in there?"

"Still there," Jerome said. "Sitting at the back table. Tall, skinny dude with a fedora on."

Griffen glanced at the two silent men in the backseat. They gazed back at him without expression.

"What's with the extra talent?" he said. "I thought we agreed I would handle this personal and quiet."

"Never said I agreed," Jerome said. "For the record, I still think this is a bad idea. I brought along a little backup in case you're wrong. The man usually carries, and he's probably got some friends in there."

"Suit yourself." Griffen shrugged. "Just let me try it my way first."

He turned and stared at the bar and grill. Anywhere else,

it would be described as seedy and run-down. Here at the edge of the Quarter, it was about average. Taking a deep breath and blowing it out, he headed for the door.

The brightness of the afternoon sun outside barely penetrated the dimly lit interior. There were about a half dozen people, all men, scattered around the room and sitting at the bar. A small television set high on the wall behind the bar was tuned to ESPN, but no one seemed to be paying it any attention.

While nobody stopped talking or looked around, Griffen was sure that everyone in the bar was aware of his entrance. If nothing else, he was the only white person in the place.

The man he was looking for was easy to spot. Sitting alone at a back table reading a newspaper. As Jerome had said, he was a good six and a half feet tall, skeletally thin, and sported a black fedora. There was a squat butt of a cigar smoldering in an ashtray on the table, along with a half-empty cup of coffee.

The man looked up dead-eyed as Griffen approached.

"Little Joe?" Griffen said, coming to a stop, carefully keeping his hands in view.

The man took a big drag on his cigar before answering.

"I know yah, white boy?"

"My name is Griffen McCandles," Griffen said. "I run a couple card games around town. Something has come to my attention, and I thought it would be a good idea if we talked about it. May I sit down?"

Little Joe shrugged and gestured to the chair across from him. Griffen took the indicated seat, painfully aware that it put his back to the door and the rest of the room. Keeping his concerns from his face, he took a deep breath and began.

"About a week ago, your little brother, Willie, sat in on

one of my games. He had a bad night, and dropped about four hundred dollars."

"I heard 'bout that." Little Joe nodded.

"It happens," Griffen said. "Some nights a man wins, some nights he loses. The problem is, I've been told that you've been talking around, telling people that Willie got taken in a crooked game. I thought I'd take the time to meet you face-to-face and ask if it's true?"

Little Joe took another drag on the cigar.

"Which? If I been talkin 'round, or if the game was crooked?"

"I guess if you've been talking around," Griffen said. "I already know the game wasn't crooked. More important, if it's true, I'd like to know what makes you think the game was crooked. As far as I can tell, you've never sat in on one of my games."

"All I knows is what Willie told me," Little Joe said.

"Uh-huh." Griffen grimaced. "Tell me, Little Joe, I've heard you're a pretty sharp card player yourself. Have you ever noticed that if someone wins, they're a great card player. But if they lose, then the game's crooked or someone was cheating."

Little Joe flashed a quick grin.

"Yeah, you right. Had to fight my way out of the room a couple times when the losers thought my luck was a lil' too solid."

"Well, the fact of the matter," Griffen said, "is that Willie isn't that good a card player. He had no business being in that game . . . way out of league, betting wild against a table of better players. I'm pretty sure you already knew that. You're a better card player than Willie is."

"And how do you know that?"

"I try to keep track of who the better players in town

are," Griffen said. "Besides, it's obvious just from sitting and talking with you. You give away less in normal conversation than Willie does when he's playing cards."

"So why'd you let him play?" Little Joe said.

"I suspected he was a weak player, but I wasn't sure until I actually saw him play," Griffen said. "One of our regulars brought him in and vouched for him, so there wasn't much I could do."

"So where does that leave us?" Little Joe said.

"It leaves us with a problem," Griffen said. "I'd like to convince you that it was an honest game so you'll quit saying that I run a crooked operation. Right now, though, it's just my word against your brother's."

Little Joe took another drag on his cigar and leaned back.

"I've heard about you, Griffen," he said. "Lots of folks say that you're not someone to get on the wrong side of. That you've got some serious muscle covering you, and that you handle yourself pretty good all by your lonesome. What surprises me, and I been listenin' real close, is that it don't sound like you're telling me to shut my mouth or it'll get shut for me."

"As I said, I'd like to convince you," Griffen said with a smile. "Threatening you would only make it look like I was trying to pull a cover-up."

"So, what do you have in mind?" Little Joe said, genuinely curious. "Somehow, I don't think your plan is to just give Willie his money back."

"As a matter of fact, for a while I considered doing exactly that," Griffen said. "Four hundred just isn't that much money, and if it could kill a bad rumor, it could be worth it."

"But yah changed your mind?" Little Joe smirked.

"Correct." Griffen smiled. "Giving the money back would be as much as admitting that we cheated him out of it. I'd be out the money and still have it being talked around that I run a crooked operation. There's a different solution I've come up with."

He patted the side of his jacket.

"I've got Willie's four hundred right here," he said. "What I propose is that you and I play for it. We both know you're a better card player than Willie. I figure if I can prove to you that I'm a better card player than you are, it will convince you that Willie lost the money honestly."

Little Joe eyed him narrowly.

"You're carrying four hundred dollars in cash? Alone? In a place like this? What makes you think I won't just take it away from you without bothering to play for it?"

"That wouldn't prove much of anything, would it?" Griffen said. "Except maybe that you're tougher than I am. If I read you right, you'd rather take it away from me with cards. Besides, I never said I was alone."

Little Joe's eyes darted around the room, then he raised an eyebrow.

"Waiting outside," Griffen said. "Just in case I read you wrong."

Little Joe nodded slowly.

"I don't have no four hundred dollars on me," he said. "If I did, I wouldn't risk it all in a game against a player I don't know."

"How much do you have?"

"Lil' over a hundred."

"Fine." Griffen nodded. "You put up a hundred and I'll do the same. If you can take my hundred before I take your hundred, I'll pass you the other three hundred as a bonus."

Moving slowly, he pulled a new deck of cards out of his pocket and tossed it on the table.

"You seem real confident 'bout this," Little Joe said, not reaching for the cards. "It occurs to me you're asking me to risk a hundred of my own dollars using your deck."

"I don't think there's enough light in here to see the marking if it was a rigged deck," Griffen said drily. "If it will make you feel better, though, we can see if the bartender has a deck, or we can wait while you send someone out to buy a new deck from a place of your choice. It shouldn't make that much difference, though. I'm going to insist that you do all the dealing. We'll just take turns calling what the game is."

Little Joe frowned.

"You still seem awfully sure."

"I think I'm a better card player than you," Griffen said with a shrug. "You don't give away much, but it's enough for me to beat you."

"Then you probably know I'm still thinking it might be a better move for me to just take the money." Little Joe smiled.

Several of the others around the bar turned around meaningfully. Though no one actually reached for anything, Griffen could clearly see bulges under coats and shirts. A trained gambler, he knew not to bet that the bulges were cell phones, not guns. Of course, there was what Little Joe had said about his reputation to handle himself.

Griffen sighed, then reached over and took Little Joe's cigar from the ashtray. He blew on the glowing end until it was red hot, not flame, just stoking the embers. Then keeping eye contact with his opponent, he slowly ground it out in his own palm.

"I think you'd be wiser to play cards," he said.

It took Griffen less than an hour to win Little Joe's hundred.

The two men shook hands when they parted company.

Twenty-six

It is surprising, for an area that comes close to worshipping food, just how understocked its average grocery is. True, the physical confines of the Quarter were prohibitive. A massive chain supermarket simply would not fit in one of the refurbished old buildings that were the norm. So small groceries and delis stocked the basics, as well as an erratic supply of specialty goods and ingredients. And, like so many other Quarter businesses, many were open 24/7.

Valerie had finished her morning jog earlier than usual, and found herself more in the mood to cook up something than stop into one of the early morning restaurants. No, she realized, it was more than that.

The run had done very little to relieve her frustrations. She was worried about Griffen, and what had him distracted that he obviously wasn't up to telling her. Sitting in a restaurant when she was still restless would be torture. But beating a few eggs into submission? Yeah, that could work.

Unfortunately, that meant she needed to get some eggs.

Like so many people visiting and living in the area, her fridge held very little in the way of supplies. A few leftovers, some soda and favorite snacks, and a bottle of good wine, because one never knows when it could come in handy.

So, she stopped at the local A&P, the closest thing to a proper grocery, just a few doors down from Yo Mama's. As she approached, she saw some of the average early morning crowd on the street. A drunk passed out in a doorway, a few musicians and street performers resting against a building and sharing a cigarette, and a few shopkeepers in the process of hosing down the sidewalk and opening up their fronts. There always seemed to be more people who hadn't gone to bed yet than there were early risers.

She was just about to enter the store when she caught the rank smell of too many cocktails and not enough bathing. She started to turn abruptly, but before she could finish found a hand palming her rump. Valerie stiffened, letting out a hiss that was as much rage as shock, and finished her turn.

"Hey, baaaaby."

The man before her was dressed in filthy jeans and a shirt that seemed more a collection of stains than actual cloth. His matted hair and almost black fingernails would have suggested he was homeless, but his shoes and watch were both high quality. All this was a secondary observation to Valerie. First was the fact that even facing him he was trying to maintain his balance and his grip on her behind.

Valerie grabbed the man's wrist and jerked hard enough to fling him into the wall. He stumbled and cracked his face against the brick, long scratches embedding in his cheek. Whirling, back to the wall and braced, he jerked out a knife that even Valerie knew was substandard. A little pocket knife that probably couldn't open an envelope.

"I am not your baby," she said.

"Bitch, I kill you for that!"

"Baby, no. Bitch. I can do that."

She reached out as if to grab the knife, and he slashed at her hand. While he was focused solely on the weapon, she took a half step forward, and slammed her other foot into his crotch. He sank to the ground, eyes shut and groaning. She ripped the knife out of his hand blade first, reversed it, and pressed it under his nose. His eyes popped wide again.

Which was, of course, when two police officers stepped out of the A&P with a bag of groceries.

"Now, there's something you don't see every day," one said, looking at the man on the ground with Valerie standing over him with a knife.

"Miss, could you drop the blade! Now!" said the other, one hand resting on the butt of his gun.

Valerie did as she was told, and stepped away from him. The man gratefully shut his eyes again and rolled into a ball. The police stepped forward, guns still in holsters but clearly ready to clear the leather.

"Whoa, whoa. You best be holdin' it."

The officers and Valerie glanced to the side, and one of the street performers had stood up and was striding across the street to join them. He was a tall, thin man with very dark skin and very white clothes. Bleached so well they practically shone. The police saw his approach, and actually relaxed marginally. One nodded his way.

"Slim, you see what happened?" the officer said.

"Sure did. Dude saw Ms. Valerie here looking all fine in her workout clothes and then forgot everything he ever did know about manners. When she reminded him, he thought he would cut her for the trouble."

The two officers looked from Slim to the man and woman. Valerie, tall, attractive, and in sweat-stained but otherwise clean apparel. The other, filthy, dirty, and obviously still drunk. They nodded to each other and relaxed more fully.

"Ma'am, do you want us to run him in? The little weasel might try to push for assault, but I doubt it."

Valerie caught Slim's shake of a head out of the corner of her eye.

"No, that's all right. I got mine in," she said.

"That you surely did."

The officers shared a grin, and picked up their forgotten groceries. Valerie and Slim watched them head around the corner and out of sight.

"Thanks, Ms. Valerie. I knows this idiot, and the last thing he needs is more trouble with the po-leece. We both owe you," Slim said.

"You're welcome, but how come you seem to know me so well?"

"Ah, well, to answer that . . ."

Slim bent down and picked up the knife, looking over it with an expression of disgust. He shrugged, and pressed it against the downed man's belly. The drunk gave a pathetic squeak, and tried to curl tighter into himself.

"You open your eyes right now!" Slim said. "Right now, I say. Good. You think you seen some tourist babe fresh from the hotel and you'd have some fun. Right? Well, I gots news for you, son. This here is Griffen McCandles's sister you tried pawing."

The man's eyes shot wider still as he looked from Slim to Valerie. He tried to blubber an apology, but his words still would not come. Slim nodded and straightened up, and without looking chucked the knife squarely into the nearest trash can.

"That should take care of things. Good morning to you, Ms. Valerie." Slim nodded and sauntered away, and Valerie stood watching him go. A mixture of emotions warred through her, holding her in her spot. By the time he was gone, her eyes had narrowed dangerously. She started to leave, turned back, and kicked the man once more in the stomach, then stomped off.

The other performers cheered from their perch across the street.

Twenty-seven

Once in a while, everyone needs advice.

Valerie found herself pacing back and forth in Mose's living room, which wasn't really large enough for her stride. After about four steps, she had to turn and start back the other way. Mose watched her progress and leaned back in his chair, seemingly completely relaxed. It was a good act, considering her nervous energy had him practically twitching. Being in tight quarters with an agitated female dragon was something he had learned from long experience to avoid. He was thinking that he either needed to calm her down or jump out the window and seek cover.

"What am I doing here?" Valerie said.

"Well, not to put too fine a point on it, but I was about to ask the same thing," Mose said.

She waved off his comment with an impatient gesture.

"Oh, I didn't mean here, Mose. I meant here!"

"Thank you for clearing that up."

Valerie drew her self up sharply, but saw his twinkling

eyes and the laughter lines on his face start to deepen. With
an exasperated sigh she folded herself into a chair. Sitting
stiff backed and wire tight, she seemed to tower over Mose's
relaxed form. Her expression, however, had relaxed marginally, and she clasped her hands in her lap to keep them from
fidgeting.

"I'm not making much sense am I?"

"Well now, I wouldn't go that far. Let me take a guess."

Mose steepled his fingers and looked over Valerie closely.
She didn't realize some of the changes that showed in her.
Her strength and natural confidence had grown, as had her
pride. Though she hadn't changed dress habits as drastically
as her brother, what she wore began to cling to her differently as she began to hold herself differently. More noticeably, though, she had a new light burning in her eye, that
even with Mose's long experience he couldn't quite place.

He looked over her long enough, that she felt like getting up and pacing again. Finally he opened his hands wide
and spoke.

"You meant here as in New Orleans. Big Brother Dragon
has been changing and growing and coming into his own,
and you're wondering where yours is. Feeling restless."

"More like useless. I came down here to protect Grifter,
even if he thinks it was his idea to protect me."

"And you've been doing a fine job at it by my reckoning."

In a flash she was up on her feet again and Mose fought a
reaction to wince. She tried to pace, gave up on it, and con-
tented herself to lean against the back of the chair. Her
hands gripped it so hard it creaked, but she didn't seem to
notice.

"Fine! How do you figure fine! I haven't done a single
thing, and he's got his other protectors now."

"Jealous?"

Mose braced himself, but it was a necessary risk. Instead of another outburst, Valerie looked shocked, and with the shock came serious consideration. She sighed and leaned more against the chair, folding her elbows under her to brace herself.

"Oh, hell, I can't be. It's good that he's got things working so well. It's only; I don't seem to have a place in it right now. Grifter doesn't even realize that we are seeing each other less and less each week, and he doesn't even think to ask what I've been up to in between."

"Which brings up a damn fine question. What have you been up to? More to the point, what got you so agitated that you found yourself at my door?"

"Er . . ."

"Are you blushing?"

"No! Of course not."

She turned away from him, and as a gentleman, Mose discreetly looked out the window. After several moments passed, she spoke again. This time her voice was softer than he had ever heard from her, and more than a little lost.

"Let's just say I'm not used to being saved in my brother's name. It should be the other way around."

"Ah. Now you are being a silly little girl."

"WHAT!?"

Now she really did tower over Mose, seeming to have swelled several inches. Her already well-defined muscles strained in tension, and Mose had to quell his imagination. For just an instant, it had felt much warmer in the room. As if a blast of heat had come out of her mouth with the exclamation.

"I'm sorry, did I say 'little girl'? That was wrong of me."

Mose watched carefully as she seemed to deflate, and carefully kept his tone mild and bland.

"No, it's usually the boys that have such easily bruised egos. The insecure, overly macho ones at that. Surely you don't have anything in common with that sort; do you, dear?"

"Okay, no need to rub it in. Make your point."

"First, sit down. And try to relax a bit. You're impressive enough without having to try and intimidate an old man."

"I wasn't trying—"

"Sit!"

Valerie found herself sitting without realizing it, and looking deep into Mose's eyes. They flashed in a manner she hadn't seen before, and his relaxed pose was gone. Now he was straight and tall, and seemed filled with strength that normally lay quiet and dormant in him. He made sure he had her attention, then leaned back again, not quite going as relaxed as before.

"Now it's my turn to talk and yours to listen. Okay?"

He waited for her to nod and gave one in return. As he spoke, he ticked points off on his fingers.

"First of all, you don't know what a mark you have made here. And not just because you are Griffen's sister. I bet there isn't a doorman, shill, or bartender who doesn't nod to you when you walk by. And considering from what I've heard you haven't been spending most of your time in their establishments. But you are known just the same."

"What do you mean you've heard?"

"And that's the second thing. If you haven't figured out by now that everyone talks about everybody in this town, you aren't as smart as I know you are. Big Brother doesn't ask after you? That's because if anything goes wrong, you can bet he would hear about it in twenty minutes flat. Good news takes longer, and gets a bit more respect privacy wise, but that filters in, too."

Mose held up a finger as she began to interrupt again. She shut her mouth sharply.

"Third, none of that matters. If you think you aren't keeping Griffen safe, you're underrating yourself. And I don't just mean like with Gris-gris."

He sighed and shook his head, then stood and walked over to a small bureau. After a few clinking sounds, he walked back over to Valerie and handed her a glass filled with rich brandy. He sat again, cradling his own glass and took a long sip.

"In some ways, you've got it a lot harder than he does, Valerie. You've got a tighter line to walk. You wonder what you are doing in New Orleans, and how that helps your brother. Well, I'll tell you, you are keeping him safe, by being safe yourself. Wouldn't be the first damn time a dragon went through family to manipulate or hurt another one. Not to mention in some circles you would be considered a prize and target on your own merits. Here, he knows you're safe, and you know you're keeping him likewise."

He took another sip and this time she joined him, rolling the amber fluid around in her mouth thoughtfully.

"See, the thing is, the more active you are in his operations, the more danger you put yourself in. I know that isn't easy to accept, but you really have to balance out how much you are helping him in the long run, by sticking your neck out in the short. And if you went anywhere else, he'd have his attention divided, and as good as he seems to be adapting that would be downright deadly."

Silently, Mose pondered that those were exactly the reasons he was glad Griffen hadn't told her about the most di-

rect threat to him. What help she could offer would be out-
weighed by his own worry.

"I think I understand," she said, and leaned back in her
chair, thinking over and over his words.

"If you don't, you will. I want you to think hard about it,
and we'll talk again. The best thing you can do is live your
life, well and happy. 'Cause you are the boy's joy and hope,
and if something happened to you, everything we've been
working to build would crumble to the winds."

Valerie rose wordlessly and set her empty glass on the
table. She looked over Mose thoughtfully, and leaned down
and kissed his cheek. As she turned and walked out he
watched her very carefully, and at least part of his attention
was on just how nice a sight he was watching. He chuckled
to himself as the door closed and shook his head.

"Mose, you're getting too damn old for those kind of
thoughts," he said to himself, and rose to pour another
drink.

He was doubly glad now that he had advised Griffen to
keep his sister in the dark about the George.

Twenty-eight

As soon as Griffen rolled into Yo Mama's, Padre caught his eye and jerked a head toward the back booths. Detective Harrison was already there, nursing a cup of coffee and studiously ignoring the other customers.

Griffen briefly considered reversing his course and easing back out, but it was too late. Harrison had already seen him and beckoned to him with a small motion of his hand.

Heaving a silent, inward sigh, Griffen complied. He really wasn't feeling up to dealing with the detective tonight, but it seemed he didn't have much choice.

"Okay, McCandles," Harrison said without preamble. "I think we've gotta plan here. I've been talking to a couple a boys down at the precinct, and they're willing to give a hand. Lucky for you they don't like the Feds any more than I do."

"Okay. Lieutenant." Griffen nodded. "You have my undivided attention."

The detective glanced around, then slid a slip of paper across the table.

"That's my own cell phone number," he explained. "When you spot one of these jokers following you, give me a call with the location and a description. I'll relay it on to whoever's closest, and we'll handle it from there."

"Wait a minute," Griffen said. "I have to call you? How am I supposed to spot these guys? They're professionals. I don't know anything about tailing people or how to spot someone following me."

"It's not all that hard." Harrison shrugged. "It's actually pretty hard to tail someone if they're watching for it. Ask your buddy Padre there for a few pointers. He used to be a private investigator. I'm more worried about what we're going to do with them once we catch them. I mean, we can always find some reason for bracing them, but unless they declare themselves to be federal agents, it might be tough to tell them from some of our homegrown muggers."

"I might be able to help you there." Griffen dug into his pocket and produced his own cell phone. "Remember I told you I talked with Stoner? Well, before he walked up on me, he called me on his cell phone. That means I've got his number."

"Okay. What does that get us?" the detective said.

"Well, I figure these people watching me have to report in somehow, and it's my guess they're using cell phones themselves. When you stop them, see if they have Stoner's number in their directory. Even if they don't, there should be one central number they all have to report to."

"That could work," Harrison said. "Not bad, McCandles. Well, let's see what we turn up in a week."

He rose to leave, then hesitated.

"I know I've asked this before, Grifter," he said, "but do you have any idea why this Stoner guy has it in for you? I mean, this whole terrorist thing stinks on ice. What's his real problem?"

"You wouldn't believe it if I told you," Griffen said with a smirk.

"Try me."

Griffen looked at him levelly for a moment, then shrugged.

"The way it was explained to me," he said carefully, "Stoner is a dragon. As such he collects power and has done a pretty good job so far. The problem is, he has it in his head that I'm a dragon, too, and am just coming of age. He's afraid that I may be more powerful than he is, so he's having me watched and tracked in case I become a threat. I try not to think about what he would or could do if he decided I was dangerous."

Harrison stared at him.

"This is a joke, right?"

Griffen leaned forward and blew gently on the detective's now cold cup of coffee. A small column of steam rose from the cup. He looked at it, then back at Harrison.

"I know," he said. "I have trouble taking it seriously myself."

"I didn't know you had been a private eye," Griffen said.

He was still finding that a little hard to believe. Even though he was getting used to the idea that almost everyone he met in the Quarter had a story behind them, Padre just didn't seem the private-eye type. He was in his mid to late forties with longish hair pulled back in a ponytail. It had some streaks of gray, as did his mustache and goatee, and combined with his thin, wire-frame glasses, he looked more like a hippie than like anyone vaguely connected with the establishment.

"That was a while back, while I was in Texas," Padre said, wiping down the bar.

Griffen had gone cruising for a while and was now back when the place was nearly empty. Early evening, Yo Mama's was usually jammed with people ordering burgers, but if one came by late enough, after the grill was closed, say after three in the morning, the action had usually died down and conversation with Padre was easier.

"I don't know what you said to Harrison before you took off," Padre continued, "but it made an impression. He must have stood there looking at his coffee for five minutes before he finally left."

Griffen ignored the unasked question.

"So, can you give me any tips on how to spot someone who's tailing me?"

"It depends on who's doing the tailing," Padre said. "When I was a PI, it would pretty much be a one-man operation. Usually, they weren't expecting it, so the main trick would be to keep them from noticing you."

He paused to gather the dirty ashtrays along the bar.

"There are ways to make small changes in your appearance. You can wear a jacket you can take off, even better if it's reversible. Sunglasses are good, and so are hats. You can also switch sides of the street every so often, so if they glance back, they aren't always seeing someone behind them at the same distance."

He gave a quick bark of laughter.

"Of course, all that doesn't help much if something happens to bring you to the attention of the subject. I remember once I was tailing a guy through the downtown strip joints during his lunch hour, and a bunch of kids came up to me and asked if I was Weird Al Yankovic. Of course, I told them I wasn't, but they kept crowding around and asking for my autograph. In no time flat a crowd had formed . . . including the guy I was following who turned around and came back to see what the commotion was about. Talk about blowing your cover!"

Griffen laughed along with him, enjoying the joke.

"Okay. I can see that," he said finally. "But what if it's a larger organization following you. Say, the Feds, for example."

Padre shot him a narrow-eyed glance, then turned his attention again to washing the ashtrays.

"That's a rather interesting example," he said. "But . . . okay. Outfits like that have a lot of manpower. If you're playing in that league, they'd be expecting you to be on the lookout, so they'd probably assign a whole team to the job. They'd probably have radio or cell phone hookups and use rotating front and back tails."

"Whoa. Hold up for a minute," Griffen said, holding up a restraining hand. "Rotating whats?"

"Front and back tails," Padre said. "People following you from ahead of you as well as from behind you."

"How could they do that?" Griffen said. "I mean, how could the ones ahead of you know where you're going?"

"Easier than you think." Padre smiled. "Let's take an example. If they were on you tonight, they'd probably have teams spotted in bars or in one of the fast food places . . . except most of those are closed right now. Unless I miss my guess, they'd have window seats and be ordering their drinks in go-cups. As soon as you leave here, they all put it in motion, pausing in the door or on the sidewalk, say to light a cigarette. If you turn right toward Bourbon Street, they start moving in that direction and have you bracketed. The same thing if you turn left toward Royal."

"But how do they know which way I'll turn when I hit an intersection?"

"They guess, but it will be an educated guess. If they've been on you for a while, they already know your main stops and the routes you take to get to them. This time of night, they'll probably be expecting you to head to your apartment, which means you'll turn left and head toward Royal, then left again on Royal. Even if the front team guesses wrong and you keep going toward the river, there's no problem. Either the back team keeps in touch with them and they run parallel for a while, or the back team passes you and the old front team falls in behind as the new back team."

Griffen sighed and shook his head.

"The way you put it, they'd have me in a box," he said. "So what could I do to deal with it?"

"That depends on whether you want to shake the tail or spot who's following you," Padre said. "If you want to shake them, vary your routine. Go different places or hit the same places at different times of the day or in a different order. Go to a movie and leave partway through it by a side exit. Hop a trolley car and ride it up to the Canal Place shopping center, then ride the elevators and escalators at random."

"And if I'm trying to spot them?"

Padre favored him with a long look before answering.

"Some of the same things apply," he said. "Vary your routine, but lean toward more isolated places where they can't hide in a crowd. Take a stroll along the Moonwalk at night when there aren't many people around. Walk it partway to the aquarium, then turn around and reverse your course. Keep an eye out for people you've seen before, or people who suddenly stop when you come back at them. Sometimes grab a cab and go to a bar off your usual prowl pattern. Then grab a window seat and see who pops up that you've seen before . . . particularly if they're getting out of a car or cab. Oh, and do all those things a bit at a time, so it just looks like a blip in your routine. If you start doing a lot of evasion or backtracking all at once, they'll know you're on to them and bring on extra team members to make it harder for you."

Padre paused to pour Griffen a fresh drink, then leaned his elbows on the bar.

"Of course, there's another way they could be handling it," he said.

"What's that?"

"The easiest way to tail someone is from beside them," Padre explained. "You could pick up a new friend or two while you're hanging at the bars. Someone who laughs at your jokes and buys you drinks, then asks to tag along to your next stop. Someone, say, like a good-looking woman who finds you fascinating. Then they don't have to follow you at all. You'll be looking for them to hang around with and will probably tell them what your plans are for tomorrow . . . or the next week. That makes their job real easy and it's a lot harder to spot."

Griffen started to protest, but then he thought of Fox Lisa. What Padre was describing was exactly how Jerome had set him up with her originally. If Stoner was keeping an eye on his group, wasn't there a chance he already had it infiltrated? How many people was Fox Lisa doing favors for . . . maybe at the same time?

"One more example, Padre," he said. "What if, instead of a surveillance team, I had a hit man after me. What would be the story then?"

Padre stared at him hard before answering.

"You do come up with some unpleasant examples," he said slowly. "Could make a body nervous about hanging out with you. If a hit man was after you, he wouldn't have to track your every move. Instead, he'd try to identify your usual patterns . . . what bars you hang out at, where you live, what routes you walk between them. Then, all he has to do is sit and wait and pick his time."

Suddenly, Griffen's drink didn't taste as good as it had originally. He drank it anyway.

Twenty-nine

The next day, Griffen decided to try out some of the tactics Padre had coached him on. As far as routines went, Tuesdays were when he usually hit both Virgin and Tower to shop for new DVDs, so it would make a good test.

As he emerged from his apartment complex, he paused to look around with new, suspicious eyes.

There was a street entertainer sitting on the far side of the avenue playing a guitar. Griffen had seen him there often, but had usually ignored him as the man really wasn't that good a musician. This time, just to change his pattern, Griffen crossed the street to speak with him.

"Keep seeing you out here," he said, dropping a five into the open guitar case, "but never had the time to stop. You work hard for your money."

"Hey! Thanks, man. Really appreciate it." The guitarist smiled back.

The man had a cell phone in his guitar case, and his hair was noticeably shorter than the norm for the Quarter. Also, even though he was wearing denim pants and jacket, they seemed very stiff and new.

Griffen strolled toward the Square, but glanced back before he had gone half a block. The musician had stopped playing and was talking on his cell phone.

Uh-huh.

There was a moderate crowd of people on the street, a mixture of tourists seeing the sights along with a scattering of locals going about their daytime errands.

Griffen strolled along at a leisurely pace, pausing occasionally to look at the displays in the shop windows, then took advantage of the cover of a knot of tourists to duck into a used bookstore he had never been in before. With a quick glance around, he selected a place where the shelves hid him from the street, but he could see out. Then he selected a book at random, opened it, and waited.

In the next several minutes maybe two dozen people passed the store headed for Jackson Square. Again, they were mostly tourists, but a few stood out. A trio of gutter punks went by with a small puppy on a rope arguing about something with exaggerated gestures. One young woman, a tourist by the look of her, was pausing every four or five steps to snap a picture of something . . . anything apparently. Lampposts, Dumpsters, storefronts, anything. A delivery man from one of the delis or restaurants came by with a basket on the front of his bike. He was walking the bike instead of riding it, which was a little strange, but Griffen realized he recognized him and turned his attention elsewhere.

A Latino male caught his eye, walking by at a normal pace wearing the uniform black pants and tuxedo shirt of the service industry. A green jacket topped his ensemble. A waiter. From the Court of Two Sisters, by the jacket. What was unusual was that it was the wrong time of day for him to be going to work. Too late for the breakfast and lunch crowd, but too early for the dinner crowd. Still, maybe he had gotten a call to fill in for someone.

Finding nothing he could definitely label unusual, Griffen was about to give up and move along when he spotted the Latino again. The man was returning on the far side of the street, but moving slowly and looking through the windows of la Madeleine, a restaurant Griffen sometimes stopped at for a late lunch. He reached the end of the windows, then turned and stared back toward Jackson Square. Finally, he produced a cell phone, keyed a number, then spoke into it briefly.

Within minutes, another man appeared. This one was wearing a suit complete with a convention badge displayed prominently on the lapel. The only thing that made him vaguely distinguishable was that he wore a wide green tie and was carrying a bright orange shopping bag. Normally, Griffen wouldn't look at him twice on the street. The man went into a brief huddle with the Latino, then they both walked hurriedly toward the Square and the video stores, splitting so that they were moving some fifteen feet apart.

Bingo!

Griffen smiled and reached for his own cell phone.

By the time he reached Yo Mama's, Griffen was in a foul mood. After waiting on pins and needles for over six hours for some kind of word as to what, if anything, had happened, this summons to meet with Harrison seemed almost anticlimactic.

The detective was there ahead of him, holding down a booth, and waved him over as soon as he walked through the door. The fact he seemed to be in a good mood did nothing to ease Griffen's disposition.

"Sit down, Griffen," the detective said. "You got a steak dinner coming to you courtesy of the NOPD."

"I didn't know they served steaks here," Griffen said.

"They do," Harrison said. "They're just not as popular as their hamburgers. Mostly, the hoi polloi prefer to eat cheap."

"Actually, I've already eaten," Griffen said.

"Well, it's paid for in advance," the detective said. "Just tell Padre the next time you're in the mood for a steak."

"I'll remember that," Griffen said.

Harrison peered at him.

"Are you okay?" he said. "You sound kinda peeved. We don't buy steaks for people every day, you know. As a matter a fact, that steak dinner bonus was supposed to be for me. I decided to pass it along to you instead."

"It's been six hours," Griffen said. "You could have called."

The detective leaned back in his seat and scowled.

"Did I miss something here?" he said. "Am I reporting to you now on the chain of command? Jeez, you sound like my wife."

Even though he was young, Griffen knew enough to be aware that when someone compared you to his wife, it wasn't a compliment. He decided it was time to lighten up a little.

"I didn't know you were married," he said.

"I'm not. Not anymore." Harrison sighed. "I'd forget to call her, too. She didn't like it either."

All of a sudden, the detective seemed more like a man and less like a cop. It made Griffen uneasy. He preferred to think of Harrison as a cop.

"I'm sorry to hear that," he said. "So what happened after I called you?"

"Oh, it was beautiful!" Harrison said, regaining his good mood. "First of all, we managed to pick up all three of them . . . good descriptions, by the way. I was a little worried about the Latino . . . afraid we'd get tagged for profiling . . . but they were all carrying, which made it real easy. Seems that someone told them that this town of ours is dangerous."

"Slow down a little," Griffen said, holding up his hand. "Profiling?"

"Sorry," the detective said. "I keep forgetting you're not in the business. Profiling has been all the rage ever since 9/11. Homeland Security is real big on it. Basically, it means keeping a special eye on people who fit the profile of a terrorist or a career criminal. It's not a bad technique, and you can build up a nice case against a suspect using it, but the civil rights groups don't like it. All too often, the profile includes a reference to a racial or national group, so we get accused of treating anyone of that group as a criminal. Now, I'm sure not going to try to say that *all* blacks are criminals or that *all* Arabs are terrorists, but the records do show that a disproportionate percentage of criminals or terrorists do come from those groups. Trying to ignore that fact when you're looking for potential perps is just plain silly."

Griffen actually had a fair idea of this from reading the newspapers, but after having gotten off on the wrong foot with Harrison, he figured it wouldn't hurt things to give the detective a chance to show off a little. From the extent of the speech, the longest he had heard from the otherwise gruff cop, it worked.

"So the fact that one of them was a Latino was a problem?" he said.

"As I started to say, it never came up," the detective said. "All the boys did was stop them and ask for some identification. We had plausible stories for doing that if they had raised a hassle, but the fact that they were all carrying firearms moved everything past that point in a hurry. That meant they had to show not only identification, but their permits to be carrying, so it became readily apparent that they were federal men from the get go. Then the only question was what they were doing in New Orleans."

"What did they say?"

"One of them . . . the street entertainer . . . tried to bluff his way through, saying he was just here on vacation. Yeah, right. Like federal agents always spend their vacations standing on the street in the French Quarter playing guitar for loose change. The other two admitted they were on assignment, but wouldn't say what it was. That's when things really got fun."

"What did you do?"

"Took 'em down to the station on Royal and let them talk to the chief. He had them get this guy Stoner on the horn so he could confirm their story. Stoner admitted that he had an operation in place down here, but refused to tell the chief any more about it claiming it involved national security."

The detective broke off and laughed.

"I wish you could have seen it," he said with a grin. "If there's anything the chief hates more than Feds on his turf, it's being told that it's none of his business."

"He told Stoner in no uncertain terms to get his team the hell out of town, and that if he ever ran an operation down here again without going through proper channels, the chief would personally see to it that any agents he caught would do time as well as getting their pictures plastered all over the *Times-Picayune*."

"What did Stoner say?"

"He didn't like it, no. Not one bit, but there was nothing he could do but agree. With the chief in the mood he was, if Stoner had tried to bluster his way out of it, the chief would follow through, startin' with the three already in custody. Of course, he had to get in one good lick before he hung up."

"What was that?"

"He said something to the effect that the chief had better hope that Homeland Security never got the chance to return the courtesy that the NOPD had shown them."

Griffen scowled and shook his head.

"That doesn't sound good," he said.

"Just a little face-saving bluster," the detective said dismissively. "There isn't much he can do against the whole city . . . or the police force, for that matter. If he tries, he's in for a surprise. The chief had him on the speaker phone and taped the whole conversation."

Griffen sighed and shook his head again.

"What is it?" Harrison said.

"I don't know," Griffen said. "I mean, I've heard about how local cops don't like the Feds coming into their territory, but it all seems . . . I don't know, a little petty is all."

"You've never had to deal with them like we have," the detective said with a snort. "Come in throwing their weight around and treating us like dirt. They act like the whole force is incompetent, on the take, or both."

It occurred to Griffen that he had met Harrison when the detective was growling at him about having to put up with protected gambling operations, but it didn't seem like a good time to point that out.

"Well, enjoy your steak," Harrison said, sliding out of the booth. "I've got to run. The boys are getting together for a little celebration, and I told them I'd stop by. We owe you one or two for this one, McCandles."

Griffen sat staring for a long time after the detective had left. He was still staring when Padre came up to the booth.

"So, do you want that steak now?" the bartender said.

"I'll take a rain check on that," Griffen said. "Sit down for a second, Padre. What all did Harrison tell you?"

"Enough that I could tell they caught the ones shadowing you and that they were Feds," Padre said. "He seemed really happy about it."

"Yeah," Griffen said, making a face. "Tell me, is it just me or does all this seem a little too easy to be true?"

"It's not just you," the bartender said. "Remember what I said about the possibility of an infiltrator? It could be that whoever's running this show is pulling a little misdirection. Let you catch the obvious tails so you relax and don't look around internally."

"I remember, and I'm keeping an eye out," Griffen said. "Of course, it doesn't really matter."

"It doesn't?" Padre said.

"No, it doesn't," Griffen said. "We really aren't doing anything that merits federal attention. The only reason I said anything to Harrison was to switch his focus from our operation to the Feds, and that seems to have worked out just fine."

Thirty

Nighttime Bourbon Street was the usual kaleidoscope of color and sound. Even on a slow weekday night it swirled with energy unmatched by the "hot spots" in most cities even at their most celebrative. Some of it was because there was so much packed into a small area. A lot of it was both due to the no traffic, pedestrian nature of the street after seven o'clock, and the go-cup ordinances that allowed the revelers to wander from club to club with their drinks in hand. Most of it, however, was because of the mood. People came to Bourbon Street to have fun. To see and be seen and party like there was no tomorrow. If, at times, the gaiety was a little forced or strained, well, they were there to enjoy themselves and were bound and determined to do just that.

Tonight, Valerie was on a mission, and had convinced Griffen to escort her as "a change of pace from the rut he was getting into." He had gone along with it partly because he agreed that he needed to do something different, and partly because he enjoyed the music clubs.

That was Valerie's mission. She had met a musician, sort of helped him haul stuff into his new apartment, and he had invited her to come hear his band play. The trouble was, she couldn't remember which club he was playing in, the name of the band, or even his name for that matter. Then, too, there was the minor detail that there were two to three dozen clubs along an eight-block stretch of Bourbon Street that had live music.

By Griffen's calculations, there was no way they could stop and have one drink at every club without running out of energy, money, or both. Not drinking really wasn't an option. With the overhead, mostly rent, the Bourbon clubs paid out every month, they couldn't afford to have people taking up the limited seating and floor space without their contributing to the coffers. There was a one-drink minimum at most places, and even a Coke would cost you six dollars.

He pointed this out to Valerie, but she waved him off. To start with, what she did remember was that the musician in question played with a "cover band." That is, a band that mostly played popular rock and rhythm and blues music made popular by name bands. That meant they could bypass the clubs that played Dixieland, Chicago blues, Cajun, or folk music. That substantially reduced the number of clubs, but it still left a lot. Griffen, however, had long since learned to recognize when his sister was set on an idea and didn't bother trying to argue. Instead, he just drifted along with her, enjoying the night and the company.

"I still can't believe we're doing this when you can't even remember the guy's name," he said as they paused at a cross street that let the cabs cross Bourbon.

"You know how it is, Big Brother," Valerie said with a shrug. "He mentioned his name when we first met, but I didn't really make a mental note of it. After we spent some time together, I was embarrassed to ask him to repeat it. That's kind of why I'm trying to find him again. I want to see if the first impression holds up. If it does, I can catch his name when you introduce yourself."

"Is that why you wanted me to come along?" Griffen laughed. "Not that I mind, but . . ."

A soft shove in his back sent him staggering forward a step. Catching his balance, he turned quickly, expecting to find a clumsy drunk or a bad pickpocket.

Instead, he found himself looking at the horse of a mounted policeman, which was looking back at him with soft brown eyes.

Startled, Griffen took another step backward.

The horse followed, ignoring its rider's attempts to rein it in.

Valerie, of course, was laughing hysterically.

Griffen looked sternly at the horse.

"No!" he said firmly. "I can't even have a cat at my apartment. There's no way they'd let me keep a horse."

The horse looked hurt and shook its head.

"I think you broke its heart, man."

Griffen looked around.

Standing a few feet away was a street entertainer, a mime by the look of him. He was tall and skeletally thin, wearing an all-white outfit crowned by a top hat decorated with red, white, and blue stripes.

"Hey, Slim," Valerie said, stepping forward. "How's the crowd tonight?"

"So-so, Ms. Valerie," Slim said. "There are a lot of 'em, but they ain't parting with their money. Guess they think 'tipping' is a city in China."

"You two know each other?" Griffen said, still tracking the horse, which was now being turned away by the officer on its back.

"We've met," Valerie said with a smile.

Griffen wondered about that smile but decided not to ask.

"You must be Griffen McCandles," Slim said, holding out his hand. "I've been hearing things about you."

Griffen shook the offered hand.

"I hope that none of it is that I'm a horse thief," he said.

"Oh, the beast just took a shine to you, is all." Slim laughed. "It happens sometimes."

"We're out to do a little club crawling, Slim," Valerie said. "Want to tag along?"

"It's tempting," Slim said. "But I got rent due soon. I'd better keep working the crowd."

With that he waved and wandered off down the street.

Griffen didn't take too much note of his passing. Instead, he was thinking about the horse.

Something hit him a sharp blow high on his back, staggering him a few steps. Catching his balance, he turned quickly, but there was no one behind him close enough to have hit him. Scanning the crowd, he realized his back was wet.

"Here it is, Big Brother," Valerie said holding up a large plastic go-cup. "I think someone threw it at you from one of the balconies."

Griffen shifted his gaze and studied the crowds on the balconies that bracketed the street. They seemed to all be tourists, with no familiar faces visible.

He realized he smelled of beer. He also considered how it might have been if the go-cup held something other than beer.

"Ya gotta love this town, even if it does get a bit crazy from time to time," Valerie said, waving at the crowds.

Griffen found himself wondering if it had been the George counting coup on him, or if it had really just been a drunken tourist blowing off steam.

He was starting to see what Mose meant when he said the George's stylish approach could make his victim jittery, jumping at shadows.

They never did find Valerie's musician.

Thirty-one

Griffen was sitting on the Moonwalk, the half-mile-long pedestrian walkway that wound along the Mississippi River from the cathedral to the Aquarium of the Americas, watching the sun rise over the Mississippi. Because of the bend in the river that gives the crescent city its name, in the Quarter, one could experience the unusual phenomena of watching the sun rise over the "West Bank." Though the locals had long since taken it for granted, Griffen was still new enough to the area to find the paradox amusing and often prolonged his night an extra hour or two just to witness it.

Also, he was idly watching the activity of the wharf rats along the edge of the pier. Maybe he was just starting to notice things more, but he didn't recall them being this active when the sun was up.

"Seems like every time I see you, you be stirrin' up the wildlife."

Griffen looked around and found the lanky black street entertainer standing behind him in full costume.

"Hey, Slim," he said. "Are you up early or late?"

"Early," the man said. "Competition's getting pretty heavy for street space since they started regulatin' where we can entertain."

There was an ongoing fight in the Quarter between the street entertainers, particularly the tarot readers, and the painters, as to who did and didn't have the right to set up shop on Jackson Square.

"Is it just me," Griffen said, "or are the rats along the wharf more active than normal?"

Slim peered dramatically at the foraging rodents. "Naw." he said firmly. "They be just trying to grab some food before the heat of the day sets in. Don't take it personally. I was just pullin' your chain a little. Well, hang loose, Grifter. I gots to be gettin' to work."

"Watch yourself, Slim," Griffen said, waving good-bye.

Turning his attention to the rats again, Griffen found himself frowning. Until the street entertainer made his comment, it had never occurred to him that his presence might be affecting the local wildlife.

Staring hard at them, he tried to will them to go away. They steadfastly ignored him. Glancing around, he tried again.

His cell phone rang, starting him out of his exercise. Glanced at the caller ID, he flipped it open.

"Hey, Mose," he said. "What's up?"

"Didn't think you was going to be awake, Grifter," came the old man's voice. "I was going to leave a message on your voice mail, but this is even better. When y'all went shoppin' a while back, did you happen to pick up a suit?"

"No, we didn't. I've got my sports coat and slacks that I

used to use for interviews and theater dates, but never figured I'd need a full suit," Griffen said. "Why? What's up?"

"Well, try to pick one up today or tomorrow."

Griffen frowned slightly.

"Okay. Any particular reason?"

"We got us a funeral to attend," Mose said. "A suit isn't
really necessary, but it's a nice gesture."

"Whoa. Hold on a minute, Mose," Griffen said. "Sorry,
but I don't do funerals. Weddings either, for that matter."

There was a moment's pause before the answer came.

"I can understand that, Griffen. Nobody really likes to
go to funerals. Still, I think you should go to this one. It's
one of our people."

Griffen was now very attentive.

"Who? I mean, what happened?"

"Do you remember Reggie? Works as a spotter for us at
one of the hotels in the CBD?" Mose said.

"Older guy? White hair and mutton chops?" Griffen said.
"Yeah, I remember him. I didn't even know he was sick."

There was a short snort of a laugh at the other end.

"Not sick. Lead poisoning," Mose said.

"Excuse me?"

"New Orleans plague," Mose said. "Went and got himself shot last night."

Griffen was stunned. He looked out over the river again,
the scene now having taken on a slightly surreal aspect to it.
Then he remembered he was on the phone.

"Sorry, Mose," he said. "That freaked me out for a second.
Remember, I'm just a kid from the Midwest who's led a
sheltered life. This is the first time someone I've known has
been shot."

Griffen turned from the river and started to walk away, heading toward Café Du Monde and Jackson Square. He held the phone to his ear as Mose talked.

"I hate to say it, but start getting used to it," Mose said. "It's not all that uncommon in New Orleans these days. Just be thankful you live in the Quarter."

"What happened?"

"Jerome will fill you in on the details," Mose said. "Talk to him while you're picking out a suit. Like it or not, you should be at that funeral. He was one of ours, and folks will expect you to be there. It's one of the downsides of heading up a crew down here."

"Sure, I'll talk to Jerome, but can't you tell me a little mor—"

Griffen felt a featherlight tug at his pocket. Instinctively, his free hand went to his pocket and he twisted to look behind him. He hadn't had his pocket picked yet in his time in New Orleans, but his mind flashed the suspicion that he had just had that new experience.

If he hadn't been distracted by the phone, he would have been more aware of the stairs in front of him.

He never caught the barest glimpse of his assailant. Body twisted and off balance, a hard shove threw him forward. He barely registered that the shove had been two handed, one just above his hips, the other between his shoulder blades, guaranteeing he wouldn't recover. Then he was in the air.

The stairs leading from the Moonwalk down to Decatur Street are a flight of curved, amphitheater like steps. Made out of concrete.

His first impact was on his side, but the force of the hard steps into his ribs jerked his body, and his head hit a moment later. The cell phone dropped from a hand that shot out to try and stop his fall, but he was already rolling. Nails scraped on concrete, and felt as if they would tear. Three more steps went by, each a sharp pain as his body twisted.

Griffen lay stunned. Blood pounded in his ears. Dazed, his eyes caught upon his hand, gripping the step above him. His nails were long, almost claws, and had dug the smallest of grooves into the concrete. They slowly receded back to normal.

"Griffen! Griffen what's happening!?"

Mose's voice called from the fallen phone, snagging his attention and jerking him back into focus. He pulled himself up, intending to stand but groaning and sitting down as pain shot through his ribs and side. He scrabbled for the phone and put it to his ear.

"I'm here," Griffen said.

"God, lad, where'd you go?!"

A few people were rushing toward him, not many. More kept walking, not seeing him. Wouldn't be the first drunk to fall, even in daylight. He waved off those who approached.

"I fell, down the stairs."

"Griffen, the thickest skin in the world won't save you from a broken neck."

"Now he tells me. Mose, I was pushed."

"By who?"

"I don't . . . wait."

Griffen reached into the pocket. He realized, the tug he had felt had not been where he kept his wallet. Hand shaking slightly, he pulled out a long card that had been slipped in before his fall. The Knight of Swords.

"It seems," Griffen said, fear momentarily numbing his pain, "that the George has taken things up a notch."

Thirty-two

"I'm telling you, Jerome, I'm even less thrilled about going to a funeral now."

"Hey, at least it's not yours," Jerome said

"Yet," Griffen said, neither one of them had much humor in his voice.

They had gotten together as planned to pick out a suit for Griffen. A cheerless chore nowhere near as interesting as their last shopping excursion. His mind kept going back to the fall, and how easily it could have been much, much worse.

Of course, Griffen's mood wasn't improved by the ache in his ribs. Mose had checked him out, and declared nothing broken. They still protested every time he lifted his right arm too high. He winced as he tried on a somber jacket.

"Sure I can't help you with that?" Jerome said.

"Yes."

Griffen waved him off stubbornly and shrugged the jacket on. They were more or less alone, having told the

salesperson they didn't need assistance. Griffen wanted free-
dom to talk.

"You can help me understand about Reggie. How he
died and why you and Mose seem to be treating this as business as usual."

"Can't really treat it as anything else. It's the drug
gangs," Jerome said. "Most murders are within family or
friends when someone gets drunk or mad and goes for a gun
or a knife. The so-called 'killer' is usually still sitting there
when the cops come. It's the drug gangs that are pushing
the murder rate so high in this town."

"Wait a minute," Griffen said. "Are you saying that Reggie was part of a drug gang?"

"No. Nothing like that," Jerome said with a half laugh.
"He sold a little pot and coke on the side is all. Dude was
just stopping by his supplier to replenish his stock and got
caught in the cross fire is all."

"That's all?" Griffen said, a vague note of hysteria creeping into his voice. "You make it sound like it's an everyday
occurrence."

"It is." Jerome shrugged. "There are a couple areas of
town that are combat zones for all intents and purposes.
That's where most of the nondomestic killings happen. The
gangs have been fighting it out for who supplies what sec-
tions of town, and when the shooting starts, they don't care
much who's in the way."

"Why doesn't somebody do something about it?"

"Like what?" Jerome said. "As long as there are folks taking drugs for kicks or to try to make themselves feel better
about their lives, there are going to be people making
money off selling the shit to them. When there's a lot of
money involved, they're going to fight over who gets how

much. You kill off or lock up one bunch, and someone else will be there to step into the vacuum."

"It just doesn't seem right, is all," Griffen said, almost to himself.

"Right or not, that's the way things are," Jerome said firmly. "Welcome to the real world, Young Dragon. You can't save everyone, especially not from themselves. The most we can do is try to take care of our own . . . and in this case that means showing up at the funeral to pay our respects."

"Well, at least from what I hear your funerals down here are livelier than in other cities." Griffen sighed.

"Don't believe all the hype, Grifter," Jerome said. "Not all funerals down here are jazz funerals with second lines. Most of them are as sad and depressing as funerals anywhere."

The funeral had been as low-key and sad as Jerome had predicted. There were no colorful brass bands or people dancing with parasols and handkerchiefs on the way back from the cemetery. Just long-faced people who spoke in low tones and cried from time to time.

The crowd was mostly black, but there was a fair spattering of whites and Latinos in the gathering. Griffen supposed that they were people from the hotel where Reggie had worked, but never got a chance to converse with any of them to confirm or deny his assumption.

He had tried to hang back in the group, but Mose had taken him by the arm and brought him forward to meet Reggie's family. They all seemed to know who he was, and were genuinely pleased to meet him in person, effusive in their gratitude for his attendance.

Afterward, he and Jerome accompanied Mose back to the latter's residence for drinks and conversation.

"This may not be the right time to bring it up," Griffen said, contemplating his glass, "but there's something I want to discuss with both of you."

"And what would that be, Young Dragon?" Mose said, leaning back in his easy chair.

"I want to implement a new policy in our organization," Griffen said. "I want to set a rule that people can either work for us or deal dope, but not both."

Mose and Jerome exchanged glances.

"I don't know, Grifter," Jerome said carefully. "We don't pay our spotters enough for them to live on. I'm not sure it's fair to cut them off from a source of income."

"I don't care," Griffen said firmly. "They're already getting paid by the hotels and clubs they work for. If that's not enough combined with what we pay them, there are other ways of making money in this town without selling dope on the side."

"You've been down on dope ever since you got down here," Mose said. "There's no way you're going to get people to stop using it."

"I know that," Griffen said. "I'm not trying to reform the world or even the town."

He paused for a moment to gather his thoughts.

"I don't get the whole drug thing," he admitted. "I've never used them myself, and I don't understand what the attraction is that draws people to them. Fine. There are lots of things that people do that I don't understand or take part in. People are different, and differences make the world go 'round. But this drug thing . . ."

He hesitated again, then shook his head.

"Aside from the fact that drugs are illegal and dangerous, from what Jerome says there are people getting killed over them. I can't stop it, but I don't want to contribute to it either. Gambling I don't mind, but I don't want to be the head of a group of dope dealers, even if it's only a sideline. More specifically, I don't want to go to any more funerals for our people, meet their families and watch them cry, because they were dealing dope on the side. Maybe it's selfish of me, but that's the way I feel."

Jerome looked at Mose, who scratched his head, then ran his hand over his face.

"All right, Young Dragon," he said at last. "If you feel that strongly about it, we'll give it a try. We'll put the word out and give our people a week to make up their minds. One thing you should remember, though. After the fall the other day, it's definitely the George on your tail. Can't think of anyone else, including most other dragons, who could have done that to you without you even seeing their face. I'd think that was trouble enough without your looking for some more by stirring up the locals with a no-drug policy."

Thirty-three

Griffen couldn't sleep.

He'd tried calling it an early evening . . . well, early for him, anyway . . . and had called it a night around 2:30 a.m. He had even managed to go to sleep.

Now it was quarter to four in the morning and he was wide-awake. He didn't know what had awakened him. There was no apparent noise, either inside or outside his apartment, but he was awake and felt no inclination to go back to sleep.

He considered reading for a while, but realized that for some reason he was feeling restless. Yielding to an impulse, he pulled on his pants and pair of shoes and headed out again.

The courtyard of his complex was quiet. Valerie's apartment was dark. Either she had also crashed early, or she was still out.

Glancing idly around, he noticed the usual contingent of the complex's stray cats were also nowhere to be seen. Apparently it was an off night for everyone.

A scratchy rustling caught his attention. An oversized cockroach, nearly half the size of his fist, was crawling across the flagstones heading straight for him.

Grimacing slightly, Griffen decided to try his so-called animal-control powers one more time. Frowning, he focused his mind into sending the insect a message, specifically to go away.

The cockroach hesitated, then continued to approach.

So much for animal control. Turning his back on the beast, Griffen crossed the courtyard and let himself out of the gate onto the street.

Pausing for a moment, he considered his options. Harry's Corner was close and open twenty-four hours a day, but he didn't really feel like a drink just now. Instead, he decided to take a stroll along the Moonwalk. Sometimes walking along the river helped to clear his mind. Even if it didn't, perhaps the exercise would make him tired enough to sleep.

Turning south, he sauntered slowly along the street, enjoying the quiet of the early morning.

Jackson Square was deserted when he reached it. Even the late-working street entertainers had called it a night and packed it in, even though the floodlights in front of the cathedral lit the area to near-day brightness. Griffen didn't mind. Sometimes having the familiar streets to himself was a pleasant change.

"I believe we need to talk."

The words were soft spoken, but came to him quite clearly.

Looking around, Griffen saw a woman sitting on one of the benches that circled the Square. He hadn't noticed her before, but she was partially in shadow so that was understandable.

His first thought was that she was a panhandler, and that he was about to be approached with yet one more pitch to separate him from a few dollars. On second thought, however, he reconsidered. She didn't look like a panhandler. She was black, in her late twenties to early thirties, and dressed in a white cotton blouse with a light fabric, multicolored full skirt. There was a dark handkerchief wrapped around her head, but he could still see that her hair was long, halfway down her back.

"I'm sorry, do I know you?" Griffen said, stalling slightly for time.

"We have never met," the woman said, "but I have heard much about you, Griffen McCandles. There are those who are concerned about your presence in town and what it might mean to them. I felt it was time to meet you in person and to form my own opinion."

Despite his normal wariness, Griffen was intrigued. If this was a pitch for a handout, it was an approach he had never encountered before.

"You seem to have me at a disadvantage," he said, wandering closer. "You know my name, but I know nothing about you."

"My name is Rose," the woman said, gesturing for him to join her on the bench. "I am a practitioner of Santeria . . . what you would call a voodoo queen."

It occurred to Griffen that a month and a half ago, he would have found such a claim to be ludicrous. Now, he was merely curious, and a little cautious. This woman didn't look like a threat to him, but how could he be sure? It was amazing what even a short time of living in the Quarter could do for one's outlook on life.

"I don't understand," he said, taking the indicated seat.

"While I'm not a practitioner or a believer, I have some friends who are, and to the best of my knowledge I've never been opposed to or even disrespectful of your religion. Why should my presence be noticed, much less be of concern to anyone?"

"Because you are a power," Rose said. "A new power here in this area. We know of dragons, and have kept ourselves apart from their machinations. Word has been passed around, however, that it is your intent to exert your influence on all of us, to attempt to unite the various supernatural elements of this area under you control or command. You can see why this would cause some concern."

"But that's ridiculous," Griffen protested.

Griffen had to consciously keep his jaw from dropping. He was having a hard enough time coming to grips with all that was around him. The idea of trying to control anyone, much less people he's never met, had never occurred to him.

"All I'm doing is trying to learn about Mose's gambling operation. The main reason I came to town is to try to get away from dragons who either want to recruit me or kill me."

"I can see that, now that we've met," the woman said. "I look into your heart and I see no greed or even ambition there . . . at least not so far. I will attempt to reassure those who will listen, but you can understand why there are those who are afraid of . . . what is it?"

Griffen forced his attention back to the conversation.

"It's nothing," he said. "Please. Go on."

"No. Tell me," Rose pressed. "What is it that concerns you?"

"It's silly, but it's that cockroach," he said, pointing to an oversized insect determinedly making its way toward them. "I saw one just like it when I was leaving my complex and . . . I know it sounds crazy . . . but I'd swear it's the same one. I think it's following me."

"I see," Rose said, leaning forward to stare at the indicated insect. "Well, if you like, I can do something about that."

"Could you?" Griffen said. "I'd appreciate it."

He didn't really believe Rose could do anything, just as he didn't really believe the cockroach was following him. Still, he was curious to see what kind of hex or ritual the voodoo queen would come up with. He didn't have long to wait.

Rising from her seat, Rose poised for a moment, then took a long step and stomped hard on the insect with her foot.

"There," she said, resuming her seat. "That should take care of it. Someone will have a headache for sure."

"I'd say more than a headache," Griffen said, stifling a grin. "I doubt it has a mind left at all after that."

"Not the bug, Mr. Griffen," Rose said, shaking her head. "I'm talking about whoever was using their mind to control it."

"Control it," Griffen said, staring at the insect's remains.

"Remember I told you that some of the folks down here are afraid of you?" the woman said. "Well, there's one group that has a rapport with animals. Even more than the witches and their familiars. It would not be unlike them to use various animals to spy on you . . . or even to attack you if they were fearful enough."

"Well, you said that you would tell them that I'm harmless. Right?" Griffen said. "That should take care of everything."

"I said that I would try," the voodoo queen said. "Not everyone listens to Rose. I have something here that might help you with those that don't."

She dug into her handbag, and produced something that she handed to Griffen, who examined it. It was a double strand of small black and red beads.

"You put those on now, and wear them all the time," she said. "They will give you some protection, and mark you as a friend."

Griffen followed the instructions, then hesitated, suddenly awkward.

"Um, look," he said. "I don't want to be disrespectful or insulting, but may I make some sort of a contribution to your temple or whatever to show my thanks for your help and advice?"

"No need for that," Rose said with a laugh. "You just remember who your friends are while you're sorting things out. You may need some allies, and there are times we might need to call on you for assistance as well."

"I see. Sort of 'Someday I owe you a little favor.' Right?" Griffen said.

"Something like that. But without the hokey sound track." The woman smiled. "Now, you go along home. You won't have any trouble sleeping now that we've talked."

Griffen was leaving the Square before it occurred to him that he hadn't said anything to Rose about not being able to sleep. He turned and looked back, but couldn't see her anywhere.

"Hey, Grifter."

He spun around to find Jerome approaching.

"Jeez! You startled me, Jerome," he said. "Don't sneak up on me that way."

"Since when was walking down the street 'sneaking up on you'?" Jerome said. "I swung by your place to see if you were still up, but when you didn't answer I thought you were already asleep. I was just going to have one last one and call it a night."

"Sorry," Griffen said. "I guess I'm just a little jumpy. I was just talking with one of your voodoo people and I'll admit, it spooked me a bit."

"Really? Who was it?"

"She said she was a voodoo queen, name of Rose. She gave me these beads to . . . what is it?"

Jerome was staring at him.

"Excuse me. Did you say 'Rose'?" he said softly.

"That's how she introduced herself," Griffen said. "Why? Is she someone important?"

"Grifter," Jerome said carefully. "Rose has been dead over eight years now."

The beads suddenly felt very cold around Griffen's neck.

"I don't like that. No, suh. I don't like that one bit."

Mose was pacing back and forth in his living room as Griffen and Jerome watched. Griffen noticed that the more upset the old man got, the more he slipped into a black southern accent.

"I don't know," he said. "She seemed nice enough to me."

"I'm not talkin' 'bout Rose," Mose said sharply. "She was always a fine lady. I'm talkin' 'bout what she told you. 'Bout the animal folks gettin' stirred up against you."

Griffen frowned.

"But she also said that she was going to talk to them and try to calm them down. Won't that take care of it?"

"She said she'd *try* to calm them down," the old man said

pointedly. "That's not the same thing. What's more important is who stirred them up in the first place. That sounds
like dragon work to me."

"You think it's Stoner?" Jerome said from where he was
leaning against the wall.

Mose thought for a moment, then shook his head.

"Naw. It's not his style," he said. "Stoner is more one to
use his own people. He doesn't have the patience to work
with locals."

"Any ideas, then?" Jerome pressed.

"My first thought is that it might be Malinda," Mose
said. "But she normally sticks to the northeast."

"Who's Malinda?" Griffen said.

"Old-school dragon," Mose said. "She works with her
family. The dragon equivalent of Ma Barker. Greedy as hell.
Her main thing is building up wealth . . . and I don't mean
with investments. She gets her money the old-fashioned
way. She steals it."

"She's a thief?" Griffen said.

"More like a pirate," Jerome said. "She's a corporate
raider. Buys up weak companies, then breaks them up and
sells them piecemeal. It's the white-collar version of a stolen
car chop shop."

"The thing is, I don't see where she'd profit by going after Griffen," Mose said. "He's not a threat to her. And there's
not enough money in our operation to interest a high roller
like her."

"Don't forget she's got those kids," Jerome said. "She
may be looking for something for them to sharpen their
claws on. If she thinks our operation is weak and ripe for a
takeover, targeting Griffen as a backdoor in would be taking
care of two birds with one stone."

"Could be," Mose said slowly. "That kind of two-pronged attack, creating a diversion so you don't notice her marching up on you, would be just her style."

"So, what are we supposed to do in the meantime?" Griffen said.

"I'll put out a few quiet feelers in that direction and try to get a fix on what's going on," Mose said. "We don't want to put any moves on her until we're sure she's the one stalking you. If we're wrong, then she'll see it as an attack, and we'll have to deal with both her and whoever it really is coming at us."

"I guess I meant, what am I supposed to do?" Griffen said. "Do I just sit around and play decoy? Or should I be trying to talk to these animal people myself?"

"Leave that job to Rose," Mose said. "I think it's time to work on your animal control skills a bit. Just in case they won't listen to Rose."

"I don't know," Griffen said. "I mean, I'd love to get some training. But I've fooled around with the animal control thing a bit since I got down here, just for curiosity and because it sounded neat. Frankly, I haven't had much luck with it."

"It's like any other muscle or skill," Mose said. "You've got to work with it, practice it, and develop it before you can rely on it. Besides, you might have been playing into a stacked deck. If you've been trying to control the animals that you see hanging around you, they could be the very ones that are already under someone else's control, watching you."

"Just what animals have you been trying to control, Grifter?" Jerome said.

"Oh, there's a bunch of feral cats living in our courtyard," Griffen said. "I've been trying to work with them, get them to come to me or something. Mostly, they just stare at me or ignore me completely."

Jerome threw back his head and laughed.

"Cats?" he said. "Man, Grifter, you can grow old and die before you can get a cat to do what you want it to. Even with a dragon's life span. Those are some of the most independent beasts God dumped on the earth."

"It's better to start with dogs or maybe birds," Mose said. "Tell you what. Come on by tomorrow night and I'll show you a couple exercises."

"Um, actually I have a date with Lisa tomorrow night," Griffen said.

"Cancel it," Mose said. "Either that or meet up with her later. Right now we have to keep our priorities straight, and our highest priority is to keep you alive."

Thirty-four

Griffen was suddenly awake, but he didn't know why.

Turning his head slightly, he cracked an eye and focused on the large numbers on the digital clock on his bedside table. 1:30. Okay. Now the question was morning or afternoon. There were no windows in his bedroom, and the door was closed, so daylight or the lack thereof was no clue.

Then, he heard the music. "Singing in the Rain," played on a calliope. That made it one thirty in the afternoon. The calliope was on the steamboat *Natchez*, serenading the tourists boarding for the two o'clock cruise up the Mississippi. "Singing in the Rain" meant that it was raining out, or soon would be, and there would be very few tourists for the cruise.

That was one of the things Griffen loved about the Quarter. Where else could you not only tell what time it was, but also the weather conditions without even looking out a window.

Of course, that still didn't let him know what had woken him up.

Tap, ta tap tap.

He started to sit up, only to find his arm was pinned under Fox Lisa. He tried to ease it free, but she only snuggled closer to him, pressing her velvety nakedness against him. Okay. There were other reasons than calliope music that he loved the Quarter.

Fox Lisa had turned out to be a delight as a bed partner. She was as playful as an otter, and as inventive as a monkey on fifty feet of greased grapevine. Without thinking, he started to respond to her pressure.

Tap, ta tap tap.

"Hey, lover," he said softly, pulling his arm free. "There's someone at the door."

"Mmmmrphl," she said, rolling over and burrowing into their mound of pillows.

Griffen hesitated, then leaned over and kissed the back of her neck, biting it gently.

"Mmmmhmm," she breathed, raising her rump slightly and wiggling it.

Tap, ta tap tap.

Griffen disengaged himself with a sigh and got out of bed. He fumbled in the dark for a moment to find his pants, then eased out of the bedroom, closing the door behind him.

Even though, as anticipated, the sky was overcast, there was still enough light pouring through the windows to make him squint. Swaying slightly, he managed to pull on his pants as he made his way to the door.

Tap, ta tap tap.

"Who is it?" he called, trying to keep from snarling.

"It's Jerome, Grifter," came the response.

He should have known. With the security gates on the complex, the only ones who could have reached his door without getting buzzed in from the street were his sister and Jerome.

Opening the door, he stepped back to admit his visitor.

Jerome swept in brandishing a paper bag, an ovenlike blast of hot, humid air entering with him.

"Brought us some breakfast, Grifter," he said. "Fresh from la Madeleine. French roast coffee and a couple of napoleons."

"Terrific," Griffen said, hastily closing the door against the day's heat. "Just got up. Be with you in a second."

Rubbing his eyes, he made his way into the bathroom to take care of his morning business.

"You're getting to be a real Quarter rat." Jerome's voice came to him through the door. "It's the middle of the afternoon and you're just getting up."

"Nothing new there," Griffen said, zipping up his trousers as he emerged from the bathroom. "I've always been a bit of a night owl. That's why I paid other people to sit in on my morning classes and take my tests back in school. Remember? And keep your voice down. I have company."

Jerome glanced at the closed bedroom door.

"Fox Lisa?"

Griffen nodded.

"Glad to see the two of you are hitting it off," Jerome said. "Watch yourself, though, if you start stepping out on her. You can't keep nothing secret in the Quarter. Wherever you go with another woman, you're going to run into a bartender or a waiter or a busboy who knows you. Even just walking down the street you'll be spotted by a cab driver or a rose vendor or a Lucky Dog seller. You might as well just assume that the Fox there will know about it the next time you see her."

"No big deal," Griffen said, opening his coffee and taking a cautious sip. "There's nothing permanent or exclusive going on with Fox Lisa and me. We're just hanging out buddies and occasional lovers."

"Uh-huh." Jerome smiled. "The question is, does she know that? I don't recall seeing her with anyone else since she's taken up with you."

"Whatever," Griffen said, suddenly uncomfortable. "So what brings you here so early? I have a feeling it wasn't just to share breakfast or to talk about my love life."

"Got some good news for you." Jerome dug in his pocket and produced a set of keys which he tossed to Griffen. "You've got your car back. Fixed up good as new. Even had it tuned and its tires rotated."

"The Goblin?" Griffen said, his mind still fuzzy from sleep. "Where is she?"

"Got her stashed away in a garage," Jerome said. "I'll take you around and show you where when you can spare the time."

Griffen was startled to realize that he hadn't even thought about his car for nearly a month. He had been so busy learning the ins and outs of the gambling operation and the Quarter, not to mention hanging with Fox Lisa, that he had had little leisure time to think about much of anything else. The Goblin seemed like something from another time in his life . . . pre-Quarter.

"I dunno, Jer," he said. "I mean, I appreciate your taking care of getting her fixed up and all, but maybe I should just sell her."

"Sell the Goblin?" Jerome said. "Why would you want to do that?"

"Well, she doesn't really fit into my current lifestyle,"

Griffen said. "I hear it's expensive to keep a car here in the Quarter, and you were right, I haven't really needed one. I can walk or cab it anywhere I need to go. Besides, weren't you the one who told me that a distinctive car like the Goblin would make it too easy to find or track me?"

"As I recall," Jerome said, "Stoner has already found you. And as for the expense, you can afford it now. Besides, she might come in handy if you want to duck out to the burbs for a movie or a bit of shopping. Why don't you keep her for a while before you make up your mind. Once you sell her, there's no way you can get her back. Don't worry about it right now. You've got enough on your plate. I'll see she's taken care of."

Griffen took a long sip of his coffee as he studied his friend.

"I know I've asked this before, Jerome, but why are you doing this?"

"Doing what?"

"All this," Griffen said. "Getting my car fixed, taking me clothes shopping, defending me when the high rollers question whether or not I'm up to taking over things, all that. In general, playing second banana to me, even though you'd be the natural choice to take over for Mose. Why?"

Jerome rolled his eyes and sighed.

"I thought we had gone over this already."

"Well, let's go through it again. For my benefit," Griffen said. "I've got to admit, Jer, I still don't get it. It's like I've been given the starring role in a play, but no one has bothered to give me a copy of the script. What am I supposed to be doing, anyway?"

"All you got to do is just be you," Jerome said earnestly. "That's the beauty of it. You're a high-blood dragon, and it's in your nature to gravitate toward building power. I can't tell you how you're going to do it. I don't know. The other night at the big game, I wasn't lying. Since you've signed on, more and more of the independent games are wanting to join our organization. Our network hasn't changed. The only difference is you. Do you know how you did it?"

"Not really," Griffen admitted.

"Neither do I," Jerome said. "But it's happening. And you haven't even been around for two months. I don't know where it's all going or how it'll get there, but I'm in for the ride."

"Okay, Jer," Griffen said. "I guess I'm in, too. I don't pretend to understand, but I'm in. You're the one who knows dragons. Hell, two months ago I thought dragons were as make believe as vampires and werewolves. Now, I not only am dealing with them, I'm . . . what?"

He was suddenly aware that Jerome was staring at him with a bemused expression on his face.

"Sorry, Grifter," Jerome said, shaking his head. "I keep forgetting how new you are to all this."

"Okay. What am I missing now?"

"It was what you just said, about dragons being as make believe as vampires and werewolves." Jerome smiled.

"Yeah. So?"

Jerome kept smiling.

"Wait a minute," Griffen said. "Are you trying to tell me that there really *are* vampires and werewolves?"

"If you mean the movie-type vampires that bite people's necks and drink blood, the answer is no," Jerome said. "What we do have, though, is people who feed off other people's energies."

"Feed off them like how?" Griffen said.

"There are actually at least two different kinds," Jerome explained. "One kind is your classic depressive that can suck the energy right out of another person or even an entire party and leave them feeling down, nihilistic. Those people lack a certain kind of energy, the kind that lets you enjoy life, but they need it so they drain it out of the people around them. The problem is they're kind of a living black hole that just keep absorbing energy without ever being filled themselves."

"And the other kind?"

"Those are the entertainers, glad-handers, and politicians," Jerome said. "They can infuse the people around them with energy, effectively multiplying the energy they give off, then feed off that accelerated energy. You can particularly see it with actors or singers when they're working an audience. When they've got a good crowd, they work it into a controlled frenzy. That energy buoys them and inspires them to even greater heights to a point where they lose track of time or even how tired they really are. If you're ever backstage to see them when they finally come off, it's like someone cut the strings on a puppet. Once they're away from that massive outpouring of energy from the audience, they're left with their own store of energy which is depleted because they've been feeding it to the crowd to get it going."

He paused and grinned.

"That kind of an energy rush is as addictive as any drug. The only way they can get that high again is to go back onstage and perform again. You hear about people who have been bitten by 'the stage bug,' well, that's what's happened. They've been 'infected' and 'live' for that heady feeling they get from a curtain call or a crowd of autograph hunters."

Griffen shook his head.

"I never thought of it that way," he said. "I mean, I know the high-energy feeling you get at a rock concert or a football game, but I never connected it with vampirism."

"'You say po-ta-to and I say po-tah-to.'" Jerome shrugged. "The werewolf thing is the same way. We all know people who go through wide swings of mood and temperament . . . almost Jekyll and Hyde transformations. That's not even going into the 'chameleons' that change their wardrobe and speech patterns to fit various social situations. Most of us had to do that to one degree or other just to survive our teen years."

"But there aren't really people who can literally change their shape," Griffen pressed.

Jerome cocked his head at him.

"Not to belabor the obvious, Grifter," he said, "but *you're* a shape-shifter. Remember?"

"But . . ."

"Both you and your sister . . . Or don't you remember what happened the first time you met Gris-gris?"

Griffen frowned.

"I've been meaning to ask you about that, Jerome," he said. "I mean, we both saw scales on my arm for a minute there at the end. From what my uncle Malcolm told me, I thought the big lizard thing was just a disguise the old dragons used unsuccessfully to spook the humans."

"That's what I heard, too," Jerome verified. "The thing is, because of the movies and television, you've got the big lizard image locked in your mind when you think of dragons. The way I see it, when you're stressed or get excited, that's what your subconscious defaults to when it goes to shape-shift. With Valerie, what with her being so athletic and all, she seems content to just get larger."

"But you're saying there are others who have this power?" Griffen said.

"If you look around the world, almost every culture has some sort of shape-shifter mythos or legend," Jerome said. "There are stories about werewolves, weretigers, and werebears. There's even an old story about a chimera, which is supposed to be able to take on one of several different animal forms. I've never run into one, though."

Griffen pursed his lips.

"You know, it occurs to me, Jer, that a shape-shifter, especially one of those chimeras, would make a pretty effective George."

Jerome frowned and cocked his head.

"You know, I never thought of that," he said. "Of course, it's only since you hit town that I've had to think of the George at all."

"Go ahead. Rub it in," Griffen said with a grimace. "It just seems to me . . ."

The bedroom door opened and Fox Lisa emerged, bleary-eyed and yawning. She was wearing one of Griffen's shirts with a couple buttons buttoned, giving an alluring view of her cleavage and legs.

"Hey, Jer. How's it going?" she said in a slurred voice.

"Hey, yourself, foxy lady." Jerome smiled back. "Sorry. Did we wake you?"

"Not to worry," Lisa said with a vague wave of her hand. "I can sleep through an air raid. Nothing like a full bladder to get you moving, though. I'll just wander into the sandbox and go back to bed."

She headed into the bathroom with short, unsteady steps, shutting the door behind her.

"Sandbox?" Griffen said.

"Yeah," Jerome said with a grin. "I don't know who started it or where it came from, but it's doing the rounds. I think it's kinda classy."

The toilet flushed, and Lisa reappeared.

"I'll go back to bed now and get out of your hair," she announced, groggily. "I'll even shut the door so you and Young Dragon can talk in private."

The two men looked at each other.

"Wait a minute," Jerome said. "What did you call him?"

"Hmm? Oh. Young Dragon. Some of the crew have taken to calling him that, and I guess I sort of picked it up."

"Who's calling him that?" Jerome pressed. "How did that name get picked?"

Fox Lisa paused in the door of the bedroom and squinched her features into a grimace.

"Oh, com'on, Jerome," she said. "I know I'm not in the inner circle of things, but it doesn't take much to figure out there's something going on down here. To quote what's his name . . . Morgan Freeman . . . in *Batman Begins*, 'I know there are things you can't tell me, and I won't ask. But don't treat me like I'm stupid.'"

With that she disappeared into the bedroom, shutting the door behind her as promised.

Griffen looked a question at Jerome.

"Uh-huh," Jerome confirmed. "Definitely dragon blood there. Probably not as much as me, but it's there. Somehow, though, no one's gotten around to mentioning it to her. Remember what I said about female dragons?"

Thirty-five

There are certain moments in a person's existence when they realize they have made a mistake and could very well die in the next few seconds.

Griffen had experienced one such moment back in Michigan when he had accepted a challenge to road race with an acquaintance of his in the dead of winter. As they piled into a curve, his car had suddenly lost traction and began to slide sideways toward a thin line of trees with an iced-over river just beyond. Rather than feeling petrified with terror or shouting like people do in the comedy movies, a sudden calm descended over him. He knew he had lost control of the situation, but there was nothing for him to do but watch as the events transpired. In that particular instance, his wheels had suddenly found traction on a patch of gravel and with a surge of power the event was past.

Stepping into the bar's dimly lit interior and seeing the scene awaiting him, he felt that same calm as he realized that again he had lost control of a situation and could very well die for his mistake.

It had started innocently enough. He had been shooting pool with Maestro at the Irish pub when a small black kid came through the door and looked around. Griffen assumed that it was one of the tap-dancing panhandlers that worked the Quarter and figured the bartender would handle it.

Before the bartender could move, however, the kid made a beeline for Griffen.

"You Mr. Griffen?"

"On my better days," Griffen said with a smile.

"Huh?" the kid blinked.

"Never mind." Griffen sighed. "Yes, I'm Grif . . . Mr. Griffen."

"Little Joe sent me to find you," the kid said. "He needs to see you and said to tell you it's important."

"When and where?" Griffen said.

"He said the same place you two talked last time . . . right now."

Griffen started to reply, but the kid spun on his heel and pushed his way back out into the sunlight without another word, his mission accomplished.

"Sorry, Maestro," Griffen said, leaning his cue against the wall. "It seems something has come up."

"You want company?" Maestro said, looking up from his shot.

"Naw. Where I'm going, they aren't wild about strangers."

"Suit yourself," Maestro said and turned his concentration back to the pool table.

The bar was only three or four blocks away, and as Griffen strolled the distance, he wondered idly what Little Joe could want.

Maybe he was being called to demonstrate his poker skills again. Then again, it just might be that Little Joe wanted to introduce him to someone.

As Griffen's notoriety had grown, he had noticed that more and more people stopped him on the street to introduce him to their friends or family or whoever it was that they were dating. There seemed to be a certain status attached to just knowing him these days.

What was more, he made a point of going out of his way to greet people, rather than staying in one place and making them come to him. As a young white man taking charge of a predominately black group, he wanted to make the impression that he viewed himself as the first among equals rather than a boss man who expected others to run and fetch at his command.

When they had first talked, Griffen had leaned on Little Joe pretty heavy. He didn't think it would hurt their relationship if he unbent and responded to the summons as a demonstration of friendship and respect.

Two steps into the bar, however, he realized that he had misjudged the situation badly.

Little Joe was at his normal table all right. But sitting with him were two other young black men. They were both decked out in the "home boy" look that movies and television had made popular, with oversized shirts and shorts and bandannas wrapped around their heads. In short, they had "dope dealer" written all over them. But these were the real thing, not some Hollywood pretty boys. Confusing them with their wannabe suburban imitators would be the same as confusing a timber wolf and a toy poodle.

Griffen did not think they were here to play cards. Not unless the games they were used to sitting in on included having automatic pistols sitting on the table next to their hands.

Then, too, there was the table full of look-alikes in the corner, with an additional three sets of eyes boring into him.

He thought back to what Jerome had told him about shape-shifting and deliberately fought back his rising panic. He really didn't know if he was bulletproof, but would just as soon not find out today. Somehow he knew that if he startled this group by going into an involuntary shape-shift, they'd shoot first and not bother about asking questions.

There was nothing for Griffen to do but stay relaxed and try to bluff it through. Maybe the wheels would catch a patch of dry gravel.

"Little Joe," he said by way of greeting as he approached the table. "I heard you wanted to see me?"

"Griffen." Little Joe nodded back. "Got a couple folks here who want to meet you. This is TeeBo and Patches. They're brothers."

From the family resemblance, Griffen assumed the two really were brothers. What was surprising, however, was how young they were. TeeBo was about Griffen's age, while Patches was a good half dozen years younger.

He nodded politely at each of them in acknowledgment of the introductions.

"TeeBo. Patches," he said. "Is there something I can do for you gentlemen?"

"You can keep yo' white-ass nose outta our business . . ." the younger man began, but his brother cut him off.

"Patches!" TeeBo said. "Remember I'm gonna handle this."

He continued to stare at Griffen.

"Little Joe here tells me that you're a reasonable man who

likes to talk things out if there's a problem," he said finally. "So let's talk."

"Do we have a problem?" Griffen said.

"That's what we're here to find out," TeeBo said. "I've been told that you won't let your people deal our product. That true?"

"I'm afraid you've been misinformed," Griffen said.

"I have?" TeeBo seemed genuinely surprised.

"Well, only partially informed," Griffen said. "I'm not telling them not to handle your product, as you call it. I'm telling them not to handle anyone's product. At least, not while they're working for me. If they want to deal, fine. I can't stop them. But not while they're on my payroll."

TeeBo leaned back in his chair and cocked his head to one side.

"So you ain't doing this to give someone else an exclusive with your crew," he said. "Maybe like someone named T.J.?"

"Never even heard of the man," Griffen said.

"See. I told you," Little Joe said.

"Shut up," TeeBo said. "I'm talking to Mr. Griffen here. I wants to hear about it from him."

"He's lying." Patches put in. "Everybody's heard of T.J.!"

"I've only been in town a couple of months," Griffen said. "To be honest, I never heard of you two until just now when we were introduced. We travel in different circles. All I'm interested in is learning Mose's gambling operation."

"So what you got against dope?" TeeBo said. "You want us to cut you in or somethin'?"

"I'm not wild about it personally," Griffen said. "But that's not the point. I'm not stupid enough to try to stop it or to waste a lot of time and energy trying to save people from themselves. I only brought in this new policy when it started to interfere with my operation."

"How you figure that?" TeeBo said.

"Do you know an old gentleman named Reggie?" Griffen said.

"Oh, yeah. I heard 'bout that," TeeBo said. "He worked for you?"

"Only part-time as a stringer," Griffen said. "But working for me isn't what got him killed."

"So it's like that, huh," TeeBo said.

"I hear that you're fireproof," Patches said. "Are you bulletproof, too?"

"I really don't know," Griffen said. "Am I about to find out?"

"Shut yo' mouth, Patches," TeeBo said. "You might learn something."

He turned his attention back to Griffen.

"If you don't mind my asking," he said, "what's that you're wearing around your neck?"

Griffen reached up and fingered the beads.

"This?" he said. "It's a charm someone gave me."

"Someone *gave* you that?" TeeBo said.

"A woman named Rose," Griffen said. "Why? Do you know her?"

"Heard of her," TeeBo said. "Mr. Griffen, you get those before or after your little trip?"

Griffen blinked, both at the "mister" and the reference. He shouldn't have been surprised considering how rumor spread in the Quarter.

"You heard about that?" Griffen said.

"Yeah, word is, someone's real mad wit you."

Another surprise. Griffen realized that the George could

use a rumor mill as yet another way to taunt. Or even as a weapon.

"After."

TeeBo nodded as if that had been what he expected.

"You see what I'm talkin 'bout, Patches?" he said to his brother.

"Well, lookee here!"

A middle-aged black man in a suit had just come through the front door. Following in his wake were four young athletic looking blacks. What was notable about them was that they were all wearing long trench coats despite the heat outside.

"I had my suspicions, but now I know," the man continued.

Tension danced through the room like chain lightning.

"Chill out, T.J.," TeeBo said. "You just think you know. We had our suspicions, too. That's why we're here."

"So you're telling me he's not cutting me out to deal with you?" T.J. said.

"He's cutting us all out," TeeBo said. "We thought he was makin' a deal with you, but he told us he never even heard of you."

"Bullshit," T.J. said. "Everybody's heard of T.J.!"

"Well, he's not dealing with us and he's not dealing with you," TeeBo said. "He says he's making his people choose between working for him or dealing because of what happened to Reggie."

"That a fact?" T.J. said. "And you believe him?"

"That's right," TeeBo said. "You want to know why? Ease over here and take a look at what he's wearing around his neck."

T.J. glanced at his men and gave a quick jerk of his head.

They moved sideways, fanning out along the bar to give them a clear line of sight, and fire, to both the brothers and the table of their supporters. Then he sauntered casually up to Griffen and peered at the beads . . . then jerked suddenly erect as if he had seen a snake.

"Is that for real?" he said to TeeBo.

"He says that Rose gave it to him," TeeBo said. "He's a white boy only been in town a couple months. I don't see him making up a story like that."

"If he is or if he's lying, he's too stupid or too bold to be afraid of anything we might run at him," T.J. said, stepping back.

"That's the way I read it," TeeBo said.

The two men looked at each other, then nodded.

"Mr. Griffen," TeeBo said. "I thank you for taking the time to clarify the situation. Now, if you'll excuse us, T.J. and I have a few matters to discuss in light of this new information."

Griffen took this as a dismissal, and, nodding respectfully to the principals, headed out at what he hoped was a dignified pace.

He had caught a gravel patch . . . again!

The air never seemed sweeter nor the colors as bright and reassuring. Even the glare and the heat were welcome.

Thirty-six

Valerie had started her morning with another sweet breakfast at Café Du Monde. This time, she was a bit too distracted to properly appreciate her surroundings, though she couldn't think of anything that could quite block it out completely.

Some of the artists and the performers Valerie had grown used to seeing. Others seemed to alternate, or just appear randomly. Calliope music filtered over from the river, and blended oddly but somehow appropriately with a bagpipe player on the corner of the Square. A man on stilts was juggling and pacing, while a woman with six small poodles circled the Square again and again. Valerie wasn't quite sure whether the woman was a local, or a tourist, but she couldn't help noticing her hairdo matched that of her dogs.

What distracted Valerie from her meal and the events around her were a small notebook and a folded newspaper. It was a local publication, distributed free in bars and coffeehouses, and it was currently folded to the jobs section. She had decided to take herself out of her worries.

If Griffen wanted to keep her in the dark, she would find something else to occupy her time. The notebook held numbers of want ads Valerie had noticed throughout the Quarter, as well as a few she had been passed by locals. She mulled over the list, unsure of what, if anything, she planned to do about it, and sipped the last of her hot chocolate.

The waiter was just clearing away her plate when new movement caught her eye. A man came around the far corner of the Square. It wasn't his mere appearance that caught her eye, though he moved with a certain amount of casual grace that she found herself admiring.

The real attention getter was the horde of small girls scurrying around him. Over a dozen girls, all dressed in navy blue skirts and starched white blouses, the oldest of whom couldn't have been more than ten. They clamored and giggled around him, a sea of smiling faces, tugging at his pant legs and otherwise scrabbling for his attention. Pant legs that Valerie noticed were extremely well tailored, as was his dark red shirt with a rubylike sheen.

Behind the group, dressed in full nun habit, was the obvious watcher of the little horde. She stood back and shook her head, face holding a look of barely concealed amusement.

The man turned and threw his hands up, making a fierce face and bellowing. All with the predictable results of sending the giggling girls scattering all around him, not in the least bit afraid. One of the braver ones tugged on his pant leg again, and Valerie leaned forward a bit watching his reaction.

He rolled his head and presumably his eyes to the sky, flung his hands out to the side, and made a magician's pass with them. Suddenly in one hand, he held a bamboo rose of the type that get made and sold on the street all over the Quarter. The girl shrieked and clapped her hands, and he bent low and handed it to her, blowing kisses into the air by her cheeks. She turned, clutching her prize, and fled, the rest of the pack chasing after her.

The nun gave him a glare, shaking her finger and not really meaning either, and strode off to try and return some order to the group. Valerie couldn't help but to give off a full, throaty laugh.

At the sound, even though he was across the street, his back stiffened and he turned on his heel, eyes searching. There was no way for Valerie to hide that she was watching, but she didn't bother. Something about the way he moved, and now he moved toward her like a man with a purpose, captivated her eye. She noticed the well-muscled build of his shoulders, and the well-styled line of his hair, and the way people moved out of the way for him. He strode across the street, apparently ignoring the passing cars, and stopped a few steps from the rail separating the café from the street.

"Do it again," he said in a voice that was soft but compelling, even through the early morning hustle and bustle.

"Do what, precisely?" Valerie said a little cooly.

"Precisely? That wonderful, rich laugh that cuts through the world and was worth more applause then a hundred little girls."

"Oh, that." Valerie tried for dismissive, but could feel a flush creeping up her neck. She covered it well. "Perform for little girls a lot do you?"

"Ah, well, I used to give out candy, but for some reason the words 'want some candy, little girl' set off all kinds of people these days."

She smiled at him, and gave him points for picking up her tone, and rolling with it.

"Well, if you want a laugh from me, I don't think another fake rose will do it."

"Ah, but for the lady, the real thing is a must."

And just like that he was holding a red rose, stem trimmed off but petals bright and fresh. He held it out for her, not letting his eyes break contact.

"What do you do, stuff them up your sleeves before you go out just in case you need a handy pick-up bit?"

"I think I've got pearls up my other sleeve if you'd rather," he said.

At that she did laugh. She couldn't help it.

"You try giving me pearls in the first fifteen minutes of a relationship, and I'm going to start looking for your sexual predator file."

"Then the relationship is already started? Oh, goody."

"You don't go half fast do you? And no one says goody," Valerie said.

"I thought joy and rapture might be pushing things a bit," he said.

Valerie was used to strong come-ons, and dealing with them, but more and more she was becoming interested. Seeming to pick up on it, he straightened and tossed the rose over his shoulder.

"Not pearls or roses then. Dinner perhaps? Name the place and time and I shall be there."

"You haven't even asked my name, or offered yours."

"Which line would you prefer? A rose by any other name, or something along the lines of Dulcinea. As for mine, I'm Nathaniel."

"Nathaniel what?"

"Oh, Mother won't tell us, just in case we should ever try to track down Father."

"Ha! Oh, you won't get to evade that easily for long Nathaniel."

"Quite right, but you must come to dinner if you want to try for more." Nathaniel grinned.

He pulled a business card out of his left pocket and flipped it onto the table casually. He had yet to close the final distance, and he still didn't. Instead he turned and walked back toward the Square, without a backward glance.

Valerie thought for a moment and pocketed the card.

Thirty-seven

It was early August, and the New Orleans summer had descended with all its sticky, humid splendor. The ever-present construction crews started working early in the morning . . . *very* early in the morning . . . so they could knock off and be off the roofs and out of the sun before the temperature hit its peak around two in the afternoon. All the shops, restaurants, and bars were running their air conditioners at full blast to provide a lure and a refuge for the tourists who weren't used to summers in the South. Locals ran their air conditioners full blast to keep from going crazy and killing each other. (Those who couldn't afford air-conditioning went ahead and went crazy and killed each other.)

If at all possible, one avoided going outside until after the sun set. Unfortunately, it didn't make that much difference. The semiregular afternoon cloudbursts didn't cool things off the way they would up north. They simply added more moisture so that when one did go out, it had the same feel as stepping into a sauna.

It was early evening, and Griffen was at Mose's place getting a crash course on sports betting. During a break, as he was staring out the window, he realized something he had only noted in passing before.

The difference between the temperature inside the house and outside was so extreme that moisture was forming on the *outside* of the windows. This was, of course, the exact opposite of what he had experienced up north.

He pointed this out to Mose.

"You know, I had a buddy up north who wore glasses. In the winter, every time he came inside out of the cold, he'd be flying blind for about five minutes because his glasses would fog up. Here, it works in reverse. He'd step outside leaving a bar and his glasses would fog . . . except instead of being inside where it's warm and safe, he'd be stepping out onto the mean streets of the Quarter in the wee hours of the morning. Not the best time to be flying blind for five minutes."

He laughed wryly and shook his head.

"I don't understand how people live like this," he said. "I mean, I'm doing it myself, but I don't understand it."

"After a while, you get used to it." Mose sighed.

"Uh-huh," Griffen said. "They used to tell the freshmen at the University of Michigan the same thing during orientation . . . 'You get used to the cold after a while.' The problem was, they never really did."

"That's funny," Mose said. "That's what folks down here say about living up north. How can people live like that? So tell me, if you never really get used to it, how did you deal with the cold up there?"

"That's easy," Griffen said. "It's not like we sit out on our front lawns in it. We do the portable environment thing.

We go from our heated homes to our heated cars to a heated office or shopping mall."

"Well, it's kinda the same thing down here," Mose said. "We go from our air-conditioned homes to our air-conditioned cars or cabs to an air-conditioned office or bar. See what I mean?"

"Okay. You win. Still, I don't think I'll ever get used to having an accent."

Mose laughed.

"Griffen, just because you don't have the local accent, doesn't mean you have an accent. Flip through any channels on any TV, and ninety percent of the people onscreen will sound like you. Midwestern is accepted American bland and normal."

"Well . . . but you sound that way, too . . . most of the time."

Mose smiled, eyes crinkling a bit more at the edges.

"Tha' suh, 's 'cause I practice mighty fine."

Griffen noticed that the accent didn't sound like the usual New Orleans accent. No, it sounded older. He decided not to pursue it, for now.

"You win, again." Griffen laughed. "So let's get back to my lesson. I'll tell you, Mose, all this stuff with the sports betting is crossing my eyes."

"Just be thankful you came down here in June when things were slow," Mose said. "Not much happening in sports during the summer . . . except baseball, and not many folks bet on that. In about a month, football season will start and the action gets heavy. Then, when basketball cuts in, you'll have your hands full. Most of the money comes from football betting, though."

"So let's start there," Griffen said. "How do you set the

betting lines? I mean, some of those point spreads get pretty exact. How do you come up with them?"

"Don't worry about that," Mose said. "We've got experts to do that for us. You're going to be primarily working the management side."

"Well, could you give me a rough idea of how it's done?" Griffen insisted. "Even if I don't get directly involved, I'd like to have some notion of the process."

"Well, it used to be harder in the old days," Mose said. "Today, with the Internet and other electronic communication, it's a lot easier. There are a couple services we subscribe to that have stringers and informants all across the country. They keep track of everything from the physical and medical condition of key players, not to mention their love life and family relationships, to the condition of the fields, weather forecasts, and the history of the various coaches and their staff members when they've gone up against each other before. All that data gets plugged into computers and they spit out what the most likely outcomes will be."

"They can actually calculate things that close?" Griffen said.

"Sure. Of course, different services have different formulas they use or different things they consider. I mean, there's one that factors in who the referees will be and their track records for making bad calls. Because of that, the results aren't always the same. That's where our experts sit down with the service results along with the latest betting lines from the newspapers and Vegas and come up with the spreads we'll use."

"And then you take bets based on those point spreads?" Griffen said.

"Oh, we take some direct bets on single games," Mose said, "but most of the money comes from the bar cards."

"The bar cards," Griffen repeated. "I've seen some of those around, but never really got into them myself. How do they work?"

"It's a really sweet system," Mose said. "Whoever came up with it should get some kind of reward. I'd say they should get a piece of the action, but there would be no way to control it."

"What we do is print up a bunch of cards that list all the NFL games and the top fifteen or twenty college games along with the point spreads. We have runners that take them out and drop them off with certain bartenders around town. If someone wants to play, they take one of the cards, circle the teams they think are going to win, put their name or a nickname on it, and give it to the bartender along with their bet. The runners pick up the cards and money and bring them to us before the games are played. After the results are in, they take the money for the winners and drop it off at the bars for the players to collect."

He paused to laugh and shake his head.

"The thing is, most people kill themselves getting greedy. You see, on the back of the card are the payoff odds. The more games you pick and the more you bet, the more you stand to win. Folks would usually be okay . . . break even or come out a little ahead . . . if they stuck with picking just three games. Instead, they get sucked into picking five or seven games because the payback is bigger. Of course, to win all their picks have to be winners . . . and the more games they pick, the worse the odds are that the games will all go the way they think. Folks like us who run gambling operations just love the players who go with long shots and try to buck the odds."

While Mose was speaking, Griffen got up, unasked, to freshen their drinks. Returning from the kitchen, he set his mentor's drink in front of him, then resumed his seat.

"So, when you say I'll be working the management side," he said, "what exactly does that entail?"

"Well, first of all, you'll have final say on who we take on as runners," Mose said. "That can be harder than it sounds. The people we want representing us have to be dependable, presentable, and able to interact with folks from all walks of life and levels of income. People like that aren't all that easy to find these days."

"You forgot to mention 'honest,' " Griffen said.

Mose sighed.

"Now that's another part of management," he said. "Every so often, one of your runners is going to try to steal from you. You're going to have to sort it out and decide what to do about it."

"I'm missing something here." Griffen frowned. "How can they steal from us with the setup you've got going?"

"The most common way is when they start skimming," Mose said. "As you can see, most of the people who do the bar cards don't get any money back because they lose. A runner can figure that out, so he gets the idea to hold a couple cards back along with the money instead of turning them in. If the cards are losers, he gets to pocket those bets free and clear. Of course, if there's a winner in there, he has to cover the payoff out of his own pocket."

"How do you catch something like that?" Griffen said.

"Just like the players, the skimmers get greedy," Mose said. "If they settle for a couple cards a week, they can probably get away with it. If they do, they start holding more and more back. That's when we can spot it. A runner's take is pretty consistent from week to week with some minor variations for big game weekends. If someone's turn in starts consistently falling short of what we've learned to expect, there's probably some skimming going on."

"Then what do you do?"

"What *you* get to do is investigate." Mose smiled. "You have to check around and find out if there really is some skimming going on, and if there is, if it's the runner or the bartender or both who are doing it."

"And if we find out that someone is skimming?" Griffen said. "What do we do?"

"Now don't be thinking Hollywood gangster scenes again," Mose said. "If it's the runner, we fire him and put in a replacement. If it's the bartender, we just take that stop off our list . . . or recruit another bartender."

"That seems fair enough," Griffen said. "Do we do anything about recovering . . ."

Just then, his cell phone started ringing.

"Excuse me a minute, Mose."

He glanced at the caller ID, but didn't recognize the caller. For a moment he debated letting it go to voice mail, but decided it might give Mose the wrong impression about his diligence.

"Griffen here," he said into the instrument.

"Mr. Griffen? This is Jumbo. You may not remember me."

It took a second, but Griffen placed the name and voice. If was the man who had been serving as Gris-gris's bodyguard when they first met.

"I remember you, Jumbo. What's up?"

"Something's happened I thought you should know about," Jumbo said. "I hate to bother you, but . . ."

"No problem," Griffen said. "Tell me what's happened."

He listened for several minutes, his mouth tightening into a grimace.

"Okay. I think I get the picture," he said at last. "Are you on a cell phone? I'll get back to you in a little while and let you know. Thanks for the call."

He flipped his phone shut, cutting off the connection. Then he leaned back in his chair and thought for a few moments.

"Okay, Mose," he said. "You've been saying that we have to take care of our people. Exactly how far does the definition of 'our people' extend?"

"Why? What's happened?"

"Well, it seems that Gris-gris has been picked up by the police under some rather strange circumstances," Griffen said. "Is he considered one of 'our people'? Should we do anything about it?"

"You tell me," Mose said.

"Excuse me?"

"Gris-gris pulled out of our network under my management, then signed back on directly with you," Mose said. "Since then, he steered a lot of new independents our way. More important, Jumbo called you, not me. I figure that makes it your call as to whether or not he's one of ours. *He* thinks so, and *Jumbo* thinks so. The only question now is if *you* think so."

Griffen took a deep breath, then blew it out slowly, puffing his cheeks.

"In that case, I guess he's one of ours," he said.

"In that case," Mose said, "there's an attorney and a bail bondsman we usually use when our people get into trouble. Hang on and I'll get you their numbers."

"Actually, Mose," Griffen said, "let me try something else, first."

He flipped his cell phone back open, scrolled through his directory, and hit the "send" button.

After four rings, there was a pickup on the other end.

"Yeah?" came a gruff voice.

"Good evening, Detective Harrison," Griffen said with a smile, even though he knew it couldn't be seen at the other end. "This is Griffen McCandles."

There was a brief pause. Mose's eyebrows went up and Griffen smiled at him.

"Okay, Griffen. What's up?"

"Something has come up, and I was wondering if you could check into it for me."

Another pause.

"It seems that one of our people has been picked up by your colleagues," Griffen said. "He's known as Gris-gris, but his real name is . . ."

"Yeah. I know him," the detective said, cutting in. "What's the charge?"

"That's sort of what I was hoping you could check for me," Griffen said. "According to the information that was passed to me, they haven't charged him with anything."

Again, a pause.

"Actually, they can do that," Harrison said. "Legally, they can hold someone for seventy-two hours for questioning without charging them."

"I've heard that," Griffen said. "This seems to be a special situation, though. From what I've been told, he was picked up because he was walking down the street arm and arm with my sister. Strangely enough, they let her go."

He could hear a deep sigh at the other end.

"Look, Griffen. I don't know what you've heard, but we don't do that kind of crap anymore. This town runs on tourist dollars, and that would go away real fast if the cops started hassling every mixed race couple they saw in the Quarter."

"That's what I figured," Griffen said, winking at Mose. "As a matter of fact, the way I heard it, the officer that picked him up was also black."

"So what's the problem?" the detective growled. "Am I missing something here?"

"The interesting thing is, the way I hear it, that officer also happens to be the older brother of a girl that Gris-gris was dating before he took up with my sister."

This time, the pause was lengthy.

"You know, Griffen," the detective said at last, "you have a bad habit of pushing my buttons. If there's anything I hate worse than protected gambling operations or the Feds messing around on my turf, it's cops who abuse the power of their uniforms. Okay, I'll check into it . . . and this one's worth a beer, not a lousy cup of coffee."

Thirty-eight

The Irish pub had never been so damned noisy before. It wasn't people noise either. Griffen had yet to live through a Mardi Gras, but had run into some nights when even the slightly out-of-the-way pub had been packed enough that there were no seats available and the press of strangers had pushed him out into the night to find something a bit calmer. So he could have lived with a certain amount of uproar in the form of men and women looking for a good time.

Dogs on the other hand. That was another story.

It was one of the strange customs of New Orleans, particularly the Quarter. Apartments were so small, open spaces so rare, that those with canine companions tended to bring their dogs everywhere. Everywhere. Outside restaurants, groceries, and shops one could often see an animal or two tied up waiting for its owner. Bars, though, bars were notoriously lassie fair, or was that laissez-faire?

There were seven of them in the pub that night. Not only in, but unleashed and running free. As one, they started barking when Griffen walked in. From the incessant yap yap yap of something that looked like it should be at the end of a mop, to the deep rawlf of a Great Dane whose head was easily higher than the pool table. They moved toward him, barking their heads off, as various owners tried to quiet them down. Their shouts, and those of the bartender, were almost enough to drive Griffen back out.

Stubbornly, he ignored them and pushed his way over to where Jerome sat at the bar. The dogs quieted eventually, except for the little mop that followed Griffen the whole way and sat on its haunches as he took a seat. Yap yap without end. Jerome's eyes were shiny with mirth, and his smirk was broad and annoying.

"What's so funny?" Griffen said.

"Just thinking that maybe Mose needs to start giving out report cards to his student, Young Dragon," Jerome said.

"Oh, shut up."

"And the parrot says, 'Mine, too, must be the salt water.'"

Jerome's smirk broadened, and Griffen glared. Those who knew the abominable and obscure joke Jerome was referencing glared as well. A balled up napkin hit him from parts unknown. The little dog kept yapping.

"I didn't even try anything to set them off," Griffen said sourly as his drink arrived.

"Ah, but did you try and quiet them?"

"Didn't occur to me. That racket hit, mainly what I thought of was that it was time for a drink."

"We need to work on your reflexes more."

Which was the perfect time for the fight to break out.

Scuffles in the Irish pub were damned rare, and even more uncommon were serious ones. Whatever had triggered this one had started at the back of the pool tables. A shout, the sound of flesh hitting flesh, the screech of chairs as those around responded and rose from their seats. By the time the bartender was out from behind the bar and headed toward the trouble, a man, easily six-five, was pulling a pool cue back. It was clear that he intended to strike his much smaller opponent, and equally clear that the other wouldn't be able to do anything to stop it.

The big man started to swing. Those closest started to move forward, knowing they would be too late. Griffen and Jerome were on their feet, too far back to do any good, but moving forward like everyone else. And before the man could get any momentum, his arm stopped with such a painful jerk that the entire room heard his shoulder pop.

The room seemed to stop as one, taking in the scene. The big man, turned around, fist raised to strike whoever had grabbed his cue. The sight before him stunned and stopped him just as quickly as it had done everyone else. Holding on to the end of his cue, in a jaw that would have done a horse credit, was the Great Dane. Its tail was wagging.

Later reports, unconfirmed, claimed the dog waggled his eyebrows.

What came next was one of the reasons Griffen enjoyed this pub so much, and why it had so few incidents like this. Both parties in the fight were not locals, but everyone who had rushed forward was. Together, under the guidance of the bartender, the two were pushed outside where they couldn't damage the bar. The big man in particular got a lot of attention. Outside, shouting erupted as he tried to pick the fight back up, but the momentum of the anger had been broken. It was clear the smaller man wanted no part in more, and the larger was persuaded to head off before police patrolled by and got involved.

Slowly people began to filter back in. Of course, they were talking about the events. Drinks were picked back up, and several people patted the Great Dane, who seemed content to curl up in one corner and receive adoration. Griffen was one of the first back to his seat, and Jerome wasn't far behind. The little dog sat back in his seat, and began barking. Griffen looked hard at the dog, and it rolled over sticking all four legs in the air and going quiet.

"Not too shabby, Grifter," Jerome said.

"Thanks."

"But don't get cocky. Dogs is easy. They want to make people happy."

"Thanks for the pep talk. Sheesh."

The room went quiet again as the smaller man from the fight walked tentatively back into the bar. Usually, if anything like this happened, all parties were eighty-sixed, or banned, for the night. Repeat offenders, or those who pissed off the bartender too much, were banned forever. The bartender, and most of the bar, gave the man a hard stare. Finally, shyly, he spoke.

"Uh . . . sorry for the trouble. I'll leave if you want. Only . . ." he said.

"What?" The bartender said.

"Before I go, could I buy that dog a drink?"

It was unanimously decided that the rule about eighty-sixing could be waved. Just this once.

"Gots to admit, the man has style," Jerome said with a grin.

Griffen didn't say anything, staring into the "water back" for his drink.

"What is it, Grifter?" Jerome said. "You look like you've seen a ghost. Well, another one."

Still silent, Griffen slid his glass of water over to his friend. There was a slice of lime floating in it that hadn't been there when they had followed the fight. More to the point, it was impaled by a plastic toothpick in the shape of a sword. Needless to say, the Irish pub never used plastic swords with their garnish.

Thirty-nine

Griffen had found that adjusting to his new life had been surprisingly natural. Both his status as a young dragon, and his reeducation and relocation into the French Quarter. All right, his stomach tied up in knots if he thought too hard about having an assassin after him. Or about the possibility of failing those who were coming to depend on him. Still, that later fear started to fade a little more with each incident.

He wasn't the only one surprised for that matter. Though they kept it largely to themselves, those he encountered, including Jerome and Mose, were continually impressed by the obvious transformations he was experiencing, and dealing with in stride. However, some surprises hit him harder than others, and with the surplus of distractions around him, he had a tendency to forget that his life wasn't the only one in upheaval.

He was in the Irish pub, playing pool on the back tables. His opponent, Padre, had proved to possess years of serious experience, as well as a knowledge of position play and strategy that kept him well in the lead. Griffen had no problems asking for tips and pointers, nor Padre giving them. Losing gracefully at pool did nothing to hurt his local status. Though every once in a while Gris-gris would look up from the bar and indulge himself in some gentle ribbing. After writing his name on the chalkboard for next game.

Griffen had just tried for a hard slice, and scratched, when he heard the corner doors swing open noisily. One thing he especially liked about the pub: no one left or entered without being heard. The creaky doors on both streets made sure of it. This time, the doors were unnecessary, as the laughter that filtered in identified the newcomer right away.

Griffen had never heard his sister Valerie laugh quite like that before she had met Gris-gris, but now he heard it more and more often, and liked it. It was a throaty, merry laugh full of enjoyment and contentment. Only, Gris-gris was still at the bar, and Valerie was not walking in alone.

Griffen hid his surprise and slowly straightened from the table to look over her companion.

The first thing he noticed was how the man moved. Well no, to be honest the first thing he noticed was that he was a man, and had his hand around Valerie's waist. The second thing he noticed was how he moved, with a graceful, relaxed stride very similar to Valerie's own. He was a few inches taller then her, with dark hair styled and combed back.

His clothes, which Griffen found himself noticing more and more in the Quarter, were well tailored to his body. Dark pants and a richly colored shirt with one button too many unbuttoned. If the body language had been any different, one might have thought he was gay, he had that excellent sense of style and materials, but there was no mistaking his preferences as he held the door for Valerie and helped her inside.

With a wave to his sister, Griffen set aside his pool cue

and took a step forward. He didn't have time for another step; she had crossed the distance with a fast, light step and scooped him up into a crushing bear hug. He caught a glance of his pool partner as he was swept up, but Padre was already smiling and sitting back with his drink, the game on hold. The man who had come in with Valerie followed in her wake, standing to the side with a slightly amused expression at her exuberant greeting.

"Val! Air would be nice," Griffen said and pushed on her shoulders.

She laughed, not the same laugh she had used before, and set him back on his feet.

"You are such a wimp sometimes, Big Brother."

She grinned in a way that made Griffen think she was about to ruffle his hair, so he took a protective step to the side and offered his hand to her friend.

"Hi. Griffen McCandles, long-suffering brother to this overgrown Valkyrie."

"A pleasure. Nathaniel. I was all prepared to be jealous over that greeting, but the brother part changed my mind. Besides, I am just not sure that my spine is up to it."

He took Griffen's hand and shook it with an easy grip. His voice was like his grip and posture, smooth and unforced, with just a touch of rolling accents that caught the listener's attention.

"Hmm, am I surrounded by fragile things then? Will everyone break so easy? It is to sigh," Valerie said.

"Absolutely. We are but paper tigers to you. You shall just have to get used to it," Nathaniel said, and Griffen couldn't help notice the smile the two shared.

"Can I get you two a drink?" Griffen said, but Nathaniel waved him off.

"Oh, by no means. First round is on me."

He turned and strode off to the bar, leaving brother and sister more or less alone.

"You're scowling, Big Brother." Valerie nudged his ribs gently. He would have bruises tomorrow.

"I am not; he seems very . . . nice."

"Don't you believe it. He was giving a nun all sorts of problems when we met." She made sure her voice carried, and Nathaniel turned around with a mock grimace.

"I did no such thing, and you shouldn't spread stories. Mr. McCandles here is liable to take exception to my attentions to his sister."

"Griffen please, and I'd love to hear this story."

"He was seducing young girls away from the church," Valerie said.

"I was being followed by a herd of ragamuffins who could barely read *See Spot Run*," Nathaniel said.

He walked back with a drink for Valerie and gin for himself. A plastic cup or "party hat" was set next to Griffen's drink, a marker of a drink already bought.

"Minors! Pedophile. And he offered them illicit treats for following him."

"Such nasty talk from so lovely a lady. You really will be the death of my reputation." Nathaniel was still smiling, and if anything the shine in Valerie's eye was increasing as they bantered back and forth. Griffen managed a quick glance at Gris-gris, but found he had disappeared.

"Deny it if you can."

"I do. Since when does a bamboo rose count as an illicit treat? I told you, they won't let me give out candy anymore. Besides, it would have taken eight of them to make one of you, what are you worried about."

"Is that a comment about my weight?"

"Oh, no! Someone save me. Griffen, how do you manage to appease your sister?"

"When she wants you trapped? You are on your own. If you manage the trick, tell me how it's done."

"Neither of you is to give the other one pointers. It would be cheating," Valerie said.

She sipped her drink and Griffen tried very hard not to notice that she held it with her left hand, and that her right was under the table.

Gris-gris had come out of the bathroom and had settled into a far corner of the bar with his drink. Valerie seemed not to have noticed him at all, which was odd for her, but all her attention seemed to be on Nathaniel. Griffen shrugged; maybe they had had a falling out.

"Are you a local, Nathaniel?" Griffen said, trying to make conversation.

"Sort of," Nathaniel said. "My family does a fair amount of business here in New Orleans and owns a condo here in the Quarter, which has me in and out of town several times a year. Right now my brother and I are in town for a couple weeks, maybe a month."

"And what business is that?" Griffen said.

"Liquidation mostly. And yourself?"

"I do as little as possible; life seems to work so much better that way."

Griffen had yet to figure out just what to tell the average person about his occupation. Somehow, running an illicit gambling ring just didn't strike him as proper conversation.

As the three talked, Griffen found himself liking Nathaniel more and more. He really didn't seem anything special, but he certainly seemed to hold the attention. The conversation was easy and amusing, for all parties, and Griffen found his initial tension easing away from him with every sentence. Besides, Valerie truly seemed to be enjoying his company. Still, something kept nagging at the edge of his attention. A faint kernel of worry that wouldn't go away.

After their drink, the couple left. Valerie explained that she only stopped in to introduce the two of them before taking Nathaniel to dinner. That started off another bit of banter over who was taking who to dinner. They were still at it, with Nathaniel looking like the eventual winner, as the door closed behind them. Griffen shook his head, and finished his drink, walking back over to the pool table where Padre was already chalking his cue. After another few moments, Gris-gris got up and joined them.

"Hey, Grifter, got a minute?"

"Of course, Gris-gris."

"Grifter, I strike you as a jealous sort?"

"Well, to be honest . . ." Griffen paused and thought it over very carefully. "I don't know you well enough, Gris-gris. You could be. How we first met and all, yes, that was a form of jealousy among other things. But that was a long time ago, relatively speaking. So I'm willing to give you the benefit of the doubt."

"Hmm . . . can't say you don't got a point. And that's fair. I want to be clear, though. I ain't."

"All right, I'll give you the benefit of the doubt. Still, I was surprised. I thought the rumor mill would have gotten news of a new man in her life to me faster."

"In case you have forgotten, Grifter, only a few days ago I was dating her. They haven't been together long enough even for the Quarter gossips."

Griffen mulled this over, and it worried him. Valerie

seemed awful . . . attached, for so recent an acquaintance. He didn't have time to think it over as Gris-gris went on.

"Way I figure things, me and your sister had some laughs, I figured we'd have a few more, but if she wants to laugh with someone else, that's her business."

"A very good attitude, Gris-gris, though I hear a 'but' coming, don't I?"

"You sure do. I don't trust that guy. Been around the block a few times, and he sets off all my bells. It's not just who he's with, I want you to understand that. It's him."

"He seemed nice and polite and, well, harmless to me," Griffen said.

"Yeah, and my gut tells me that's because that's how he wants to seem. It was all just too damn smooth. With your permission, I'm gonna check him out."

"Gris-gris, you aren't someone I can order to do or not do something. You don't need my permission. But if you do, and you really think you need to, you be careful. The last thing I want is you in trouble, and thinking that it was my fault."

"Com'on, Grifter. You gotta be kidding me. I'm the only one responsible for me, that's how I like it. Just want to make sure we all know who this guy really is. Besides one smooth damn dude."

"Some people," Padre said even as he sank the eight ball, "just have a natural charm."

Griffen looked at him close, and felt that kernel of worry grow a bit. If nothing else, Nathaniel was the only out of towner who had made an effort to penetrate their group.

Was his little sister dating the George?

Forty

Griffen had to admit to himself, grudgingly, no place was perfect.

The French Quarter had food, music, endless variety. It was damn near impossible to grow bored there. Just the other day he had been wandering to his apartment when fireworks had burst to life above him. Grand, professional displays fired from a barge on the river just a few blocks away. No holiday, no special festival, just one of the countless conventions that decided to light up the night for the whole Quarter.

If festivals and fun grew boring, one could simply sit back and watch the young tourists, or at least the young tourist ladies, sweating away in their tank tops and shorts. As the old joke went, nice scenery in the Quarter, the buildings aren't bad either. Everyday there was something that tugged at Griffen's attention, and made him glad that, as bizarre as his life had turned, it had brought him here.

Despite this, Griffen had one vice that this delightfully

sinful place didn't begin to address. It supplied him with constant booze, delightful sights, and excitement both tame and dangerous. Yet, he felt himself yearning for just one thing.

If only the damned place had a decent movie theater within walking distance!

Okay, so it was a petty complaint. He got enough fresh DVDs that if he chose to he could plunk down in his apartment and never leave. Not to mention that the bartenders in his favorite pubs would pass him the remote controls to the TVs there without batting an eye. Still, it wasn't the same.

Griffen loved movies. His tastes ran to the classics. Old comedies, action movies, musicals. But he would watch anything in a pitch, and had. Some of his favorites were pure camp, and the proper place to see a movie the first time was the theater. Sure he preferred older films, but the experience of the theater, surrounded by others, eating cheap popcorn, and losing oneself in whatever new world the screen presented. It was one of his simplest pleasures.

He had mentioned it to Jerome one day, because he realized being crammed in a dark room with a bunch of strangers wasn't exactly safe. It would be the perfect opportunity for the George to try something.

Jerome had looked at him for a long time before answering.

"Griffen, as soon as you let his threat dictate whether you do or do not live and enjoy your life . . . well, I figure by then he might as well just stick a knife in your ribs."

Griffen had to admit, he had a point. In fact, for Jerome, it was absolutely eloquent.

"All right, then I'm going to call a cab and . . ."

Griffen trailed off, Jerome had started laughing at him. Hard enough that tears were beading in the corner of his eyes.

"Oh, hell, Grifter! Sure have been down here too long. Tell me when you want to go and I'll get the Goblin pulled out of storage."

Oh . . . yeah.

That was a plus.

Griffen found himself grinning a few days later. It had been too long since he had driven his car. Actually, it had been too long since he had seen his car. Apparently Jerome had found a place outside the Quarter with secure parking, and the equivalent of valet service. They had his spare keys and would just park and lock it at a given time and place. Surprisingly, this was actually cheaper then the garages inside the Quarter.

The Goblin had been parked on the side of the street, waiting for him. Whoever had delivered it had already headed back to their other duties, and Griffen stood for a while just looking over her. The clean lines of the car, the gleaming green. He missed the old Sunbeam Tiger more than he had realized. Sitting there, looking to his eye as eager as he felt.

Maybe the movie could wait after all, a few hours on the road, just tooling around, and a later show. That sounded about right. Sometimes it helped to have a reminder that there was life outside of the Quarter.

He unlocked the door and slipped inside. For a few moments he just sat, hands on the steering wheel, feeling the texture under his fingertips. Maybe movies in the theater wasn't the only vice that the French Quarter wasn't quite built to indulge. He sighed happily and slipped the key into the ignition. Turned it.

Nothing.

The smile slowly slid from his face. He turned the key again, absolutely nothing. Not even the engine trying to turn over. Like the starter was broken, disconnected, or cut. Griffen took the key out, made sure it was the right one, slipped it in again. For a third time there was no result.

With a grimace he slammed his hand into the dash. Not hard enough to damage his beloved car, but he was just so frustrated. Now instead of a night out, he would have to call a mechanic. He sighed and leaned his head back on the seat. He rubbed his hands over his eyes, as if that could really ease the tension. As he pulled his hand away, though, his eyes caught on something

There was a small white triangle sticking out of his visor. He hadn't noticed it. In fact, he doubted it had shown before. It was more like his strike on the dashboard had shaken it just enough to emerge. He reached up, pulled it, and found himself holding the corner of a Knight of Swords tarot card.

Griffen's mind flashed in an instant, even as his hand reached for the door handle. This didn't make sense. What skill was involved in this? Cutting an ignition when he was nowhere near the car? Or was there something worse in store? A bomb perhaps, that would have detonated if the turn of a key had worked? And a card he wouldn't have seen without the impact of his hand . . .

The door was open just a crack when the crash slammed it shut again.

A beer truck, easily four times the size of the Goblin. It had been parked half a space back, Griffen had noticed it only in passing. Plenty of clearance to back up.

That clearance was closed in half a second, with the roar of the larger engine. It crunched into the back of the Goblin and threw Griffen forward against the dash. Only his awkward position of trying to open the door saved his head from cracking against the steering wheel.

The second crash came a few moments later. The truck backed up enough for another rush. Griffen clung desperately to the steering wheel of his car, not trying to escape, just enduring. If he allowed it, the whiplash from the impacts could have snapped his spine.

Metal screamed and buckled. The strongest part of the Sunbeam Tiger was its massive engine. Compared to the truck behind, the back of the car was as sturdy as tissue paper. Griffen felt the seat smash into his back as the car folded. He was pinned, trapped. He cursed himself for not being faster. One more blow and . . .

Another blow never came.

Griffen saw the truck drive away, but blurrily. He couldn't focus on the license, or the details, and realized he had blood in one eye. A scalp wound, he didn't know when or how it had split. Nothing is perfect it seemed, not even dragon skin.

The visor hung crookedly. The blow of the truck would have dumped the card. Nice to see the George planned things out. Griffen forced the door open, metal shrieking again. It took all his strength to pry himself free from the car.

People gathered, a hand landed on his shoulder. He almost struck out, but realized at the last moment it was a police officer. He couldn't quite make out the cops questions, his eyes were all for the Goblin. A crumpled, broken mess of metal in black and racing green.

Griffen knew he should be afraid. But looking at his prized possession shattered and bent, his car, his friend, he trembled. Not with fear. With fury.

Forty-one

Griffen soared.

Everyone had dreams of flying, or of falling. Of hurtling through the air, currents buffeting over skin. How much control one had often depended on the type of person.

This wasn't like that. Griffen wasn't at the mercy of the winds, wasn't free flowing through the air. He could feel the power of muscles straining with each powerful beat of his wings. Muscles that he knew, on some level, he didn't have in the waking world, but here they felt right. He didn't question them, just exulted in the pounding of his blood through them, the effortless strength that kept him aloft.

He cut through the currents of the air as a shark did through water. Utterly confident, fulfilled, free. He was as much a part of the world as the clouds that passed under him. Sunshine beat down, and felt odd against his skin. As if it weren't skin at all, but something rougher that soaked in the light and sent small waves of pleasure through his body.

He twisted in the air, tucking arms and legs beneath

him, folding wings around him, unquestioning suddenly being a six-limbed being. Dreams have logic of their own. He dived under the clouds, saw a city before him. Lines of energy coursed, etching their own pattern above the webwork of streets and buildings. The city called to him, pulled at him. He gave into the pull and sank lower in the air.

As he circled over the city, making lazy patterns through the air, he saw a part he recognized. A small patch of lower buildings, older; a square of green in front of a great cathedral; river on one side. It was like the cities garden, if one had planned out a garden in brick and iron. Several lines of energy ran through it, met, throbbed.

Griffen looked upon the French Quarter and saw something beautiful. Something his. Warring emotions mixed in the young dragon's beating heart. A need to explore, to protect, to build. He looked down from the skies and saw his territory, his home.

He landed in Jackson Square, and for the first time something about the dream disturbed him. He was alone, completely. No people stirred in the Square, no sounds of cars or carriages filled the air. It felt lonely, wrong. In so many ways, the Quarter was the people inside it.

Griffen lifted his head high. Now that he had been unsettled, he slowly became more conscious of himself. His head was higher off the ground than it should have been. He could see farther; he could smell the river beyond Decatur Street. In the odd silence of the empty Quarter, he could hear the lapping of the water. Something about the scent and smell drew him.

Without consciously moving, he found himself at the waters edge. He stood on the set of wooden stairs that led from the Moonwalk to the shore. He found himself drawn more and more to the water, fascinated by the swirling currents and small waves. The river smelled of mud and of age and of power. An ever-changing steam, that had lived and ran and thrived long before there was ever a city.

Griffen peered closer.

He fell into a trancelike state. No longer could he feel the body he inhabited. No longer did he smell water or city. It was as if the swirling reflection of himself in the water became the entire dream, his entire world. It swelled in his sight. Obscure, detailless, just a green blob in the muddy waters.

Then it cleared, and a scaly monster stared back at him.

Griffen awoke with a start, lurching up in bed. Then smashing back down as his head cracked into the ceiling above. Stars burst into his already blurring vision, and the bed collapsed under him.

He lay, absolutely stunned. His head throbbed, whether from the dream, the surge of adrenaline, or the impact, he couldn't be sure. His vision swam and he had to close his eyes tightly, waiting for things to settle before daring to open them again. It took several hard blinks for his sight to focus.

The clock showed five thirty. He reached up, clumsily and groggily, trying to turn the lamp on and only managing to drop it off the dresser, earning his head another impact. He finally got it turned on, lying on its side on the floor, and by then Valerie was pounding on his front door.

"Hold on!" Griffen called and pulled himself to his feet.

"You alive in there?" Valerie yelled back, not managing to hide her worry.

"Think so. Hang on."

Griffen stepped out of the wreckage of his bed, still more than a little shaky. He leaned on the wall and surveyed what was left of what had been a lovely piece of cherrywood furniture. Griffen had always thought a bed should be more than a few bars of metal to stick a box spring and mattress on. Sadly, he looked at several planks that had been broken right in two.

Then he looked upward, and the last remnants of sleep slipped away.

"Griffen! I will break this door down!" said Valerie.

Hastily, Griffen grabbed a bathrobe and wrapped it around himself as he went to let his sister in. She looked him over from head to toe, even turning him by the shoulder as she surveyed for any obvious damage. Seeing no blood or bruises her expression quickly changed from worry to anger.

"What did you do?" she said.

"I was dreaming . . . I was flying. I saw my face, a dragon's face, and it scared me awake."

"And that resulted in a crash that probably woke people up three streets away how?" his sister said, unrelenting.

"I'll show you."

He led her into the bedroom and she stared at the mess. Confused and concerned, she walked carefully around the remains of the bed, face tight with worry. When her eyes finally flicked upward, he watched with some satisfaction as she did a full double take, then stared.

"Huh," she said after a long moment, "so dragons have horns?"

The ceiling was dented, a large dimple in the plaster about the size of a football. The apartment didn't exactly have high ceilings, but even so, Griffen would normally have to stand on his bed to touch it. What was more worrying was a series of small punctures, as if several objects had punched right through. Bits of flaked plaster fell even as they watched.

"You don't think you really?" Valerie said, still looking upward.

"I don't know, what else could have happened?"

"I don't know . . . this is more than a little freaky, Big Brother."

"I would have said frightening, maybe terrifying, but freaky works. Thank god I was in bed alone."

Valerie shook her head, finally looking back at her brother. He seemed no worse for wear, though his eyes were just a little too wide. Considering how little he usually showed, that was enough for her. She put an arm around him and hugged him tight to her.

"Poor wittle brother had a nightmare?" she teased, trying to lighten his mood.

"Actually no, it was kinda fun. I still don't understand why that last moment spooked me so."

"Well, I'll say this, you need to work on your control. Imagine if you were flirting with Fox Lisa in the bar and suddenly your emotions triggered another change. You might split your pants!"

Griffen, startled, jerked his head toward his sister. Even his control couldn't stop the smirk that spread to his lips. She thought for a second about what she had just said, and promptly cuffed her brother on the back of the head.

"I meant with a tail!" she said.

"Sure you did, Sis."

"You're sick sometimes, and I'm going back to bed!"

She stomped off, slamming his door behind her. Griffen hadn't seen his sister blush in years. It was almost worth having to replace the bed.

Forty-two

For couples, especially young couples, there are few places in the world that can compare with New Orleans. Depending on where one looks, a fledgling romance could find the elegance of any Paris street, the exclusivity of the New York club, or even the hint of dingy danger found in the London Underground. And that was just in the Quarter. No matter what one's tastes, it could be found in New Orleans. Besides, while looking, a pair was almost certain to find a few surprises.

It was now many days, and dates, from when she had first introduced Nathaniel to her brother, and Valerie and Nathaniel were following their ears. Drifting from street to street, stopping by the doors of bars and clubs to scope out the music inside. There wasn't a manager in town who didn't try and pipe at least some of their music into the streets. It was a more guaranteed way of getting bodies in the door than any club barker.

They had met at a jazz club on the corner of Bourbon and

St. Peter. The prices on the drinks had surprised Valerie, even with the lack of a cover. Though the music was absolutely amazing, it was also competing with the hard rock cover band across the street. When Nathaniel noticed that her tapping foot was in time with the music outside the club, he left generous tips for the waitress and the band and eased her out the door.

The quality and variety was astounding as always. In just a few blocks they had sampled an Irish trio that kept trying to one-up each other; a blues singer who had to have weighed three times the couple put together; and a solo female singer with a deep raspy voice. And those were only the ones they had stopped in to listen to for an extended period. The last was the most fun, at least as far as conversation was concerned.

"She has to be a guy," Valerie said.

"I hate to disagree, but she isn't."

Nathaniel shook his head, and was silently glad they had grabbed one of the back booths. Valerie's voice tended to carry, even when they weren't trying to talk over music. The subject of their discussion was blissfully unaware of it all. She was in her own world, and happily butchering a show tune beyond recognition.

"Don't defend him; I didn't say it was a bad drag job," Valerie said.

"That is because it isn't a drag job. Just because she has a somewhat rough voice . . ."

"That voice could grind glass into powder."

"Lots of women have deep voices."

"And more men."

"I am amazed you haven't gotten us thrown out of somewhere by our ears by now."

"I haven't been trying to. Would you like me to?"

Valerie gave a sly smile over her drink, and Nathaniel returned it, with only a momentary roll of his eyes. The song ended and the singer took a long drag on her cigarette, and then started up on the next. Valerie winced and thought about leaving, she actually liked this song. Still, the conversation wasn't done.

"It isn't the voice so much," she said. "It's the jaw you could open walnuts with and the calves of a none too fit horse."

"You're just defensive because she's taller than you."

"Oh, now you are in for it, buster."

"Promises promises. In this town it is ridiculous to wonder, we will just wander down to the clubs where you are guaranteed to be right."

"Tempting, but no. Let's wander back to see if the Irish guys have started brawling yet."

"Oh, no, you are not going back to flirt with the band again. Bad enough you got them dueling onstage."

"Little ol' me?"

"Little?"

Valerie reached under the table and pinched his ribs. Nathaniel returned the favor, and then was out of his seat and moving toward the door before she could retaliate. She followed, sweet murder in her eye, and they hit the streets again.

Valerie bounced through the Quarter with the curiosity of a kitten and the energy of a puppy. It was all Nathaniel could do to keep up, but his smile never faded. If anything, as she became happier and more enthralled with the evening, he seemed to relax and go with the flow more and more.

Finally she decided it was time for a rest, and they paused in one of the quieter bars. The band, most likely a cover group from their general appearance and instruments, were taking a brief break. The couple found seats at the end of the bar and ordered drinks. Valerie leaned past Nathaniel to snag a bowl of bar peanuts, and he was enjoying the view too much to comment.

"Hey, Val!"

The voice came from behind her, and startled she froze for a minute, still outstretched. She tried to regain some dignity, pulling the bowl back and smoothing her hands down her sides before turning around. Coming toward her from the direction of the stage was Kid Blue.

"Valerie McCandles! You finally got around to coming to hear me play," he said.

"Well, of course I did," Valerie covered. "I said I would, didn't I?"

"Why, Valerie, you didn't tell me a friend of yours worked in this club," Nathaniel said smiling.

Valerie tossed him a warning glare, and if anything his smile widened.

"I wasn't sure he was playing tonight, but thought we should check," she said.

Kid Blue looked from one to the other, and his face clouded a bit with disappointment and confusion. He shrugged it off.

"Hey, let me get you two some drinks."

"No need," Nathaniel said. "I've already picked up this round."

"Then the next is on me, hear that?"

The bartender nodded to Kid Blue and put out empty cups to mark the next round bought. Nathaniel nodded and stuck out his hand.

"I'm Nathaniel by the way, and yourself?"

"Kid Blue."

The two shook hands, and held the contact looking over each other.

"I think your band's about ready for you."

Nathaniel nodded to the stage, where the other musicians were indeed gathering. Kid Blue looked hesitant, casting a glance toward Valerie. However, he quickly shrugged again, and when Nathaniel finally released his hand turned back to the stage. Nathaniel leaned in to Valerie.

"Musicians, hmm?" he said.

"Oh, shush, I helped him move a couch." Valerie turned back to her drink.

"How much did it move?"

"Oh!"

Valerie punched him in the shoulder, and it wasn't very playful. He rubbed it and looked from her to the stage and back. By now the group was warming into their first number.

"Let's leave," he said.

"I can't, not now that he thinks I came here just to listen. In a little while maybe."

"I don't want to stay." Nathaniel leaned in to her, his voice a little more forceful than she had heard it before.

"Well . . . neither do I really . . . anymore. But it would be insulting, and maybe hurtful. We'll just finish the drinks first."

"This round, not the next."

They looked each other in the eye for a long moment. Valerie shook her head, breaking the contact first. Then she shook it harder, almost as if clearing it.

"No, that really would be an insult. But only these two rounds."

"Fine."

Nathaniel sighed and leaned back, seemingly more put out than Valerie understood. He kept glancing at her a little oddly, but the booze and music helped ease them back into a cheerful mood. By the time they left, they were arm in arm.

Kid Blue watched them go, not even getting a wave from Valerie in parting. He shrugged, and started a blues riff for the next song.

Forty-three

Griffen opened his eyes, and instantly regretted it.

Despite thick drapes over his windows, light had pierced through. Not soft afternoon or early evening light either. The direct, harsh light of noon. Which meant he had only had about six hours of sleep, if that. What was worse, he knew he was fully awake, even if regretting it. He didn't have a clue what to do with himself, but trying to force sleep was worse than useless. It wouldn't have been such a conundrum if this hadn't turned out to be one of the rare mornings he awoke alone.

So he forced himself up, and a hot shower took care of the last dregs of sleep. Surveying the fridge was nearly as hopeless as trying to sleep. Besides, his stomach wasn't quite recovered enough from the night before to want food. What he really could use was the hair of the dog. Even if he didn't usually drink so early, one glass sipped slowly would do a world of good. That decided, he headed out the door.

And back in the door.

"Shades, shades would be good." He rubbed his hands over his eyes and went rummaging. Moving faster than he should have, he banged his shin on the edge of the coffee table . . . hard. Gripping the injured limb with his hands, he swore savagely. All he needed on top of his headache was . . .

He froze, looking at his hands. The scales were back. Remembering what Jerome had said, he forced himself to calm down and breathe slowly. The scales faded from sight.

He would have to be careful of that and work at controlling his temper. All he needed was to involuntarily shape-shift in a public place.

Moving now with careful deliberation, he located a pair of sunglasses and put them on.

Once he was better equipped against the noonday sun, he left his apartment again. On his way out, he stopped by Valerie's door and knocked. He knew she led more active a day life than he did. He thought it might be nice to share a little company. Besides, she could help him find just what there is to do in the Quarter before five p.m. Unfortunately there was no answer, and he was left to hit the streets alone.

From Griffen's perspective, the French Quarter by day was a whole new world. By the time he normally got out and about, galleries and shops were closing, restaurants had already switched to dinner menus, and happy hour specials were nonexistent. Always before, when he had been out and about in the day, it had been with a specific purpose in mind. The shopping trip to improve his wardrobe, for example. Now he was just wandering, adrift and curious.

Bourbon Street showed some of the most dramatic changes. Oh, there were still tourists wandering in search of beads and booze. They were fewer, though, and seemed just a bit out of place. As if everyone else had gotten the menu of when the party started, and they missed the note.

What surprised him were the trucks. Bourbon was foot traffic only at night, so it was during the day that deliveries got made. Trucks delivering beer and soda, food and supplies, or just UPS delivering the occasional package were parked up and down the street. Strong men with pushcarts loaded with kegs and boxes moved in a steady stream, preparing the businesses for the night to come.

After a few glances into various bars and hot spots, Griffen decided against visiting the Irish pub. He didn't really want to see it empty. Or worse, occupied with that certain kind of drunk who really had no place to go. Those desperate, lonely souls were depressing drinking company at best, and though they were around at night, they seemed to disappear into the throng. In the light of day they seemed more apparent. Though he didn't really expect them in the Irish pub, he decided against taking the chance.

He wandered toward a little bar half a block off Bourbon. At night, it was a homey kind of place, full of service-industry workers, locals, and low-key tourists with more sense than most. He was curious, as close as it was to Bourbon, just what it would be like during the day. Especially since they didn't serve food, so wouldn't be attracting much of the lunchtime crowd.

It was empty. The music from the jukebox was turned down low, the twin TVs were muted, and not a soul sat at the bar. The daytime bartender sat engrossed in a novel. She carefully turned the page, put in a marker, and set it down before looking up. When she finally saw Griffen, her face split into an impish grin. He was so surprised he hadn't yet managed a second step into the bar.

"So, what will it be, Big Brother?"

"Valerie?!"

"No, I'm her evil twin, hidden from you for all these years. You're letting all my air-conditioning out. Come in and shut the door."

Valerie stood and started to pour Griffen's usual. He closed the door, and dazedly took a seat at the bar. As she put the drink in front of him she looked him over critically, smile fading slightly.

"Wow, I didn't expect you to be near this shell-shocked. I'm going to be charitable and attribute it to a hangover," she said.

"Well . . . that is part of it. Just surprised; why didn't you tell me you got a job?"

Just what she needed, Griffen thought. A regular schedule. All the easier for an assassin to find her.

"Mmm, maybe because I just got it yesterday, and you didn't get in till seven this morning. I thought sleep just might be a good thing before I joined the workforce."

"Congratulations, Sis. I didn't even know you were looking for work."

"I noticed. That will be four-fifty for the drink by the way. And you better tip. I know where you live."

Griffen couldn't help but laugh as he pulled out his wallet. He watched as she made change, and had to admit to himself that she could probably make a killing at the job. Personality, wit, and tight jeans would pretty much guarantee her popularity, with local and tourist alike. Still, something bothered him slightly about the whole thing. She pretended not to watch him as he laid a few bills out of his change for tip.

He also quelled his fears, helped with a few sips of his

Irish. The George seemed good enough to find her regular schedule or no. Not a comforting thought, though a little amusing. His personal stalker and possible murderer was professional enough he didn't have to worry more. Griffen felt like toasting the irony.

"So, how's the job so far?"

"Are you kidding? Daytime shift may be the most boring thing I've every experienced. I've sat through English lit classes more thrilling."

"How long till they get you on nighttime then?"

"Well, I'm swing shift relief now. So I'll play bar back till I learn the ropes. Figure a couple of weeks to a month."

"Don't you need some type of licensing or paperwork in this town for a bartender's job?"

"Well, uh . . . let's just say you aren't the only one who can enjoy this dragon game sometimes. The paperwork has been 'taken care of' for me."

Brother and sister shared a laugh and Griffen sipped his drink. The alcohol really did help him shrug off the lingering effects from the night before. As he rolled it around on his tongue, he looked over Valerie again, more speculatively. She quirked an eyebrow at him.

"What?" she said.

"No, I think the question was why."

"Why what?" Her tone was just a bit hard-edged, just a touch dangerous.

"Why this, why the job? It seems just a bit . . . odd."

"Yeah, well, so does most of our lives for the past several weeks."

Valerie started pacing behind the bar, fidgeting with the bar rag and searching for words. She stopped and looked over Griffen, just as he had her. She shrugged her shoulders and leaned against the bar, seemingly at ease. The tension in her shoulders and back was obvious, though.

"Mainly, I was bored."

"More bored than this?" Griffen waved at the empty bar.

"Well, a different kind of bored I guess. I mean really, Griffen. I dropped out of school; I hopped down to New Orleans. There is only so much lounging around a girl can do."

"Well, how about going back to school? Transferring credits into LSU or Tulane?"

"Oh, please. I had given up on my degree a while ago; it didn't interest me in the least anymore. I just didn't know what else to do with myself, so was going through the motions. Then you needed help, and I had something to do with myself.

"Ah . . . I left you in the lurch didn't I?"

"And Big Brother snags the gold ring."

Griffen nodded and started to frown. He hadn't really considered that. That Valerie had come to New Orleans because of him and then he had gotten distracted. Hadn't even known she was looking for work, how out of touch could he be? Valerie watched his expression, reached over, and clouted him on the ear hard enough he almost fell out of his chair.

"Stop that!"

"The hell, Valerie!" He grabbed the side of his head protectively and rubbed it.

"You needed that. No sulking gloom for you."

"But—"

"Don't 'but' me, Big Brother. Even if mine did get me this job."

"Sis!"

"Oh, you are so easy to tease. Look, you left me in the

lurch, yes, but I left myself in it more. I was back to not doing anything with myself. That's what this job is about. It
works or it doesn't, that doesn't really matter. There are
other jobs. In the meantime, I've got something going, and
no reason to mope anymore."

"Okay, I can understand that. It's just . . . you can do
more than bartend."

"Of course I can, stupid. I am Valerie, hear me roar. But
what's wrong with bartending? Just because I can do more
doesn't mean I should. I'm bored, not a work fanatic."

"Oh, no, it's true, the Quarter does corrupt absolutely."

"Just figuring that out are you? Besides, other than tour
guides, bartenders get the best dates. Of course, I could try
tour guide next!"

Griffen shared the laugh with his sister.

"I just wish there was something I could do to help," he
said.

"There is, if you don't mind sharing," Valerie said, still
smiling.

"What's that?"

"You could let me know what's going on that you're not
telling me about." Valerie was no longer smiling.

The request caught Griffen off guard.

"What . . . I don't . . ." he stammered.

"Let me make it easy for you," Valerie said.

She moved to her purse, fished in it for a few moments,
then returned to where he was sitting.

"I'm betting it has something to do with this."

She laid a tarot card on the bar in front of him. It was a
match for the two in Griffen's wallet except it was a bit
faded and distorted . . . as if it had been wet and then dried
out.

"Where did you get that?" Griffen said.

"Remember when we were walking down Bourbon and you got hit by a go-cup?" Valerie said. "Well, I found this in the go-cup when I picked it up."

"And you didn't say anything?"

"Look at who's talking," she challenged. "I remember what you said about getting one of these up in Detroit, but you've been ducking the question every time I asked about it. Then someone trashes your car and you are jumping more and more at shadows. I kept waiting for you to fill me in, but I've given up. So talk to me, Big Brother. What's going on?"

Pushed into a corner, Griffen filled her in on the situation with the George, trying to keep it as casual and unimportant as possible. For example, he left out that he was in his car when it was ruined.

"I see," she said when he had finished. "So why couldn't you tell me about this sooner?"

"Well, Mose and Jerome . . . it's just that female dragons have a bad reputation for overreacting," Griffen said weakly. "We were afraid that if you knew, you'd try to take an active hand and maybe get hurt."

"Uh-huh." she said, deadpan. "Do you see me storming around or getting angry? I agree, this sounds way out of my league. I'm more than content to let you and Mose deal with it."

Griffen felt muscles relax that he hadn't known were tense.

"You don't know how much of a relief that is to me, Val," he said sincerely. "Not telling you has been bothering me. If nothing else, now that you're on board, I can bounce some things off you."

"Like what?"

"Well, like Nathaniel, for one," he said. "It seems to me that . . ."

Valerie was suddenly looming over him.

"You leave Nathaniel out of this," she hissed. "I care for him and he cares for me. End of story. Go off and play whatever dragon games you want, but keep away from us!"

With that, she marched back to the end of the bar and picked up her book, pointedly ignoring him.

After a moment, Griffen finished his drink and left without saying anything more.

So much for female dragons not being temperamental.

Forty-four

At first, Griffen took little notice of the spatters on the side-walk.

Mostly, he was coming to grips with exactly how spooked he was by the events of the last week. He didn't usually come in this early, but somehow cruising the Quarter late at night had lost its appeal. He realized now that he had been reluctant to come out at all. It wasn't so much that he was scared. Just totally out of his depth.

Voodoo queens and dope dealers. People using animals to spy on him or perhaps even to attack him. Life on the University of Michigan campus in sleepy small-town Ann Arbor had failed to prepare him for this.

The now familiar scenery of the Quarter suddenly seemed a bit ominous and threatening. Was the rolling boom box that had cruised past him a few blocks ago just showing off, or was it one of the packs of dope dealers keeping tabs on him? Was it his imagination, or did the tarot readers on the

Square stop talking to each other to watch him as he walked past?

He suddenly focused on the splatters on the sidewalk. Originally he had dismissed them as splashes or a leak from some tourist's go-cup. But the red was too dark for a hurricane, the lethal rum drinks they served at Pat O's. Besides, they were too regularly spaced.

It was blood! Someone who passed by recently was bleeding!

Griffen stopped in his tracks and studied the splatters. Squinting slightly, he tried to see how far ahead of and behind him they extended.

The immediate problem was, they seemed to be the same size in both directions. Was he walking away from whoever was bleeding, or walking up on them from behind. Given a choice, which would he want it to be?

Lacking any data or plan to base his moves on, he decided to continue on home. It was a block and a half farther, and if he made it without incident, it would be someone else's problem.

Watching the street around him, he proceeded. There was someone sitting on the curb at the corner ahead. Griffen was about to cross the street, when he recognized the figure as Gris-gris.

"Hey, Gris-gris," he said, approaching the man.

"That you, Mr. Griffen?" Gris-gris said, looking up.

"Yeah. Say, did you notice . . ."

Griffen suddenly realized the man was hunched forward slightly, pressing his hand against his side.

"Hey," he said. "Are you all right?"

"Some dude stabbed me," Gris-gris said. "Just walked up and nailed me as I was walking along."

"Hold tight. I'll call an ambulance," Griffen said, reaching for his cell phone.

"Don't bother," Gris-gris said. "I've been stabbed before, and worse than this. Couple stitches and some tape and I'll be fine. It's more embarrassing than anything."

Griffen had run into this before in the Quarter, but still wasn't used to it. Where he came from, if you were hurt you went to a doctor or an emergency room. Here, people tended to doctor themselves, up to and including setting broken bones.

"Who did it? Did you recognize him?"

Griffen was thinking of the dope dealers he had tangled with recently.

"Never saw him before," Gris-gris said. "That's why he caught me flat-footed. Just some white dude. 'Bout your height, military haircut, built like a football player. Thing was, he knew me. That's why I come looking for you."

"What do you mean?" Griffen frowned.

"It's what he said after he stabbed me," Gris-gris said, wincing slightly. "He said, 'Stay away from Valerie. This is to let you know I mean it.' Then he just walked away. Didn't even run."

"Valerie?" Griffen said, trying to absorb the information.

"That's how I know he knew me, or leastwise that I've been seeing your sister. I thought you should know, so I came looking for you."

With a stab wound in his side, Griffen thought.

"You sure you don't want me to call an ambulance?" he said aloud.

"Naw. Jumbo's working door tonight on Bourbon," Gris-gris said. "He'll patch me up. Bouncers keep a pretty good first-aid kit on hand all the time."

"At least let me walk you there," Griffen said.

Gris-gris flashed a smile.

"That'd just be embarrassing," he said. "Like I say, the dude shouldn't have been able to walk up on me that way. The fewer that know about it, the better I like it. Just help me up and I'll be on my way."

Griffen thought as he watched Gris-gris walk away, no more unsteady on his feet than half the drunks in the Quarter.

What exactly was going on?

From what he had heard of the George, it wasn't like him to threaten, much less injure a bystander. What was more, the comment about Valerie would make no sense.

He had met Nathaniel, the guy Valerie was currently dating, but Gris-gris had seen him as well and would have recognized him. Was she seeing someone else? Was it just another jealous clash, or was there something deeper involved. Because she kept a low profile, Griffen tended to forget that she was a coming-of-age dragon, too. Maybe there were others not as inclined to forget.

He realized something else as well. He wasn't spooked by what was happening anymore. Instead, he was getting mad.

Forty-five

Wednesday was pool-league night and the Irish pub was crowded when they rolled in. Jerome was trying unsuccessfully to explain to Griffen about the Saints.

"I know it's crazy," he said. "But that's the way it is. However lousy their last season was, the fans still hang in there and follow them. I am; last year was one of their worst seasons ever, and people are still lining up to buy season tickets." ·

"But that doesn't make any sense," Griffen said. "I mean, if it's basically the same team and the same coaching staff, won't the fans bail out on them?"

"The publicity people always manage to cook up some line, and everybody eats it up. The starting quarterback, Aaron Brooks, had an injured shoulder during the final games of last season and gave a piss-poor performance. The fans wanted him replaced, but Haslett insists that now that his shoulder is better, he'll be his old self again. People believe it because they want to believe."

Griffen shrugged.

"If you say so."

"You've just been spoiled cheering for the Wolverines." Jerome laughed, elbowing his way to a spot at the bar. "It's always easy to cheer for a team that's a perennial winner. It takes a special kind of fan to keep cheering for a team that usually ends up in the bottom third of the division."

The bartender set their usual drinks in front of them.

"These are on the lady at the table by the door."

They craned their necks around for a look, then turned quickly back to the bar.

There was a moment's silence, then Griffen spoke.

"Didn't you tell me something about how the locals here in the Quarter will never give you away to an outsider?"

"That's the way it usually is," Jerome said softly. He beckoned the bartender over. "What did you tell her . . . exactly?"

"I didn't tell her anything," the bartender said. "She came in an hour ago and ordered a white wine, then said that when Griffen came in, she'd buy the first round for him and anyone he was with. I assumed she was someone you knew. Why? Is something wrong?"

"Oh, we know her all right," Griffen said. "I just didn't expect to see her here."

He glanced over at the table again, and made eye contact this time. The woman waved gaily and beckoned him over.

He gathered up his drink.

"Well," he sighed, "I might as well find out what she wants."

He picked his way through the crowd, pausing for a moment to let someone complete their shot on the pool table, then pulled up a chair at the woman's table.

"Long time, no see, Mai," he said. "What the hell are you doing here?"

"Watching them shoot pool," Mai said easily. "Some of these shooters are really good. You got a piece of this action?"

"It's a pool league," Griffen said. "They're shooting for trophies . . . and you haven't answered the question. What are you doing here? Don't try to kid me that you came all the way to New Orleans to watch the locals shoot pool."

Mai cocked her head like a bird and looked at him.

"Isn't it obvious?" she said. "I came down here to see you."

"Right," Griffen said with a grimace. "Just like old times. If I recall correctly, though, the last time we saw each other you walked out on me in the middle of dinner."

"Sorry about that," Mai said, wrinkling her nose. "I had to report in that you not only had been brought on board with your dragon heritage, but that you suspected that I knew more about dragons than I had let on."

"So now you admit it," Griffen said.

"Of course." She shrugged. "Now that you've had some time to get used to the idea and to settle in down here, I thought I'd drop in and say 'Hi.'"

"That's all? Just say 'Hi'?" Griffen pressed.

"Don't be silly," Mai said. "I'm supposed to do what I was doing before. Keep an eye on you for the Eastern dragons . . . like Jerome was doing for Mose."

"I see," Griffen said. "And now that I know you know, and you know I know you know, I'm supposed to just ignore all that and let you hang around as a self-admitted spy?"

Mai reached across the table and took hold of his hand.

"Don't be like that, lover," she said. "That's only what

the Eastern dragons think I'm doing. I've got my own agenda this time around."

"And what would that be?"

She sighed and pursed her lips.

"Well, I was going to work up to this slowly," she said, "but since you've asked I might as well cut to the chase. In a nutshell, there's a faction of the Eastern dragons, specifically the young ones, who want to throw their support behind you. I'm here as their spokesperson to approach you and see if we can work something out."

Griffen leaned back in his chair and stared at her. Suddenly, the noise of the pool matches seemed far away.

"I . . . I don't know what to say, Mai," he managed at last. "That's something that had never even occurred to me. I'd have to hear a lot more about what it entailed before I could even start thinking about it."

"Of course," Mai said. "In the meantime, though, I have a present for you. Call it a token of goodwill."

She rummaged in her purse for a moment, then produced a small notebook, which she shoved across the table to Griffen.

"You know how Asians love to gamble?" she said. "Well, here's a list of local Asians who run various gambling concerns. After I talked to them, they all want to sign on with your organization."

Griffen blinked at her.

"What exactly are they expecting from me?"

"Just to be included in your network," she said. "They want to use your spotters to steer tourists into their games . . . and maybe get included in the police protection you've set up. In return, you get a percentage of their action."

Griffen felt a quick spike of greed. If Mai's offer was legitimate, then not only would it mean some major monies for the operation's coffers, it would be a feather in his cap for bringing the new games on board.

"Am I expected to help run their operations?" he said carefully. "I mean, I've heard of mah-jongg and fan-tan and pai gow, but I don't have the foggiest idea of how they're played."

"I can teach you enough for you to get by," Mai said, laying her hand on his arm. "It'll be fun."

"Hi, lover."

Fox Lisa was suddenly standing there. Though she spoke to Griffen, her eyes were locked on Mai.

"Who's the fortune cookie?"

Griffen rose to his feet, shedding Mai's hand as he stood.

"Mai, this is Fox Lisa," he said. "Lisa, this is Mai, an old friend of mine from college."

"With the emphasis on the 'old,'" Lisa said, baring her teeth at Mai.

Mai flowed to her feet. To Griffen, it almost looked like a cobra raising its head and spreading its hood. Even though Mai was a full head shorter than Fox Lisa, she suddenly looked larger.

"With the emphasis on the 'we've been lovers for a long time,'" she corrected. "Little girl, you don't really want to go sideways to me. I don't mind sharing once in a while . . . and that could be fun, too . . . but nobody takes from me. You may have a bit of the blood in you, but you aren't dragon enough to go head-to-head with me."

"How about me?" Valerie was suddenly there, looking at Mai over Lisa's head. "Am I dragon enough to qualify?"

"You must be the sister," Mai said with a smile. "*You* I've been looking forward to meeting."

A hand fell on Griffen's shoulder, pulling him backward. It was Jerome.

"I need to talk to you, Grifter," he said. "Now!"

"But . . ." Griffen gestured weakly at the three women, but they didn't even spare him a glance.

"Now!" Jerome repeated, leading Griffen the few steps to the bar.

"What is it?" Griffen said, craning his neck to try to watch the confrontation.

The three women were seated now. Mai and Valerie were maintaining an erect posture, eyes locked. Fox Lisa was leaning forward, speaking rapidly.

"Remember what I told you way back when about female dragons?" Jerome said, stepping to block the line of sight. "Well, believe me, Young Dragon, you do *not* want to be in the middle of that right now."

"Uh-huh." Griffen said absently.

"Damn it. Pay attention!" Jerome snapped. "Think of the Chicago fire. The San Francisco earthquake."

"Yeah. So?"

"So bad things happen when female dragons get together and start quarreling." Jerome said. "In fact, there's only one thing I can think of that's worse."

There was a sudden burst of laughter, and both men turned to look. The three women were sitting with their heads together now, grinning and giggling like schoolgirls.

"Don't tell me," Griffen said. "Let me guess."

"Got it in one," Jerome said with a sigh. "The only thing worse than female dragons quarreling is when they get together and really hit it off."

Forty-six

Griffen had started to make semiregular visits to Mose. Part of it was updates and planning sessions for the organization. Griffen had free rein for the most part, but he also had the sense to use Mose as an experienced mentor and sounding board. Besides, it was expected that they should meet, a sign of respect. Somehow the Quarter rumor mill always seemed to know when Griffen had passed through Mose's gates, though never any hint of what was discussed inside.

The other part of these meetings was further training and learning about just what it was to be a dragon. After all these weeks, Griffen still had more questions than answers. Though Mose claimed not to have all the answers the young dragon would need, he certainly had more than the young man had. In fact, it didn't hurt to have Mose around just while Griffen practiced on his own. The older man knew what signs of progress or problems to look for.

Today Griffen seemed more preoccupied than most.

Mose had to keep repeating himself to get his attention. It was as if something had been nagging at Griffen, and he just didn't know how to put it into words.

"So just spill it already," Mose said.

"Huh?"

Griffen shook his head and realized that Mose had been giving him a piercing gaze for about five minutes. He flushed a bit and shook his head.

"What do you mean, Mose?"

"Well, something sure has you distracted today. New gal in your life?"

"Old one come back again . . . but no, that's not quite it."

"So why don't you tell me what it is, so we can stop wasting both our time. I swear you haven't heard half what I've said since you came in."

"You'd probably be right. Okay, Mose. Tell me about glamour."

It was Mose's turn to say "huh" and give Griffen another hard look. He gathered his thoughts carefully.

"That's some random train of thought you've got, Grifter. Before I start, though, I've got to ask, who you thinking of putting the glamour on?"

"What? No no no, other way around maybe. How do you tell if it's being done? How do you counter it? That sort of thing."

"Ah . . . Well, damn, son, if it will set your mind at ease, I can see right off that no one's got a glamour on you."

"You can see it?"

"Yes and no, you can see the change in the person, maybe something in the eye. The heavier it's been laid, the longer it lasts, the more you can see the signs."

"Okay, this is a good start. But, Mose, it wasn't me I was worried about."

"Damn, that might change things. Okay, let's start with the basics. What do you know or think you know about glamour?"

"Nothing really. It's only been mentioned in passing, I'm honestly surprised I remembered the name. From what I can tell, it's something between supercharisma and the Jedi mind trick."

"Okay, give me a moment, this isn't going to be easy."

Mose leaned back in his chair and half closed his eyes in thought. Every once in a while his lips would purse, as if he were trying on a word for fit. Griffen watched, his curiosity growing. None of his questions so far had required quite this level of thought. He wondered why this one topic was so different.

"Glamour is a tricksie thing," Mose said finally.

"Tricksie?" Griffen couldn't help himself.

"Back off, we're talking about glamour for crying out loud. Just be glad I'm not going to bring elves and fairies into the damn mix."

"Good . . . I don't think I want to know."

"Me neither. And that's part of the problem. I don't do glamour; I don't know many who do. It's not anything as simple as your growing scales or fire breathing."

"Simple?"

Griffen didn't try to keep the irony and sarcasm out of his tone. His experience with such powers had been all involuntarily, and down right awkward. Hearing it referred to as simple added to his frustration. Mose narrowed his eyes.

"Yeah, simple. Look, things like that, it doesn't matter much how it happens. As long as you know how to trigger it. Like your muscles, does it matter the chemical exchange that makes one tighten and another loosen so your arm bends? Not really, as long as you can bend your arm at will, and instinctually if in danger."

"And glamour is different?"

"Yeah, it is. There are a handful of powers out there . . . well, that doesn't matter just now. Glamour is all about perception. Part of it is the dragon's natural charisma. But that becomes augmented, and just how depends on the person who's doing it."

"What do you mean?"

"Well, to be blunt, I don't think I could teach you glamour if I tried, I'm not even sure you could manage it. Because part of it is a lie to the victim, but another part is lying to yourself. And lying to yourself on purpose is a tricky business. You have to believe what you are making them believe, but, of course, a part of you knows it's just the magic. You can see the pitfalls in that?"

"I think I need a drink; I almost understood that."

"Yeah, pour us both one. And remember, this ain't exactly my area. I'm passing on thirdhand knowledge at best."

Griffen got up and poured the drinks. As he passed one to Mose, he raised his in silent toast and they both drank. Griffen sighed as he sat back in the chair.

"I would never have believed I'd run into something that made fire breathing seem simple," he said.

"You're still young; you'll run into a lot more," Mose said. "In the oldest legends glamour and illusion were almost the same. One could be made to see monsters and nightmares and all sorts of things. Though I haven't heard of anything like that in the modern world, so it's probably just myth."

"Okay, this is all very confusing. Let's get back to basics; how can you counter it? Does just knowing it is happening act as defense? Or does it take more."

"Knowing what's going on helps, and can keep you protected against casual leakage. But against a direct attack, it takes a bit more. Glamour of your own is the best. But really all you need is an exertion of will to reassert your personal perspective."

"Which is done how?"

"Well, for you, you could probably just think hard. But actually this is where some of the old legends about counter curses and protective charms pop up from. You can use an object, some words, or even a hand gesture to focus your will behind. A physical reminder of what you are doing."

"Oh, great, psychic cue cards."

"Something like that. Also, if you are real good, with the physical aide you can disrupt them entirely. Their own lie falters, so if they are spreading their attention and affecting a room a little push from you can free the whole group. But it's harder if they are just focused on one individual."

"Could glamour be used to force someone to kill another?"

"Not that I know of, at least not if that killing goes against the person's deepest nature. Again, the old legends . . . well, you might trick someone into thinking the person they were killing was someone or something else. Still, I think that's pure myth, though."

"I'm finding this real hard to believe," Griffen said.

"But it fits what you've already suspected," Mose said.

"Yeah. Yeah, it does. I think Valerie's taken up with someone who's more than he seems."

"Huh, well, maybe I could take a look at her; see if she's under a 'fluence."

"From what you've said, only a few people have serious talent at this, even in dragon circles. Any idea who might be targeting Valerie?"

"Too early to say, I might know better when I see her. It's such a style thing that if I've seen their work before I'll recognize it."

"And can I use my will to break her hold?"

"Yes and no, you can help, but with a dragon of her stature, you will also have to teach her how to break it. As soon as it comes from within, everything that he has laid on her should crumble like a badly made house of cards."

"Good."

"One more thing, Griffen, and this is purely from what I've heard. If I had a guess, touch would amplify it. Don't ask why, pheromones directly, a direct channel to the psyche, I don't know. But keep your guard up. Story goes, when two glamour users touch and go to war, the effects on the loser are devastating."

"How devastating?"

"Well, the loser is pretty much stripped of his will, and the winner's own is imposed directly."

Mose paused and sipped his drink, and a small tremor ran through his body. If Griffen didn't know any better, he would have thought the man was afraid.

"This here being New Orleans. Ever heard of zombies?"

Forty-seven

It was Monday night. Actually, it was twelve thirty in the morning on Tuesday, but by Quarter reckoning that was still Monday. As was becoming his habit on Mondays when there wasn't a game on the schedule, Griffen set aside the night to watch a movie or three on DVD.

The reason for this was simplicity itself. Officially, new DVDs were released nationally every Tuesday. The Quarter, being the Quarter and fiercely competitive for every dollar, had devised a way around this rule. Both the major multimedia stores in the Quarter, Tower and Virgin, stayed open until one in the morning on Mondays, allowing them to sell the new releases to the late-night Quarterites that didn't want to wait until the next day.

Griffen had done his shopping this week at Tower. Even though it was a couple blocks farther from his complex than Virgin, they often had better prices. There was also a better selection of the old movies that he traditionally favored.

Walking along the riverside of Decatur Street, he mentally

reviewed his selections with no small degree of self-satisfaction. Of particular pleasure was finding the old Danny Kaye movie, *The Five Pennies*, on DVD. Ever since stopping in to listen to Steamboat Willie and his band play in an open-air bar on Bourbon Street, Griffen had been slightly nostalgic for the old big-band sound, and this movie about Red Nichols was just the thing to satisfy that craving.

As he walked, however, he slowly became aware that someone was behind him. Whoever it was neither fell back nor closed the distance, but seemed content to match his pace. That in itself was noteworthy, since, as a transplanted Northerner, Griffen tended to walk faster than most of the leisurely strollers in the Quarter.

His recent experiences had made him wary, so he decided to try one of the techniques Padre had coached him on to check a tail. Pausing in midstride, he set down his bag of DVDs and stooped down, loosening and retying his shoelace. The follower didn't stop, closing the gap between them. Reclaiming his purchases, Griffen straightened and looked back. The approaching figure was instantly recognizable.

"Hey, Slim," he said. "How's it going?"

"Actually, I was kinda lookin' for you, Mr. Griffen," the street entertainer said. "Can we talk for a few? Maybe over by the river?"

A small alarm sounded in Griffen's mind.

"I'm sort of in a hurry," he said casually. "Can we do it another time?"

"It's really important," Slim said, his voice flat.

Griffen stared at him for a long moment.

"Do we have a problem, Slim?" he said.

"That's what I want to find out," the entertainer said. "Shall we?"

He gestured toward the Moonwalk.

Griffen continued to hesitate.

"You know, Slim," he said carefully, "I haven't had much luck with surprise meetings lately."

"Yeah, I heard about that," Slim said. "But I ain't no damn dope dealer ambushing you. I'm coming to you head on and axing to talk."

Griffen made his decision.

"Lead on," he said, gesturing for Slim to precede him.

The two men walked through the parking lot beside the Jackson Brewery, now a small shopping center of stores, crossed the railroad and cable-car tracks, and emerged on the Moonwalk by the paddle wheeler, *Natchez*, silent and deserted at this hour.

Slim motioned for Griffen to sit on one of the benches lining the Moonwalk, while he himself stood staring at the river and the tour boat. After a minute or two passed, Griffen began to grow restless.

"So. What can I do for you, Slim?" he said, breaking the silence.

"I've been hearing a lot about you, Mr. Griffen," Slim said, not turning around. "Some of it good. Some, not so good. Been watching you myself trying to figure you out, but I can't make up my mind. I've finally decided to talk with you direct."

The man turned and faced Griffen, his arms folded across his chest.

"What is it you're doin' in my town, Mr. Griffen?"

"I thought that was common knowledge," Griffen said. "Mose has asked me to take over his gambling operation, and he and Jerome have been teaching me the ropes."

"And what else?" Slim pressed.

"Might I ask, first, what your interest in all this is?" Griffen countered.

Slim gave him a smile that held no humor at all.

"Take a look over your shoulder and figure it out your-self."

Griffen turned slowly in his seat and looked back.

Rats! Twenty . . . no, closer to thirty of the large wharf creatures were arrayed in a loose half circle with him at the focal point. They weren't snuffling around or foraging for food. Instead, they were sitting silently and staring at him.

A totally inappropriate thought flashed through Griffen's mind—he was glad he hadn't picked up the remake of *Willard* on DVD.

With an effort, he broke off his examination of the ani-mals and turned back to Slim.

"So," he said. "You're one of those. The animal control people or hoodoos or whatever."

The street entertainer grimaced.

"Never did like that name," he said. "We aren't really a group. We don't have meetings or conduct rituals or any-thing. We're just a few people with the same skills who know each other. Can't rightly see why anyone would want to try to take us over."

"Me neither," Griffen said. "Least of all, me. I've got enough on my plate already."

"That ain't exactly the way it was told to me," Slim said.

"Yeah. I heard that someone had given you folks some cock-and-bull story about my having a hidden agenda,"

Griffen said. "Well, I'm telling you, man to man, that I have no interest in controlling your group or trying to use it in any way. I might like to sit down and talk with you some-day, but that's pure curiosity. If you didn't want to share your secrets, well and good. That's your call."

"Uh-huh," Slim said. "Of course, that's what you'd say if you *were* hatching some kind of plan."

"So, what am I supposed to do to prove it?" Griffen said. "I'm already doing nothing. I haven't even tried to contact any of you, much less cozy up to anyone."

"Isn't that what I told you before?"

Both men turned. Rose was sitting on the next bench. Neither man had seen her approach.

To say the least, Griffen was relieved to see her.

"Are you in this, Rose?" Slim said. "Are you taking his side?"

"Don't need to," Rose said. "The man's a dragon, and a strong one. He doesn't need any help from me."

Suddenly, Griffen was less relieved.

"Well then, have you maybe got an idea 'bout how we can resolve this?" Slim said.

"I've been thinking on it," Rose said. "Seems to me the only way Griffen here can convince you that he's not after you folks is for him to prove to you that he doesn't need you."

"And just how is he supposed to do that?" Slim said.

Rose turned her attention directly on Griffen for the first time that night.

"Show him," she said.

Griffen blinked and cocked his head at her.

She gave him a small wink and nodded her head.

He turned his attention on the rats.

They moved forward in a loose line, passed under the bench he was sitting on filtering by his feet, then stopped in their original formation . . . but halfway between Griffen and Slim with their eyes focused on the entertainer.

Slim moved back a step. The rats followed.

The entertainer looked at Griffen and nodded slowly. Griffen nodded back.

Suddenly the rats scattered, disappearing into the shadows and over the edge of the pier.

Silence reigned for a long minute. Then Slim stepped forward and held out his hand.

"I appreciate your takin' the time to speak with me, Mr. Griffen," he said as they shook hands. "If you'd like to talk about this further sometime, I'll be happy to exchange information with you."

Turning, he walked away down the Moonwalk without looking back.

"How did you know I was strong enough to do that?" Griffen said after the entertainer had gone. "I've never tried anything like that before."

"I didn't know for sure," Rose said. "I knew Mose had been working with you, though, and it seemed like a good time to see how far you had developed."

She stood up and started to walk away, then turned back.

"You know, don't you, that this isn't the real problem," she said. "The big question is who pointed these folks at you and why."

"Mose is working on it," Griffen replied.

"Tell him to work harder."

Forty-eight

"I miss the cards," Griffen said.

"Who are you kidding, lover, you are just fighting the urge to stack up the dominos and knock them down like a kid," Fox Lisa teased from his left side, carefully arranging her hand.

"He is, isn't he? I'm amazed you've lasted this long, lover," Mai put in from his other side.

The two women paused a moment to narrow their eyes at each other, as they seemed to do every time one of them used that pet name for Griffen. But they were too busy smirking to hold it long.

"If everyone is done over there?" Mose said.

He was sitting opposite Griffen at the table, and was amused as hell by the whole setup.

"All right," Mai said looking at the hands. "Griffen loses outright, Fox pushes, and Mose wins. Again. You've got to be cheating."

"How could I cheat? You brought the dominos." His eyes twinkled.

The group was at Griffen's apartment and playing pai gow, or rather learning it under Mai's careful instruction. Though usually it was played with more, Mai had handled the invites. That had triggered a few warning bells in Griffen's head, but he was glad that Mose was getting a chance to look her over. He wanted advice later on the whole situation with the Eastern dragons. Tonight, though, dragon talk was kept to a minimum. Mainly because of Fox Lisa's presence. Instead, they talked gambling, and played.

Each hand used, instead of cards, four Chinese dominoes, with pairs being made and scored. To win, both pairs in a hand had to meet the dealers pairs, but a "push" was achieved if the front hand, or lower scored pair, beat the dealer's front hand but the rear hand, the other pair, lost. Then the player broke even. If neither pair beat the dealer's, as in Griffen's case, it was an outright loss and away went his money. Mose was building quite a stack of Griffen's money, and enjoying it.

Mai dealt the next round, and went through a brief reminder of the Gee Joons, Gongs, Wongs, and pairs. Griffen watched the shuffling of the tiles, which was itself intricate and fairly ritualistic, and once again failed to remember the pattern. He just hoped he never had to play dealer for out of town gamers. In a lot of ways, he felt like he was back in school again.

Well, except in school, he hadn't ever been between two such interesting and unpredictable women. He was getting damn confused by all the mixed signals floating around—between the gentle teasing, the taunts at each other, and the occasional wandering hand under the table. He also had them laughing about him over his head, helping each other cheat him out of money, and pulling Mose into their act when he made any serious mistakes. He should have run when he found out that Mai had arranged the seating.

"Fan-tan was easier. Let's go back to that," he said.

"No way, Grifter, it's easy because it's far too close to pure chance. I like a little strategy," Fox Lisa said.

"Besides, you need to learn this, at least well enough that you can fake it," Mai said.

"And you quit too easily sometimes, youngster. Stick that chin up for another blow and put more of your money on the table."

Mose's eyes shone more and more. With Griffen as a convenient target, he could lean back and enjoy things completely. The ladies were having far too much fun tormenting him. Fox Lisa leaned over and poked the bills Griffen pulled out and put on the table. She winked at Mose.

"I know whose pocket this came from, but whose money is it really?" she said.

"Oh, my, that was a low blow," Mai said.

Mai was purring.

"It'll be mine soon. Mose, you are dealing for a while," Mai said.

"Ha! Wondered why you invited me," Mose said.

"Why to discuss my connections interested in your gambling ring, honored sir."

Mai batted her eyelashes, and Griffen choked on his drink.

"Honored sir! That's it; I'm heading to the nearest bomb shelter," he said.

Griffen started to rise and the girls, laughing, grabbed his arms and yanked him back into his seat. Mose laughed with them as Griffen pretended to struggle. He decided to dodge the inquiry.

"That's between you and Griffen, I'm just here to play."

Mai nodded her head gracefully, and pushed the dominoes his way. If anything, he shuffled faster and with more skill than she had, and Griffen once again failed to be able to keep track.

The night progressed at about that speed, though despite being outclassed and distracted, Griffen did pick up the rules fairly quickly. It was not a highly complicated game, though it had touches based more on aesthetics than anything else. Which made it highly different from anything commonly seen in Western gambling.

After about an hour more, Mose rose and stretched. He started to gather up his winnings, and his coat, and took his glass to the kitchen sink.

"Well, kids, it's about time I moseyed home. Can't keep up these late hours anymore," he said.

The others exchanged a glance, not believing it in the least.

"Need an escort home, Mose?" Griffen asked, rising from the table.

"Lad, you are a fool if you'd part such charming company for an old man. I can take care of myself. Though I will have a word outside with you if you'll pardon us."

Outside, Mose paused to look up at the sky. Despite being in a city, there were always a few stars visible in the fairly subdued lighting of the Quarter. A bright sliver of moon hung over the sky. He didn't look at Griffen as he spoke.

"Young Dragon, you be careful with that one," he said.

"Which one?"

"Don't get cute, Grifter. I'm serious. My dealings with the Asian dragons hasn't been much, but that is one dangerous lady. She will always have her own agenda, and you will never, ever, know what it is in whole. I think she honestly likes you, but that doesn't make one bit of difference. And when dealing with her, don't ever think that what you say is exactly what she hears."

"Yeah, I had figured that out. I think."

"Good. Now forget it for a night and go back in and enjoy yourself. Those two are planning the kind of night that is inevitable. Don't fight your destiny."

Mose smiled to himself and walked away. Griffen blinked and turned back into the apartment.

Fox Lisa and Mai watched him with a gleam that made him think of women looking at an intricate, seven-layered, chocolate confection. Something sinful and sensual but when all is said and done, something to be devoured. He closed the door behind him and surrendered to destiny.

Somehow, strip pai gow really did make it easier to remember the rules.

Forty-nine

One thing that Nathaniel truly seemed to revel in was taking Valerie out to dinner. She was such a contradiction at the dinner table. Poised and elegant, but with the same enthusiasm in indulgence that she always showed. Every reaction to each new treat was magnified, and for some reason her palate seemed to be fairly limited. He kept managing to find new dishes that she had never tried, and each time she attacked the new dish with childlike glee and ravenous hunger.

That evening, they were dining at the Rib Room, the hotel restaurant at the Omni Royal Orleans. It was New Orleans elegant, without the coat and tie rule of Antoine's.

They had just gotten through their appetizers, chatting companionably, when Nathaniel stiffened violently. Valerie paused, forkful of crab cake halfway to her mouth. She rarely saw such sudden reactions in him, and this one left her puzzled. She turned in her seat, and if anything her expression became more confused. Coming through the door were Griffen and Mai.

"Nathaniel, what's wrong?"

"Well, uh . . ."

By now the maître d' had stepped up to the two and started to lead them to a table. Griffen saw Valerie, and a surprised smile lit his face. She realized that was a good thing, for if he had been coming just to check out her and Nathaniel on a date, she would have been seriously pissed. Griffen leaned over to whisper into Mai's ear. She turned toward Valerie and Nathaniel, and the smile that had started to blossom froze instantly. So did her step.

Nathaniel and Mai stared at each other as the McCandles looked from their dates to each other, uncertain.

Mai straightened her back and an angry hiss escaped between gritted teeth. Nathaniel winced, and pushed his chair back. Just enough to stand and run without hesitation. Mai stalked forward, and suddenly every eye was on her. She dripped with anger, but the sway of her hips and the arc of her step was as sensual as it was dangerous. Griffen's jaw dropped noticeably as he watched her from behind, and even Valerie was captivated.

"Nathaniel," Mai said, voice dripping venom.

"Careful, Mai, you will corrode the silverware."

Nathaniel made a negligent wave with his hand, and suddenly attention all around the room drifted away from Mai. The sudden and instant allure she had was broken, and conversations started up again. Griffen approached cautiously, shaking his head as if to clear it. Mai hissed again.

"How dare you," she said.

"Compensate for your lack of control? It isn't as if I don't have practice."

Nathaniel's tone was almost unchanged. His usual confidence leaving it seemingly unhurried and unworried. However, his eyes kept drifting to the door, and to Valerie.

"Almost as much practice as you have in causing others to lose theirs."

Mai's eyes fell on Valerie directly. She stopped and stared, and comprehension dawned in her eyes. For an instant, her composure softened, then she turned back to Nathaniel and, if anything, her anger was magnified. Griffen thought he should interfere before someone got hurt.

"I take it you two know each other?" Griffen said.

"You might say that," Nathaniel said.

"I know more than he wants you to know," Mai said, then addressed Nathaniel. "How's Malinda?"

It was Griffen's turn to stiffen.

"That was unnecessary, and probably very unwise." Nathaniel sighed. "But since you ask, Mother is fine."

"What is going on here!?"

Valerie slammed her hand into the table. The fork, forgotten, buried itself into the surface and permanently imbedded a bit of crab cake into the wood. Nathaniel reached out and rested a hand on hers, talking a bit more quickly, though very soothingly.

"Nothing, my dear. A jealous and very ex-associate who wants to ruin an otherwise fine evening."

"Stop that," Mai said, looking at Valerie. "Stop it right now or I swear I'll kill you like I should have last time."

"Oh, really, there is no need to be so melodramatic," Nathaniel said.

"I am not quite sure what you two have between you.

But if you are doing anything to my sister at this moment, I will do worse than anything Mai can think of.".

All attention went to Griffen as he spoke. His voice was both cold and hot at once, and he seemed to swell with anger. His hand, which had been resting lightly on Mai's waist, had begun to show the first signs of scales. Nathaniel very, very carefully let go of Valerie's hand, and leaned back in his chair again.

"Very well, then it is over," Nathaniel said. "You understand, of course, Mr. McCandles, this will change the game between yours and mine. Though not immediately."

"I'm not sure which of you three I am supposed to be angry at just now. So someone just answer my question." Valerie's hand clenched and Mai sighed.

"I suppose this is not the place. Well, time for an age-old escape. Valerie, let's head to the ladies' room. Lover, don't kill the twip in public. We'll be right back."

Valerie let herself be led away, and the two men stared at each other for a long moment. Griffen bristled, rage and suspicion rolling in his blood. Nathaniel merely looked slightly put out, which irritated Griffen more and more. Nathaniel was the first to speak.

"Yes, Malinda is my mother. However, this was not about you and your little empire. My sole interest at this point was your sister. The whole thing with the animal people was a diversion to hold your attention while I courted her. We had a vague idea of trying to lure her into joining our family."

"Of course, you left her completely free to make up her own mind. Not influencing her in any way."

"Of course not." Nathaniel laughed, and Griffen almost broke his nose right there. "That is not how these things are handled. I did what came naturally to me. It is not my fault that your sister was all but unprotected."

"No, but that is no longer the case. I think you should be leaving now."

"Ah, quite so."

Nathaniel rose, leaving money on the table for the check, and headed out the door. Griffen stared after him, still reining in his own impulses.

It was a good ten minutes before Mai and Valerie emerged. Valerie was red with fury, and stalked right past Griffen without a word. Mai and he exchanged a glance and followed after her.

Fifty

It was clear that Valerie's path was taking her back to the complex where her and Griffen's apartments lay. So, Mai and Griffen felt a bit more at ease hanging back some and giving her some space. As they approached the complex, the first thing Griffen noticed was that Valerie had left the gate open wide, maybe with a few new dings in it from being slammed much too hard, he thought. The door to Valerie's apartment was half-open, and the crashing from inside left no doubt that she was still in.

Griffen and Mai exchanged another glance, and she took a step back to lean against the nearest wall. He nodded, and proceeded forward alone. At the door he pushed his head in slightly and knocked lightly. Valerie was bent over and digging for something in her closet.

"Val?"

She swung around, half-surprised, but mostly just still very angry. The shotgun in her hand finally came clear of whatever obstructions she had been clearing from the closet. It swung around with her.

"Jesus!"

Griffen yelled and ducked back out the door, but no gunshot rang out. He tentatively stuck his head back in the door, but Valerie was already coming out, pushing past him and heading toward the gate again.

New Orleans may be laid back in some respects, but a very pissed off woman holding a very large shotgun stalking through the streets was bound to attract attention.

Mai stepped between Valerie and the gate, standing straight and radiating outward calm. Valerie stopped in front of her, eyes narrowing. Griffen made a fast decision and stepped next to his sister, grabbing her hand tightly in his. The muzzle of the gun was pointed more or less safely at a patch of empty ground for the moment.

"Val, you have to stop and think," he said.

"Too busy. I'll save that for later, Big Brother."

Her voice was oddly detached, and not like his sister at all. Griffen half wondered if it was some sort of backlash from the glamour breaking. He also fought the urge to glance at Mai, wondering if she had triggered this somehow. He quickly dismissed that idea, though; she was the one standing between Valerie and the gate after all.

"Valerie, this isn't the way. Killing isn't going to solve a damn thing," he said.

"How about kneecapping?" she said.

"Little harsh for the crime, don't you think?"

"No! No, I don't!"

She whirled to face Griffen fully, and in a gesture of her anger hurled the gun away from her. It hit and chipped a brick under the impact. Thankfully it again did not go off.

Though maybe, just maybe, the barrel was slightly bent now. She yelled into his face.

"How can you say that Griffen! That bastard completely invaded my mind, my personality! What punishment could ever be equal to that!?"

"Probably none can, so any you try is just going to leave you unfulfilled and unsatisfied," Griffen said.

"Yeah, well, I'm feeling pretty damn hollow right now! So I won't be any worse off."

"You would be and you know it. Not only inside, but think of the trouble. Forget that this scumbag has family, dangerous family. You could wind up in jail, Sis. If you were lucky, it would be for one night for toting that damned gun around. If you succeeded, a damn sight longer."

"So what am I supposed to do!?"

"Act like a dragon," Mai said, and stepped forward.

Both McCandles looked at her. She took a step past them and found herself a seat in the open courtyard. With a passing glance at each other, brother and sister followed. Griffen gently but firmly took Valerie's arm and helped her sit. She glared at him for a moment, but was grateful for the seat. Adrenaline and rage had made her muscles tense and unsteady.

"You do not slay a dragon by killing it," Mai said. "Especially not one like Nathaniel who has many relatives who would avenge him. You are a dragon, you have the time, the ability, and the cunning to wait and plot. You find when he is most vulnerable and take from him what he took from you."

"Take what?" Valerie said softly.

"Power."

Griffen looked at his sister carefully, mind racing. Pieces

clicked into place, and he found himself nodding without realizing it.

"We forget sometimes," he said. "Being a dragon is more than just how we act or what we can do. It's what we are. I've never seen you this upset, and that's because Nathaniel attacked something that every dragon seems to deeply love. In their bone and blood."

"Power," Valerie said softly, and nodded.

"So you wait. You plot. You think! And when the time comes, you will make Nathaniel feel every inch what you are feeling now," Mai said.

"Yeah. That I can do."

Valerie's eye gleamed, but it was a gleam Griffen knew and was happy to see. She was still pissed, but her spark was back. Silently he hoped Nathaniel had the good sense to never, ever come within a thousand miles of Valerie again. For his own sake.

"And in the process you are living your life, building your own power back, growing and learning. So that when the time comes you will already have moved so far beyond this that he is nothing but a tiny flea to you. A flea you will squash anyway, because you are a dragon, and we do not tolerate vermin."

Mai's eyes burned, too, as she spoke, and that was an entirely different spark. One that Griffen wasn't sure he was comfortable with at all. He wondered just how long Mai had been waiting for her own retribution, and just how safe it would be to be near the two female dragons, as allies.

He decided to change the subject.

"Now, where the hell did you get a shotgun?!" he said.

"Oh, umm . . . Gris-gris gave it to me. Just in case."

Valerie flushed a bit, and it was such a change in her that

Griffen was almost happy enough to drop the whole thing right there. Almost.

"We live in the French Quarter, behind security gates, and under protection. And you need a shotgun in your closet that you couldn't even get out quickly?"

"Hey, I didn't say the idea was great, but it was a present," she said.

"And just where were you marching off to with it?"

"He pointed out his condo to me one time when we were out walking," she said. "I figured I'd start there."

"Sis . . ."

"Leave your sister alone, Griffen. In fact, I think it is time you let her alone for the night. She needs to decompress," Mai said.

"What about you?" he said.

"If she doesn't mind, I will stay with Valerie. We will have girl talk and ice cream and single malt scotch. Important healing things. No men allowed."

"Hey, that doesn't sound half-bad," Valerie said.

"Okay, okay, I can take a hint. Hell, it's not like I ever got dinner. Val, you sure you're okay?"

"No, but I will be."

Griffen nodded and left. Mai watched him go, but Valerie was looking down at her hands. When the gate had shut, Mai let out a long sigh.

"Men. They have no understanding of closure."

"Huh?" Valerie blinked, surprised by the change of tone.

"Come. We shall pay Nathaniel a little visit."

"What about all that crap you just said about power and waiting?"

"I meant every word. That does not mean you let the little shit slip away scot-free thinking he is safe. Leave the silly gun. It won't come to violence. But you deserve more resolution than ice cream."

Valerie looked at Mai closely, and slowly smiled. She nodded and stood, heading into her apartment to grab a coat. And maybe to run a comb through her hair. Never let them see you less than perfect. Mai grinned, and whispered to herself a bit breathlessly.

"Besides, if there is one thing all dragons crave besides power, it's drama!"

Fifty-one

The two didn't have much trouble getting into the building. Or perhaps it would be more accurate to say that Mai didn't have any trouble getting past security gates and locks. Valerie wondered more and more about her brother's ex, but was more intent on the current goal. That goal was clear. To confront Nathaniel, and let him know she was no longer under his thrall. Also to let him know there would be a reckoning in the future.

They climbed the stairs to the top floor of a fairly upscale condo, one that in the Quarter could easily rent out for twenty-five hundred dollars plus. The two looked at each other as they reached the actual apartment door. Mai smirked, and stepped to the side, gesturing that it was all Valerie's.

Usually it is not practical or often possible for an ordinary person to kick a door in on one go, but Valerie had motivation.

The door slammed open and stayed open. The two strode

in, both looking utterly confident. As if they owned the
building and anything, or anyone, inside. Mai hung back a
few steps, letting Valerie take the lead, but it had been
agreed between them that Valerie would not be left without
backup. Mai was perhaps enjoying her role as wingman a bit
too much.

The place was well-appointed, but empty of personality.
All the furniture had to have come with the apartment, laid
out with a designer's touch and not a trace of personal
warmth. Likewise the art and decoration. There wasn't a
single sign of the man who lived here. No personal pictures,
not a spare book on the table, not even a dish in the sink.

It could have been a show apartment, completely unlived
in. For a moment Valerie thought that was just what it was.
Then Mai nudged her and brought her attention to a small
coffee table.

Sitting on it was a string of pearls, and a bamboo rose.

Valerie picked up a piece of boring statuary, and brought
it down on the pearls as hard as she could. The rose splin-
tered and flew through the room as so much shrapnel.

"I always liked violence in women," a gruff voice said
from the doorway.

The man blocked out the doorway, and was not
Nathaniel. He had the build of a linebacker, or a very dangerous marine. He had to have been six foot six, with short
blond hair and a nasty glint to his eye. Valerie drew herself
up to her full height, but she didn't have his bulk. She rarely
felt dwarfed by anyone, and though he wasn't that much
bigger than she was, he managed.

Mai, a doll compared to either of them, was more used to
it, so took a step forward and spoke first.

"Was that in, or to?"

The man ignored her and took a step forward, still blocking the main exit entirely.

"I had wanted to be sitting in the chair waiting for you. Maybe with the curtains drawn and a single lamp for back light. But Brother wanted you to find his little gift first. He always was too soft."

"Brother? Nathaniel?" Valerie said.

"Yes. You may call me Thor."

"Or you could call him what his mama named him. Theodore," Mai said.

The big man, Theodore, turned his head to glare at Mai. The expression made it quite clear that graphic and nasty and not particularly imaginative things were happening to her in his head. She didn't blanch, or appear to react at all, but just glared back. After a time he turned back to Valerie.

"If the Asian slag says anything about my ma again, I toss you both out of the window," he said.

"What do you want?" Valerie said.

"What I want doesn't matter. Not in any of this. Ma said to watch Brother's back, I watched his back. And he still gives me shit for jumping the gun with your other boyfriend. The little card runner. Not that it matters."

"What did you do to Gris-gris?"

Valerie took a step forward, anger starting to boil back. Theodore, or Thor, looked marginally impressed. Or maybe just pleased.

"Damn, Brother had you under good. Didn't even hear about Gristle or whatever you call him getting a bit of steel between the ribs. Don't worry, babe, he lived."

"Get to the damn point," Valerie said.

"I was, before you interrupted me. Despite all that, I'm still watching Brother's back. Now this was his game, top to bottom, I just was here in case things get rough. Maybe another game starts now, maybe not. Up to Ma and the others. I could give a shit. But if you try anything, anything at all, you can bet it won't be touchy-feely glamour and expensive dates next time."

"I don't care how tough you are, threatening me is not a good idea right now," Valerie said.

"I'm not threatening, I'm telling. You don't want to find out my idea of a date, babe. This mess is done. If you try to come back at us, you or yours, then me and mine are going to roll over and bury you."

He turned and left, just like that. Didn't even bother to close the door behind him. Valerie took a step forward, and stopped. She didn't see the point, didn't see what it would accomplish. Mai looked her over and sighed.

"So? Scotch and ice cream was it?" Mai said.

"Emphasis on the scotch."

Valerie was still staring at the door.

"You know, that family is really starting to piss me off," she said, and strode out the door.

Mai nodded, cast one last glance to the smashed pearls, and followed.

As Thor left the condo, he failed to notice the two figures standing in the shadows across the street. With no apparent haste, he sauntered leisurely toward Bourbon Street.

"That's him," Gris-gris said. "That's the dude."

"He's all yours," Griffen said. "You might want to use this. I've got a hunch he has tough skin."

He passed a large pocket knife to Gris-gris, who quickly

thumbed the blade open. The blade caught the light, and showed a series of deep serrations along the cutting edge.

Gris-gris took a step in pursuit, then paused.

"How did you know?" he said.

"Once Nathaniel showed his true colors, I remembered that he had mentioned he and his brother were staying at the family condo," Griffen said. "I thought that Valerie had caved in a bit too easily, so I hung around outside our complex and tagged along when they left. Called you on my cell phone so we could hook up along the way, and here we are. Maybe it was a long shot, but we are into gambling, after all."

"Are you sure this won't cause trouble with Nathaniel's family?" Gris-gris said, still hesitating.

"After what they did to you and Val, I don't really much care," Griffen said coldly. "Just don't mess him up too bad. I think they're about to blow town and wouldn't want that delayed by a stay in the hospital. Oh, and don't mention this to the girls. Let's keep it between the two of us."

Fifty-two

After everything that had happened, Griffen felt obliged to take Valerie out to a nice dinner. If nothing else, he felt they both deserved a relaxed evening in each other's company.

Tonight, their restaurant of choice was the Desire Oyster Bar in the Royal Sonesta Hotel on Bourbon Street. While he normally avoided Bourbon Street except for listening to specific groups, he had developed a taste for the turtle soup they served at the Desire. That coupled with half a roast beef po'boy sandwich made for a very satisfying, filling meal.

As they were reaching the end of their meal, Griffen noticed an Asian gentleman and two young white men being seated at a table a short distance away. He specifically did not make eye contact or wave a greeting, but the Asian spotted him and nodded in smiling acknowledgment. Griffen nodded back.

"Who is that?" Valerie said.

"He's a player from one of our games," Griffen said. "He's a really nice guy. A chef who relocated here from Atlanta and opened his own restaurant over on Decatur."

"I notice you waited until he nodded to you before you nodded back."

"I figure it's basic manners," Griffen said. "I don't know who he's with or why they're here, but it could be awkward. If I waved at him, he'd either have to explain that he knows me from an illegal card game, or make up a fast story on the spot. If he faked it, they might stop me for conversation at a later point. Since I wouldn't know what he told them, I could easily mess things up for him. It's easier to let him acknowledge the acquaintance first."

"I see," Valerie said thoughtfully.

A well-dressed black man approached their table.

"Excuse me. It's Mr. McCandles, isn't it?"

"That's right." Griffen said, rising and shaking the offered hand. "Only I prefer 'Griffen' in informal situations."

"Griffen it is." The man smiled. "Sorry to interrupt your meal, but I was hoping you could do me a small favor."

"It depends on the favor." Griffen smiled back.

"Nothing illegal, I assure you," the man said with a laugh. "You see, I don't get to spend much time in the Quarter lately, and the young lady I'm with this evening wants to hear some real New Orleans music. I was hoping you could recommend someplace."

"Well, it depends on what kind of music you want," Griffen said. "If you like the old classics like "Basin Street Blues," Steamboat Willie and his combo are playing just down the street here, in the courtyard across from the hotel's main lobby. If you want Cajun and zydeco music, then go down a couple blocks across Toulouse to the Steak Pit.

Denny T. is playing there tonight, and he's the best Cajun fiddler I've heard in the Quarter. Plays a lot of Doug Kershaw material. On the other hand, if you'd like to try something a little different with more ambiance, Sean Kelly's on St. Louis between Bourbon and Royal would be my suggestion. Beth Patterson is playing in there tonight, and she always puts on a great show. Some traditional Irish music with a lot of parodies, and her own material. It's not like anything you'll hear anywhere else."

"I'll try that. Thanks a million."

The man waved and returned to his table.

"You're really settling into the Quarter scene, aren't you, Big Brother," Valerie said. "Should I ask who that was?"

"Another one of our players," Griffen said. "I think he's one of the local politicos."

"I notice you didn't introduce me," Valerie said.

"To tell you the truth, I couldn't recall his name," Griffen said. "Besides, I noticed that he didn't bring his escort over to introduce her to us either. Of course, that's probably because the young lady that's with him isn't his wife."

Valerie choked on her drink, then dabbed at her mouth with her napkin.

"Is everything all right, folks?"

The waiter, a stout, white-haired black gentleman, was hovering at the table.

"I think we're fine," Griffen said. "Just a little more coffee and the check, please."

"I'll be right back with the coffee, but there's no check tonight, sir."

"Excuse me?"

"No, sir, Mr. Griffen," the waiter said. "There'll be no

check for you tonight or any other night you come in on
Amos's shift. Amos, that's me, sir."

"Pleased to meet you, Amos," Griffen said. "This is my
sister, Valerie."

"I thought that's who it might be." Amos smiled. "Nice
to meet you, Ms. Valerie."

"I'm still a little confused, Amos," Griffen said. "How is
it that you know me and why are you comping us this
meal?"

"Well, sir, I knew who you were when you walked in tonight. A lot of the folks here in the Quarter know who you
are and what you do," Amos said. "I guess I just know a little more than most. You see, Gris-gris is my sister's boy, and
the whole family is grateful to you for helpin' him out when
he got in that scrape with the po-leece."

"You're Gris-gris's uncle?" Griffen said. "No fooling?"

"No, sir. I wouldn't joke about a thing like that," Amos
said earnestly. "Gris-gris always was a bit of a wild one, and
we've always been a little worried for him. It's a big load off
our mind that he's workin' with a fine gentleman such as
yourself, Mr. Griffen, and seeing a fine lady such as yourself,
Ms. Valerie. Anyway, anytime you come in here on my shift,
your money's no good. It's the least I can do to say thank
you."

"That's very nice of you, Amos," Valerie said.

"I appreciate it, Amos," Griffen said, "but it presents me
with a bit of a problem. You see, I really like the turtle soup
here, and was planning on coming in more often. The trouble is, if I do that now, with you comping me, I'll feel like
I'm taking advantage of your generosity."

"Don't you worry about that none, Mr. Griffen," Amos

said. "You come in here as often as you like. I'd like nothing better than to see you in here every day."

"All right, all right," Griffen said, throwing up his hands in mock surrender. "I know when I'm beat. But I insist that if I bring a party in here, I pay for it, not you."

"We'll have to see about that." Amos grinned. "I'll just get your coffee now."

Griffen laughed and shook his head as the waiter retreated.

"What do you think about that?" he said.

"I think you're really getting into this whole dragon thing," Valerie said, without smiling.

"What do you mean?"

"The whole thing with people catering to you . . . waving at you and coming up to your table and giving you freebies. You're really starting to enjoy it."

"Hey. It's all part of the business," Griffen said. "You know, contacts and cocktails. It's the same in any business. It's just a bit more exaggerated here in New Orleans."

"And since when did you concern yourself with business?" Valerie shot back.

Griffen studied her for a moment.

"Is something bothering you, Little Sister?" he said at last. "You've been making little comments like that all through dinner."

"Yes . . . No . . . I don't know," Valerie said, shaking her head. "It's just that you've changed since we got down here. Maybe you can't see it because it's happening gradually, but only seeing you every now and then, it's apparent to me."

"Changing like how?"

"Think back, Big Brother," she said. "When you were in school, you never thought beyond today. You liked the soft, irresponsible life and only lived for the next card game or woman. Any attempt to get you to take anything seriously would have you running for the horizon. Now look at you. You're heading up an entire gambling operation, schmoozing with the local bigwigs, and working at setting policy and procedures. That's a big change no matter how you look at it. The thing is you seem to be enjoying it. You're taking to it like a duck to water."

"So, are you saying this change is a good thing, or a bad thing?" Griffen said thoughtfully.

"I don't know yet," Valerie said with a grimace. "The jury is still out on that one. It's good to see you enjoying yourself. On the other hand, we already know you're in the crosshairs. Actually, we both are. The weather may be cooling down a bit, but I've got a feeling things are going to get hot for us."

Griffen considered what his sister had said for several moments, then rose from his seat, tossing some money on the table for a tip.

"Hate to eat and run, Little Sister," he said, "but I think I need to have a chat with Mose. Maybe catch up with you later."

"She's right, Young Dragon," Mose said with a smile. "Of course you've changed. You've had ideas and opinions ever since you got here. The difference is, now you're doing more telling than asking."

Griffen frowned.

"That makes me sound pretty pushy and arrogant," he said.

"No. That makes you sound confident," Mose said. "It makes you sound like a dragon."

He leaned forward in his chair.

"Look at all you've learned and done in a little over two months," he said earnestly. "You've got a good handle on our operation. You've handled a couple of potentially nasty situations pretty much by yourself. You've even made some changes in policies that have been in place for decades. Everybody in the crew looks to you for leadership . . . and a lot of folks outside the crew as well. For a new dragon, fresh out of the box, you're doing yourself proud. If I had any doubts about turning the leadership over to you, they're long gone."

"I guess." Griffen sighed. "Say, Mose. About the whole thing with taking over the leadership. How long do you figure it will be before I'm ready for that?"

Mose threw back his head and laughed.

"Young Dragon," he said, "you haven't been paying attention. It's already happened. I just said that everyone is looking to you for leadership, and that includes me. For all intents and purposes, you *are* the dragon of this crew."

Fifty-three

Griffen was still thinking about what Mose had said as he unlocked the front gate and let himself into the complex courtyard. Behind him, the now familiar sounds of the city faded. The clip-clop of a passing carriage being the loudest as he shut the gate.

It was true that he was pretty much running the gambling operation now. But did that really make him the local dragon? He had nowhere near Mose's experience or wisdom. More important, on many levels he knew he lacked the confidence and his abilities to truly be a leader. The head honcho.

Suddenly, the lights in the courtyard, those fake gas lamps New Orleans was famous for, went out.

Griffen stopped in his tracks. He had been so absorbed in his thoughts that he had relaxed his now habitual scan for trouble or tension. This, however, was too blatant to ignore.

The courtyard was not completely dark. There was a bit of ambient light from the street, and a little coming from between the curtains of his upstairs apartment where he usually kept a light on in the living room, even when he was out. There was also one gas lamp on a post still lit, creating a ten-foot pool of light.

A figure stepped out of the shadows in the courtyard and into that pool of light and stood there, waiting. It was a short, slightly built man. It took a moment, but Griffen finally recognized him as the man who had been in the fight at the Irish pub the night someone had slipped the lime slice into his water back.

"Mr. McCandles? I believe we have some unfinished business."

"And you would be the George," he said, keeping his voice level.

The man bowed slightly.

"So you have heard of me. I was starting to wonder there for a while."

"Is this it, then?" Griffen said. "The showdown at high noon?"

"Considering the hours you keep, I felt that the wee hours of the morning would be more appropriate," the George said. "But basically, you're correct. This is it."

Griffen began walking along one of the paths between the flower beds, more to be doing something and to hide his nervousness than anything else. The George watched him, turning slowly to match his progress but not leaving his pool of light. There was something about the way that he watched; a tilt of his head, or the shine of his eye, or perhaps just his stance that made Griffen's stomach knot. This man was a predator.

"Before we start, do you mind my asking a question?" he

said. "Are you out to kill me, or just to test my powers? We never have been able to figure that one."

"Does it really matter?" the George said.

The George made a gesture, a wave of his hand that struck Griffen as a bit too theatrical. Especially under the circumstances. Beneath the predator lurked a showman, and a cocky one at that.

The lone lamp flickered and blinked out.

"It does to me," Griffen said, trying to adjust his night vision to the new darkness. "I've never killed anyone, so I'd like to know if I'm fighting for my life, or just to defend myself."

"In either case, you'll be defending yourself," the George said. "If it eases your mind, though, I don't think you *can* kill me."

The voice had shifted locations, now coming from the shadows behind Griffen. The move had occurred far too fast and silently to be natural.

"How—" Griffen said without thinking, then caught himself. Now was not the time to admit ignorance. Too close to weakness.

"How do you think?" the George said.

The voice was at yet another place, closer, but not close enough for Griffen to find him in the darkness. The George chuckled, enjoying the chance to taunt Griffen directly. Griffen drew himself up, mind working quickly.

"Teleportation," Griffen said. "Very impressive."

"Over short distances," the voice replied from a different pool of darkness. "It takes up a lot of my energy, so I don't do it often. Though it did allow me to push you down the stairs and get myself in a position to see your face as you landed. It's the simple things one enjoys."

Again the voice shifted.

"I just wanted you to realize what you're up against. I can also see in the dark better than you."

Griffen fought back a surge of panic.

Panic doesn't solve anything, and it can get you killed.

Mose's words came to him as if the old man were in the courtyard with them. He forced himself to remain calm and to focus on analyzing the situation.

The George had picked the time and place for the confrontation, and was using the darkness both to conceal his location and to unnerve his opponent. Well, he wasn't the only low-light specialist around.

Griffen let his own mind flow out, seeking for the feral cats that frequented the courtyard. He couldn't see through their eyes, but could gain some awareness through them. And cats are aware of everything. He made contact, and reached out a gentle probe.

Uh-huh.

He turned his back on the direction the voice had last come from and spoke directly to a spot some fifteen feet away.

"You may be right," he said. "Somehow, though, I expected something a bit more to the point than a game of hide-and-seek."

There was a pause, then all the courtesy lights came back on, revealing the George precisely where Griffen had anticipated.

"If you will," the George said with a shrug. His lips curled slightly, displeased with being so easily called out. "I've always had a weakness for the dramatic, and was a huge fan of film noir when it first came out."

"That's a neat trick with the lights, I'll admit," Griffen

said, stepping into a clear space. "Is that another power, or do you have a mechanical gimmick?"

"It's a power," the George said, circling slightly to maintain the distance between them.

Yet, Griffen felt, he was also stalking him. The man moved liquidly, much like a cat himself. Though one larger and more dangerous then the feral cats of the courtyard. The whole time he maintained eye contact, and his lips curled in slightly mocking amusement.

"Like the teleporting, it's only good over short distances and uses up a lot of my energy."

"Feel free to drain as much of your energy as you want," Griffen said. "I've always liked special effects."

"Don't worry. I have more than enough energy for the task at hand."

The speed with which he moved was absolutely shocking. This wasn't teleportation, just pure physical quickness. Griffen raised his hand to ward off the blow he saw coming, but it was a feint. The George's other hand cracked in a backhand slap that rocked Griffen's head back and sent him staggering back.

"My," the George said, fifteen feet away again in an eye blink. He was rubbing his hand with a faint wince. "You are tougher then most of those I encounter. I'm mildly impressed."

Griffen steadied himself, but he could taste blood in his mouth. A tiny trickle slipped from the corner of his lips, and the George nodded. Satisfied.

"First blood to me. Feel free to try a return blow."

"And if I refuse to play your game?"

"Why, then this will grow tiresome quickly, and my temper will grow short."

But Griffen hadn't waited for him to answer. He reached out, and the George turned about at the snarling yowl of two scarred old tomcats that leaped through the air at his face.

His eyes widened, a mistake. Claws raked at his cheek, drawing blood, before he could knock the beasts aside. They landed heavily, and crouched back, hissing at him.

He hissed back, and they cowered more.

Griffen tried to make use of the distraction, rushing the George and swinging a blow at him. Again with greased quickness the George moved away, foot catching Griffen lightly on the ankle and dodging. Griffen stumbled, but not much and the George stepped away, bringing the gap between the two men wide again. Griffen brought himself back around as the George postured.

"Oh, very good, second blood and quite unexpected. Really, boy, I've known dragons three times your age who hadn't done so much."

"What are you, anyway?" Griffen said, fishing for information, and searching for tactics. The cats were no longer responding; they were closed off to him. "Other than an enforcer for hire, that is."

"From where I stand, he's dead meat," Valerie declared loudly, emerging from the door of her apartment wearing a loose-fitting sweat suit. Her eyes shone with rage.

"Stay out of this, woman!" the George ordered, not taking his eyes from Griffen.

"Not a chance," Valerie said, starting forward. "That's my brother you're smacking around."

As she moved, she began to grow visibly until she was nearly half again her normal height. The sweat suit, first loose, now strained against her proportions.

"I warn you," the George snarled. "You are not strong enough for this contest."

Valerie came to a stop ten feet from the George.

"You're probably right." She smiled. "That's why I brought a friend."

From behind her back she produced the shotgun Grisgris had given her. At her new size, it almost looked like a toy in her hand. Still, its roar was deafening in the silent courtyard as she fired it point-blank at the George.

The man was blown from his feet and went sprawling into one of the flower beds.

"Heard the cats. I've told you before, Big Brother," Valerie called, "you worry way too much about fighting fair."

"Val! Don't . . ." Griffen called, but he was too late.

The George was on his feet standing behind Valerie. Grabbing the back of her sweat suit, he pivoted and threw her five feet into a wall. He snatched and wrenched the shotgun from her hand even as she flew. She rebounded and lay in a boneless heap on the pavement of the courtyard.

Griffen's vision began to blur. He could feel his skin tightening and his muscles shift as blood pounded in his ears. He didn't need to look to know his arms now had scales.

"She'll be all right," the George said, tossing the weapon away dismissively and turning back to his main target. "I don't hurt bystanders. She'll be bruised when she wakes up, but . . ."

With a roar, Griffen charged him . . .

. . . And the George was gone!

As Griffen lunged through the space the George had occupied a moment before, something struck him hard from behind, driving him to his knees.

"Sorry if it's not a sword," came the George's voice, "but that would be a bit obvious to carry on the street."

Looking back over his shoulder, Griffen saw that the George was holding a metal baton, one of the collapsible ones popular with some policemen. Turning his head was a mistake, even as he registered the weapon, the George's foot slammed into his face and knocked him fully down, sprawling.

"I thought about the sword. I saw the little toy you use for your fencing practice. But, it would have been like daring an infant to attack me with a fly swatter. Hardly sporting."

For a moment Griffen was held rigid with paralyzing anger. Again he felt his body tighten as fury changed him.

"Besides, it takes a special blade, and this really does more dam—"

With a snarl Griffen pushed himself to his feet, twisting toward his tormentor in the motion. Even as he turned, his tail lashed out for the man's head.

His tail?

A surge of joy surged through him as Griffen found his powers responding to his need. The moment's distraction cost him his advantage.

The George was gone again.

This time, the blow came low on his back, drawing a gasp of pain as he stumbled forward.

"See, thick skin doesn't protect you from broken bones. Not even plated with scales," the George said from across the courtyard. "You should know . . . Hey!"

Valerie had wrapped her arms around his legs from where she was lying on the ground. She tightened, so strong that the George's face twisted with pain.

"You talk too much," she growled, rolling like the athlete she was and . . .

. . . They ported again, both of them. This time barely ten feet from where Griffen stood.

He seemed to sag for a moment with exertion. Valerie grinned savagely and took the opportunity to wrap her legs around one of the trees in the courtyard. For a moment, they blurred, the George trying to port again, but only for a moment—he was stuck.

Fighting for balance, the George struck at her with his baton, she sagged, but if anything her grip clenched harder . . .

. . . And Griffen had him.

Taken off guard by the sudden violence of the attack, the George barely had a chance to give a yelp of surprise before Griffen's hands closed on his neck.

The George's baton went flying as Griffen lifted him bodily into the air, ripping him from Valerie's grasp, and slammed him down on the walkway . . .

And he was holding a large spotted cat, a leopard, by the throat. Ignoring the claws raking his arms, he tightened his grip . . .

And he was holding a giant snake that writhed in his grip and hissed viciously. It bit into Griffen's arm, but fangs could not penetrate scales.

Enough was enough.

Griffen took a deep breath, and exhaled a jet of his strongest flame full in the creature's face. The creature redoubled its struggles, then suddenly went limp.

Griffen didn't trust it, he lifted the beast and slammed it down one more time. Reptilian head knocking against the ground.

Releasing his fallen opponent, Griffen moved quickly to his sister's side. She was just starting to stir, slowly trying to get her hands under her so that she could rise.

"Just lie still, Little Sister," Griffen said soothingly. "It's all over. Take a few to get yourself oriented."

"Held on to the bastard," Valerie said weakly, eyes flashing.

"Yeah. Yeah, you did. My Valkyrie."

"I told you I don't hurt bystanders."

Griffen whirled to face the voice.

The George was standing in the center of the walkway, apparently unharmed. Even the scratch from the cats had vanished.

"I also said you couldn't kill me," he said, smiling at Griffen's expression.

"What are you?" Griffen said almost to himself.

"The important thing is that I'm defeated," the George said, holding his hands up, palms out in surrender. "The test is over, and you've won. Someone badly underestimated you . . . I suspect it was me."

"But I . . . you . . ."

"As to the other, the current name for what I am is a chimera. That's someone who can shape-shift into multiple animal forms, though you didn't give me a chance to really show off most of them. Also, I have extremely rapid regenerative powers. As an added bonus, as you may have noticed, I'm fireproof. It comes in handy when one's hunting dragons."

"I see," Griffen said, rising to his feet. "And after all you've been putting me through, including tonight, I'm supposed to just let you walk away?"

"I seriously doubt you could stop me," the George said.

But tell you what. Just to save wear and tear on both of us, 'll make you a deal. I'll tell you one truth. If you agree it's valuable enough, you let me walk without any further non-ense."

"You mean like who sent you after me?" Griffen said.

"Sorry. That's a professional no-no," the George said. But remember, you have to agree that what I tell you is valuable. Otherwise, it's no deal and we're back at where we re now. What have you got to lose?"

"Okay," Griffen said. "Let's hear it."

"This is completely confidential, you understand," the George said. "Just for you and your sister, since she got her-elf involved."

He glanced at Valerie, who had managed to prop herself p on her hands.

Griffen nodded.

"All right, here it is. The whole George legend thing? How no one knows what I look like or how I do the things I do? It's really very simple. I'm only one of a team. Together, ve operate under the name of George."

"I can see where that would give you an advantage," Griffen said.

He now realized how the lime had gotten into his water ack without the man he was facing having been anywhere ear where he had been sitting.

"This could be important to you in the future," the George continued. "As I said, the current contract is over. If omeone decides to pony up to send us after you again, it von't be me you'll be seeing. Understand?"

"All right. Fair enough," Griffen said.

"No!" Valerie snarled. "You are going to just let him alk?!"

She started to push herself onto her feet, size swelling
again.

The George tensed.

Griffen put a restraining hand on her shoulder.

"Let him go. It's not worth killing for," he said softly.

Valerie looked him over, emotions warring in her eyes,
but nodded grudgingly. For once the George stayed silent.

"Do you need me to let you out?" Griffen said.

The George looked at him with a tolerant smile, then
winked and bowed, flourishing with his baton. He vanished.

Griffen shook his head and helped his sister to her feet.
As the two of them walked back toward their apartment
proper, Griffen realized that he was no longer lacking in
confidence about his abilities and powers as a dragon.

Epilogue

Griffen was sprawled in his living room watching a DVD when his cell phone rang. He flipped it open without taking his eyes from the screen.

"Griffen."

"You disappoint me, Mr. McCandles."

It took a moment to place the voice. When he did, a chill ran through him and he sat bolt upright, muting the movie with the remote.

"Stoner? What now?"

There was the briefest pause and it took that break for Griffen to realize he had snapped at this powerful man. Nothing like a brush with death to increase one's confidence.

"I was under the impression that we had reached a tacit agreement the last time we spoke," Stoner said as if Griffen had not spoken. "That you would limit your activities to your local gambling operation and, in turn, I would leave you alone."

"We did. I mean, I have," Griffen said He took a deep breath and centered himself before continuing. "Excuse me, sir, but is there a problem?"

There was a long, pregnant pause at the other end.

"Am I to understand that you feel there has been no change in the scope of your activities?" Stoner said at last.

"No, I don't," Griffen said. "If you have information to the contrary, could you please explain it to me? Believe me, sir, I have no wish to go sideways to you."

"I'm referring to your renewed contact with your little Asian friend."

"You mean Mai?"

"Precisely," Stoner said. "You're aware, of course, that she is a dragon. More specifically, an Eastern dragon. Did it not occur to you that forming an alliance with the Eastern dragons goes well beyond the scope of a local gambling operation? That now you're involving yourself in international matters, and in doing so, infringing on my particular area of interest?"

"Whoa. Hang on a minute," Griffen said. "I haven't formed any kind of an alliance. Mai has used her influence to bring some of the local Asian games into our network. That's all. There's nothing international in that."

There was another pause.

"Nothing was said to you about forming an alliance?"

"No. Well, she said something about some of the young Eastern dragons being interested in my leadership. I said I'd think about it. That's all. I haven't agreed to anything."

Stoner sighed heavily on the phone.

"I'm afraid you still have a lot to learn about group dynamics, Mr. McCandles," he said. "Especially when it comes to the Eastern dragons."

"I don't understand," Griffen said. "I haven't agreed to anything."

"More to the point, you didn't say 'no,'" Stoner said. "In some cultures, if one does not immediately refuse a proposal, it implies that they'll agree if certain details are worked out. Apparently, that is how your response was taken."

"What makes you say that?"

"I have reliable information that there is active recruiting going on within the Eastern dragons," Stoner said. "More specifically, the recruiting is being done in your name. I'm told the response has been enthusiastic . . . to the point where the old-guard Eastern dragons are quite upset over it."

"But I haven't done anything!" Griffen protested. "I had no idea that Mai was going to do anything like this."

"Unfortunately, part of the job of being a leader is that you are eventually held responsible for the actions of those under you," Stoner said. "The Eastern dragons now consider you to be a threat. Someone who is actively working to undermine their power base. Under the circumstances, I have to agree with them."

"You mean you see me as an enemy now?" Griffen said.

"That's why I was giving you this courtesy call, Mr. McCandles. To inform you that we are now at hazard."

Griffen heard the words like a sentence of doom. All that had passed, and he still wasn't out of danger.

"What am I supposed to do now?" he said carefully.

"I am not the one you should look to for advice in this situation," Stoner said. "I am, however, sympathetic enough to your dilemma to offer up a couple friendly suggestions."

"And those would be . . . ?" Griffen urged.

"First, look to your defenses. I don't believe you are anywhere near powerful enough or prepared enough to consider going on the offensive."

"Anything else?"

"Yes." Stoner hesitated a moment before continuing. "I am not the biggest threat to you at this time. If my information is correct and the Eastern dragons are uniting against you, you have bigger things to worry about than me."

Griffen started to thank him but realized the connection had been cut off.

He sat staring at the wall for a while. It slowly dawned on him that the George had only been the first challenge in his new life as a dragon.

ROBERT ASPRIN was raised in the university town of Ann Arbor, Michigan, home of the University of Michigan Wolverines. This, combined with his Philippine-Irish heritage, gave him a rich wealth of characters and stories to draw upon in his writing. Though he wrote several stand-alone novels, such as *The Cold Cash War*, *Tambu*, and *The Bug Wars*, he is best known for his humor series, such as the Myth novels and the *New York Times* bestselling Phule's Company books. He also edited the groundbreaking shared-universe anthology series Thieves' World.

A devoted fan before he turned to professional writing, he founded the Dark Horde in the SCA and the Dorsai Irregulars in fandom. He was inducted into the Filk Hall of Fame. He died at his home in New Orleans in May 2008.